"Naoné óra baría...

...kar freon."

*"Courage cannot awaken without fear."*
-       *Sergeant Jason Kale*

Visit author's website at www.authorkjharrowick.com.
Visit publisher's website at www.portalworldfantasy.com
Visit Teacup Dragons cooperative at
www.indiestorygeek.com.

Published by: K. J. Harrowick & Portal World Publishing
Identifiers: LCCN 2021911642 | ISBN 978-1-955532-04-
4 (digital) | ISBN 978-1-955532-00-6 (paperback)
Subjects: Fantasy | Romance | Science Fiction
Book cover illustrated by: Rebecca Wilcox
Book cover design: K. J. Harrowick
Edited by: Carly Hayward of Book Light Editorial
Copyedited by: Jeni Chappelle of Jeni Chappelle
Editorial
Interior design by: K. J. Harrowick
Interior illustrations: Rebecca Wilcox

THE HIDDEN FLAMES ARTIFACT

# BLOODFLOWER

To (the real) Dusty Inman
Your loss will never be forgotten.

# BLOODFLOWER

## CHAPTER 1

*The North*

The Rakir were still on their trail—tower soldiers with orders to arrest Captain Jon Ayers and his men. Trained to be an army of mercenaries and assassins, Rakir guarded the north under the rule of the high council.

Until six weeks ago, Jon had been one of them, something he wasn't proud of. They'd executed his family—three sisters, his parents and his nephew burned alive over a jeweled hunk of metal.

Jon gripped the bloodflower and crouched at the edge of the plateau, surveying the valley below for any sign of Rakir. The pendant's four metallic leaves dug into his skin, the central ruby warm against his palm. He needed to get south of the Forbidden Mountains where his men were waiting.

This was his life now, exile or death. Cursed to always be on the run.

"Guardians be damned." He needed a cigarette. Already out of shadeleaf, it was still half a day's ride to the next village, a small cluster of buildings nestled in the gap between the far mountains.

The heavy rainfall soured his mood further as he shoved the bloodflower back inside his shirt and moved away from the edge. Lichen slick with rain covered a labyrinth of crumbling stone walls across the muddy plateau.

"What do you think this place was?" Mather, his best friend and second in command, crouched on a broken wall, bow in hand. The dark green of his wool clothing camouflaged him against the lower tree branches. With his hair wet from the heavy rains, the tattoo on his forehead was a beacon for any Rakir hunting them. As if reading Jon's mind, Mather mussed his hair until it covered the inked mark.

"Observatory maybe. Though with a spyglass that large"—Jon gestured at the rusted metal tube in the center of the ruins—"someone could probably see all the way to the land of the Guardians."

Such a place was no more than legend, and Jon cursed himself for even speaking it. If any protector of their world existed, they sure as shit didn't care about anyone in the north.

Patting his horse on the cheek as he passed by, Jon entered the labyrinth of stone and metal.

"We need to get moving." Mather leapt down from the wall. "Those scouts have likely found our trail."

"Not yet." Jon traced his fingers along a wall made of metal with long, worm-like vines draping from a heavy crack. He and Mather had barely saddled their horses for the day's ride when something had tugged at Jon's instincts, calling him to this place.

Be it destiny or fate, he could never ignore that sixth sense. It had saved his life on more than one occasion, even if it did take them an hour out of their way.

Jon brushed dry dirt off a spidering crack, a few granules whispering away on the breeze while the remainder plopped to the ground. Long ago, a mudslide had covered the floors of this place, packing hard earth against stone. But as the rains of gensana·darak, the season of leaves, fell heavy on the mountain, everything turned to slick ground mat over the forest ruins.

"What are you hoping to find here?" Mather fingered his bow as if expecting an attack.

"I'm not certain." But the instinct pushed at Jon's senses. It must have something to do with the bloodflower. At least he hoped it did. Something was here. He just had to find it.

Cold wind sliced through his clothing, chilling him as he slipped partway around the next wall. The muddy ground glowed with a green reflection, and he froze, not daring to move another step.

"Dalanath."

The ghost-like apparitions were a terror every northerner grew up with. They were common around the north, many believing the sleepers to silently damn the misdeeds of this world. At least one must have been just out of his sight, its eerie green glow reflecting in the muddy puddles.

Jon clenched his fist—he didn't need their judgment today.

He already bore the guilt of his family's death. He'd arrived too late, forced to hand over the bloodflower, only to receive a box of his family's ashes.

Jon would never let the high council have the pendant now. After stealing it back, he'd barely escaped to the mountains. Biting back the pain in his heart, he was tempted to reach for his weapons, but in the thirty-three years of his life, no dalanath had ever awoken. That he knew of, anyway.

Yet the hairs on his neck stood stiff. He was probably just on edge from the Rakir bearing down on them.

"Aren't we done with this place yet?" Mather muttered.

Jon edged around the corner in plain view of the ghosts, the soft green glow of their sleeping faces floating against the stone wall. It was always the same, half-formed bodies that tapered to a smoky mist below the waist.

"Looks like someone tried to seal them in." Mather patted a mud-brick wall covering several of the apparitions. "Long before our time."

"Probably didn't want to be judged." Jon slid his hand over a pane of glass buried in smooth, metallic stone, the surface chilled in the morning storm.

A thin line of blue light slid across the glass.

Jon jumped back. "Shit, did you see that?"

Magic, it had to be.

Mather yanked an arrow from his quiver and slid it onto the bowstring. "Guardians be damned, Jon. What did you do?"

Blue light spread across the pane, illuminating ancient symbols nobody alive could read.

"I barely touched it." Jon's voice fell away as a figure walked onto the glass. Unlike the dalanath with their green glow, the full-grown man looked like he could step out of the wall into the real world.

"Vamahéa heriakór Jason Kale," the figure said, strain lacing the desperation in his voice.

Jon gripped the hilts of his sheathed daggers and stepped closer, wishing he could understand the tiny man's words. "Who are you?"

As if unable to see beyond the barrier, the figure kept speaking, rubbing a hand across his short, blond hair. Releasing the grip on his weapons, Jon touched the glass. Still the same smooth chill, and the man kept talking as if Jon wasn't there.

"You think he's a Guardian?" Mather traced a finger along his arrow's fletchings and eased the tension.

Jon couldn't imagine he was. Only seven Guardians remained, the others deserting Sandaris when they disappeared into the night sky.

Human-like beings from the old world, their language could still be seen etched into stone ruins, but it wasn't enough to ease the cultural scar of their desertion. While those in the north shattered many of their statues long ago and turned their backs on the Guardians, the southern lands still worshipped them, hoping to one day call them back.

"Maybe he's trapped." Mather slid the arrow back into his quiver. "Maybe that's where they all went, into some unknown land of metal and glass."

Jon waved at the talking figure to get his attention, but the blond didn't budge.

"If he's trapped, we can try to get him out." Maybe this man was exactly who he needed to find.

Jon gestured to the figure to stand back then slammed the hilt of his dagger against the pane, a jolt sizzling up his arm as the glass remained uncracked.

The figure kept talking, then disappeared into blackness.

"Dammit, what is this stuff made of?" Jon said. "I can't crack it."

Smoke poured out of the seams between glass and rock, fire-sparks erupting from the corners.

"Shit, Jon, I think you made it worse," Mather said. The dalanath flickered, disappearing for an instant before they reappeared. "What the fuck?"

Jon stepped back to avoid the sparks. The closest dalan was an old man who looked meaner than a rabid wolf. His ghostly green body disappeared, nothing but smooth metal wall behind him. Where were these figures disappearing to?

"This has to be magic." He touched the smooth surface scattered with raindrops, a pulse whispering beneath his fingertips. "You ever seen anything like this?"

"No." Mather scanned the trees. "But we need to get out of here. Not even the wind speaks to these woods now."

The breeze had died down, the woods too quiet. And there was an unmistakable edge to Mather's voice. That could mean only one thing: Rakir were close. Mather was right. They needed to get the fuck out of here.

Except Jon couldn't make his feet move.

Lights flickered on inside the metal wall, illuminating a hollow space filled with glowing green liquid.

A woman floated inside, colorless worms or vines growing out of the interior and digging into her body as if to trap her. Long hair obscured some of her features as the strange pulse passed under Jon's fingertips again, this time stronger.

Her body jerked as if she'd been struck from behind.

As her hair threaded away from her face, the woman opened her eyes wide, terror and anguish in their depths.

There was something familiar about her features. He couldn't place it, but he'd seen her before. Or maybe his lack of cigarettes was muddling his thoughts.

"Jon. We have to move." Mather smacked his shoulder. "Now."

She pressed a hand against the glass and opened her mouth wide as if screaming, but no sound came out.

*Guardians.* That's what struck him about her features. Even with her hollow cheeks, she bore a striking resemblance to Herana, the Guardian of Lost Souls.

Jon had seen her statue before, though always with part of her face shattered. Someone long ago named her after the cold emptiness of a derelict world, and that meaning had become something of an ache to his own lonely heart.

He laid his palm against hers on the barrier, discarding the idea of the woman as a Guardian. It was ridiculous.

She mouthed something as if trying to speak to him, but he couldn't stay any longer. Not without putting himself in more danger.

"Captain!" The strain in Mather's voice said time was up. Run or fight. There might be two scouts or a dozen, and he didn't need another close call.

The woman seemed lost, desperate. Jon didn't want to leave her stranded. He unsheathed his sword and slammed it against the transparent wall to shatter it so she could escape.

Tension rippled up his arm, and he didn't even put a dent in it. "Fuck."

He'd have to lead the Rakir away and hope they didn't get blocked in.

"Get the horses!" he said to Mather then slapped the glass to get the woman's attention. "I'll lead them away."

His instincts fought what his training told him to do. And the terror in her eyes was like a knife to his heart.

"I'll come back, I promise," he said.

Jon really hoped she wasn't Herana as he bolted back to his horse. It was uncanny how similar the woman's features were to the old statues. The last thing this world needed was mercenary soldiers with a Guardian's power behind them.

## CHAPTER 2
*The North*

"Help me."

Jàden pressed against the glass. Green stasis serum held her weightless as a man with a bushy beard stared back. Gone almost as fast as he appeared, she screamed and pounded the glass, heavy grief clutching her chest. She had to get out. Even hypersleep couldn't erase the most traumatic day of her life.

But waking jolted like the touch of an electric fence during a bad chest cold. The final pulse hit her heart with the grace of a hammer shattering glass.

Fully awake now, the system opened the cover. Liquid rushed out, and she dropped into a huddled ball. Her hands shook so hard she had to clench her fists to make them stop.

A bracelet circled her wrist, stone laced with a honeycomb of metal.

The electricity provided a barrier between her and the Violet Flame, the universal energy source used to fuel starships. Except she'd been born with the ability to touch the Flame without the use of technology.

She reached for the well of liquid fire, but a static buzz blocked her. Jàden yanked on the bracelet, trying to rip it off. Too weak to pull it further than the base of her thumb, she slammed the walls of her pod in frustration.

Every inch of her body ached from those final horrifying minutes before the darkness and her last moments with the man she loved. An exploding fireball of twisted metal flashed across her memories.

"Kale!" She tried to scream her anguish at his death, green goo burbling down her chin. Her brain refused to believe he was gone.

Gripping the edge of the hypersleep capsule, Jàden squirmed onto the ground, a mire of rain puddles and thick mud riddled with footprints.

Someone had been watching her.

Before she could hold onto that thought, she heaved green ooze, clearing stasis fluid from her searing lungs. Her hands sank into the chilled earth, and she gripped the mud until her fingers were frigid, sobbing her grief. "Kale."

He'd been in the cockpit when his ship hit the ground, crushed under two tons of metal. A faint shout reached her ears, the sound far away but still sending a jolt of panic through her. The men who'd killed Kale would be close.

She had to run.

A difficult task with a tangle of plastic tubes dangling from the needles in her body. She scanned for the plumes of smoke from Kale's ship, but silence and heavy rainfall pressed in on her from a forest of thick sequoias. Nothing looked familiar, and the man who'd been watching her was nowhere in sight.

Maybe she could figure out where she was and how to get out of this place. Jàden crawled to her pod's control panel and wiped the mud-splattered screen until four red numbers stared back at her.

3,793 years.

*That's not possible.*

A row of pods stretched to either side, the closest ones buried beneath crumbling stone blocks, as if someone had built around them before fading into history. Ghostly green faces formed the exterior laser illusion of each occupant's features, a way for families to keep watch over loved ones who chose the long sleep between worlds.

Red numbers flashed on the exposed chambers: 3,654, 3,722. Each one was different, noting the passage of years since each occupant stepped—or was forced like her—into hypersleep.

No one survived that long in stasis. There must be a mistake. Jàden pressed her thumb to the screen's bottom corner. *Please still work.*

Thin blue lines scanned her biometrics, tracing across the glass to form her personal welcome message. *Jàden Ravenscraft. Bioengineering Guild, Class 3, Blue Sector - Hocker Hills. 1,365,480 days since your last login.*

That number was too large to comprehend.

"Where am I?"

Maybe the central computers could tell her. The screen flashed blue with a single black ring in the center.

*Hàlon*, one of the last human starships.

But the image zoomed in on the orb in the center of the ring, a moon trapped in the starship's theric energy web.

"Sandaris." She couldn't be on the moon's surface. With her feet planted on its rocky surface, Jàden should have sensed its beating heart. Last time she'd visited, the entire landscape was rock and water and refused to be terraformed. The computer had to be wrong.

The data map stopped on the smallest of the three central landmasses. Nashéoné, "the forbidden zone."

The only place on Sandaris no one could go without security clearance. She'd never been to this region of the moon, though Kale had many times over the years.

Jàden's hands trembled with fear. If the Enforcers found her here, she'd be imprisoned or killed for the power that flowed through her veins.

If Frank found her...

Terror gripped her heart. She needed to get back to *Hàlon* where she had thousands of places to hide. But she couldn't fly a damn starship to save her life.

Voices caught her ear again from a different direction, and this time they were closer.

*Run first*, she prodded herself.

Time to pop the tubes free and yank the needles. She'd hide where no one would find her. Kale's hidden ship. *Their* ship.

"Release hypersleep tubes."

The screen went dark.

"No." Jàden slapped the glass. "Please, just work!"

The image of a young man faded onto the pixels, his skin pulled tight around a distraught expression.

"Kale." She traced the glass, leaving a streak of glowing mud on his cheek. 3,793 years.

How many lifetimes had he lived without her? She'd always wanted to share her future with him, to fly among the stars and travel to new worlds. Finding him in the next life should have been easy with the right technology, but twenty lives…

She pressed a hand to her mouth to suppress a sob.

Raindrops splattered against her hand and dotted the screen as a pre-recorded video of Kale played.

"I wish I could see your face," he whispered, rubbing a hand across his buzz-cut blond hair. Kale's thin-stretched voice was no match for the haunted pain in his eyes. "Do you remember what I told you? About courage and fear?"

She nodded, tears in her eyes as someone shouted again. That was three directions now, an invisible noose closing around her neck.

But she couldn't leave Kale. Not yet.

Kale rubbed his head again, something he did when under a lot of stress. Even his pale complexion seemed dull with exhaustion. "I know what my father's done to you, Jàden. It's not your fault."

She leaned her head against the pod. Frank—Kale's father. Thanks to that asshole, she'd spent two years before hypersleep locked in a cage without so much as a glance at another human being. The lights on bright through day and night cycles. He'd tortured her with sensory deprivation to unlock the strength in her power while simultaneously making her weak.

So much time had passed. She could only hope Frank had suffered a long and horrible death, but some deeper instinct told Jàden she'd never be that lucky.

Kale's voice pulled her thoughts back to the present as he pressed a button on his console.

"I'm going to get you back to our ship. It won't be easy, but you're not alone. I'll be with you every step of the way." An image appeared below his face— a zankata with its wings spread as if about to take flight. The bird's black feathers faded to bright indigo fletchings beneath its wings. "This is your symbol now. Here is where you'll find safety."

"Not after four thousand years," she muttered. Raindrops splattered against her cheek to hide the tears.

"No matter what happens, know this: I'm out there somewhere, reborn into a new life."

A new body, a new face. How would she ever know who he was if she couldn't recognize his features?

"I'll find you, baby." She needed a pilot to take her back home, to *Hàlon*, and he was the only man she trusted.

Kale pressed his hand to the screen. "Find your zankata and go back to the beginning. I'm coming for you."

The bands of light disappeared.

"Kale?"

She smacked the empty transmission panel to bring it back to life as grief swelled in her chest. Glowing hypersleep serum smudged the dark screen as she slammed her shoulder against the glass.

"Don't leave me!"

A surge of electricity frizzled across the screen, flames bursting through the metal welds and dissipating into wisps of smoke.

"No!" Jàden pounded the glass. "Don't turn off. Don't—"

She couldn't handle his loss again, not so soon after his death. Clutching her head, Jàden screamed the ache in her heart.

"Come back, please."

Sparks trailed through the connecting walls, and one by one, the other pods hissed open. Hypersleep serum splashed to the ground, followed by several waking sleepers crashing to the mud.

Voices shouted in the distance, and something pounded against the ground. It sounded like horses, the noise so familiar from her childhood that Jàden whipped around.

The last pod hissed open. An old man fell to his hands and knees, vomiting up stasis fluid. The others sleepers crouched, gagging up green ooze as if unaware of the danger.

"Run," she whispered. *Before Frank catches us.*

She needed to move her ass too.

Jàden had barely stumbled a few steps when the pod tubes tugged at the needles still embedded in her skin. She winced in pain.

Midnight black horses charged across the clearing, riders in woodland browns and greens with hoods over their faces. One looked right at her, and she shrank against the smoking console. The other held a wooden bow with the arrow pulled tight. The weapon was legendary in the hands of Saheva, Guardian of the Breaking Sun, but Jàden had never seen a real person use one before.

As the rider fired the arrow, both hooded figures and their horses disappeared into the trees. Which was exactly where she should be headed— somewhere to hide.

In their wake were half a dozen more riders in black leather uniforms closing in from all sides, a silver emblem on their shoulders but not one Jàden recognized. One of their company fell to the ground, an arrow buried in his neck.

Fear gripped her, but Kale's voice echoed in her head. *Go back to the beginning.*

Of what?

She'd figure it out later. First, she had to get out of this place before she was captured again. Jàden yanked a hypersleep needle out of her arm, wincing at the sting.

"Dalanath san drapo!" a rider shouted and pulled back hard on the reins. His companions wrangled their horses around and raced back into the clearing.

"Shit, shit, shit."

All of them carried weapons and looked meaner than an angry pilot with an itchy trigger finger.

A uniformed rider fired an arrow into the old man still coughing up fluid. His withered hands clawed the shaft, and he fell to the mud, lifeless eyes staring at Jàden.

If they tried to capture her, she couldn't defend herself, not without the Flame. She pressed her back against the empty pod as the uniformed man strung another arrow and turned it toward her, his companions spreading out to corral her and all the other sleepers in. She jammed the needle between the seams of the bracelet to trigger it open. But the metal shaft snapped. The stone was too hard or the needle too thin.

A black horse charged into the clearing. The hooded figure on its back unsheathed two long daggers and crashed into the bowman.

The arrow loosed and plunged into her shoulder.

Pain ripped through Jàden as she crashed to the mud. The long, thin rod wedged into her body like a giant rock into her joint. Hot agony seared in her arm as she cried out in pain.

She grasped the shaft to yank out the arrow, but a dagger sliced to the ground next to her hand.

The hooded figure stood amid uniformed men who circled him with their horses. They drew their swords, and he raised his hands in surrender. His eyes met hers, filled with a deep-seated anger masked by strong determination.

It was the same man who'd stood outside her pod before it opened. Maybe he wanted to hurt her too.

Or to help. Clinging to that thought, Jàden grabbed the dagger and dug the blade into the bracelet's seam until the circlet sprang open.

The Flame's light rushed into her veins like unbridled fire.

Breathing in her power as the hooded figure pulled a man off his horse, she dropped the knife and gripped the empty pod.

She hesitated, not entirely sure how strong her power was anymore, only that it had grown during her years in captivity. A hand went flying past her head and smacked the smoking console, spraying blood against Jàden's cheek.

Without another thought, the Flame's energy surged through her arms into the metal, sparks shooting in a dozen directions until the tubes holding each sleeper burst from their seams, releasing them from their pods.

"Run," she blurted out, her voice faltering when a muscular woman in Enforcer grays attacked a rider.

Four silver petals lay against her shoulder around a red orb.

The bloodflower. An emblem of peace and protection.

Except every Enforcer on *Hàlon* had orders to kill Jàden because of the power she wielded. Terror seized her heart as other Enforcers yanked out tubes and scrambled to their feet, their hardened bodies healthy and muscular. One woman with short-cropped hair yanked a dagger off a rider's hip and shoved it into his back.

Power surged through her, riding the wave of fear and pulling enough of the Flame's energy to power a starship. White light crackled along every vein and capillary until she could no longer keep it contained.

*Oh, shit.*

Too weak to fight like the others, the more blood she saw, the harder it was to control the Flame. She clenched her eyes shut.

*Please don't kill them.*

The ground rippled beneath her feet. Metal hypersleep pods shattered, tearing along the wall and shaking loose wires into the mud. Horses screamed and pounded away as fountains of rock burst from the ground, swirling up to jagged points.

Jàden opened her eyes, for one single moment her body free of all pain.

Dust rained down over bodies scattered in the mud, both uniformed men and the sleepers they'd killed.

The last from her world had swords buried in their chests.

Only one uniformed man remained, a silver ring around his arm below his emblem, likely their leader. He swung his sword at the hooded figure, who barely ducked the blade in time. The two men circled one another, feinting attacks and dodging each other's blades with the occasional punch to the face.

The Flame's power swirled in her veins as she leaned against twisted metal and shattered rock, pulling needles out of her skin.

The leader roared in pain as the hooded figure clutched his wrist.

In half a breath, he had the black-clad figure on his knees with a giant knife buried in his throat.

For one moment, she considered what it might feel like to have his knife in her throat. To end her pain and the anguish of Kale's tragic death.

Nothing but peaceful bliss until her next life started.

But Kale might already be in his next life with no memory of their shared past. If she died now, she could lose him in the seas of the afterlife and forget all they were to one another.

The hooded figure yanked his weapon out of the leader's throat and twisted the knife against the flat of his arm, speaking words she couldn't understand.

Jàden scrambled backwards along the line of pods, now shattered metal and glass with rain-soaked sparking wires. The discarded dagger lay on the ground, but maybe she could rip the arrow out and use it to protect herself.

He advanced cautiously toward her as she grabbed the wooden shaft.

"I don't want to die. Not yet."

Quick as lightning, he closed the gap between them and opened a hand in surrender, his blade dropping to the ground. He pushed the cowl off his head and held up a hand for her to stop.

"Ekki." His voice was deep, guttural.

She glanced toward the Enforcers and uniformed men, unmoving on a mat of dirt and pine needles. "Are they..."

"Herana." Eyes as dark as rich tree soil stared back at her from a tan, weathered face.

Blood leaked from Jàden's shoulder as he wrapped his hand around hers. Warmth flooded from his gentle touch into her skin as he lifted her face to meet his.

He whispered a few words, his tone gentle despite the harsh dialect. "Herana, sanda le."

Then pain sliced through her neck as he snapped the arrow shaft in half. She cried out, gripping the bearded man until the sharpness eased.

The stranger cupped her chin.

Jàden froze under his grip, a gentle warmth she hadn't felt in nearly four thousand years. None of her captors had ever touched her, a thick barrier of glass always dividing them. And that didn't include her long millennia in hypersleep. Their shared heat triggered a longing in her heart, like coming home to a lost family after years in exile.

"Please, don't let go." She clutched his hand, pulling it against her forehead.

Flecks of blood splattered the bracer on his arm. He'd killed those men with barely a scratch on his cheek, and he hadn't harmed her.

A man like him could kill Frank before the bastard had the chance to capture her again.

And Jàden didn't want to be alone anymore.

She couldn't bear another day with no one to talk to.

Desperation won out over fear of the stranger as she gripped him tighter, sobbing against his dirt-stained fingers. For the first time in years, she had someone to touch. A voice to hear that wasn't on a computer screen or spouting useless data.

"I need your help." She grabbed the stranger's forearm, his muscles solid beneath the soiled garment. A small voice in her head warred against what she was about to do, but she needed protection. Just for a little while.

*Don't leave me.*

The Flame's energy crackled along her arm and illuminated her fingers before the light absorbed into him.

"Forgive me," she said. The guilt was already there, taking the choice away from another, but she had no way to communicate with this stranger. Without his help, she had no doubt she'd die. "I promise I'll reverse this and untie the threads of energy."

"Melin oné. Herana, ekki." The rest of his words were a garbled mess to her ears, but his features hardened. Jàden sensed he was trying to stop her from using the Flame, but she'd been forced against her will for far too long.

She hated forcing another, but desperation squashed the tiny voice in her head. "I won't hurt you."

Guilt tugged at her chest as a current of energy threaded through her skin, carrying a wave of strength she'd never possessed. Luminescent trails lifted from her arms, digging into his neck and binding the core of her essence to the stranger.

His strength flowed back, shielding her like a suit of armor.

Jàden savored the feel of him, a connection nearly as strong as the fire surging through her veins.

Wincing at the pain in her shoulder, she wrapped her other hand tight around his wrist and leaned her forehead against his chest. Warmth, the touch she craved, beat rhythmically underneath his thick clothes.

Jàden breathed him in and twisted her palm skyward. Flecks of light and shadow swirled together above the deep-cut lines in her palm.

"I tied your energy to mine," she whispered.

A forbidden bond, but she was no longer under the jurisdiction of *Hàlon's* laws, and she needed help.

Pushing aside her guilt, she lifted her gaze to the stranger. *Just a few days*, she promised herself. Long enough to find food and water, and get her wound bandaged. Then she'd release him. "Please, help me."

## CHAPTER 3
*Meridan*

Jàden's shoulder screamed in agony each time his horse bounced too hard or leapt over a fallen log. She didn't know where he was taking her or long they traveled, only that it was away from her hypersleep pod and all those dead people.

Away from Frank.

*Go back to the beginning. I'm coming for you.* She clung to Kale's final words as she lost all awareness of her surroundings or any movement. She didn't need to sleep anymore, but she couldn't stay awake.

"Don't leave me," she muttered, a trace of incense in the air, but something wedged her mouth open.

She spit out the stick and screamed as sharp pain sliced into her shoulder. Bright light flickered in a dozen lanterns hanging from wooden beams.

*Frank found me.*

A red-haired woman with freckles on her nose stepped into the light, a bloody dagger clutched in her hand.

Panic clutched Jàden's chest, and she knocked the blade out of the woman's hand. "Stay away from me."

She rolled off the table and fell to her knees, fingers brushing soft earth as she searched for a door. Wood shelves lined with herbs and small bowls circled a central table. Two years in a cage of steel and plexiglass, the earthy smells and woven hangings didn't spark any recognition.

Until a new stranger crouched in front of her, a line symbol tattooed across his forehead and hair shaved on the sides. He gestured to her shoulder, but she dug into the dirt.

He had a mohawk, just like Frank.

"I won't go back!" Jàden threw dirt in his face and scrambled backward, sharp agony ripping through her shoulder when she put weight on her arm. Bruised skin lay sliced open with half the arrow still embedded, blood streaking down the black lines of her birthmark, a zankata in flight engulfed by flames.

*Find your zankata.* Kale's voice was a mere whisper through the blinding pain.

She grabbed the bloodied arrow shaft. The reverse points lay exposed, something that might have torn her open if she'd tried to pull it out earlier. Jàden slid the last bit of the arrow free and tossed it at the tattooed man. Blood streaked down her arm as she bit back a cry of agony.

The new stranger uttered a few words and pointed to the injury.

No, she wouldn't let him cut her again. Scrambling to her feet, Jàden yanked the thin blanket from the bed and pressed it against her shoulder to stop the bleeding.

Both the new stranger and the woman put their hands up as if to calm her down. The same gesture the lab doctors gave her each examination.

As if she were the wild animal.

Jàden leaned against a hanging cloth between the shelves to be as far from them as she could and stumbled through the makeshift door onto frost-bound earth.

Cold air bit into her bare skin as she gazed across a central plaza. Circular huts with sloping roofs clustered beneath giant oaks, their branches twisting in a dozen directions to form a sheltering barrier. Men and women walked along the plaza carrying trays of food, blankets, or small pots.

White stone arcs jutted out behind the huts, many of them cracked and crumbling. The glistening telen stone, forged by *Hàlon's* engineers and strong enough to withstand millennia, jutted to jagged points, cracked at their midspan as if something ripped them apart.

Telen was no simple stone, forged and compacted until it was tougher than steel. Something only a high-powered bomb could destroy. All she needed was a single firemark to power any remnants of this base that might still be intact.

This had to be a hallucination or maybe some kind of holodeck.

"Herana." A deep male voice made her jump, and Jàden edged away from the hut. The bearded stranger whose energy flowed through her tossed aside a cigarette. A horse bridle over his shoulder, he held up his hands in surrender and cautiously stepped toward her. His strength wove through her veins alongside the Flame, breathing his essence through her very core.

*Not alone,* it seemed to whisper.

The tattooed man stepped out of the hut and ran fingers through his shaggy hair, the red-haired woman beside him. Both shared a concerned glance as blood dripped down Jàden's arm.

"You stay away from me." She stumbled into the central area, keeping the clutched blanket over her bare chest.

Groups of people stared back at her. Many of them made a gesture with their hands she didn't understand then dropped to their knees.

One woman hummed a low melody, others picking up the tune. Something about the song itched at a familiarity from her childhood, at a memory of her grandmother singing to the Guardians as she lit small incense sticks.

This had to be a trick. Everything was white, from the thin layer of snow on the hut roofs to the frost on the orange oak leaves to the strips of white fur on everyone's clothing. Why did everything have to be white?

Two years under the glare of fluorescents and still Frank taunted her. Maybe she really was still in her cage. "Let me out of here, Frank!"

The strangers moved to either side of her, the one with the mohawk keeping his distance.

"Herana, sanda le." Her protector closed the gap between them. His voice tempered to a soft calm as if soothing an anxious horse, and he laid a hand on each of her cheeks. "Níra."

Gentle yet strong, his warmth bled into her skin. Jàden desperately wanted to believe this wasn't a cage, that this man was real and would keep her out of Frank's clutches. "Please. I don't want to go back."

"Sanda le." He caressed her cheek.

She frowned at his strange words, so different from the smooth flow of *Hàlon's* common speech.

Yet, one word stood out: sanda.

"Safe," she whispered. As the icy air blew across her neck, she recalled the red numbers on her pod: 3,793 years.

Everything had changed.

She scanned the villagers, dressed in thick clothing lined with fur and leather. They weren't attacking her, and none of them wore a Guild patch or any emblem of office.

This wasn't an illusion or a cage. This was life.

"Where's Frank?"

Maybe this stranger knew something, but he held no recognition of the name in his eyes.

As her shoulder throbbed, she leaned into the stranger and buried her head in his chest. His warmth eased her terror as he lifted her into his arms and walked her back to the small hut.

"Please don't let them cut me." But as she glanced at her injury, it became evident why the woman held a bloodied dagger. She'd been cutting Jàden open to remove the arrow.

Incense twisted to a gentle blend of mountain pine and warm air as he set her on the table. Crackling flames heated the room from a small hearth, and Jàden leaned against her protector's shoulder. A gentle voice and warm touch were far better companions than a sea of endless white fluorescents.

This time, she bit back her pain as the red-haired woman stitched the wound with an efficient hand. As the last remnants of blood were wiped away and her arm bound in a sling, her stomach growled. Jàden couldn't recall the last time she'd eaten anything resembling food.

Kale was the only thing that mattered now, and she wouldn't get far without a bite to eat and warm clothes.

Her protector wrapped a thin blanket around her shoulders, then pressed something warm into her hand as if reading her thoughts. "Borda."

Jàden uncurled her fingers, poking at the cooked flesh with bones poking out of it. She touched an orange beak then lifted the creature to her nose and sniffed. Her stomach turned at the dry, oily scent of whatever bird it had once been.

For two years, Frank's lab technicians only gave her a daily ration bar—barely enough to keep her alive. She'd always preferred the taste of real fruits and vegetables from her grandmother's garden, but after so long with only synthetic meals, her body might reject anything else.

If she wanted to be strong enough to find Kale, she couldn't be picky.

Jàden tugged away a small strip, touching it against her tongue. The dry meat and strong flavor triggered her gag reflex. She winced and pushed the fire-cooked flesh into her mouth.

The bearded stranger laid a bowl of water into her hand as the red-haired healer retreated from the hut. The cool liquid soothed Jàden's throat as she sipped and handed it back, but he set it down beside her. He gestured something silent to his companion.

Jàden eyed the man with the tattoo across his forehead. He didn't look anything like Frank now that she studied him. His face was much younger and his body lean. Only the color and cut of his hair held any similarity.

But she still didn't trust him.

The tattooed man gestured something back that seemed to satisfy her protector then disappeared out the cloth door.

"Don't let him come back." She slid another piece of meat onto her tongue, chewing the rubbery texture and crinkling her nose as wind blew fierce against the hut.

The bearded man pointed to his chest. "Jon." He touched her hand. "Herana."

Jàden furrowed her brow then understood. His name.

"Jon," she whispered, rolling her tongue around the sound. Her frown deepened at the other word. She grabbed his hand and pulled it to her cheek. "Jàden."

The moment his warmth touched her, Jàden's chest tightened. Desperation pulled at her senses, the need for human interaction blanketing her desperation for Kale. She should have pushed Jon away, but his thumb traced the curve of her cheek, deepening the lonely ache in her chest.

Or maybe it was the food.

Her insides twisted, cramping. She shoved the half-eaten animal into his hand and dropped off the table. Grabbing a small bucket, she heaved up the few small bites she'd eaten, the strain shooting pain to her injury.

Two years with nothing but ration bars and her stomach couldn't take anything else. Her insides twisted again. She clenched her jaw to hold the nausea back. She needed strength if she was going to survive long enough to find Kale, which meant she'd have to learn how to eat again.

And she needed to know if Frank was still alive.

Jon crouched beside her. He lifted her chin and put a bowl of water to her lips.

She drank deeply, her throat burning with the animal's bitter taste. "I haven't eaten real food in..."

3,973 years.

Jon wrapped a bodice around her chest and snapped the seams closed so she was no longer half naked. His dirty, calloused hands brushed her side, a gentleness in his touch despite the heavy scars on his knuckles.

Her gaze trailed along his muscular arms before she closed her eyes. So many years alone. Jàden couldn't bear the weight of the emptiness inside her, so she reached for her only companion left.

Sandaris.

With the circlet gone from her wrist, the moon's gentle heartbeat echoed alongside hers. She'd forged the connection long ago, at a time of desperation when her power first became more than a small party trick.

Opening her eyes, Jàden unfolded her hand, flecks of light and shadow twisting away from her palm. She could feel Jon's energy like an intimate embrace. What would Kale think of what she'd done? Forging a forbidden bond without an Enforcer contract.

Jon grabbed her wrist, tracing his thumb across her palm. "Balé?"

*Why.*

He'd just spoken her language. Or had he? Perhaps the Flame's bond seamlessly translated the word in her head. Or maybe she was finally listening now that the pain from her injury didn't overshadow everything else. She scratched behind her ear at an imaginary tickle against her brain. Strange words and meaning melded together as one. "Because I need your help. I have to find Kale. Go back to the beginning."

And she couldn't do it alone. Not when she was so broken.

Jon stuck a cigarette between his lips and pulled a block of brushed steel out of his pocket. Blowing on the glass orb, illumination traced outward along thin lines in the casing.

"A lighter."

Before he could light the tip of his cigarette, Jàden snatched it from his hand and popped the small orb out. The glow faded. Cupping her hands around the firemark, she blew until it illuminated again. Trillions of bioluminescent bacteria flared to life inside the transparent sphere.

Like her, they directly touched the Flame. Creatures of pure biotheric energy used to power starships and all human technology.

"Do you have more?" she asked.

Jon reached into his pocket and tossed her a leather pouch.

Loosening the string, she dumped the contents onto her hand. More than a dozen firemarks—blue and violet, amber and green. She clutched the marble-like orbs. She'd seen the bacteria beds once, long ago, and never wanted to go back.

Each bacteria-filled sphere glowed with her touch. Pushing the memory out of her head, she shoved a blue firemark into the lighter, the glow tracing thin lines of light along the brushed steel.

Power. It didn't matter where it came from.

She could go home.

## CHAPTER 4
*Meridan*

Every muscle in Jon's body tightened as he leaned his knuckles against the worn table. He had enough shit of his own to deal with—his family dead, soldiers on his ass, and his men in danger.

Except now he had a new problem, a half-dead Guardian in his care. He didn't want to believe it, but the statue at the head of the village left little room for doubt. Maybe he should walk away now and leave her with the healers. Most certainly she'd be safer with them and have a chance at a real life without dragging his problems into it.

Someone had tortured the woman. That much was clear from her emaciation. He'd spent too many years inside the Tower prison as a captain not to understand what starvation and long years in a cage did to a person.

Jon clenched his jaw tight as Mather stepped inside the hut. "Is she asleep?"

"For now."

They'd tried to lead the Rakir away from the observatory, but the bastards corralled them in. While he'd tried to protect the Guardian, Mather was ambushed in the woods and barely missed a hoof-kick to the head.

Jon pulled the blanket up to Jàden's chin and tucked it beneath her uninjured arm. The woman's softness breathed into his skin, her magic spreading through his body as if she'd woven her essence into his veins.

He'd always ached for a woman of his own, one who saw past the terrifying soldier to the deepest parts of his heart and loved him anyway. Most only saw the darkness, the Tower patch, or his inability to relax enough to ever be 'off duty.' He supposed it was his fault for the deep shadows hanging over his life and the need to be constantly alert.

But he never imagined a woman would bind him as a husband before she even knew his name, especially a Guardian.

He should be angry at her. Shit, he should be furious. And yet the softness of her breath on his skin tugged at an ache deep in his soul.

How long since any woman let him close enough to touch her hand? Or to caress his fingers through the softness of her hair? Jon pulled the sensation in like a lover as he traced a thumb across her cheek, a deep connection he'd craved nearly all his life.

"Healers are in an uproar." Mather crouched near the fire to warm his hands.

"Because we found a damn Guardian." Not surprising. By the singing outside the hut, they'd want to keep Herana for themselves.

Never at peace with his Guardian sign, Jon had always considered himself one of the ranasen, those who followed the lonely path to Herana, the Guardian of Lost Souls. The only moonless Guardian of the seven.

Except she couldn't be real.

Guardians were no more than an idea to give comfort to those on the edges of death, though Jon often heard rumors that the southern cities built great towers to honor them. While the north destroyed all trace of the Guardians in favor of one central power: the Tower of Idrér.

"Worse," Mather muttered. "One of their border men spotted Rakir on the east ridge."

"Fuck." Their hard ride through the canyon pass should have put enough distance between them and where he found Jàden. So much for any rest. Jon lit a cigarette and brushed past Mather to step outside. "Don't let her out of your sight."

"Yes, Captain."

Dropping the door back into place, he trudged across the plaza toward the stables. The previous day's gentle shower turned back to freezing rain as a sharp wind blew across his cheek. The season of leaves was nearly at an end, and soon the season of the deep freeze would blanket the mountains under a veil of white. He needed to get to the other side before they were trapped in the passes.

Tied to an outside post, his and Mather's stallions tossed their heads. Both northern-bred Tower horses ignored him as farriers brushed them down and offered each one treats. Unlike other equines, norshads only traveled in brother-herds and would kill most mares outside of mating season. The stable keepers had to keep them away from the smaller mountain horses, but neither stallion seemed to care under the farriers' attentions.

Jon stepped beneath the long eaves and crouched near their gear to assess the remaining supplies. Barely enough food to get them through another day.

Healer Feira, the village leader who'd cut the arrow out of Jàden's shoulder, emerged from the shadows and shushed away the others as the last of the four suns dipped below the horizon. "Let the horses rest."

Bright red hair glistened like dying embers of a spent fire as she stepped beneath the eaves and offered him a cup filled with steaming liquid.

"Thought you could use this."

The rich smell of ground coffee teased his nose. Jon grabbed his saddle and blanket and set them on the back of his horse. Never one to pass up a fresh cup, he couldn't shake the news of Rakir nearby and needed to have the horses ready to run again. He'd never want to bring the wrath of the Tower soldiers on a peaceful healer village.

"Thanks," he muttered but ignored her outstretched hand as he pulled the cinch through the buckle.

"You're leaving already?" Disappointment laced her tone as she set the cups aside and blocked him before he could grab Mather's saddle. "The Guardian must have time to heal."

He didn't have time for the woman's stubbornness. Jon tried to step around her, but Feira grabbed his arm.

"You are not like the other soldiers." Her sharp eyes bored into him. "Rakir only show kindness to their brothers, never to outsiders."

Even without their horses, he and Mather could never hide what they were—Tower soldiers. At least until six weeks ago.

The pain of that last day burned in his chest, but he pushed it down. Now wasn't the time to relive his family's death. "I'll get rid of the scouts your border patrol found, but don't get in my way again."

"You have no supplies, Captain, and I daresay you used most of your shalir to pay for the Guardian's healing." She squeezed his arm to hold him in place as if she had some important piece of news. "I want to make you a trade."

Jon took a long drag on his cigarette. Now what in all of Sandaris could she want to trade him? Few women were ever so bold around him or showed no fear. As his curiosity prickled, so did the hairs on the back of his neck. "Go on."

"I want a child. A daughter with the strength of a warrior and the gentleness of a healer. Since the Guardian has no physical means to help me"—her eyes traced downward—"I want you to give me that child."

Jon stared at Feira as if she'd gone mad. There were women in his home city who sold their bodies to soldiers as part of a bond-contract to produce an heir, a common practice since Rakir were forbidden to have wives. Many wanted to leave a blood legacy in this world, so they'd pay for a woman to be their companions—housing them, feeding them, and caring for them during the pregnancy and first year of nursing. Once the contract was complete, the woman left to sell her body to the next person and left the child behind.

"You want me for a bond-contract?" Jon had never considered it before, and the woman couldn't have picked a worse time to make such an offer.

"No contract," Feira practically hissed. "One night and the child is mine. You will leave in the morning along with your companion and all the supplies you need. The Guardian stays with us."

Jon's chest tightened as each word from her mouth hit him like a hammer. Of course she didn't want him. But as soon as the healer mentioned Jàden, the hairs on his neck prickled in warning.

Tossing his spent cigarette aside, Jon pulled Feira's hand off his arm. "Find someone else. I already have a wife."

He brushed past her and picked up Mather's saddle and blanket, setting them on the back of his friend's horse. As he tightened the cinch, he tried to suppress the irritation creeping in. Only Jàden's magic weaving through his senses kept him calm.

Fate indeed. Maybe he should have ignored his instincts earlier that day.

"I thought Rakir were forbidden to have wives." Feira's voice remained neutral.

But Jon still felt the underlying sting. It reminded him of the last time he saw his father alive. They'd argued because his father wanted him to bond a woman and keep her hidden on the family farm, but Jon would never cage another to satisfy his own needs.

Not that a woman would want him for a husband. She'd have to be out of her mind.

Feira seemed undeterred. "The Guardian must stay, Captain, even if you will not. Promise me."

"Ain't gonna force her, healer." Jon untied the horses and fixed his gaze on Feira. "You did the job you were paid for. Now I'm gonna do mine."

Although he didn't feel like a husband because he knew almost nothing about the Guardian apart from some scattered mythologies, he'd already lost one family to the Tower's orders. He wouldn't lose another—not the men he called brothers, nor the wife now in his care.

Jàden might not ever be the woman he ached for in his life, or see him as more than a bodyguard, but even Jon had to admit he found comfort in the connection to another person.

As he tied off the horses in front of the hut where Jàden slept, he patted each one on the cheek. "Rest while you can. I'm going to take care of a little problem."

# CHAPTER 5

*Meridan*

Jon climbed the sharp incline out of the healer village, thorned berry vines tugging at his breeches. Silent as a fox, he crept through the denser brush onto a smooth trail. The wind blew fierce without the trees to shield him.

Rakir scouts camped nearby, their large fire easy to smell each time the wind blew. If he didn't silence them before they picked up his trail, he'd likely spend his next few weeks in chains as they dragged him back to the Tower of Idrér. The heart of Ìdolön's power.

Jon would rather die than let anyone chain him.

He crept along a line of large, rocky crags, scrub trees growing through the gaps. A campfire flickered in an alcove, bordered on one side by a steep cliff.

*Idiots don't know how to hide their presence.* Any scout worth his spit would've kept the fire underground to avoid detection.

Only one soldier sat near the flames, an older man with a bald head shouting at the two picketed horses. Scouts always traveled in pairs, so the other must be nearby.

Jon slid between a gap in the rocks as a second soldier joined the first.

"Picket the horses over here." The older man gestured toward his companion. "They're too loud, and I need me some sleep."

"Move 'em yourself. I'm going on watch." Jack Bonin, one of the street patrol soldiers, spat at the ground. His tower and two moons emblem glimmered in the firelight.

Jon knew the symbol as well as the back of his hand. He'd been part of their ranks, his long years spent securing prisoners in cages. His body remembered the scent of leather armor and how the wool uniforms fit tight across his chest. While he'd never gotten used to the smell or the screams inside the prison, he'd been damn good at his job.

Jon despised men like Bonin, who was rumored to hold children ransom until their merchant parents paid him to 'protect' their shop. He edged into the deeper shadows as the bastard strode by muttering under his breath.

Slipping from the gap in the rocks, Jon shadowed Bonin toward his perch near a cluster of tall redwoods. Time to rid the north of one more asshole.

He stepped into the deep shadows and crouched low, whistling softly enough that the noise was barely a whisper above the wind.

Bonin perked up, a dagger clutched in his hand. He slipped between the trunks as his footsteps faded to silence.

Jon kept still, the woods silent.

Rakir were trained to be smart, deadly. Only a whisper of wind on the back of Jon's neck alerted him to Bonin. He twisted back, slamming his elbow into the bastard's nose.

"You fucking cunt!" Bonin spat blood at his cheek and slashed his silver blade.

Jon dodged the blow and hooked his arm, swiping Bonin's feet so the bastard crashed onto his back. He stripped the dagger and pressed it to Bonin's neck. "One sound and I'll slit your throat."

Bonin's mouth stretched into a bloodied grin. "Jon Ayers. I hear your sister screamed when they lit her on fire."

The pain of his family's death still too raw in his heart, Jon slammed the dagger into Bonin's hand. The bastard was one of a thousand assholes oppressing citizens of the north, all in the name of serving the six—old, powerful rulers who imprisoned and killed anyone with a hint of magic in their blood.

He could never let them get their hands on Jàden.

Pulling the dagger out of Bonin's hand, Jon punched him hard in the nose and pressed the blade to his throat again. "How many Rakir in these mountains?"

Bonin gasped for breath, pain etched across his features. "Thousands."

Fuck. Ìdolön must have sent half its army to track him down. That bastard Éli Hareth would probably be one of them.

As if reading his thoughts, a devious grin curled Bonin's mouth, exposing blood-stained teeth. "Commander Hareth has a message—"

Jon slid his dagger across the man's throat before he could finish, his muscles tightening into a hard knot at the name.

He dragged Bonin into a shadowy thicket to hide his body, but his eye caught a half-muddied emblem chicken-scratched on a piece of paper—a perfect circle around a red orb, four silver leaves spread out from the center.

The bloodflower. Rakir were after his family's pendant.

He stripped Bonin's weapons and retreated into the darkness. Keeping tight to the shadows, he retraced his steps to the remaining scout who hadn't bothered with the horses. Already he was curled up in his blanket, snoring loudly. The guy must be half deaf not to hear Bonin's shouting, or he simply didn't care.

There was nothing honorable about killing a man in his sleep, but Jon had tried to stay honorable over the course of his life and it got him nothing. Plus he didn't have time to be picky.

He tromped across the small camp, almost hoping the man would wake up, but the bastard snored until Jon's blade dug into his throat.

After hiding the body behind a knot of trees, Jon extinguished the fire and hid all traces of the inhabitants as best he could. If there were any more scouts on this ridge, maybe they'd pass right by and never find the trail. Likely these two were headed straight for the healer village and planned to be there by midmorning.

"Looks like you're coming with me." As he secured the scouts' weapons onto the saddles, he mounted one of the horses and held the other one's line as he rode back to the healer's village.

He'd been up for two days now, and exhaustion tugged at him as gray streaked the early morning horizon. The horses hung their heads as he plodded past the statue of Herana, the sharp angles of the Guardian's face so much like Jàden, or what he imagined if someone hadn't starved her.

Feira came out of her hut, a shawl wrapped around her shoulders to fend off the morning chill. "I thought you were leaving."

Dropping to the ground, Jon placed the reins of both horses in her hands. "Here's your trade. I'll take those supplies now."

## CHAPTER 6
*Meridan*

Someone wouldn't stop screaming. Jàden curled tighter into the pillow as heat washed over her, reminiscent of the fireball from Kale's crash.

"You're safe," a voice whispered to her.

It had to be her protector. But when she opened her eyes, the man with the tattoo across his forehead laid a hand on her arm.

"Wake up. You're safe."

The screaming stopped. Jàden's heart raced as if some terror chased her out of a peaceful slumber, but she didn't remember dreaming. "Where's Jon?"

He furrowed his brow then seemed to understand. "Soon as we check that shoulder, I'll take you to the captain."

On cue, the pain seeped into her wound, pushing away the cold. But as she sat upright, Jon's strength flowed through her veins. She could feel him now as if he held her tight.

Jàden had never tied anyone to her before, as such energy bonds were forbidden. If the two people became intimate, the tie became irreversible, sealing them as a bonded pair.

Guilt pressed on her slowing heart as the tattooed man set a bundle of clothing beside her.

"I'm Mather, Jon's best friend," he said. "Gonna re-bandage your shoulder if that's okay." He had a gentleness to his tone as the Flame slowly translated his words.

Jàden nodded and looked away, trying not to focus on the shaved sides of his hair.

*Not Frank*, she told herself.

Wincing as he tugged the last bit of fabric away from her skin, she glanced toward her swollen shoulder and the purple bruising.

"How—" She tried to find the right words in his language as a dictionary of bizarre sounds and meanings unfolded in her head. "How long before it heals?"

"A few weeks." He wiped green paste across the stitched threads, a cool tingle dimming the soreness. "You're lucky it was your shoulder and not between the eyes."

Jàden shuddered. The old man in the other pod had barely gotten the hypersleep serum out of his lungs when the arrow had struck. That could have been her, lying in the mud and left to rot.

Tears burned in her eyes. "Why did they want to kill me?"

Mather tightened his jaw as he placed a fresh bandage and rewrapped her shoulder. "They were chasing me and Jon. I suspect they only stopped when they saw dalanath waking up."

"Dalanath." Jàden didn't quite understand the word, but the Flame's energy pulled in meaning— sleep, glow, faces. "You mean sleepers."

"Ain't never seen a sleeper wake up. 'Specially not a..." Mather looked her over then turned away to stoke the fire. "Get dressed. I'll take you to the captain."

Jàden slid off the table and very slowly untied the front of the sleeping dress. Perhaps she should have been more wary of a stranger in the room with only underclothes on, but she'd lost any dignity over her body years ago. Frank and his scientists poked and prodded her while she slept with no regard for her feelings.

She was nothing now and had lost so much weight she was barely more than a skeleton. Refusing to look at herself, Jàden dressed the best she could, getting help from Mather to slip the thicker overshirt on.

By the time she finished, Jàden itched to explore and find a working computer. She could use the firemark to give it power.

"Come on. Captain's outside."

Jàden followed him out the hanging door, relief washing over her that the frost had disappeared under dark storm clouds sprinkling a light mist. The world was now filled with brown, amber and green, and Jàden pulled the hood over her head to keep off the weather.

Villagers stared at her and made their gestures, but she ignored them and trudged across the muddy plaza, scanning all the old pillars behind the huts to piece together the size of the Enforcer base. In her time, it probably held no more than a few hundred people, and the landscape beyond the oaks must have been a shipyard to move Enforcers on and off Sandaris. Kale would have known the base better than her since all she had to draw on was her knowledge of a few public militant areas.

But if she read the landscape right, there would be a statue nearby of the Guardian Élon.

Most of *Hàlon* didn't believe in Guardians or how they were deified, but Élon was a symbol of strength and bravery. His statue was placed in central areas where Enforcers could pass by on their way to a patrol mission and press two fingers against the stone for luck.

"You coming, Jàden?"

She turned back toward Mather and spied a statue on the far corner near the road into the village. Jàden needed to see Élon's features for herself so she had a familiar starting point.

But as she edged around the other side, lead dropped into her stomach. A woman's dress flowed toward the edges of a grand circular pool, the water long gone and replaced by fallen leaves and muddied lichen. High cheekbones and an angular face sharpened beneath hair pulled back into a long tail with bangs fringed across her forehead.

Jàden pressed a hand to her mouth, staring at the familiar features as if her Guild photo had morphed to stone. "It can't be."

Someone had turned her into a Guardian.

And these villagers must believe it as they sang a haunting melody, crossing the plaza toward her and gesturing signs across their cheeks.

Except she'd done no great deeds of heroism. She'd screamed and begged for mercy in her cage like a child. With a statue this large, Frank would find her in seconds.

This had to be his fault. He'd made sure she could never hide from him.

"You fucking bastard." Jàden picked up the closest rock and lobbed it at her own face. "I'm not going back in the cage. I'll find Kale, and we'll get the fuck off this damn moon."

Mather laid a hand on her good shoulder. "Easy, Jàden."

"No." His gentleness offered no comfort, nor the same strong tug Jon did each time he laid a hand on her cheek. Where was her protector anyway? Jàden searched the crowd for Jon's thick beard and shaggy hair, but everyone was clean-shaved with their braids slicked back.

As the tears burned in her eyes, the sonorous melody halted. The red-haired healer who'd cut her arrow out stepped from the crowd and made a gesture across her cheek. "Herana, welcome to Meridan. We would be honored if you would stay with us."

As the red-haired woman finished her words, the others bowed. If the woman had any sense, she'd see the tears on Jàden's cheeks and know something was very wrong.

"My name is Feira." The red-haired woman grasped Jàden's hand. "I understand your companions are eager to leave, but you would be most welcome to stay as long as you like."

Feira's expression and body language held an edge of anger. Jàden had seen that look before on one of her ex-boyfriends when he got into his childish moods, a stubborn edge between digging his heels in and throwing a tantrum. And Feira had a similar intensity to her features.

Jàden pulled back. She couldn't stay in this place now, not with a giant statue of her practically screaming for Frank's attention. "No, I can't."

It might be better to search the ruins for a working computer, but that would be like waving her arms in the air on a deserted plain.

Frank couldn't miss her.

She'd have to find another base, maybe one that still had power. Tugging her hood lower to cover her face, Jàden turned away from the others.

But Feira caught her arm. "Herana, wait—"

"The Guardian said no." Mather had his sword against the healer's neck. The change in his tone from gentle to deadly toward the healer shot a shiver down Jàden's spine. How had he drawn his blade so fast?

Light sizzled into Jàden's veins at the woman's tight grip. She may crave the touch of another, but the way Feira's fingers dug in repulsed her. The Flame's light crackled through her veins, and Jàden clenched her fists as the unbidden power leaked between her fingers.

Fear often triggered the Flame, pulling it like silk into her veins with destructive intent. Jàden didn't want to hurt these people, and she couldn't lose control again. She just wanted to hide.

As Feira released her arm, Jàden stepped out of reach.

Anger burned in Feira's eyes as she spat at Mather's feet. "Rakir don't believe in Guardians. He should not speak. This man will only lead you into death, Herana."

"Woman, you must have cotton in your ears for how well you listen." Jon trotted through the crowd on his horse, pulling Mather's along beside him. Both mounts were loaded with blankets and sacks. He pushed himself in front of the healer, forcing her away from Jàden as Mather re-sheathed his sword. "The Guardian chooses her path, not you."

Relief flooded into Jàden as she wiped a stray tear from her cheek. "Get me out of this place."

As Jon lowered his hand to her, Jàden grabbed his forearm to steady herself. She was too weak to climb up, but Mather grabbed her waist and lifted her behind Jon.

She always felt safe on the back of a horse, even as a child. Wrapping her arms around Jon's waist, she leaned against his back, inhaling deeply of his masculine scent—pine and smoke and mountain all blended together. This was her safety now.

"Herana, please." Feira's voice held a note of desperation.

Jàden pitied the woman, but she couldn't stay.

Only one thing mattered—finding Kale and getting off this damn moon—and she couldn't do that inside a cage.

*Go back to the beginning.*

But the beginning of what? A dozen different things popped into her thoughts—their first dance, first kiss. But one day stood out among them as the worst, the beginning of her nightmare.

"I know where to start." Ignoring the healer, Jàden tightened her legs around the stallion as Jon turned them away from the gathering crowd.

"Remind me never to come back to this place." Mather wrangled his horse alongside, and they trotted onto the road, every small jolt sending pain into her shoulder.

"Jon," she muttered. "We have to go south to Ironstar Gate. I need to start at the beginning."

The Bloodflower Gate was closer, but she couldn't risk running from Frank straight into the arms of Enforcers. If she was lucky, the Ironstar Gate would be open and she could get home unseen. At least long enough to track Kale in his new life.

## CHAPTER 7
*The Forbidden Mountains*

Jàden traced her fingers along the ridges of a bark mushroom on a tree, slimy after the day's downpour. Between the pain in her shoulder and puking up most of what she ate, everything since Meridan had been a blur. After so long shut down, her body and mind were finally waking up, so she'd found a quiet spot to gather her thoughts.

Jàden was eager to keep going, but even she had to admit the horses needed rest. Especially Jon's black who now carried two riders.

Plus, she still hadn't found another base. They could be heading in circles for all she knew. Only trees and mountains were their constant companions. Without technology to navigate her toward Ironstar Tower, one of six gateways between the moon's surface and *Hàlon*, there was no telling how long before she'd be home, and she needed to reverse her energy tie with Jon.

Hopefully the gate was still open. She'd never seen a gate key. Always surrounded by an entourage of Enforcers, the Keepers kept each key hidden in a secret location no one could access.

It might take her months to reach the tower. Even though the Bloodflower Gate was closer, she couldn't risk it. The security would be high, and the area surrounded with Enforcers. At least, so the rumors went before she'd been shoved in her pod.

If only she could find south. But the heavy storm clouds provided a constant barrier between her and the stars.

Until tonight.

She broke the mushroom off the tree and leaned against the trunk as darkness blanketed the cloudless sky. Maybe another hour and the first of the sister moons would rise, or at least the simulation of it.

The bionet—*Hàlon's* energy field. It shielded the moon from losing atmosphere and generated day and night cycles—complete with four suns and two moons to simulate the old Alliance worlds.

Except the stars were gone.

Jàden closed her eyes, using the mushroom's wet dew to tap into the moon's lifeblood. Water ran though this world's oceans and rivers like a system of veins, and if she listened hard enough...

There.

The moon's heart beat a faint rhythm alongside hers. There was a time no one believed her, that Sandaris was so sick it couldn't hold any of the terraforming. Something plagued it like a bad virus, killing everything that tried to root in its soil. Unable to find a cause, or even proof of the sickness in her data, Jàden had offered herself as a final voice to ease its passing.

But she opened her eyes once more to the scent of pine on the wind. This world hadn't found death but life.

"Let's take a look at that shoulder." Jon's deep voice jolted her thoughts as he strode toward her, sweat glistening along his forehead. He untied the laces on her sleeve. "How's it feel?"

"Same." The pain constant now, a deep ache blossomed from her neck to her elbow. As he towered over her, she fiddled with the bark mushroom to distract herself from the lonely ache in her heart.

Jàden knew nothing of Jon except the black-uniformed soldiers wanted to hurt him, yet his energy was so intimate. Every step closer wrapped around her senses like a lover's embrace.

She missed Kale so much it hurt, and the stirring desire for another companion sliced her with guilt.

Jàden traced her thumb across the fungus, its symbiotic relationship with the tree one of shared energy so both lifeforms could flourish. It's what she'd become, the fungus on Jon so she could survive this world. As her guilt pushed to the surface, she tossed the tree fungus aside.

"You've barely said anything the last few days. Is the language still hard?" Jon unwound the bandage from her arm. Stitches held her wound closed around a blood-crusted scar.

"A little." The Sandarin language worded everything backwards, but once she understood how some of the phrases morphed from common speech, it became easier to pick up patterns and flow. She tried to use their words but sometimes fell back on the ease of her own dialect. If it weren't for her energy tie with Jon, she'd barely be able to string together a greeting. "Are you sure we're headed south? I have to get to Ironstar."

She had no reason to distrust him, but now that the fog of pain had lifted a bit from her thoughts, she was eager to find a computer and start her search.

Jon's unreadable gaze met hers, a stubbornness rooted in its depths. "Ironstar can wait. We find my men first."

"No. I need to find Kale first. I can't go tromping all over Sandaris waiting for you and Mather to listen." At least if she was headed south, she wouldn't be so anxious waiting for another base to appear on the horizon.

Jon seemed almost irritated by her words. His eyes lost focus for a moment, as if recalling some inner turmoil. "My men are in danger. Them first, then Kale."

"He's in danger too." The words flew out of her mouth like a petulant child, even if Kale could take care of himself. But Jàden sensed the Flame's hold on her growing stronger, the very thing Frank wanted to happen. And she'd already lost control the day Jon found her. If she lost control again, someone might get hurt. "If I don't find Kale—"

"He your husband?" The words had a bite that sent a chill through her.

She could re-bandage her own arm without his help and pulled away. "Does it matter?"

Jon leaned his shoulder against the tree and crossed his arms. "He's important to you though. A lover perhaps, or a sibling."

The pain of Kale's death bled into her heart. Clenching her hands tight to stop the trembling, she gazed out over the valley.

"Kale is everything." Friend. Lover. The brightest light she'd ever encountered in another person. Even from the grave, his gentle voice rang strong in her mind.

*"I need you to be strong," he'd whispered the last day she'd seen him alive. "I love you, baby, since the first time I saw you." Tears slid down his cheeks as his fighter roared, the engines nearly drowning out his voice. An orange glow flickered across his features as the flames rose higher in the cockpit. "When you wake up, go back to the beginning. I'll find you there."*

"Kale knew he was going to die." That awful explosion echoed through her head. "I have to find him. Get him home where we'll both be safe."

Or at least closer to safety.

Jon brushed her arm, tracing his fingers along her zankata birthmark as he checked the injury. "Hard to find a man who's already dead."

She turned away to hide her tears. "I could find him if I had a computer."

*Hàlon's* core systems kept records of every birth and death for thousands of generations, connecting energy signatures of each person from one life to the next. Some people chose to look through their previous lives and access lost memories, but most were content to live in the present.

Sometimes accessing the past could cause emotional complications and family bonds to be broken. Jàden once considered digging into her past, but when she met Kale, nothing mattered anymore except him and their future.

She couldn't talk about Kale any more, not without breaking down into a sobbing mess, so she wiped her cheeks dry and turned the questions back on Jon. "Mather said those riders are after you."

Tying off the bandage, Jon kept his silence as the wind howled across the plain, bringing a cold chill to her exposed arm. Folding the two halves of her sleeve back together, he tightened the laces and tied them off near her elbow.

She clutched his hand before he could release her. "Why were they chasing you? Who are those men?"

"Ìdolön soldiers." Jon tightened his jaw as if mulling over his words and how much to tell her. Small raindrops clung to the hairs on his thick beard. "I'm a deserter."

"You're a soldier?" It made sense, with how quickly Jon killed his pursuers. Yet she sensed a deeper story behind his words, some terrible tragedy she couldn't quite put her finger on. "Can I ask why you left?"

He gripped her hand as if needing a lifeline to hold onto. "They executed my family. Burned them alive."

Pain speared straight to her heart as she pulled away. What had she done, binding her energy to a man with a spouse? "You have a wife."

"Three sisters and a nephew. My parents too. All killed before I could save them." Jon untied the laces of his leather gauntlet and pushed up his sleeve, exposing a red orb with four silver leaves inked into his skin. "Because of this."

"The bloodflower." Jàden grabbed his arm and pushed the soft fabric higher, his skin warm and sweaty. "You're an Enforcer?"

Her hands trembled as she traced over the familiar mark. *Shoot to kill*—the order every Enforcer had received before Frank abducted her.

"How long have you been awake?" she asked.

"It's my family's mark, that's all." Something in Jon's tone held a dangerous edge as he pulled away. He wrapped the bracer around his forearm and tied the ends. "I was born on Sandaris, and when I die, I'll go to the land of the Guardians, just like my sisters."

It was the second time he mentioned them, and his voice seemed to hang on the word. His sisters must have been the most important thing in his life.

"This lover of yours, if he's dead, you won't find him here." The edge in his voice sharpened as he met her gaze, the soil-rich eyes filled with a grief so deep it tugged at her own heartache.

"There is no land of the Guardians," Jàden whispered. "That's a myth from the old world. Kale's alive in a new life, and if I don't find him—"

"We'll find your lover." Jon's voice was razor sharp this time, sending a shiver down her spine. "But I ain't changin' my mind. My men come first."

"Lighten up, Jon." Mather rode into the clearing, a small pheasant tied to his saddle. "Ain't her fault we haven't found the others yet."

A dark cloud descended over Jon's features as he lit a cigarette and trudged toward their makeshift camp. "Get some sleep, both of you. We leave in a few hours."

Jàden wrung her hands together, a painful knot tightening her chest. "I've angered him."

Mather chuckled and dropped from his horse. "Nah, that's just Jon being Jon. You'll know when he's angry."

She furrowed her brow and tried to suppress the uneasiness in her gut. She hated confrontation or any kind of heated argument, and yet she itched to smooth things over. "How do you know? I must have said something wrong. He seems really upset."

"You see that sword on his back?" He lifted the saddle off his horse and held it across his shoulder. "When the sword comes out, he's angry. It's the only time he ever unsheathes it."

Jàden couldn't imagine anything more terrifying than to have Jon aiming his weapons at her. As Mather's stallion pressed his nose into her hands, she scratched along the velvety fur, content with some equine affection.

"His name's Agnar." Mather set the saddle down and patted the rump of his mount. "He's yours."

"What?" Her hands froze as the horse nudged her to get more attention. "You can't give me your horse."

He scratched the back of his neck, his eyes clouded over. "I love Jon. He's like the brother I never had, and I owe him my life. But I got a wife back home I never should have left. I'm going back, and I can't take this old boy with me."

"Why not? He's strong and surefooted with a gentle temperament." And a desperate need for attention. She half-smiled as the stallion shoved his head into her chest like he wanted to climb onto her lap.

"I ride home on a soldier's horse, every Rakir in the city will know I'm a deserter. I'll be killed or stuck in a cage the rest of my days." Raw pain flashed across his features. "Tomorrow we'll pass through the last village before Nelórath. I'd be honored if you'd find me a good horse, Herana. One with a strong spirit who will take me home to my wife and child."

Jàden nodded, not sure what else to say. "Thank you for everything you've done for me."

"I have one more favor to ask." Mather laid a hand on her shoulder and looked deep into her eyes. "That dead lover of yours ain't never gonna be the man you remember. He'll have a different life with no clue who you are. If you really care for him, don't go lookin'. You'll just be draggin' him back into the same mess."

A deep ache uncurled in her chest. She'd discovered the same truth about recycled lives long ago. Every child did. Of course he'd be different, but *Hàlon* possessed technology to help people remember their past. Memories were contained in the essence. With the right connections, their bodies could access lifetimes of data. Maybe Kale hadn't been able to save her from the cages, but he'd told her to go back to the beginning.

So that's where she would go.

Jàden refused to let the life they created together be gone, not when she loved and trusted Kale more than anyone else alive. Besides, he needed her, and she needed him. "I'm all he has."

Kale's father sure didn't want him, and his mother died long ago on the Alliance rim worlds.

"Jon's life ain't been nothin' but trouble since he first rode a horse, but he's a good man with a kind heart and he'll always have your back in a fight." Mather stepped away and shouldered his saddle again. "All I'm sayin' is I ain't never seen a woman show him so much kindness. When I'm gone, it'll be up to you to take care of him."

## CHAPTER 8
*The Forbidden Mountains*

No land of the Guardians.

Jon couldn't shake Jàden's words, the pain of his family's loss deep in his gut. His older sister would have been devastated by such news.

At some point Jàden had switched to her own dialect, the softer tongue rolling through her impassioned words.

*Kale is everything.*

Her revelation stung the deepest part of his soul, and he couldn't push aside the thought of her with a lover. Jon would give up the bloodflower in a heartbeat to hear any woman say such a thing about him. He glanced over his shoulder to where Mather and Jàden lay curled in their blankets on either side of the fire pit. But he didn't want those words spoken from any woman.

Jon wanted to hear them from her.

Clenching his jaw, he squashed down the ridiculous notion. He lit another cigarette and leaned against a tree trunk, scanning the woods for any movement. Normally he kept watch like a hawk, but tonight his thoughts boiled over with memories of his family, the old farm, and the last argument with his father.

Both stubborn to the point of ridiculous, Jon and his father had battled all the time. But those final words between them ate at Jon. "Without a wife, the bloodline is lost, boy. You and your sisters will be the last of the Ayers name."

Jon became Rakir—soldiers forbidden to have wives—to right a wrong from his past. Except he'd made a mess of his family name and bungled the debt he'd set out to discharge. Now he had nothing but a broken legacy, an army desperate to possess the heirloom around his neck, and an old enemy who would kidnap Jàden just to enrage Jon.

A whisper of wind alerted him to a presence at his side. As Jon grasped his dagger, Jàden wrapped a blanket around her shoulders. Soft light from the largest of the sister moons glistened against her dark locks.

"I'm sorry about earlier," she said.

"For what? You said your words, I said mine. Ain't no harm done." His little sister would have smacked him for speaking to Jàden like she was one of his soldiers.

Jon released the grip on his weapon and bit back his frustration before he said something worse. The last thing Jàden needed was an earful about how she didn't need to be chasing a dead man.

Never mind that it made him a hypocrite. If he thought there was any chance his family still lived, Jon would do everything in his power to find them.

She grasped his arm, right over his bloodflower tattoo, and his chest tightened.

"Jon, tell me how to find south. I have no idea what direction to go without a datapad or a sky full of stars." She'd switched to her own dialect again, but with the soft breath of her magic flowing through his veins, the words seamlessly translated in his head now.

"Give me your hands." Jon turned her around to face the tree trunk and gripped her hands in his. Their delicate warmth bled into his palms, and he stifled the ache to wrap her in his arms and pull her close. He placed her hands to either side of the trunk, the bark rough against his calloused skin. "I don't know what stars are, but the trees will always lead the way."

"How will this—"

"Just wait," he whispered, the delicate scent of pine off her hair teasing him. "Every tree has two faces, one to the mountains and one to the sea. Feel the bark across your fingers, how it differs on one side of the trunk." Fine hairs rose along the trunk, brushing against his skin. "The mountain face sleeps while the sea calls to the thin fibers, like hair raising along your neck."

Jàden furrowed her brow and brushed each side of the tree, tracing the trunk's deep lines with her bony fingers.

Releasing her hands, he gazed across her soft features, so similar to the stone planes of Herana's statue. Her cheeks weren't quite so hollow anymore, but the similarities between Jàden and the Guardian couldn't be doubted.

"I feel it," she whispered then pointed away from the valley. "That's south."

"Almost." He shifted her arm a little further. "This is south."

He traced his fingers along her hand, turning her wrist so her palm faced skyward. Flecks of light and shadow drifted upward.

"Tell me what this means to you," he said.

She pressed her lips together as if she didn't want to answer, but Jon needed to know. With one bit of magic, she'd forged a bond between them, made herself his everything.

He'd spent years stifling his ache for a true companion, seeking out the company of both men and women with his need always suppressed in the back of his thoughts. Jàden's breath on his skin cracked open all those old desires.

"It's an energy tie, something only Enforcers know about." She bit her lip, clearly holding something back. "Kale taught me, though he wasn't supposed to. Soldiers tie their energy in a crisis to help one another stay alive. Its practice is forbidden to outsiders."

Her eyes lost focus as she caressed her thumb across the lines in Jon's palm, the same flecks of magic hovering over his hand. Jon clenched his jaw.

She saw him as a soldier, someone who could keep her alive. Nothing more. Not that it should have been surprising. Most women only saw him for his sword arm. One day he'd find a way to tell her what the bond meant to him, but he suspected that revelation would only trap her between a dead lover and a bodyguard she'd discard the moment she found Kale.

"Jon." Mather's voice sliced through his thoughts, an urgency to his tone. "Fire, next ridge."

As Mather pointed to the flickering lights across the valley, Jon laid a hand on Jàden's shoulder. "To the horses, quick."

Jon saddled his black and tied everything down, keeping one eye on the ridge and one ear to the woods for any change in sound patterns. He would rather have one more night of peace, even if it meant keeping the secret of their bond close to his heart, but he couldn't afford to be caught by the Rakir. He'd be in chains, but Jàden's fate would be a lot worse.

"More soldiers?" She pressed close to a tree, searching the sky as if expecting something to be there.

He lifted Jàden onto his horse. "Likely scouts. Still haven't seen the bulk of the army."

Clouds gathered in the east beyond the high peaks.

"If we can get ahead of the storm, the snow will cover our tracks." The black tattoo across Mather's forehead crinkled, telling Jon his best friend's thoughts were on Sharie, his wife. Mather had bonded her in secret and kept her safe in a small home deep in the Flower District so the Rakir would never discover their connection.

Jon always knew his friend had a lover, but he'd never known the full truth until he met Sharie, her stomach swollen with Mather's child. Forced to leave her behind when they'd deserted their posts,

Mather's gaze often held a deep longing to return to his family.

A sentiment Jon understood all too well.

Mather held the same stare now, his gaze piercing the hilly landscape to a memory of the past. Probably because he'd never made peace with his decision to leave Sharie.

"You don't have to follow, brother." Jon laid a hand on Mather's shoulder. "Go back for your wife and head north. Sharie will want to know you're alive, and Rakir won't follow you into wolf country."

They'd had this conversation dozens of times. Mather clenched his jaw. "I made you a promise, Captain. What kind of man would I be if I didn't honor it? Besides, I need to say goodbye to the others first."

Jon considered ordering him to turn back, even if he preferred Mather at his side, but once Mather made up his mind, no man could change it. A trait they often shared. "If we push the horses, we can find the others in a few days and get you on your way."

After clearing away all signs of their presence from the small campsite, they trotted along narrow roads and through snow-bound valleys, their tracks a beacon to any Rakir. He and Mather stayed sharp, always searching the terrain for anything out of the ordinary while Jàden nestled at his back.

He relished her heat and the softness of her breath under his skin. Maybe she wasn't really his to have, but Jon wasn't going to hand her back to some asshole who'd left her to suffer. Jàden had him as a husband now, at least according to northern law, and Jon refused to take the duty lightly.

Even if she didn't hail from the north.

The next day broke with another storm, snowfall so thick it practically covered their trail as they rode.

Jon scanned both directions at a crossing. Narrow ruts under a thin layer of powder showed the wider road still in use. Mountain folk with smaller, surefooted horses, but no northern mounts like he and Mather rode. "Let's keep pushing. Maybe another day."

Exhaustion from the rough terrain kept the stallions' heads hanging low, but they trudged on with their ears forward, as if they sensed the rest of their brother-herd nearby.

Jàden eased her grip on his waist and pointed to a jagged rock formation. "There's something buried there."

As she squinted toward the cliffs further along the road, snow blanketed the land under dark clouds, a weathered sign pointing the way ahead.

"There should be a village close by." Yet he followed her finger to smooth, dark metal painted with a white zankata. He glanced at Mather as if to ask if he recognized the structure, but he shook his head.

Jon didn't have any clue either, but something about the sharp lines buried beneath rock set him on edge. He lit a cigarette, the bitter shadeleaf smoke filling his lungs. But as he doused the glow on his lighter, the same sharp lines of the small block were a striking similarity as those from the cliff.

"What is that?" Surely it couldn't be a lighter hundreds of spans tall.

"It's a ship," Jàden whispered. "And that's my zankata."

# CHAPTER 9
*Nadrér*

Jàden slid off the horse and bolted across the road into a cluster of sparse trees. Kale promised the bird's symbol would guarantee her safety, so maybe the ship still had power like her hypersleep pod. She clung to the idea as snow fell silent in the stormy gloom.

"Wait, Jàden!"

Ignoring Jon, she raced through snowy pines toward a thick line of brush. The cliff face on one side partially covered the ship's tail fin, likely a buildup of dirt and storms millennia after it crashed. She wanted to find the airlock. Foliage grew around the ship, stunted trees brushing their canopy on the underside of the bridge. She crawled beneath a thick bush to a tear in the hull and climbed a rusted metal ladder, ivy clinging to the steel rails. Jàden crawled onto the platform, a long corridor leading deeper inside the ship. The pain in her shoulder flared, but it wasn't enough to stifle the guilt creeping along her spine as Jon climbed up beside her.

"You can't go running off like that." He unsheathed his daggers and twisted the blades against the flat of his arm. Fatigue pulled at the tired lines around his eyes. Jon hadn't slept for almost a full day. "Not with Rakir nearby."

"The zankata symbol is Kale. He's trying to tell me something."

She squeezed his arm, and a knot tightened her stomach. Every day she rode with her arms around his waist, or sometimes she'd guide the horse while he held her against his chest. She didn't want to admit it, but she liked the way Jon held her and the roughness of his voice when he whispered in her ear.

While hard to see most of his features under the bushy beard and shaggy hair, Jon proved to be an odd mix of gentle warmth with a harsh edge to his spirit, as if even the trees would move out of his way to avoid a fight on his moodier days.

Jàden pulled Jon's firemark from her pocket and blew the glass orb until it glowed. As an Enforcer, Kale would understand her desperate need for survival. At least she kept telling herself this each time her body ached to slide under Jon's blanket and curl up in his arms.

The comfort of another might help her push back the grief for a few hours of reprieve, but Kale still had her heart.

"All right, Kale," she said. "Show me where you are."

Jàden wasn't naïve enough to believe she'd find him amid the starship wreckage, but if any of the electronics still worked, she might be able to connect with *Hàlon's* computers.

Wires hung like vines across the shield panels as she held up the firemark and stepped inside a narrow tunnel packed with dirt. Faint illumination glowed behind the rock—a door's light pad.

Grabbing a large stone, she slammed it against the dirt, chipping at the packed granules as they fell from the glowing plexiglass.

Jàden opened the hole enough to fit her hand and pressed her palm against the door. The glow shifted from white to blue, and machinery whirred behind the dirt wall.

The door slid open. As she gripped the stone to make a bigger hole, Jon laid a hand on her shoulder.

"Let me try." He slammed his shoulder into the rock and stumbled through the opening, dirt raining across the doorway. "Fuck me."

The awe in his voice was unmistakable as Jàden stepped into a wide corridor. Rock gave way to smooth metal. She traced her fingers across the familiar nelané shield material, a metal lighter than titanium and stronger than steel. Guild engineers forged a degree of flexibility into the mined ore to withstand both deep seas and outer space, with the ability to shift from pure obsidian to transparent glass.

*Hàlon's* citizens used nelané in everything from starship hulls to machine parts to computer glass and weapons manufacturing. It was the root of all their technology, powered by the biotheric microorganisms glowing inside her firemark.

The corridor stretched in both directions, faint light glowing through the gray metal seams from the cargo bay to the bridge.

"What is this place?" Mather stepped into the hall behind her, an arrow held loose against his bow string. "I don't like it."

Jàden brushed her fingers over a rougher patch of metal where an emblem had been removed, the four petals of the bloodflower unmistakable. But someone chipped off the seal and painted a zankata in its place.

"It's a nardrér starship." Easy to spot by the tail fin and larger than Kale's Raith fighter, the nardrér could latch onto an enemy cruiser and splice a temporary airlock onto the hull in under three minutes. They were known to be flown by soldiers to enter an enemy vessel or by deep-space salvagers.

Voices laughed in the distance.

Both Mather and Jon raised their weapons, shielding her at their backs.

"Hello?" Jàden stepped between them and followed the sound deeper into the ship.

"Watch me run, Daddy. I'm fast like..."

The voice drowned under a rush in her ears. Why would a nardrér be crashed? *Hàlon* hadn't encountered an enemy ship once during her twenty-three years, and a training simulation gone bad would have been salvaged. The thought only added to Jàden's growing list of questions about why she'd been in hypersleep for nearly four millennia.

A little girl spoke from deeper inside the ship. "I'm strong, Daddy, like Jàden."

Her heart skipped a beat.

The voice came from beyond the far door. She pressed her palm against the light pad for the bridge, frosted plexiglass shifting from white to blue. The door swished open. Tree branches slapped her cheeks as she coughed on a burst of snow.

Jàden shoved aside the barbed foliage, a zankata crowing from the other side of the door. It spread its wings and flew off as she wiped the excess dirt from beneath her nose.

"Wait." Jon tried to hold her back.

But she eased through the door, alert to every sound of children's laughter beyond the thick foliage. They giggled again, and the same words repeated as if caught in a loop. "I'm strong, Daddy, like Jàden."

"Hello? Anyone there?" Jàden said.

Snow fell beyond the branches onto three seats facing a wide console. Glass cracked across the transparent shield panel, fracturing a video of children racing through the screen.

"I'm strong, Daddy, like Jàden." The unfamiliar little girl grabbed a pile of dirt in two hands, gripping it tight as a seedling sprouted between her fingers until it exploded into a burst of tiny leaves.

"Strong like Jàden," Jàden muttered, a woozy light-headedness gripping her.

The girl grew a seed from the dirt in her hands, something Jàden had never done in her life. Her power didn't fuel life. It destroyed.

As if on cue, the moon's heartbeat whispered alongside hers, a bond of connection that Jàden ultimately feared. If her power grew too strong, she could lose control and tear all of Sandaris apart.

Her breath came fast now as panic gripped her.

Jàden grabbed the nearest chair to steady herself. The seat twisted, and bones clattered—a decayed skeleton in gray fatigues. Hollow eye sockets met her gaze, and she stumbled back, knocking into Jon.

"Who are these people?" Jon's deep voice filled the chamber as he traced his fingers over the uniform's shoulder patch.

No infinite circle wrapping the drain and ladder logo. This person wasn't a guildsman but from general maintenance, fourth-class citizens banished from taking Guild exams because of their crimes. Most had almost no credits but those they earned working on *Hàlon's* sewers, garbage maintenance and a thousand other jobs.

When the little girl spoke again, Jàden eased the chair back around so the skeleton could watch the screen.

Sorrow was etched into Jon's deep brown eyes. "Is this him?"

If only it were that easy. Jàden stifled the rising grief as she recalled those final seconds before the explosion.

*"I love you, baby."* An orange glow flickered across Kale's features, flames rising higher in the cockpit. *"When you wake up, go back to the beginning."*

She winced at the memory of his final transmission.

"It's not him." She clutched Jon's shirt and leaned against him, aching for his warmth and the comfort it offered. Jàden imagined the skeleton was once a young mother who couldn't go home and wanted to spend her dying minutes with her children. "This woman was probably still alive after the ship crashed, maybe bleeding internally."

"I'm strong, Daddy, like Jàden." The little girl's voice looped again.

A life born after her disappearance. The red numbers on the hypersleep pods made more sense with each passing day. While Jàden slept, *Hàlon* lived, but where were they all now?

Stepping toward the console, she eased into an empty chair. "This pilot might be dead, but someone has to be alive."

"What are you doing?" Jon hovered over her shoulder as she scanned the different buttons.

"Calling home." Jàden pressed the HUD's heads up display button, the screen lights jumping out in a three-dimensional display.

"Holy shit, what is that?" Jon leapt backwards. He eased toward the lights, his fingers passing through the holographic display. "Too dangerous to use magic. Someone might—"

"This isn't magic." Jàden punched several keys, trying to familiarize herself once more with the console before she tugged a headset over her ear. She pressed the button to call directly to the nardrér's command unit, glancing over her shoulder. "Where's Mather?"

"Went to look around." Jon's jaw was tight.

She pressed the headset against her ear. It was standard procedure for *Hàlon* to monitor all distress calls, no matter where they came from. Jàden punched in the pilot emergency distress button.

Jon leaned against the back of her chair. "Are you sure about this?"

Her hand froze on the mouthpiece. As far as she knew, Enforcers still had a standing order to kill her. Maybe she should shut down the signal. A dozen soldiers might recognize her face and fly in to bomb the area to get rid of her for good. Or they would want to take her into custody.

*And put me in another cage.* "No, I'm not."

A voice blared from the headset, an AI monitor with an almost human voice. "Nardrér 3625-7C, what is your status?"

No going back now. Jàden turned toward the console as the HUD typed across the air, scan data from the ship showing more errors than working systems.

"Crashed," she whispered into the headset. "On the surface of Sandaris. The pilot is dead."

"Transferring to operator 573-D." The scan data disappeared and pulled up an image of an empty chair inside a tower control room, one of thousands scattered across the giant starship. Overhead lights and most of the computers were on, the narrow-focus camera showing more than a dozen unoccupied stations.

"Where is everyone?" Her stomach twisted into a tight knot. Nothing moved, not even the data on the screens, as if the room had been cleared and everything frozen. "Is anyone there? Please. I need to find Sergeant Jason Kale."

Dead air filled her headset. She covered her ears, hoping to catch a door closing off camera or any small sound, but absolute silence bled through the speakers.

"Hello, this is"—she hesitated—"the Bioengineering Guild. I need your help." Operator rooms were never left unattended. "Pan the camera. AI. Operator. Anyone."

Finally it pulled back, widening the focus to more than fifty empty stations and a silent docking bay beyond the far glass.

"We need to leave this place." Jon yanked the headset off and pulled her out of the chair. He didn't seem like the type of man who spooked easily, but one look at the hard set of his features said he was clearly rattled. "That is one creepy ass place, Jàden."

"It's where Enforcers monitor the ships coming in and out of a docking bay. Maybe they all went to lunch."

Guild command would never allow an operator room to have fewer than ten people on duty. As Jon guided her out the door, she gripped the edge and glanced toward the HUD, the little girl's voice still chatting on the looping video.

"I'm strong, Daddy, like Jàden."

Jàden clutched the door frame to hold on a little longer in case someone walked across the screen. *Hàlon* housed over a million occupants. Someone should be there.

Jon slid his arm around her waist and leaned next to her ear. "Rakir are close. We protect the living. Then we can chase the dead."

## CHAPTER 10
*The Forbidden Mountains*

Captain Éli Hareth often heard that revenge was a confession of pain. But his late brother Sebastian told him once that revenge was a liberation of anguish, if a man could target his enemy well.

As the morning storm blew off the sea into the foothills, Éli trudged across the muddy camp, the familiar tingle of the Dark Flame brushing his senses. Smooth as silk when it slid across his thoughts, the thrumming power called to him like a beautiful mistress he'd been forbidden to touch.

He clenched his fist to keep it contained, hating that he could wield his sword without mercy, but even a meager amount of magic would get him executed. Éli refused to die, at least until Jon Ayers suffered for what he'd done.

"How long do we have?" Éli said.

Granger, his second in command and most trusted ally, fell into step beside him. "Message received an hour ago. They're three days out."

Flurries blew with an icy wind as they walked the line of picketed horses. The animals hated to be tied up, and most could easily escape their ropes, which was why they'd had to use locking nuts to keep them from scattering.

Granger grabbed Éli's arm, stopping him in his tracks. Then Granger lowered his voice. "Ayers ain't ridin' with his men though. Scouts say he's got some woman with him."

"A woman?" Pain punched his gut as Éli digested this new information. It couldn't be Jon's sisters. They were all dead. "Where the fuck are his men?"

"Mather rides with him. The others disappeared weeks ago."

"Fuck!" Anger burned in Éli's chest as he clenched the dagger at his waist until his hand hurt.

He scanned the giant sequoias, half-expecting an ambush of Jon's men. "They'll be close. Find them."

He would destroy them all just for the satisfaction of debilitating Jon under a mountain of grief. "Who's the woman? Anyone recognize her?"

"She had her face covered." Granger looped his thumbs through his belt, his gut hanging over the front. "I sure could use me that whore to get warm though. Don't matter what she looks like."

Two things his captain loved most were sex and violence, and the two were never mutually exclusive.

"No one touches her until I figure out who she is." Éli wasn't about to let anything slip through his hands, especially a woman he might be able to leverage against Jon.

"There's somethin' else." Granger spat at the ground, biding his time as if he didn't want to tell Éli the news on the tip of his tongue. "Selnä's got Connor."

"What?" Éli snarled so loud half the horses startled and tugged on their ropes. He clenched his jaw so tight it throbbed. Not that he cared much for the little prick. His son was bred for one purpose: revenge.

"The boy sails with the high council barge." Granger gestured toward the sea, just out of sight beyond the woods.

"Those fucking bastards." Éli couldn't shake the notion that he'd become like Sebastian—a soldier desperate to sever all ties with the Tower and protect his bloodline from the same fate. If he didn't get Connor back soon, his son would be branded to the Tower's fate and the cycle would start all over again.

Éli slapped a nearby tree trunk, startling the horses again before he grabbed a blanket to saddle his stallion. The whole point of this mission was to ambush Jon from all sides and retrieve the bloodflower key, but Éli had no intention of killing that bastard.

Death was too good a reward. He needed to suffer, to feel the same anguish Éli had borne all these years since his brother's death. Tightening the girth on his stallion, he untied the lead rope on his horse and climbed into the saddle.

"Send a message to the scouts..." He trailed off as he glanced toward the camp and the large black tent in the middle. A whisper of power brushed against the brand on his arm, a symbol of the Tower's hold on his life.

Black threads of that power rose from inside the tent, brushing across each branded soldier as the high council member inside kept a tight rein on them all.

Only Éli could see the black threads that bound them to six hypocritical old crones. They killed any man, woman or child with a hint of magic, all to protect their own. It was why he'd asked to work inside the prison, so he didn't have to bear witness every day to the woven threads of his doom.

"Commander?" Granger nudged his horse alongside. "What message should I send back?"

"Never mind." Éli sure as shit didn't want anyone on the high council knowing his thoughts on the woman. She was probably some mountain bitch riding the same trail, but with Jon, Éli could never be sure he hadn't picked up some damsel in distress. "We need to find that blacksmith. What's his name?"

"Sproki." Granger spat at the ground again, this time a mass of mucus clinging to his beard. "You have the jewel?"

Éli patted his chest. It had taken nearly everything he owned to secure a real ruby, one that looked similar to the jewel buried inside the bloodflower pendant. "Let's go."

He nudged his horse onto a trail that would lead him toward the coast and small village built inside giant trees to the south. Beneath the giant redwoods, great holes had been cut into the trunks and served as small marketplaces. Inside the trunks, stairways carved into the wood rose to small homes. In Éli's mind, the cozy quarters might keep out the cold weather, but all an invading army had to do was light a fire to the tree and hundreds would be burned alive.

Southerners and northerners didn't like one another, and people here were no different. They stared at Éli and Granger, and most turned away quickly. Half a day's ride south and they'd be killed for wearing these uniforms. But in this place, the tree folks were used to tradesmen from the mountains and across the sea.

Éli stopped his horse in front of a blacksmith stall and slid from the saddle.

"Don't work for Rakir," the man shouted without looking up.

"You want to go home to your wife tonight, you'll work." Éli slapped a sheet of paper onto the man's workbench before the smith could swing his hammer.

Not a man—a woman who turned one eye to him, the other a hollow socket. "You deaf, northman? Your kind ain't wanted here."

She looked about to say more but glanced at the drawing on the paper.

"By Élon's light, where did you get that?" she asked.

"You see this symbol before?"

The woman dropped the hammer and crossed herself. "Not for many years."

"I know where the real one is." As soon as the woman's head shot up, Éli knew he had her. "I need you to make one just like it."

"It'll cost you, northman, and you ain't got enough money in the world to pay me." Her gaze drifted to something behind Éli as the horses snorted. "Tell you what though. That bitch across the way has been on my ass for months. Get rid of her, you and me are square. I'll make your pretty trinket."

Éli turned to a small shop barely a dozen spans away. Colorful draperies hung, each with a symbol to the seven Guardians. He clenched his fist, scanning for the emblem for Erisöl, a duplicate of the mark inked into his forearm. Éli didn't believe in Guardians, but Sebastian had been born under the signs of Élon. From the time he was little, he and his brother had been inseparable, just like the two Guardian brothers.

At nine years old, Sebastian had taken Éli to get his tattoo, binding them as brothers for life. A year later, Jon had killed Sebastian, and Éli's life fell apart.

Before he could turn away, something else caught his eye. A banner, buried behind the others and barely visible, with colorful threads woven together in a series of lines. Embroidered into it was a small diamond shape with two arms stretching outward into a circle—the sign for a dreamwalker.

He glanced at Granger. The last time he'd met a dreamwalker, the woman kept digging into his dreams and searching for secrets to blackmail him with. Maybe the smith really didn't like the woman over there, or she too wanted to see what secrets were in his head.

Éli jutted his chin toward Granger, a silent gesture to take a look around. When he turned back to the blacksmith, a sneer tugged the corner of his lip.

"Make sure that medallion is done by dawn." He handed her the ruby he'd carried in his pocket for weeks. "I'll take care of your little problem."

But not before he got what he wanted. To learn exactly who the woman was and how he could use her to strike at Jon.

# CHAPTER 11

*The Forbidden Mountains*

Jàden bitterly let go of the door frame. Chase the living, not the dead, and yet she needed to understand why no one answered the distress call and how her zankata became emblazoned on the starship.

While she hadn't expected Kale to pop out of a room, there had to be something here. A clue to lead her to him.

Ducking under Jon's arm, she dug through the pilot's pockets for a datapad, something she could take with her. At this point, she'd even settle for a gun in case someone tried to shoot her with an arrow again.

"Jàden, we need to leave." Jon's tone was so calm.

A surge of irritation gripped her. He didn't understand how important her task was. If she lingered too long on Sandaris, the Flame could cause serious damage.

She slammed her fists on the console. "I have to find Kale."

The lights flickered, and the HUD disappeared.

"No, dammit, not again," she said.

Diving back into the navigator seat and buckling in seemed like a good idea, except the ship wouldn't have access to the life archives. She'd need a datapad and the right access codes, or she'd have to be back on board the ship.

Jàden refused to give up and dashed into the corridor, slanting upward toward the tail fin. She yanked open drawers and cabinets, slowly moving aft as she searched for a med-kit, a gun, anything that might help. But someone had been here long before her. Shelves and drawers laid bare except for a layer of dust.

"Dammit." She slammed the last cabinet shut. Maybe she'd have better luck in the cargo bay.

But Mather blocked her path. "I wouldn't go back there."

As he gestured something toward Jon, she rushed past and stumbled into a cargo hold filled with glass cages. Skeletons slumped in the corners, each one alone and trapped between four panes of transparent shield glass.

"No!" Jàden rushed to the closest cell and slammed the glass. "Open the doors—"

Jon grabbed her arm. "I'm getting you out of here."

"No, they need help." Jàden squirmed in his grasp.

"They're dead."

The ice in his tone seemed to rip a blindness from her as she screamed, "Let them out!"

But they were all dead, from starvation or suffocation long after her own imprisonment.

Jon's features were tight with worry. "The dead are in their graves. Let them stay there. Ain't no good gonna come if we linger here."

Jàden's gaze stayed glued to the death cages long after they disappeared behind a closed door, her chest so tight she could barely breathe.

Thunder rumbled in the sky as they stepped onto the platform.

Mather palmed the door closed. "This place holds nothing but death. You're safer with us."

"Don't you get it? I'm not safe anywhere. Those people..." She couldn't stop thinking of the pilot. Why had someone in maintenance kept people in cages? Any empathy Jàden had minutes ago for the dead pilot shattered under the weight of what she'd seen. Wringing her hands, she glanced once more at the ship, her zankata—Kale's symbol of safety— painted on the death trap. "All of this is wrong. Kale would never lead me into death."

And yet the doubt settled in her heart as she turned away to a snow-bound landscape. Even the universe taunted her, death in a cage and a world of white.

"I'll never get home, will I?" she whispered.

Jon leaned toward her ear. "Wherever we ride, that's your home now."

Easy for him to call the road home. Jàden shouldered him away and retreated down the ladder. She didn't want this to be her home. The stars called to her from beyond the bionet, a life of peace in a sea of glimmering jewels.

Mather would return to his home, his wife, and she'd be left with nothing.

And Jon... As he slid down the ladder to land beside her, he too had no home but the road under his feet. They were a pair, two lost souls with nothing but a mission. He, to find his men, and her, to reunite with Kale.

As Mather hit the ground and met her gaze, his words came rolling back through her head. *When I'm gone, it'll be up to you to take care of him.*

She cursed under her breath and retreated to the horses. Jon could take care of himself—he didn't need her.

Jàden tried to climb into the saddle, but was still too weak to do more than stand in the stirrups. Jon lifted her onto the stallion's back, she grabbed the reins and scooted forward. She didn't want to be along for the ride anymore. She still needed to find Kale. Not only because she loved him but because he was a damn good pilot. Someone needed to fly her away from this place.

Jon climbed on behind her without a word, nudging his horse onto the road with his heels.

With a final glance at the nadrér's tail fin, Jàden tried to suppress the anger in her heart. Her zankata painted on a graveyard. It seemed fitting somehow that she'd only find true safety in death.

"Nothing you could have done for those people, Jàden." The scent of Jon's cigarette's smoke wove into her senses, but it did not calm her unease. "They died in cages, under my emblem. The sooner I get off this world, the better."

Snow fell furiously as they trotted along the road, a blanket of white surrounding them on all sides. Jàden tried to force back the grief, stifling it under her need for Kale.

But Jon didn't make it easy to keep her thoughts focused. As fatigue hit him, he slid one strong arm around her waist, his head dropping against his chest to nap. His soft breath wove a spell through her senses as she clenched the reins tighter. She'd slept near him for weeks each time they'd stopped for the night, but now it was like they were curled together in the same blanket.

"If he's too heavy, wake his ass up." Mather's features softened as he nudged Agnar closer.

"Let him rest." It was about all she could do and not be useless to them. She turned back for one last look at the ship, but it was already gone in a sea of white. "Those soldiers, how far will they follow us?"

"They should have stopped weeks ago. Something don't feel right about it, but the others will keep the captain safe."

His eyes lost their focus again as Jàden nudged the horse into a gallop. It was too easy to get lost in the pain on Mather's face. His wife was still alive and only a season's ride north while she had easily three times that distance to travel. It would be easier with a ship, even one as small as a scout craft, but it simply wasn't something she could count on anymore.

Her stomach tingled as Jon grumbled in his sleep and leaned into her head.

"Jon," she whispered, pushing him back with her good shoulder.

He tightened his grip on her waist and mumbled into her ear, "I'm awake."

"About time." Mather smacked his shoulder. "Should be at that village in a few hours."

## CHAPTER 12
*The Forbidden Mountains*

Jon grumbled against Jàden, the gentle pine scent of her hair a calming remedy as he pulled her against his chest. He'd give almost anything to start every day with her curled in his arms.

As the afternoon sky darkened, he sat up straight and lit a cigarette. No time to languish this close to a village. They hadn't seen the scouts since the fire on the ridge, but their absence didn't ease the tension in his body. It seemed the scouts intentionally kept their distance.

Which could be because they were close to warden territory.

Everything south of the Forbidden Mountains belonged to the wardens and their golden cities. While Jon never traveled this far before, he'd heard the stories about women armed as soldiers and the great towers of the Guardians.

Rakir and wardens despised one another, content to let the mountains divide their cultures. Wardens and southerners worshipped their Guardians while the north barely acknowledged their existence.

Jon and Mather intentionally tried to appear as mountain hunters with their thick beards and long, shaggy hair, hoping to escape the notice of both factions. Unfortunately, the horses gave them away, but Jon wouldn't trade his companion for a dozen mounts.

"We need to lighten our load," Jon muttered, nodding toward the furs stacked behind Mather. "Get you a horse so you can be on your way back to Sharie."

"Still need to say farewell to the others." Mather stopped his horse, clouded eyes scanning the landscape.

Shadows grew deeper, the air cooler. He glanced back several times, but still no one followed. A lonely pole stood to the side of the road, an empty lantern swinging from its apex.

"Somethin' ain't right," Mather said.

Jon listened to the silence. Watched how the snow fell without a hint of wind over the desolate road. Low mounds lined the cliff amid a cluster of trees and thick ivy.

He glanced toward Mather as they wove a twisted path among fallen pines and shrubs, sharing a silent *I sense it too*. His best friend was right— something felt off, almost too quiet. At the very least they should be able to spot hoofprints or wagon tracks, but the snow laid over the road like a fresh blanket.

"Stay on the horse and be ready to run." Jon dropped to the ground and laid a hand on Jàden's knee. The sweetness of her breath flowed through his skin, but he tightened his jaw and tried to ignore it. "Shout if anything moves."

He grabbed his quiver, noting the way Jàden searched the sky and gripped the reins like her life depended on it.

"Take Agnar." Mather tossed his reins to Jàden. Dismounting, he shadowed Jon on the far side of the road.

Something in her magic nudged his mind with a vision of metal flying high over the clouds. He shoved it away and crept along the road, holding an arrow loose against his bow string.

Tall redwoods twisted along the path, covered in fresh-fallen snow. Burn marks scarred the lantern pole. Further along the road, small mounds poked out at odd angles, a faint scent of embers smoldering.

Jon crouched and brushed snow away from a shattered signpost, a silver dagger wedged in a crack with the tower and two moons emblem on the hilt.

Zankata cawed from the high cliffs, their black feathers a smudge against the clouds. "Rakir. They shouldn't be ahead of us," Jon said.

Mather nodded. "Looks like Rakir passed through days ago. I'd bet my life that pile over there holds more than a cremated building."

He followed his friend's hand toward a larger mound. Nothing moved, but Jon could sense death lurking. He crouched near the snowy pile and tugged a charred bonding cloth from between two timbers. Grief swelled in his chest as he recalled his last day in Ìdolön and his family's death.

Mather laid a hand on his shoulder. "It wasn't your fault, Jon. Not your family and not this."

"I held their ashes in my hands," he muttered, unable to shake the surge of anger. Just like the one gripped in his hand, his parents' bonding cloths had been laid on a box full of ash.

"Another family lost because of me."

He traced his thumb across the burned fabric. Several families, if the dozen or so smoldering mounds were any indication.

Mather brushed aside the snow to reveal black cloth embroidered with a silver emblem. Rakir soldiers. "This doesn't make any sense. We have a lead on the closest scout unit. How did they get ahead of us?"

Both men glanced at Jàden, standing in front of the horses and scratching their noses. He'd ordered her to be ready to run, and she obviously hadn't listened to a word.

"I don't think they did." Jon nudged the Rakir uniform, his boot pressing on the dead soldier's frozen arm, buried under at least a foot of snow. "A fleet of ships could sail to Nelórath in half the time. These bastards have been here for weeks."

"No wonder the scouts are hanging back. They're running us right into a trap. Half the army's probably waiting for us nearby." Mather gripped his bow gripped so tight Jon thought he might break it in half. "I hope the others are still alive."

Jon leaned his forehead against his hand, wishing his father was here. The older Ayers always had a way of helping Jon think straight.

They couldn't backtrack, or they'd run right into the scouts. And east was far too dangerous for humans. Jon cursed himself for not following the coast or sticking to the high passes. He should have known Éli was clever enough to get ahead of him. "Get Jàden out of sight. I'll have a look around and meet you on the road. Be ready to run hard. I'd rather deal with a few scouts than whatever Éli's cooked up."

He re-tied his bow and quiver to his horse, then laid a hand on Jàden's good shoulder. "Stay close to Mather and keep your face hidden."

"We're in danger, aren't we?" She tugged up her hood, worry in her wild eyes.

"If there's trouble, you stay low and out of sight." He didn't need to add more stress to the anguish etched into her features. She had suffered enough.

But Mather had no horse to return home now, and who knew what they'd find on the road ahead.

"Whatever happens, don't use your magic," Jon said. "Rakir will kill anyone with a hint of power. I didn't keep you alive only to see you killed."

## CHAPTER 13

*The Forbidden Mountains*

Jàden bit down on her lip as Jon squeezed her shoulder. The small gesture sent a tingle of heat straight to her gut.

Every day it became clearer why Enforcers forbade energy ties. Even for those who had no love between them, something sparked along the shared energy. Jàden wanted to blame it on her years of loneliness. And yet something tugged her toward Jon before his strength ever flowed through her veins.

As he disappeared into the trees, she grabbed the reins and tried to climb onto the saddle, but her body was still weak from so long in a cage.

"I've got you." Mather shoved her until she could swing one leg over and sit upright. The heavy snow already covered Jon's tracks. But what if soldiers hid in the trees? Jon shouldn't be on his own.

"What if he gets hurt?" she asked.

"Captain knows what he's doing. Let's go." Mather wrangled his horse onto the road between the buried mounds.

She nudged Jon's black alongside. Charred cinders poked up from the ground. "What happened here?"

"Rakir burned them all." His shoulders tensed as he passed by a carved stick in the snow, something that looked like a child's toy.

"Jon lost his family this way, didn't he?"

Mather nodded. "Rakir are trained to show no mercy when they have a kill order."

Just like Enforcers. Jàden glanced toward the woods, aching to comfort Jon's grief. She'd lost her family as well and understood the pain that came with tragedy.

They passed the remains of a stable, several bracing poles still holding up part of a roof. She should have been there searching for a horse to lead Mather home, but nothing remained.

"Maybe the next village—" she started.

"Don't worry about it." His tone bitter with grief, Mather kept his eyes straight ahead, an arrow against his string. "I'll find a way home. Sharie ain't gonna have our baby alone."

They passed to the far side of the village, and Mather ushered her under a copse of young redwoods. The dense canopy blocked out most of the storm and the sky as she searched for any sign of a ship. Frank could still be out there somewhere.

"Captain will be here soon. Keep your voice low and try to make as little noise as possible." Mather slid off his horse. "I'll make sure you and the captain find the others. Then I'm gone. Horse or no horse."

The determination in his voice spoke volumes about his worry as Jàden dropped from Jon's horse and tied him off to a thick branch.

Mather reached over and yanked her knot loose. "These boys ain't like normal horses. Never tie them up unless you want a fight on your hands. Norshads don't stray from their riders, not even when they're spooked."

A twig snapped.

Mather turned toward the woods, tension tight on his arrow. "Hide."

She crouched between the horses. Jàden crawled beneath Agnar, some desperate part of her hoping the large stallion would kick her so hard in the head she could recycle her own life and start over. But as Jon's strength flowed through her, it pushed against the fear seizing her chest. She slipped between a large bush and a tree trunk.

Gold-armored wardens stepped through the trees and surrounded them, a black sun emblazoned on their breastplates and helms. They had no emblems on their shoulders like Guild patches. So, not Rakir.

By the way they unsheathed their swords, these were more people who wanted to kill Jon and Mather.

Or maybe this time they were after her.

"Well, look what we have here, boys. Rakir scum." An armored woman nudged her horse forward, a black band around her left arm and her hair pulled back in a series of braids beneath her helm. She spat at the ground. "I'd know them Tower-bred horses anywhere."

Jon's stallion whinnied, eyeing the wardens with his ears laid flat.

"Where's the other Rakir?" one man asked Mather. His skin was white as snow, his eyes so black they seemed to suck the light out of the air.

Jàden's heart pounded as she crouched lower, trying not to make a sound. Heat rushed into her veins, crackling along each capillary until the Flame's power tingled her palms.

*No, not now.* She didn't want to lose control of her power, nor use it against others unless she had to. But she also didn't want to take another arrow to her shoulder. The last one still ached as she gripped the tree's bark.

The moon's heartbeat thrummed in her ears. Almost as if Sandaris egged the Flame's power on. The more its power surged through her body, the stronger the connection became, and the harder to stamp it back down.

She curled her hands tight, trying to hold the energy back.

Mather held up his arms, arrow in one hand, bow in the other. The corner of his mouth tugged into a half grin. "I'm all alone, which almost makes this a fair fight."

"Kill him," the woman with the brains ordered.

Mather dropped the arrow. He grabbed a knife and threw it into the white-skinned man's neck, his helm tumbling to the ground. The warden gripped the dagger's hilt, but the light went out of his eyes and he hit the ground.

Mather attacked them like a wild dog. He shoved a second knife into the woman's knee between the seams of her armor then hammered his bow across another man's jaw.

Jàden pressed her palms against a tree trunk. Maybe a little power wouldn't hurt, enough to knock these wardens off their feet and give Mather a fighting chance.

She breathed deep, trying to focus the Flame's energy so it didn't overwhelm her. But something else lurked, a sensation easing toward her thoughts like a shadow. The strange eeriness crawled up the back of her neck until her scalp tingled.

*He's here,* a voice whispered into her thoughts.

Jàden peered through the gloom for another figure as Jon slipped between two of the armored men and slit their throats.

*Stay out of my head.* She kept stone still. If she could sense them, could they sense her too?

*Herana, run!* the voice in her head screamed.

Arms wrapped around Jàden and yanked her off the ground.

"Gotcha," a distinctly male voice said in her ear. He sounded young, but the guy was strong.

She howled and kicked out her legs, slamming her feet against the black's rump. The horse bolted, trampling over a warden and crushing her chest.

"Jon!" She tried to twist away, pain searing into her shoulder.

The attacker pressed a knife to her throat.

"Jàden!" Jon scrambled from the shadows and fixed his hardened gaze on the attacker at her back. With a knife clutched in each hand, he eased toward them with all the tension of a coiled snake. "Let her go."

The wardens who were still alive retreated, led by the woman with braids in her hair.

Fire crackled in Jàden's veins as the Flame fed her fear, nudging her open to draw on its full power.

"Don't do it." Jon's words rippled through Jàden's body, as if they could quell the fire in her veins.

She needed to protect herself, but the harshness of his voice stung. The Flame's power could uproot the trees and spook everyone away. She grabbed her attacker's pants as her power surged, clenching her fists to suppress the flow of energy.

No, she needed to do something.

Pacing back and forth with his daggers gripped tight, a terrifying anger hardened Jon's features. "Last chance, boy. Let her go, and you'll walk out of here alive."

The young man's putrid breath rolled across her neck. "I can't."

The soft, lilting boy's words deepened into a man's icy, sadistic laugh.

Even the energy changed, almost as if the boy stepped away from his body and someone else took his place. The voice turned cold and confident.

"Remember what I promised, Jon," the man-boy said. "This ain't over until I say it's over."

Jàden had only known of one other person who could do such a thing. One of the other test subjects in a cage three floors above hers.

Dreamwalker. An ability nearly as rare as her own, dreamwalkers could open a hole inside a person's psyche and manipulate their dreams. Was this boy's conscious mind asleep?

"Éli." Jon froze, his knuckles white around his daggers. "You stay away from her."

Dark energy pulsed, an oily slime gripping Jàden's senses and stifling the Flame's power. The man-boy pressed his nose against her ear and sniffed deeply. "Can't wait to meet her."

Jàden opened her hands, energy pulsing from her fingertips as she fought against the Flame. This was the man she'd heard whispers about, the one both Jon and Mather seemed to have a vendetta with.

Jon dropped his daggers, and only the hilts stuck up from the muddy snow. He unsheathed the sword on his back. The rage in his eyes chilled her.

"Say goodbye, Jon." The man-boy tossed a glowing violet firemark at Mather's feet.

A dozen black and gold arrows slammed into Mather's body.

"No!" Jàden screamed.

Steel brushed against her hair as Jon's sword plunged into her captor's skull.

She gasped. The man-boy held her tight as bone crunched sickeningly next to her ear, both of them flying back.

# CHAPTER 14
*Nelórath*

Éli hit the ground hard, pain sizzling across his back. The woods dissolved into a softly lit room, each wall covered in dozens of dark fabrics with golden dream symbols woven into the threads. The stabbing pain in his head dulled as his connection to the warden boy severed.

A sword splitting his skull was not the way he wanted to die. It took him a moment to catch his breath and be fully back in his own body. Only the scent of the woman remained, some mousy brunette who didn't have a single enticing quality save one.

Touching her enraged Jon.

A dark laugh escaped him as he pushed to his feet, his body aching from the force of the fall. Kicking aside the overturned chair he'd been sitting in moments ago, he grabbed the tankard of ale from the small table and downed it in one gulp.

Kesh Einar, a tall woman with a meaty build, narrowed her eyes and leaned an elbow on the table. "Tell me that boy is dead."

Her voice rough as chapped leather, she clenched her fist tight. The woman commanded a unit of soldiers along the mountain boundary near the redwood city, but her burnished bronze skin was only one feature that made her look almost identical to the smith across the way.

"Ain't movin' anytime soon. That warden's got a sword buried in his skull." Éli glanced toward Granger, who lounged on a chaise near the back of the shop, gaze on the two scantily clad women by the door.

The dark and cozy shop was located beneath a thriving harlot house. Even the small room smelled of sex and ale. But he gave his captain a silent gesture to say, *Keep it in your pants.*

Einar's golden armor gleamed in the low lamplight as her dark brows pulled tight over a suspicious gaze. "You're certain?"

"I'd bet your life on it." Éli refilled his tankard, the faux bloodflower pendant heavy in his pocket.

He didn't know if the two sisters were working together or if they really didn't like one another, but he no longer cared. Everything he needed to get his son back was in his pocket, and the satisfaction of Jon's rage would tide him over for a few days.

Yet, it hadn't been his magic forging the connection.

A scrawny, trembling body sat next to Einar's knee, legs pulled tight against their chest as tears streaked their cheeks. They muttered the same words over and over: "I'm sorry."

Relief flickered across Einar's features. She rapped the heavy wooden table once with her meaty knuckles and leaned back in her chair. "Good. That's one bastard out of my way."

The boy had witnessed the woman beating one of her soldiers to death when he took the Oath of the Seven to serve the Guardians in their towers. Éli hadn't even tried to find the boy's crime, but his mind flooded with memories the moment he'd connected. The boy had been right to fear for his life.

Éli didn't care. Wardens were all the same—Guardian worshipping scum who spent far too much time in their temples.

A whisper of energy brushed behind his ear as Éli sensed the presence of soldiers outside the door. Granger pulled back the curtain a fraction and clenched his fist.

They had company.

"Before I go, I want to know where you found that." Éli jutted his chin toward the form cowering at Einar's knee.

Through the dreamwalker, he'd practically stepped inside the warden's senses. The woman's soft scent and palpable fear triggered his ache for vengeance.

Thin, frightened and protected by Jon Ayers.

He'd find a way to pull her into his plans and watch Jon squirm.

Einar clenched the iron chain, locking stone cuffs onto the trembling figure curled at his feet.

"Oh, this? Found them hidden in the mountains half-starved. Most of their kind can only enter a sleeping mind, when natural defenses are down. But this one"—Einar scratched their head like she would a pet—"they can walk through anyone's waking reality. Makes them see and say whatever they want."

They shuddered, curling their knees tight against their chest. They stared somewhere beyond Éli. Soft, incomprehensible mutterings escaped through their lips.

Éli had never been inside another's head before, but the rush lingered in his senses.

Except now he wanted the woman—Jon's woman. "And the shackles?"

Granger stood calmly from the chaise. One woman slid a comb from her hair, letting her raven locks fall around her shoulders. And she was no kitten, a gleam in her eyes telling them both they'd run out of time.

Éli was starting to like the freedom of the road and the thrill of the hunt, and he never wanted to go back to stone walls and echoing screams.

Einar waved away the question. "They're from the old world. Something in the stone hinders the ability. Tried to use it on me once, but they know better now."

The dreamwalker scratched their ear, twitching at the hidden threat in their master's words.

Granger leered at the women, grinning until his yellow teeth showed.

Crouching in front of the cowering form, Éli rubbed a hand across his sparse beard. He didn't need another mouth to feed, but he had use for these abilities.

"I kept my end of the bargain, Commander." Einar slid a piece of paper on the table.

Éli picked up the parchment, everything he needed written and sealed inside. Safe passage through Nelórath for him and his men to help them capture Jon. His chest tightened, the cold slither in his senses uncoiling to a strong warning. Even Granger seemed to pick up on it as he clutched the hilt of his sheathed dagger.

Einar had no intention of letting them out of this room alive.

"I'm also going to need one more thing. Your pet." Éli unsheathed his sword and sliced it across Einar's throat before the woman could protest.

Einar stared at him wide-eyed, her mouth moving as blood poured down her golden armor. Her expression dulled, and she slumped in her chair.

Blood dripped from the silver steel blade as Éli touched the tip to the ground and crouched in front of the trembling dreamwalker, ignoring the tussle behind him. No doubt Granger would silence the two women, and he'd do nothing but bitch about it for a least a month.

Éli grabbed the pet's chin, digging his fingers into their jaw. "You're coming with us. Try your shit on me, and it will take you a month to die."

# CHAPTER 15
*The Forbidden Mountains*

Kale often warned Jàden to trust her instincts, but the thought came too late as she lay on her back, terror freezing her in place.

Jon's sword shuddered against her head, tapping her lightly as a reminder in giant neon lights how close she'd come to having her skull cracked open.

As he reached down to help her up, Jàden shoved the dead man-boy's arm away from her throat and rolled into a crouch. She wanted to scream at him, but she'd been that close to death before with Kale behind the trigger.

Jon seemed to sense her hesitation and yanked his sword free. "Hide. Now."

But she couldn't move. Couldn't breathe.

Mather fell to his knees as dozens of wardens charged in.

Everything shifted around her in slow motion: Jon killing gold-armored soldiers, Mather gasping for breath, the woman with braids on horseback watching with a sinister gleam in her eye as she tried to staunch the blood in her wound.

*Run, Jàden.* She screamed the words at herself, but her body wouldn't respond.

Gold-armored soldiers dropped dead, arrows buried in their necks with blue fletchings. She hadn't seen arrows like those before.

Someone else had to be here.

*Run!*

Her body responded sluggishly to the shock as she tried to stand. Two hooded figures appeared from the woods, each with a bow. They fired arrows into the attackers with deadly precision. A bright red beard caught the light as a hooded man charged the braid-haired woman still on horseback.

"Get down." Jon shoved her back to the ground, a knife barely missing her head.

Limbs and swords and bodies lay scattered across the ground, red soaking into white snow.

Jàden scurried backward, pulse pounding in her ears. Her fingers brushed over a weapon. She grabbed the sword hilt, but it was so heavy she could barely pull it out of the mud.

Jon dropped to his knees beside Mather and pushed their foreheads together. "Stay with me, brother." He whistled sharply, calling the horses to his side. "Let's get him up."

Mather's weapons dropped into the mud-churned snow as the two hooded figures crouched beside Jon.

Mather laid a bloodied hand against Jon's cheek. "Sh-Sharie."

That one word tore into Jàden as she sobbed. He was supposed to go home, to embrace his wife and hold his child.

"This is my fault." She clutched her head.

More than a dozen gold-fletched arrows stuck out from his chest in all directions.

Her only instinct now was to hide from everyone. To hide from all these deaths and scream her anger to the universe. She shouldn't have listened to Jon. They should never have left the crashed nadrér ship.

Blood dripped from the side of Mather's lip.

Jon smacked his cheek. "Get up. You're going home, brother. Back to Sharie."

There was no way Mather would ride home to his wife now, not even with a skilled surgeon and an ass-load of luck. At least a few of the arrows must have penetrated his organs, but even if they hadn't, Mather would be bleeding internally.

A tear slid down Mather's cheek, and the light dimmed from his eyes, followed by a howl of grief from Jon that stretched Jàden's nerves to their breaking point.

Jon's sword crunching bone against her ear. Kale's ship exploding next to Bradshaw's lab. All the rawness of those jarring sounds unfurled a manic need to escape. Hands shaking and sobs wracking her chest, she scrambled toward the horses.

But Jon's horse lowered his head and watched her, ears forward as if he accused her of Mather's death.

"He told me not to," she whispered but couldn't ignore the sting of the animal's stare.

The stallion snorted and tried to bite her then reared up in a display of dominance.

Jàden stumbled backwards, straight into someone's arms. "Leave me alone."

"Quiet," Jon hissed in her ear.

He turned her around and held the sides of her head, his palms warm against her ears. "Pull yourself together."

His words froze her, as did the anguish in his eyes.

"We need to leave before more wardens come, so get your head on straight." The biting tone in his words didn't reach his eyes, but he lifted her onto the back of his horse like she was more burden than company.

One hooded figure pushed back his cowl. Black shaggy hair fell across a young face lined with a thin, black beard. "Captain, torchlight on the next hill. Gotta move quick."

"Fuck off, Theryn." Jon's hand slid to her thigh. "You—don't fall behind."

Everything about his manner was cold and distant, except where his hand touched her. Fire ignited in her gut. So many long years without intimacy, and her body picked now to feel the stirring heat.

Shame stabbed at her heart as she laid a hand on Jon's shoulder in comfort, but he pulled away and retreated to the others, helping to snap the shafts off Mather's embedded arrows.

A knot hardened in Jàden's chest as the frigid wind blew across her cheek. Death always found her when she tried too hard to stifle her power. She should have ripped every tree from the soil and toppled them onto the soldiers.

*I could have saved him.* And then her power would grow out of control that much quicker.

The other hooded figure emerged from the trees, leading two more black horses. Bright red hair crowned a pale, freckled face, but his eyes held the same steely edge as the others. He tossed the reins of one horse to his companion and climbed onto the other, reigning his mount toward the rising moons. "This way."

Jon climbed onto Agnar behind Mather. "I'm sorry, brother."

"I'll keep them off our asses," the dark-skinned man said, an arrow readied in his bow.

Jàden clutched the reins and nudged the stallion alongside Jon. Snow fell, and she tugged up her hood, the shame of desire burning her thoughts.

His horse tried to bite her again, obviously unhappy it wasn't Jon on his back, but Jàden dug her heels in and kept close to the others.

Snow turned to sleet as they rode through the night over hills and between thick redwoods. Once Jàden dozed off only to wake screaming in pain as the red-haired man gripped her injured shoulder to nudge her back into the saddle.

She didn't doze again, her injury throbbing. Two sister moons peeked every so often between the clouds, no more than a hologram generated by the bionet.

These men didn't need her—nothing but a burden who didn't have enough strength to lift a sword. Gray streaks in the southern skies pressed back the gloom as they followed the riverbed, turning the woods as colorless as her grief.

Firelight danced in the distance, laughter ringing through the trees across the river.

Several men from a small campsite lifted their heads, and the smiles slid off their faces as they raced to the shore. Identical twins with tawny brown skin and black hair and a middle-aged man with gray hair pulled into a knot at the nape of his neck.

These had to be Jon's men.

"No!" A blond man with hair cropped close to his head splashed into the river. His piercing blue eyes fixed on Mather. He reached their side of the river and trudged onto the shore, water dripping from his dark green clothes. He rubbed a hand over his pale features. "What happened?"

Jàden winced at the razor edge in his voice. How could she face these men when their friend died because of her? She lowered her head so the hood covered her face.

"Hareth laid a trap," the black-bearded man with the bow said. "Dusty and I got there too late."

Skirting away from the others, she nudged the stallion into the river, lifting her feet as the current brushed against the black's chest. She circled toward the fire, the wind howling through the trees and scattering snow across stacked gear. These men looked ready to pack their horses and go.

"I'm sorry, brother." Jon embraced an older man with white-streaked hair, several horses lifting their heads from sparse patches of frozen grass.

She wiped a tear from her cheek and glanced at Mather, his chin drooped against an arrow shaft.

He'd never go home to his wife now, never see his child born.

The pain gutted her.

Jon laid a hand against her leg, his eyes full of bitter grief. "There's nothing to be done."

The edge in his tone sliced into her. Jàden desperately wanted to turn back the clock and succumb to the Flame's power, if only to spare Jon the anguish etched across his features.

"I'm so sorry," she said.

He pulled her from his horse into a tight embrace. "It wasn't your fault. Éli laid a trap, and we walked right into it."

She hugged him tight, burying her cheek against his neck. His warmth bled into her skin, offering no comfort to her aching heart. "What can I do to make this right?"

Jon sighed and leaned his head against hers. "Only one thing can make this right. Éli Hareth is going to die."

She recalled the boy's strange laugh, how it twisted into a man's. "I should have used my power."

"No." He wrapped his fingers in her hair and forced her to look at him. "It's too dangerous. The Rakir will hunt and kill anyone with even a hint of magic. As for the wardens, they'd lock you in a tower and worship you as a Guardian while they kept you a slave to their beliefs."

Just like home.

Everyone wanted her dead or to steal her power for their own machinations. If they only understood that she'd give it all away to have a boring, mundane life.

The Flame had caused so much grief in her past, and even now, the moon's heartbeat seemed to keep nudging her toward embracing the destruction. She had to find another way to protect herself and maybe not be a burden to Jon.

"Teach me to fight like you," she whispered. *So when I find Kale, I can protect him.* She closed her eyes, absorbing Jon's scent and the comfort of his arms, hating herself a little more for how much she didn't want to let go.

"Get some rest." Jon gestured toward the fire. "You're safe with these men. No one here will harm you."

Jàden left him to unsaddle the horses and curled up by the fire. The flames crackled in a deeper pit than what Jon and Mather usually dug, heat washing over her face.

Mather's lover would wait until she couldn't stand the ticking of a clock. Then she'd search every rock and tree until she was forced to face one of two truths: either he was dead or he didn't want her.

The same thoughts circled in her own head for years as she waited for Kale. It seemed as if any moment he'd come blazing in. Then the anger would grab hold and drive her to pace her cage again for any small fracture or hidden mechanism.

Poor Sharie might wait her whole life and never find an answer.

Jàden shed her tears behind her hands as Jon's men moved around the camp in grief-stricken silence. The blue-eyed man clenched his jaw tight across from her, the older man rubbing his forearms. He must have been in pain behind his stoic mask, but she couldn't be certain. For all she knew, it was a ritual she hadn't seen before.

Jon sat on a log nearby, a cigarette hanging out of his mouth. He sliced small sections of a reed paper with his knife and rolled each one around a pinch of rust-colored leaves. He stuffed each new cigarette into a small pouch and tied off the top.

His eyes found hers and held her gaze. Then he turned to his men, who had fallen silent. "It's time."

No laughter.

No playful banter.

The men left her alone by the fire. Each grasped one of Mather's shoulders or legs and carried their brother into the icy river.

Jon held his head while the others removed every arrow.

They cut away his clothes, washed his body and stitched each wound. Mather's hair and beard were neatly trimmed. Finally, they dried him off, dressed him in a fresh set of clothes and wrapped his bow and quiver in his arms.

Their grief coalesced with Jàden's own. She'd known men and women, brothers and sisters, colleagues and friends her whole life with the same expressions. Seen the grief on their faces when one passed or when a mother and father put their children into hypersleep.

But this devastated her heart.

These men loved Mather. The masked pain on their faces fed the guilt throbbing in her chest as they carried his body to an unlit pyre they'd built.

She was an outsider, and yet Mather's sentiments from the previous night slammed into her as she followed.

It was her duty to care for Jon now and one she couldn't fulfill.

"No more tower law, no more duty." Jon stood next to the pyre with a bow in one hand and a single arrow in the other, white fletchings on its shaft.

Each of his men held a bow and a single arrow.

Jàden peered closely at faint lines etched into their arrow shaft. They'd carved their final farewells to him.

Jon spoke again. "Mather died a free man whose only desire was to return to the loving embrace of his wife." He glanced at Jàden. "We should all be so fortunate."

Warmth blossomed in her neck.

Each man dipped their arrow tips into a bowl of pitch and ignited the ends. Flames licked the arrowheads as all seven men lined up and aimed at the logs below the pyre.

They released the arrows.

The fire danced higher, igniting bursts of sap and dried branches as it consumed the body. Jon grabbed both of Mather's swords and shoved them into the earth.

"This sword"—he touched the first one—"was given to Mather by his father. I will bind the hilt with white cloth and carry it as a sign of mourning. Every man who stands between me and Éli Hareth will feel the sting of its blade until I bury it in his black heart."

Jon touched the next one, a crafted weapon of silver steel stamped with the Rakir emblem.

"This sword is Mather's last link to the Tower. It will be bound with blood-cloth and used against every enemy who dares to cage us. Who among you will carry it?"

"I will." The blond man stepped forward and touched the blade. "We all will, until the hearts of every soldier who murders, maims and kills for pleasure no longer has a heartbeat in this world."

A shudder rippled up Jàden's spine at the ice in his tone.

They tore two long strips off a bolt of white cloth. Jon wrapped Mather's family sword until the hilt was snowy white over gleaming silver then buckled it to his back. He carried two now, as Mather had done.

The blond tugged off his shirt and unsheathed a dagger. A Guild emblem scarred his skin, the same one Jàden had seen the day she woke from hypersleep. This one shimmered black as if he'd melted obsidian into his skin. What type of man would brand his own flesh?

He pulled out a dagger and sliced open the skin near his scar, letting his blood soak the second piece of cloth. "Every time I feel the pain of this cut, I'll remember the man who killed our brother."

One by one, the others stripped off their shirts. Each was branded with the same emblem. A ritualistic practice used to mark livestock back on the Alliance worlds. Her grandfather would never have scarred the animals he loved.

They sliced open their shoulders, passing the cloth between them until it was soaked red in every corner. When it was finished, the blond man wrapped the blood-cloth around the hilt. "For Mather. May the Guardians embrace him in the next world."

"For Mather," the others echoed.

"Ash and stone, death and duty. May he be free of the Tower in every life hereafter." Jon unsheathed his dagger and walked toward the horses.

Agnar bolted toward Jàden and circled behind her.

"Grab him," Jon said.

She grasped the stallion's halter and patted his cheek.

Agnar neighed and reared up, ripping his halter from her grasp.

When his hooves hit the ground, she grabbed the reins and whispered soft words in her own language. "Easy."

"Hold him tight."

Jàden frowned. Then the meaning in Jon's words slammed into her. "You can't kill him."

"Mather's gone to the land of the Guardians until he finds a new life. I ain't sending him alone." Despite the determined tone in his words, grief lay bare in his eyes.

But Jàden ignored it and stepped between them. "There is no land of the Guardians. I told you this. Killing Agnar won't do anything except give you a dead horse. *My* horse. Mather gave him to me."

The guilt from all the lives she'd destroyed wrapped her chest like a vice. She couldn't bring back Mather, but at least she'd try to preserve some small part of him to ease her conscience.

"Step aside, Jàden."

"No." Agnar nudged her shoulder, almost as if he egged her on. "No more death. I can ride him and save the strain on your horse."

He stared at her for a long time, the pyre flickering higher behind him like a halo. Jon pushed past her before she could stop him.

Icy wind rippled her hood as Jàden reached for the blade. "No! You can't—"

He grabbed a handful of Agnar's mane and sliced the hairs.

Jon patted the stallion's shoulder. "You'd better keep her safe, horse."

Agnar grunted.

"As for you"—he sheathed his dagger and pointed at Jàden, the black and gray hairs clenched between his fingers—"horse and rider always stay together."

"Then he stays with me." She inched toward Agnar, sliding her fingers around his leather bridle. Jàden couldn't bear another life gone because of her.

"He's your responsibility now." Jon stalked back to the pyre and scattered the hairs across Mather's charred body.

The stallion leaned over her shoulder, pressing his nose into her hands. She caressed Agnar's velvet fur, her forehead against his cheek. "You're safe now."

Her words sounded hollow. Hopefully Agnar's affection meant he'd accepted her as a rider, but Jàden had no idea how to care for a war horse. The animals on her grandfather's farm, an old docking bay converted into grazing fields, were all bred for work or racing.

She hugged Agnar's nose, and Jon's men fanned out between her and the pyre.

Each one's stony gaze bored into her—tall, muscular men dressed in greens and browns and grays. Dark eyes and blue, red hair and blond. Their silence lay thick over the campsite as they appeared to size her up.

She leaned against Agnar's shoulder, noting their guarded expressions. Hiding their grief. Or maybe their hatred.

One by one, they burst into laughter.

Except the blond man, who turned away without a glimmer of kindness in his expression.

"Must be one hell of a woman to stand up to the captain like that." The black-bearded man stepped forward, tall and wiry, his hair cropped short since they'd crossed the river. He offered his forearm. "Theryn Blakewood. And that red-haired bastard over there is Dusty Inman."

Dusty nodded, fiddling with the string on his bow.

Theryn offered touch, connection, and yet she glanced at Jon, refusing to offer her arm. "Jàden."

The man laid a hand on her shoulder. "What, no family name?"

Her cheeks burned. People from her world never asked her family name more than once. Ravenscraft carried the stigma of "rich girl" to those who knew her grandfather and his work, except it was entirely unfounded. Her grandparents may have owned the bay, but it took every credit he had to keep it running.

These men knew nothing of her past, but if Frank and Bradshaw were still out there, she'd need all the protection she could get now that Mather was gone.

Jàden pushed back her hood. "It's Ravenscraft."

"Herana." The smile dropped off Theryn's face. He pressed a fist to his left shoulder and bowed his head.

The others repeated his gesture, except a shorter man with rich brown skin and small blades sheathed down the length of his chest. He shoved Theryn aside, a mischievous smile on his lips.

"I'm Ashe, and this is my brother Andrew." He slapped the identical man next to him on the chest. "Don't know how you got mixed up with the captain, Guardian, but most of us don't bite."

"I'm not..." The words died on her tongue as she recalled the statue in the healer's village. Like the others, these men had grown up with her legacy. Or at least her face carved into stone.

She was nobody, and yet she bit back the rest of her words.

Seven men to protect her instead of two. If they'd all been near the village, would Mather have suffered the same fate? Jàden wanted to believe he'd still be alive.

Ashe grinned at her then bolted as Theryn charged him.

She jumped back. What was wrong with these men? A moment ago they'd had tears in their eyes and now these full-grown warriors smacked and dodged one another like playful children.

Then she recalled something Kale used to tell her long ago. *Sometimes the only way to deal with the pain is to pretend it doesn't exist.* It was a coping mechanism. A way to handle grief when it was too overwhelming.

An older man, black and gray hair pulled into a knot at the base of his neck, edged closer. On his back, he carried a sword and a large ax, each handle bound with fine threads and dull-colored feathers. He patted her on the shoulder, his tanned skin deeply weathered but not yet showing the wrinkles of his age. "I'm Malcolm Radford. The captain told us what happened."

The lines around his features pulled tight with grief, but his blue eyes were sharp and inquisitive. She guessed him to be close to a hundred, with at least another eighty years of a strong, rich life.

"Jàden," she muttered and shouldered his hand away. She only wanted to be comforted by Jon, who stood like a horse ready to bolt for all the tension he carried.

They needed to get on the road again. Ironstar lay far to the south, and if she'd had a ship, they could fly there in less than an hour. Even with a computer, she could at least calculate how long they'd have to ride before crossing the sea.

"The captain blames himself." Malcolm pulled out a pipe and lit the bowl. The smoke curled up, offering a scent of fog and rain and hickory.

"It was my fault. Not his." And she had to untie their energy before she got Jon killed too. Just being close to her might be enough. All the more reason she needed to find Kale as soon as possible, but working technology was so hard to find in this world.

"That scream of yours is how Dusty and Theryn found you. Wasn't anyone's fault. Just damn bad luck." Malcolm talked away like they were old friends, but she barely listened. Maybe he was trying to figure her out, or his grandfatherly voice could mean an attempt to put her at ease. "It's warmer by the fire. You hungry?"

"No." She couldn't possibly eat with such a heavy weight in her chest, and this man was still a stranger—someone she didn't trust. She released Agnar's halter and hastened toward Jon to feel a little more secure. Or maybe she still needed his comfort to erase her guilt.

But as heat from the blazing timber warmed her cheek, she was reminded once again of the fireball from Kale's crash burning her life into embers.

The same devastation etched itself across Jon's expression, and she couldn't bear the pain of it. Jàden reached for his hand.

"Don't." He curled his fingers into a fist.

The hole in her chest opened wider, and she pulled her arm back. "I'm sorry. I thought—"

"I know what you thought, Jàden." His brusque voice turned hard as steel. "I ain't gonna kill a damn horse unless I have to."

She shied away from his anger, the echo resonating through their bond until every muscle in her body tightened. Jon was all she had in this world, and no one could understand more the ache he must be feeling. She swallowed a lump in her throat, recalling Mather's words as she whispered, "You don't have to grieve alone."

He stepped close and leaned toward her ear. "Always alone."

Jon pushed past, a darker edge to his voice. Wrapping his fingers in his horse's mane, he climbed onto the stallion's back and raced into the woods.

She closed her eyes, the ache burning inside her.

Always alone, the motto of her existence.

# CHAPTER 15

*Enforcer Prison*

Fire burned through Jon's veins, fueled by the heat Jàden gave off each time she stepped close to him. He wanted to shove her against the nearest tree and kiss her until he couldn't breathe. It was the only way to stifle the pain of Mather's death, but Éli's words rang in his ears: *Can't wait to meet her.*

Every muscle in his body tensed.

Éli's stunt in the woods left a black hole in Jon's gut. He had no doubt the bastard would stop at nothing to possess Jàden. Not because he loved her, but to stir the flames of a rivalry and make Jon feel the full weight of Éli's anguish.

"I'll never let you touch her."

He'd always regretted what happened, though he could never erase the image of Sebastian Hareth knocking his mother into a wall.

Jon cursed for the thousandth time that day. He needed to get Jàden somewhere safe, but now there wasn't a place anywhere on the Northern Isle he could leave her.

That only left one option: leave the north. With rahén in control of the west and the Lonely Sea to the east, the only remaining place left to disappear also bred some of the worst tales.

South. To the place she called Ironstar.

And straight into her lover's arms.

Jon tightened his grip on the reins. He'd grown fond of her company these past few weeks. At least, that's what he kept telling himself. But her essence breathed in his skin, tugging him each day into a desperate need for more that drove him mad.

And her magic bound him as a lover, a husband by northern law. He'd be damned if he let another man touch her.

Several riders melted from the darkness and blocked his path.

Jon pulled hard on the reins, and the black skidded to a halt.

Four of his men formed a solid wall as they spread across his path, their expressions grim.

"Out of my way." Jon's voice held a sharp edge he rarely used with his men, but tonight he was in no mood for their shit. He needed to resolve his conflicting thoughts before he did something stupid.

Like drag Jàden into his blanket and make love to the skittish woman.

"We have a problem." Thomas nudged his horse closer. "Found your family's mark on a dalan tomb."

Jon clenched his jaw. This was the last thing he needed tonight. Once a family heirloom passed down with each new generation, the bloodflower symbol had quickly made him a target.

The high council wanted the pendant, and after what he'd seen the day his family burned, those old bastards would have to kill him to get it.

His family's mark south of the Forbidden Mountains could mean anything. Perhaps safety, but Jon didn't put much faith in that idea. Any region patrolled by wardens was a tomb for them if they stayed. It already was for Mather, and for Sharie if she ever learned of his death.

He'd known Mather since they were children, a man forced into Tower duty when his parents died of sickness. The loss pulled at the grief of his own family's death, and tears stung Jon's eyes.

He needed to know the truth and just how bad of a shit situation they'd landed in.

"Show me." He followed Thomas deeper into the woods but could not let go of the fire in his soul. Some twisted part of Jon hoped one of his men would pick a fight with him so he had an outlet for his frustration. More than anything, he was desperate for Jàden to show him some sign of affection.

They rode in silence, keeping alert for another attack.

Moonlight illuminated the storm clouds, painting the trees with a silver edge as they crossed the river onto hard-packed dirt and ice. Branches wove together into a twisted canopy until Thomas stopped before a raised mound.

As the others dismounted, Jon slid to the ground.

Thomas lit a palm-sized firemark and pushed aside the brush.

Jon followed him through a thicket of foliage to a set of double doors forged in ancient telen, a pale sandstone created by the Guardians that never eroded and couldn't be chipped or broken by any hammer.

A raised bloodflower lay partly buried near the ground, but a large hole around it told Jon someone had recently dug out the symbol.

Generations of stories tracked his family's history across the sea to the borderlands. There was never any mention in his history that they traveled further south than the Forbidden Mountains.

He tightened his jaw and traced his fingers along the etched bloodflower. "How did you find this?"

"Tracking a warden." Thomas rubbed a hand across his jaw. "Dusty and I found it."

Jon laid his palm over the seal and a faint vibration rippled through his hand. The pendant against his chest warmed as red light traced along the seam between the doors.

"Back up." He edged toward Thomas as the bloodflower seal glowed and the doors slid open. Loose soil tumbled inward.

Jon snatched a branch to steady himself, but it snapped in half and he slid through the gap underground.

Light flickered down a long corridor to a second sealed door. Glass sheets hung along the walls to each side. Two remained dark, but the others glowed with white symbols, twisting in Jon's head until a strong impression of a word he vaguely understood filled his thoughts.

*Loading...*

But loading what?

Thomas landed beside him, one hand on his sword hilt. "What the fuck is this place?"

If only he knew. But it had the same smooth stone as the Tower of Idrér.

Jon gripped the dagger hilts strapped to his back, hoping he didn't have to see more dead people in cages.

And yet something tugged at his curiosity. The idea that the bloodflower was far more than a family emblem. Whatever the Ayers true history, no story or legend ever spoke of anything like the polished floors and glowing walls.

Light flickered again, new symbols on the glass. *Welcome to South Island High-Security Prison.*

Jàden's magic had done something to him. He could read the strange words, at least the ones that held similar meaning in his own native tongue, and one word stood out above the others on the glass.

Prison.

A place he'd patrolled for more than a decade in service to the Tower. Where piss and vomit, screams and hatred, all bled into a daily routine of fights, death threats and loneliness when a man realized he might be the only sane person left. A prison was something he understood, but it still twisted a knot of coldness into his gut.

This was not a safe place to be.

Dusty slid down behind them, an arrow on his bowstring. "Think anyone's alive in here?"

"Let's hope not." Jon should have turned around right then, but he had to know more about this place. To understand what was so important about the pendant around his neck and why the high council desperately wanted it.

Hands on his daggers, he crept down the corridor.

The glass sheets flashed again, panning across a large room like a moving portrait. Dalanath stood along every wall, mysterious green creatures who floated on mist, only their upper bodies formed as if they could open their eyes at any moment and step from illusion to reality.

Only a few months ago, he hadn't really understood the significance. After his time with Jàden, everything became clear.

"They're like Jàden—human. Someday, they're gonna wake up." And they might all possess the same powerful magic she did, but the words on the screen lingered like stones in his thoughts.

Dalanath.

Prisoners.

Captives.

Jon tried to imagine hundreds of people like Jàden all waking up at once. Anguished, starved, and who knew what else may be fueling their decisions.

"We shouldn't be here, Captain." Thomas slid the blood-bound sword from its sheath. Brash and hot-tempered, Thomas rarely showed trepidation unless his chronic muscle pain became too debilitating. Thomas had assured him earlier that it wasn't bad tonight, but Jon sensed a hesitation that mirrored his own.

"Look at this." Dusty slid his fingers across a glass sheet, and the image vanished, replaced by a new one. And another. Dusty moved through several images before Jon could really get a good look at any of them.

An illusion, perhaps the same magic that only showed the upper half of each dalan. And any place that contained magic was something Jon wanted no part of.

Except this place must hold a truth about his family's legacy.

"What do you think this…" Dusty stopped swiping as an image of Jàden reflected back at them. "Oh shit. That's Herana."

"Captain, what the fuck is this place?" Thomas held his sword out now as if he expected an army to come pouring through the sealed doors.

Jon tightened his jaw at the image of Jàden, a healthy, strong woman with no fear in her eyes. It was a far cry from who she was now, and he wondered if she'd ever been asleep in this place or if it was just one of many facilities. "It's a prison."

And he had their mark inked into his forearm.

Maybe that's all his family was, a long line of captors suppressing people with magic in their blood.

"What did they do to you?" he muttered under his breath, unable to tear his gaze away from the happiness in her brown eyes.

Jon had seen it a thousand times, innocent folks thrown behind bars for petty crimes or defending their families. Some were released again without relative harm, but others walked out of his prison as hardened criminals. Or worse, with no life spark left and ready to give up.

Usually those from Éli's sector.

He traced the image of her cheek to a small arrow with a word he didn't understand. As soon as his finger touched the word, her portrait shrank under a throng of rioters.

Shouts echoed from the glass. Crowds of people with signs stood around a central pedestal, a fiery red orb hovering overhead. As the rioters swarmed, several people disappeared into the flames. Jon tried to understand what he was witnessing but couldn't separate out the strange words.

"Are they killing people?" Ashe poked his head from the doors, a dagger in each hand.

Jon didn't have an answer, nor could he hold back the anger ripping through him. Only one thing he knew for sure from when he'd touched the bloodflower's flames his last day in Ìdolön—"That fire doesn't burn."

He'd been in that room once, and it gave him chills. The wide, empty space, the metal forged into every wall like he stood inside a giant dagger hilt.

The people who disappeared very likely fell into the high council chamber. Those old bastards didn't build the Tower like they'd have the citizens of Ìdolön believe.

The Guardians did.

"Captain." As if the world fell out from under Dusty, his tone turned hollow.

Jon hadn't taken his eyes off the image. Sheets of glass, similar to the one he watched now, flashed over the crowd. Each one showed someone screaming in pain from inside a glass cage.

As the rioters quieted, one man's shout was easy to pick out. "She saved our moon!"

Others tried to shout over him. "Flame wielders will kill us all if they can't be controlled."

"Stuff her in a starship engine and see if she can make it fly," a woman shouted, others laughing at her words.

"Anyone know what they're saying?" Dusty asked.

"They're arguing over whether to kill Jàden or not." Jon didn't understand the starship comment, but the magic tied to his body told him enough. A jest—probably meant to be funny—but he couldn't see the humor.

People were scared of her, of the power she wielded. He'd seen it firsthand the day he'd found her when she'd torn earth and metal. He couldn't imagine Jàden would try to intentionally harm others, but if the high council or the Rakir got hold of her, who knew how they'd use her.

Jàden screamed from a glass sheet, a cry of pain so desperate it burned a hole in his soul. She collapsed into sobs, bloody handprints streaked across her cage, and muttering a single plea. "Help me."

Fury tore Jon's heart. He couldn't watch anymore. "Move!"

He ripped the sword from his back and slammed it across the panels. Glass shattered. Sparks flew from the walls, and smoke curled up from the edges.

"Let's get the fuck out of this place." Whoever had tortured Jàden was going to die. He'd drive his sword into their skull or follow them into every life after to make them suffer.

# CHAPTER 16

*The Forbidden Mountains*

An ache bit into Jàden. *Always alone.*

Jon didn't want her comfort. Only Agnar seemed to understand her pain as he nudged her shoulder for attention. She wrapped her arms around the stallion's neck and leaned against his soft fur. "We're both alone now, aren't we?"

Silver storm clouds glittered across a bend in the river. The slow current swirled the pooling water. She could take Agnar and leave. Untie her energy from Jon and disappear so she'd no longer be a burden to him. But without any technology to navigate her toward Kale, following the trees would probably have her riding in circles.

Jàden breathed deeply of the frigid air and wrapped her hands on either side of a young sequoia, the fine bark hairs tickling her fingers. They were still west of the sea from what she could tell.

"We should go now, before they're gone." She grabbed Agnar's bridle, but the thought of riding anywhere without Jon tightened the knot in her chest. She ached to comfort him and feel his strong hand slide along her knee.

*You belong to Kale*, some small voice in her head chided.

Except tonight she needed Jon to soothe her guilt so her heart didn't hurt. Someone who offered warmth and connection.

When had she become so pathetic?

There had to be another way to find Kale, something that wouldn't require months in a saddle or technology she didn't possess.

The movement of the river grabbed her attention again. It was the lifeblood of the Sandarin moon, from the heart at its core to the webbed rivers across its surface. If anything could track Kale's energy in life or death, it was the water that gave Sandaris life and the essence of each person safe between lives. The moon's gentle rhythm beat alongside her heart, almost as if it heard her thoughts.

She caressed Agnar's nose then tied him to a nearby tree using a knot her grandfather had taught her years ago—one a horse couldn't slip out of.

"Help me find him." She skimmed her fingers along the surface of the water. Jàden pulled the firemark out of her pocket and used the Flame's destructive power to shatter the smooth glass.

Warmth flowed through her arms into the firemark as millions of bacteria multiplied and spread along her hands.

She couldn't see it, but the power in the tiny creatures sent shivers up her spine as she stepped into the icy water. Chill bumps rose on her skin as she moved deeper, the cold penetrating every nerve and cell until she could barely breathe. Dipping her hands into the river, the bacterium flowed away from her into the current.

The bacteria touched the Flame as she did, but their power didn't act unruly like hers.

Agnar splashed into the water, the reins loose. He grunted at her like he was showing off, and she could almost see his smugness in the way he lifted his tail.

"Fine, smarty horse." Hopefully he'd stay close because she wouldn't go chasing after him.

The river remained dark, a tingle spreading through Jàden's limbs. She turned her attention back to the water and took a deep breath, immersing herself beneath the surface. Dropping to the muddy bottom, the waters twisted around her, tugging her loose clothing and swirling her long hair about her head.

*Show me what I want to see,* she silently begged to the moon's lifeblood.

She dug her fingers into the loose dirt to hold back her anxiety. It had been years since she'd tried this, and the last time, Sandaris had clung to her psyche, binding the heart of its energy to her.

But through their connection, she'd sensed the sickness plaguing the soil and why terraforming Sandaris had failed.

Jàden closed her eyes as the familiar whisper from the heart of the moon delved deep into her mind. Branching out like tree roots, the sensation roared through her, opening neural pathways.

*I need to find Kale.*

The whisper of the moon's heart was not a true voice but a rumbling growl that vibrated her body.

Visions of rivers and oceans filled her thoughts as saw through the moon's senses. Sandaris whisked her inner sight over rocky terrain, through vast waterways and stormy seas as if searching each energy spark—both alive and yet unborn.

*Kale. Where are you? Time to go back to the beginning.*

Each crash of the ocean's waves along the shore created a gentle susurration against a lonely rock and water world, showing her Sandaris as it once was, four thousand years ago.

Seedlings sprouted. Algae and millweed bloomed. Green life burst through soil and carpeted the plains. Golden sands blazed across the Ocean of Fire, while further north of the desert, vibrant leaves opened toward brilliant azure skies.

This must have been how Sandaris healed. Jàden bit her lip at the ache in her chest from holding her breath. This time, the moon's heartbeat seemed to be a gentle agreement. Once lonely and dying, it showed her how its former sickness retreated under a blossoming, green world. Bacteria mined from its heart fed the soil, nourished the seas, restored the natural pulse until life breathed from its surface.

"Sandaris," she mouthed, her voice lost in the current. Her moon.

She slid her fingers out of the dirt and let whispers of lost souls slide across her fingertips.

Mather was here, anguished for his lost love.

Jàden clenched her hands against a wave of guilt. *No, I need to find Kale.*

But Mather's anguish brought back her own loss and the insidious words Frank used to taunt her with. *You're gonna wish you'd never been born.*

"No!" A bubble escaped her throat as she covered her ears. *Stay out of my head!*

She'd heard enough of Frank's taunts to last a lifetime, and these past few weeks, she'd fought to stay hidden from him. Sandaris rushed her mind over green fields until they gave way to dark tunnels and steel-piped hallways. The corridor widened into a docking bay, a silver ship's seams pulsing with a faint orange glow.

Kale. *He's on Sandaris.*

Jàden tried to imprint herself with every detail. Her lungs burned, but she was so close. He was somewhere near the Ocean of Fire, on the other side of the moon.

Welded steel doors opened into a narrow hall until a thick-bearded, scraggy face hovered, a green laser light effect to show a hypersleep pod's occupant. The sides of the man's head were shaved into a mohawk, deep lines wrinkling the corners of his eyes.

Frank.

Still alive. But asleep. He wasn't chasing her.

Relief ripped through her, and she nearly laughed, pressing her hands over her mouth to stifle losing anymore of her breath.

Sandaris had found the wrong Kale.

Frank Kale, her ex's father, and he couldn't harm her from the inside of a hypersleep pod. This was the best news she'd had since waking up.

*I need Jason Kale. Hurry.* Her air was running out, and she didn't want to start again.

But just as she was about to break the connection for a breath of air, Frank's hologram disappeared. His pod's cover glass faded from smoky black to transparency, hypersleep serum glowing green.

Frank Kale's eyes popped open.

"Oh, shit." Jàden let out a gasp, the water filling her lungs. Panic seized her throat as she pushed off the muddy bottom.

An iron grip pulled her above the surface, Jon's face hovering inches from hers. "Are you trying to get us killed?"

She coughed up water and gasped for air, her knees weak in the current. What had she done? Jàden tried to recall the last few details before the visions pushed her underground, but her heart pounded so hard her chest hurt.

"He's awake," was all she could manage.

And it was her fault. She'd woken him up, and once Frank realized she wasn't in her pod, he would be furious.

"I gotta get out of here," she said.

Jon grabbed her cheeks, forcing her to look at him. "How many damn times I gotta tell you, woman? No magic. We have to get the fuck out of this place."

She yanked out of his grasp. "I'll use the Flame if I want to. If you'd kept your mouth shut, I could have saved Mather."

"No one could have saved him," Jon growled at her. "Look at this shit!"

Water lifted off the surface of the river, tiny droplets glowing crimson and soaring high into the storm clouds.

Power.

The bacteria were supposed to stay dark, but they'd lit up anyway as they drew on the Flame's energy. They'd become a river of blood disappearing into the landscape.

"Now you've just told every damn soldier in these woods where we are," Jon said.

"I fucked up, okay?" The moment Frank had a ship in the air, he'd know where she was. No time to fight with Jon. She grabbed his arms and dug her fingers in. "We have to hide. Frank's waking up. He's going to hurt me again."

Jàden couldn't bear another cage. For the loneliness to tick away the years in solitude, always alone.

Fat snowflakes fell on Jon's head, scattering across his dark hair. Anger lurked in his eyes. "Frank. The man who tortured you?"

She nodded, Kale's words sliding from her tongue. "Five minutes to wake up. Fifteen minutes to the ship. Frank will be here in thirty."

Hypersleep-to-combat, something few Enforcers could do well, but all of them were forced to learn. Kale trained many of them and admitted the soldiers were given an adrenaline patch upon waking. Without one, it could take up to an hour to function well enough to fly a starship.

Jàden had no doubt Frank knew as much as his son did.

The visions rolled back through her head. Silver sands across the Ocean of Fire then the long dark hallway to a silver fighter perched in the docking bay. Frank was already inside a ship, and if it still flew, he'd be awake and in the air in under fifteen minutes.

"We have to leave." She dug her fingers in deeper so Jon would understand her desperation.

"Dry off before you get sick. Go." Jon nodded toward the shore.

Jàden grabbed Agnar's reins and trudged out of the water. Goosebumps prickled her icy skin.

"Let's pack it up. We got an enemy on our ass," Jon shouted to the others.

"Yes, Captain." His men were already packed, gathering gear and saddling the horses. Did they know something she didn't?

"Mather's clothes won't fit, but at least they're dry." He shoved a bundle into her hands before stripping off his pants.

She turned away to give him privacy and dropped the bundle near the fire. She didn't like the idea of undressing in front of seven men, but one glance at the storm clouds and her fear uncurled.

Frank could have a ship above them before they reached the next city. She stripped down and dressed as fast as she could, using one of Mather's belts to hold the oversized pants in place. His boots had burned with his body, but at least he had dry socks.

*I'm wearing a dead man's clothes.* Jàden tried to ignore the thought as she wrapped her wet clothing in a blanket.

Jon tugged his sleeves down to his wrist to wrap a bracer around his arm. "Same as last time. Stay by my side, no matter what happens. I don't want you out of my sight."

A dark shadow passed over his expression, something that hadn't been present when he'd pulled away from her earlier. Something must have happened, but now wasn't the time to ask about it.

Jàden wrapped her hand in Agnar's mane and tried to pull herself up, but she could barely get her foot off the ground. The strain burned her arms.

Jon lifted her into the saddle as if she weighed nothing. "Right by my side."

The order left no room for argument. She held no illusions about the danger they were all in. Frank would have a ship, targeting software and weapons. The kind that could blow up a base, just like in Meridan.

She tugged up her hood to hide her face.

Once Frank's ship was in the air, the external cameras could spot her. Jàden pushed all traces of her hair inside her shirt and lowered her head.

Jon nudged his horse alongside hers. "If you get tired, ride with me."

Fatigue was the last thing on her mind. Adrenaline rushed through her veins as she gathered Agnar's reins.

"Jon, listen." If Frank or Bradshaw caged her again, she might spend an eternity as a broken shell. "Don't let them take me alive. Kill me if you have to."

As the others disappeared into the trees, Jon grabbed her cheek, a dangerous edge in his eyes. "No one's going to touch you."

They raced after the others, and Jàden could only hang on as she adjusted to Agnar's gait. She searched the sky for traces of light to alert her to a ship. Only clouds and snow.

Bitter ice blew against her nose. Jàden curled one hand around the reins, the other in Agnar's thick mane hairs. His gait was so different than the captain's black, rougher with a slight off-step. Something both she and her aching shoulder would need to get used to.

Cold and fatigue already tugged at her body, but the smells and sounds of Sandaris breathed life into her soul. She wasn't about to let Frank take that away. Jàden kept one eye on the sky as they raced away from the crimson river.

"Jon." She shifted her horse closer, trying to find the right words in his language. Her head throbbed, and finally she growled and switched to her own dialect. "He'll have cameras on his ship. Object profiling. Heat sensors. I could hide in the darkest hole, and Frank would still find me. We—"

"Stop." He held up his hand, reining his horse in front of her. "I don't know half of what you said."

His men slowed their horses, something silent passing between them she didn't understand.

Jon fixed her with his steady gaze, switching the words back to his language. "We've got two options, Jàden: run or fight. Wardens in these parts kill every northerner who comes within a league of the southern cities. The Rakir are hunting us, and they've come further south than any northman has in more than a century."

"And let's not forget what will happen when the Elbren realize we have their Guardian. Those temple worshippers are fanatical in their devotion." The blond man, every muscle in his body rigid, sat astride a black-and-rust horse. "Just like those glass—"

Jon held up his fist, silencing the blond man with no more than a gesture.

"We've got enemies on every side and only one way out." Jon lowered his arm and turned his horse about to face his men. "Jàden and I are leaving these lands. We'll be sailing to the Dark Isle."

This was something she definitely agreed with and nudged her horse alongside him to show her support. They'd found those still living, and it was time to chase the dead. Whatever lay across the sea, it would give her a shot to put some distance between her and Frank.

"You can't be serious. No human has ever returned from that place. The mountains would be safer." The blond man—Thomas maybe?—had hard, angry lines tightening his jaw. "We can circle west and slip past—"

"No one's forcing you to go," Jon said. "You're all free men now, so if you want to leave this company, we part here as brothers."

The tension in Jon's shoulders gave his nerves away. Whether to leave the Northern Isle or that his men might disappear, she wasn't certain. Jàden glanced at the sky, obscured by thick sequoia branches heavy with pine needles. This conversation would only slow them down.

"We need to go," she muttered to Jon.

Thomas glared at both of them. "Of course I'm coming. That's not the point. The Dark Isle could put all of us in greater danger. You have no idea what's out there. We know these mountains—"

"Bullshit." Ashe, one of the twin brothers, kept his voice steady and hushed. He had half a dozen small daggers sheathed across his chest. "We don't know the Forbidden Mountains any better than what's beyond the next hilltop. Hareth is out there with a thousand Rakir hunting for that key. The wardens just killed one of our brothers, and now some asshole is searching for this woman, probably to make sure he finishes her off."

The word "key" caught Jàden's ears like a beacon.

Keys opened doors. Except on *Hàlon* where they were all secured with light pads and biometrics readers. Even small items like lock boxes used print scanners. Unless someone was a collector, her world had done away with all types of key—except six.

She grabbed Jon's arm. "You have a gate key?"

A computerized gemstone wrapped in coded nelané steel could open the gate fire between Sandaris and the starship. If Jon possessed a pendant, it changed everything. She could get back to *Hàlon* and use a computer to find Kale's new body within minutes.

She wanted to beg Jon to show her—she'd never seen one in person before. But the thought of Frank possessing such power only carved another wound in the terror elevating her heartrate.

"If Hareth knows we have a Guardian, Rakir are probably after her, too." Ashe's voice lowered. "They won't stop until we're all swinging from the gallows and the captain's in chains."

"Ashe is right," his twin Andrew said. "At least beyond the boundary we have a chance to survive. To stop running and put down some roots. Not even Hareth knows what lurks on the Dark Isle. I'm with the captain."

"Same here," Ashe muttered.

"Dusty and I go where you go, Captain," Theryn said.

"Speaking for your wife again, Theryn?" Andrew laughed, dodging a kick from the dark-skinned man.

"He's right." Dusty glared at Andrew. "Theryn and I follow the captain. Doesn't matter where we go as long as it ain't here."

Malcolm grunted. "We'll need a cargo ship."

Jon nodded. "Good. We ride for Nelórath."

"How large is that city?" Jàden asked.

All eyes turned toward her.

Frank would be able to see almost anything from the sky, to track their path from the campsite, count how many horses they traveled with. There wasn't much he wouldn't know from his computer readouts, but in a large city filled with people, he wouldn't be able to track a single heat signature.

"Nelórath is large enough, but it still leaves us with one giant problem, Captain." Thomas pointed at Jàden. "Her."

Irritation flushed her cheeks. This guy obviously didn't like her. Probably blamed her for Mather's death too.

Thomas clenched and unclenched his hand then stretched out his arm as if trying to relieve muscle pain, something she'd seen injured horses do in the past. "City laws are the same down here. If she's dressed like a man, wardens will arrest her and we're all done for."

Jàden glanced at her clothing, a thick, wool tunic woven with greens and browns to blend into the woods over thick riding breeches.

"Don't worry, boys. I'm the expert in women here." Theryn grinned and winked at her. "Come on, Dusty. Let's head toward the city and find a dress for Heartbreaker."

Jàden's cheeks burned with embarrassment as she turned away from their lingering eyes. She could almost feel the judgment in these men, as if she was somehow cursed to be born a woman. She wrangled Agnar away from them and edged toward the boundary at the copse of trees, searching for any light in the sky.

"Someone throw a knife at him," Jon muttered as the two men raced away. "Go with them, Malcolm. Find us a ship."

"Yes, Captain." The older man spurred his horse ahead and raced after the bowmen.

"The rest of us stick close to Jàden. From here on out, someone always has eyes on her." Jon nudged his horse out of the trees. "Let's move."

They kept to a brisk trot through thick woods, the ground covered in pine mats and snow drifts. Heavy storm clouds obscured the moons, but small lights began to dot the surrounding country.

Every few minutes she scanned the sky, certain Frank was somewhere in the clouds, ready to pounce.

"I'll teach you to fight." Jon searched the terrain ahead, patting his horse on the shoulder. "But until you're fully trained, you follow his orders." He nodded toward Thomas, who rode on her other side. "In return, I'll help you find Kale."

She clenched the reins harder as Thomas visibly tensed beside her. So far, he hadn't shown any of them an ounce of friendliness. Besides, she'd rather have Jon showing her how to hold a weapon. "What do you get out of this?"

Jon glanced at Thomas, the two of them sharing a silent conversation she couldn't hope to understand. "I get another fighter."

Something about Jon's words didn't feel like the whole story, but Jàden was far too worried about Frank catching up to scrutinize too closely. "How long will it take?"

Jon scratched his chin. "Two years."

"Two years?" she sputtered. "Jon, I—"

"And you can't use magic. That's the deal, Jàden." He clenched his hand, running his thumb along his forefinger.

"I can't wait two years to start searching for Kale." She needed to release Jon from their bond, not tempt fate that she might fall into his arms—and his bed.

But Kale needed a strong woman, not the half-starved, broken version of herself she'd become. Someone who could be the protector to him that he once was to her. She could train, but she would never stop looking. The sooner she found a way off Sandaris, the safer it would be for everyone who lived here.

"Fine," she muttered, only intending to stay long enough to find Kale. "Two years."

Thunder rumbled across the clouds, laced with a stronger high-pitched roar.

Jàden recognized the sound of a ship and turned toward the sky.

An orange glow lit the storm, tracking through the clouds until it disappeared into the north.

"Frank." She bit down on her cheek until she tasted blood. "He's here."

She dug her heels into Agnar and bolted ahead.

The others were beside her in seconds.

Jàden leaned low against Agnar's neck, and he lengthened his stride as they raced across an open plain. The stormy skies to the north grew dark as his ship disappeared beyond the horizon. Frank must be going to her hypersleep pod. It wouldn't take him long to figure out where she'd gone.

They ran until the horses panted, foam lathering along their necks. She wanted to keep running, but Agnar was struggling, slowing down into his choppier gait. "Just a little further."

Lights twinkled in the distance, stretched from one side of the horizon to the other.

A sharp whistle came from the road. Jon pushed his horse ahead and angled them into a copse of oak trees.

She slowed her horse beside him. "We can't stop."

They'd kill the horses if they kept pushing, but all she could think about was Frank. He was too close. He was awake. And he was coming for her.

"All I could find off a merchant wagon heading into the city." Theryn tossed a bundle at Jon. "The old man is headed toward the docks, but Dusty and I will hit the rooftops and shadow you in."

Theryn and Dusty slid off their horses and retreated toward the city on foot, longbows strapped to their backs.

Jon tossed the bundle toward her. "Get dressed. The rest of you, let's rearrange a bit. Don't want to give ourselves away too soon."

There was nowhere to dress. Oaks lined the avenue, cutting across a desolate landscape as it dropped out of the foothills toward the city.

Jàden slid off her horse and stepped around a wide oak, clutching the bundle of clothing to her chest. All she could think about was Frank sitting in the cockpit, zeroing in on her location. Her hands shook so hard she could barely keep the rest of her body from doing the same.

She untied the string and lifted the bolts of cloth, long lengths of gray fabric lined with dark maroon material attached to a bodice "Oh, you can't be serious. What am I supposed to do, be a tent?"

"Outside the cities, you can wear whatever you like, but we can't draw attention to ourselves." Jon spoke to her from the other side of the tree, cursing occasionally under his breath as he and the others tampered with the supplies.

*Damn sexist law.* She stripped off her clothing, the icy air blasting against her skin. Jàden fumbled with the bodice. Even as skinny as she was, it dug into her ribs. She clasped the small hooks up the front then slid the dress over her head.

The thick wool was warm and soft but heavier than her forest clothing. As soon as the wind blew up her skirts, bumps broke out along her bare legs. She slid her breeches back on for warmth. One way or another she'd be cold, but at least she wouldn't have the wind slicing against her bare skin.

"This is ridiculous." Bundling up the last of her clothing, Jàden stepped out from behind the tree toward Agnar, who whinnied and tossed his head.

A sleeping blanket stretched across her stallion's back, covering the Rakir brand on his rump. Jon tightened the saddle, now loaded down with supplies.

She shoved her clothes into a bag. "I can't ride on all of that."

He turned toward her and the half-spent cigarette fell from his mouth. Jon traced his eyes to the hem of her dress and back to her face. "You'll ride with me."

"Then we'd better move fast. Frank will be here any moment."

## CHAPTER 17

*Nelórath*

Guardians be damned, Jàden was beautiful. Grabbing a long gray cloak from the back of his horse, Jon tried to push the images of her torture out of his mind. No way would he let her out of his sight, not when that lover of Jàden's left her in a cage to suffer. Jon had half a mind to kill him again if they ever met.

He wrapped the cloak around her shoulders and fastened the clasp at her neck, his fingers brushing against her throat. Stifling a groan, he allowed his hand to linger after the clasp clicked. "Don't speak unless you have to. Can't have you slipping into your own language."

This was a terrible idea. The wilds would keep them safe, but a ship across the sea could get them far from human lands. And he sure wasn't leaving the horses behind to sail to the boundary on a skiff.

Forcing himself to pull away, Jon checked the girth on his horse one last time. They needed to get inside the city, but he and his men had to time it right. Too soon and they'd stick out among sleepy streets.

"You ready, buddy?" He clapped his companion on the shoulder then climbed into the saddle. Jon grasped Jàden's forearm and pulled her up behind him. "Let's move. The horses are tired and we still got an hour before we hit the city."

Warmth flooded into his chest as her arms wrapped around his waist. Jon turned his horse toward Nelórath as the old part of himself, a captain in full command, pressed to the surface. "Keep your hoods up and stay together."

Every shadow became friend or foe when they crossed the river into the thicker woods. Ice mixed with snow drizzled across the foothills. Through twists and turns over the hilly terrain, they rode through groves of redwoods, skirting around a series of farmhouses toward the hazy glow of the city.

The pendant lay heavy against his chest as farmers joined them on the road. Lanterns hung from the posts on their wagons pulled by teams of southern short horses and mules.

Jon slowed his horse to a walk to blend in with the merchants.

Jàden's fidgeting put him on edge. This was taking too long but the horses needed to take it slow in case they had to run again. Maybe she just needed something to take her mind off the wait.

"You're the bloodflower's keeper, aren't you?" she asked, keeping her voice low.

Jon nudged his horse ahead of the others until they were out of earshot before he answered. They plodded past a portly woman reigning a four-horse team from the top of a closed carriage. Her bright-colored dress and low hem across her bosom gave her away as a matron bringing prostitutes into the city.

"It's my family's emblem," he said, "handed down through my great grandfather more than a hundred generations back." He reached for Jàden's hand—*too intimate*—but closed his fist and pressed it against his thigh. She may be his wife, but still she'd given no indication their connection was more than just her magic. "No one knows what I carry except you and my men."

As if the words sparked some dark force, a troop of wardens trotted from the city toward the merchant line. Jon slumped a little to appear more like a farmer, his mind still on his family's heirloom. The pendant had always been a source of contention between him and his father. As the only son to the Ayers bloodline, it was his duty to gift it to his wife when their first son was born.

A decade of arguments with his father washed over Jon, the pain of Marcus's loss slicing into his chest. He loved his mother and sisters, but he missed his old man every day.

Wardens slowed ahead and shouted to the driver of a wagon. The guy must have been drunk—he yelled right back, cursing the gold-armored men with a heavy slur to his words.

"Say nothing," he muttered to Jàden.

The wardens scattered to the far side of the road, ordering the portly man to uncover his goods. Jon took a cue from the other merchants' behavior; he averted his eyes and kept moving. They were almost there.

Jon glanced back, the wardens now in a shouting match with the farmer and ignoring everyone else. "That bastard saved our asses."

Jàden eased her grip on his waist, but Jon had a question burning in his gut since the day he'd found her. No time like the present to keep her distracted from searching the sky every five seconds.

"Why'd you bond me, Jàden?" he asked.

Especially when she had another lover. The city walls loomed amid thin trails of mist off the ocean, bastions of stone lit by fiery cauldrons at their apexes. Snow dropped heavy from the lowering clouds, banks of fog rolling in from the coast.

"It isn't a bond, Jon, just tied energy." Her hands tightened into fists. Churned mud and slush glittered in tiny pools of ice, reflecting the distant glow of lanterns and silver-laced storm clouds. "I told you, I needed your help. I'm not strong enough to fight Frank."

"Bullshit." Jon glanced at the sky then back to the deeper shadows along the road. Each face leapt out at him from the merchant wagons. Tired, grim, angry, scared. Every person he passed held expressions he'd seen on any normal day. Jon searched for the outlier, for a soldier who might be in disguise or anyone who watched them a little too closely.

The last thing they needed was to succumb to Éli's dreamwalker trick again. Yet part of his attention stayed with Jàden. "I helped you before the bond, and you have magic strong enough to tear that bastard apart. Tell me the truth."

He'd seen the hesitation in her eyes that day. Something held her back, but a stronger force pushed her into the bond. Jon needed to know what it was, or perhaps he only searched for an answer he wanted. Something to give him any hint that she needed him as more than a bodyguard.

She leaned her forehead against his back as they entered the city alongside the first wave of farmers.

"I want you to kill Frank and Bradshaw so I can escape to the stars," she mumbled against him. "I can't stay on Sandaris, not without bringing death to other people, and I don't want to hurt anyone."

"Who's Bradshaw? You haven't mentioned him before."

Jàden tried to pull her arms away, but Jon caught her hands. He could almost sense her fear by the softness of her words. "He's a Guild surgeon with a specialization in biotheric energy manipulation. And Frank's partner. Or boss. I was never really certain."

Her voice trailed off as Jon tried to digest this new information. "He helped Frank hurt you?"

"He ran the lab. Bradshaw is... I don't want to talk about this." The salty smell of the sea hung in the air as icy roads turned to mud and finally to slush and cobblestones. "I'm sorry, Jon. I should never have done what I did."

She tried to pull away again, but he tightened his grip. He still couldn't mentally shake her screams or the blood smeared across her cage walls. If the situation were reversed, he honestly couldn't say he'd do any different out of desperation. "I'll kill them for what they've done to you."

But there was still something she was hiding, and Jon wouldn't let her out of telling him. He caressed his thumb across her fingers to soothe the answer from her lips. "We're leaving everything we know to protect you, Jàden. I need to you to tell me: what does our bond give you that no one else can?"

"It's not a bond." Her head lifted skyward, and she sighed deeply. "I wanted to feel more than empty glass walls. No one touched me for two years or even spoke to me apart from Frank's occasional taunt. I was alone, Jon. More alone than you'll ever know."

His chest tightened. Loneliness was a familiar friend.

"I meant to set you free when you killed Frank, but then a day turned into weeks and your energy, your strength..." She gripped his hand tight. "It's the only thing keeping me from falling apart." Fog clung to the buildings as Jàden stifled a sob. "I can't be alone anymore."

He squeezed her hand, aching to wrap his arms around her and drive away the loneliness. Or maybe to stifle his own as the grief of Mather's death clutched his chest like a vice. "You have me, Jàden. I ain't going nowhere."

She squeezed his hand tighter. "I don't want to go back to a cage. Not ever again."

"Don't you worry. Frank and Bradshaw are dead. I just ain't killed them yet." Desperate for a cigarette, Jon scanned the streets for any sign of Rakir. Most men preferred to smoke the occasional pipe, but Jon had a fondness for the taste of shadeleaf with a hint of cedar smoke flavoring the papers. Today he couldn't take the chance of a cigarette giving him away, especially if Éli lurked nearby.

Merchants stepped out of their shops to open windows. Horse hooves clopped against the road as they passed, citizens of Nelórath eyeing them warily.

A warning went off in Jon's head.

He searched each street and alley they passed and the rooftops above for clues in expressions and body language. Nothing seemed out of place, but he couldn't shake the dread in his bones. Though he hated to do it, he released Jàden so he had both hands free to draw a weapon if needed.

Thomas nudged his horse alongside. "This feels like a trap. We haven't seen a single soldier since we rode into the city, and we're nearly a third of the way to the docks."

That was why the warning went off. Wrapped up in his own thoughts, Jon hadn't noticed the one thing missing from the city streets: gold-armored wardens.

"Keep your eyes open." No chance of turning back now as the bastards likely had the city gates blocked.

Seven white towers loomed tall against the cityscape, each dedicated to a Guardian. At the top of every tower hung a large banner depicting one of the seven—Erisöl, Élon, Herbridés, Miore, Sahéva, Shelora and Herana, her symbol a tree of life curved into the shape of a moon.

"Guardians, protect us," Thomas muttered then glanced at Jàden. "Or curse us."

Jon glared at Thomas. If they weren't trying to sneak through the city, he'd punch him for that remark.

The streets slowly filled with activity. Several merchants hung stark-colored banners over their doorways, pinks and oranges and indigos all bearing the shop's trade emblem inside the golden sun.

"Those look like Guild emblems," Jàden whispered.

The crowd parted as a dozen gold-armored soldiers trotted their tawny-colored horses straight toward Jon, led by a helmed rider with a black band circling his left arm.

"There they are," he muttered. Jon nudged his horse ahead of the others.

The wardens spread out and blocked their path.

"Where you boys coming in from? Don't usually see mountain folk until the season of rain," the black-banded leader said.

Jon stopped his horse, curling his fingers tighter around the reins. "Last run before we hit the high passes."

The leader removed his helm, black hair curled tight against dark brown skin. He eyed Jon suspiciously. "Why is the woman hiding her face?"

*Because she's a damn Guardian.* Jon's instincts needled him. He scanned the streets with his peripheral. Dusty and Theryn were on the rooftops, arrows ready to fire in case trouble erupted. Jon hoped it wouldn't come to that.

"She's shy of strangers." Jon nudged the black forward.

The leader sidled his horse closer. He laid his helm on the pommel, eyes fixed on Jàden. "Let's see your face, woman."

"Why? You want her contract?" Jon pulled back, shifting Jàden away as he came eye to eye with the soldier. "Five thousand shalir."

The armored leader grimaced. "No woman is worth more than two thousand. She must have one hell of a face."

"Probably a wildcat," another soldier called out. His comrades laughed.

Jon held his hand low on the far side of his horse, palm flat toward his men: *be ready.*

He kept his eyes on the leader. "Five thousand and not a firemark less."

The leader's features hardened. He drew a spear-like weapon and nudged his horse forward, circling around behind Andrew and Ashe.

Likely searching for any reason to delay them further. If the man had half a brain, he'd know the horses were northern bred, but Jon would never give up his stallion.

The armored leader came back along the other side and finally fixed his eyes on Jon. "Furs are good. Be out of the city before sixth bell."

"Yes, sir."

Except the leader's eyes held an edge of distrust.

Jon nudged his horse ahead, the street now crowded with merchants attending their outdoor stalls. He kept his eyes forward but spoke softly over his shoulder. "Jàden, are they all through?"

She shifted behind him. Then her sweet voice rolled over his ear. "They're through, but the soldiers are watching. At least a dozen more have joined the first ones." She lifted her head to the sky. "And I still haven't seen Frank, but I know he's close."

Jon didn't like that detail. If more were gathering behind them, that meant the wardens were going to cage them along a specific route. "Be ready for anything."

The road passed between two towers, Élon and Herana. Sleek, white walls replaced merchant shops and squat buildings. Clopping horse hooves echoed off the smooth stone as the avenue turned to an open-air corridor.

A faint melody touched his ears. Singing. Jon cursed under his breath as citizens sang to their Guardians.

He tried to shake the warning in his gut, but the fog from the wharf grew thicker, obscuring the way ahead. "If we get separated—"

"Jon, don't." She tightened her grip on his waist. "We have to stay together."

He grasped her hand in his, wishing he could feel her skin instead of the glove. "Listen. If something happens, trust my men. They'll keep you safe."

Jàden clasped his hand tight, weaving her fingers through his. "If something happens, you'll never see me again."

## CHAPTER 18
*Nelórath*

Jàden didn't want to let Jon go. She may have ached for Kale's soft whispers and strong arms holding her tight, but Jon was more than a protector.

She needed him.

The soft melody of Guardian song washed over her, but it wasn't enough to loosen the knots in her gut. Jàden couldn't keep her eyes off the sky, her ears tuned to every sound of the city. Right about now, she imagined Frank screaming in rage, maybe shouting into an earpiece at Bradshaw about how she'd escaped.

She shuddered. Doc Bradshaw was worse than Frank, a cold-hearted man whose theories about human enhancements had been of great interest to *Hàlon's* Guild scientists until they found the first victims of his experiments.

Both humans and animals, tortured to the point of madness. Jàden knew firsthand what those creatures suffered.

If the doctor was awake too, he probably had a dozen monitors in front of him and lounged with his feet on the console. He'd tap on the keys as if the world held no excitement while Frank would tear apart the mountains to breathe down her neck.

Jàden clenched Jon's hand as if this were their last moment together, but the thought was unbearable. His mere presence soothed the terror and loneliness in her heart, and each time he touched her, she ached for more. For an intimacy that could make her forget all the anguish and grief poisoning her soul.

The tower walls gave way to vast courtyards. Gray and tan tile checkered across the ground through archways and around tall maple trees. A great waterfall cascaded down the side of each citadel into a crystalline pool.

Snowflakes blew across a large central statue of Élon, Guardian of Strength and Bravery, who gripped a sword in one hand and a gun in the other. Jàden had seen the statue nearly all her life, especially in the Enforcer corridors where most soldiers still idolized the great hero.

But today it sent a shiver down her spine as if the great ancestor already knew she existed between two worlds. What she wouldn't give for a gun in her hand. Not that she could hit a starship, but she could put a hole in Frank's head and end her nightmares.

"Help me, Élon," she whispered. Guardians knew she didn't have the guts to face off with Frank. Otherwise she'd have left Jon in peace.

Jàden turned to the other courtyard to see which Guardian had the unrecognized moon and tree symbol.

A woman's dress flowed toward the watery edges of a grand pool beneath the cascading falls. High cheekbones and an angular face sharpened beneath hair pulled back into a long tail with bangs fringed across her forehead.

Jàden lifted her head from Jon's back, staring at her familiar features.

Again.

Another beacon to wave at Frank and scream, *I'm right here.* She slid from Jon's grasp and dropped to the ground. Thomas's horse grunted at her, but she shoved the velvety nose away and scrambled toward the courtyard.

"Jàden, wait." Jon wrangled his horse after her.

Thunder rumbled overhead as she pushed through a crowd of golden-robed singers until she stood in front of the giant statue of herself, this one with the Bioengineering Guild's trainee seedling patch etched into her shoulder.

This statue was different from the other one, more accurate from the waist up, showing the lines of her Guild uniform.

Herana, the moonless Guardian. The lonely Guardian.

The empty, derelict, nothing Guardian.

Why would they call her that? But as she glanced at the sky, Jàden had a pretty good idea. Élon's golden sun burned bright in the north, Erisöl's lighter white sun to the east.

Four suns.

Two moons.

A Guardian for each, and she was the seventh. Jàden opened her hand, the Flame's power tie between her and Jon strong, with Sandaris's heart beating alongside hers. A symbiosis of energy streams.

Anger ignited inside her at being called empty.

Jàden screamed out her rage and fear, as if that would help anything.

Robed figures strolled through the courtyard, singing a low melody. A few heads turned her way as their soft, sonorous tune matched the darkening storm.

"You fucking bastard, Frank," she muttered, her hood falling to her shoulders. He would find her here too with a statue that large.

But the Guild patch etched into the stone nagged at her. If these people knew about the Guilds, maybe they hid some of *Hàlon*'s technology nearby. Nearly all the shops were marked with symbols of their factions or specialty, and all inside the golden sun.

Which was just an infinite circle, like the patch on her shoulder.

"It's Herana!" someone shouted.

Jon caught her arm. "We have to go. It's too dangerous here."

She yanked out of his grasp. "If these people know about the Guilds, maybe they can help. Frank is right on our asses."

Besides, what if she was wrong? Frank had a ship, guns and a whole arsenal of technology at the tip of his fingers. The stone towers might keep them safe if they could get underground.

"Enough." The sharp tone in his voiced silenced the fear burning to spill forth from her lips. Jon grabbed her hood with both hands and yanked it over her head, pulling her so close his mouth brushed against hers.

Jàden's next words froze on her tongue as heat tingled against her lips, his bushy beard prickling her skin.

Jon seemed frozen too as his thumb traced across her cheek to the corner of her mouth. A shadow flickered across his eyes but was gone before she could grasp its meaning. "Frank ain't our only problem. You said you wanted to fight, so here's your first lesson."

*Kiss me,* she screamed, aching to feel more of Jon's intimacy, but the Guardian song hushed along a tidal wave of longing and guilt. Jàden tried hard not to notice his closeness, suppressing the urge to press her mouth against his.

"Herana." The whispers rose in volume as citizens dropped to their knees, gesturing a strange series of signs across their bodies. "Our Guardian has come."

"Keep your face hidden until we're on that barge." Jon grabbed her arm and led her back to the horses.

"He's kidnapping Herana," voices shouted.

Several women bolted away, perhaps to notify the city guards, but Jàden couldn't shed the heat in her cheeks as a cold wind blew through the courtyard.

Citizens shouted their anger and rallied to their feet. Thunder rumbled in the sky. The clouds shifted from stormy gray to a bright glow. Engines roared, and a sleek, silver craft lowered beneath the clouds.

Orange lines illuminated the seams of a silver scout craft, the wings spanning the gap from one side of the courtyard to another.

"Run!" Jàden shouted. She squirmed out of Jon's grasp and raced across the courtyard, a crowd of roaring citizens on her heels. Yanking her hood across her face, she ducked behind a large pillar.

Gunfire echoed off the tower walls and ripped through the buildings, knocking down several rioters. Blood splattered across the crowd.

"Jon!"

"What is that thing?" Jon shouted over the roar of the engines when he caught up to her. He grabbed the reins and climbed onto his horse. "Come on!"

She clasped his arm and swung up behind him. "It's a scout ship."

He wrangled the stallion around and dodged into the nearest alley, Thomas and the others on their heels.

A loud voice reverberated over the city. "I know you're out there, darlin'."

Frank's voice sent a chill to the deepest part of her psyche. She tightened her grip on Jon, heart slamming against her chest. "Shit, shit, shit. Don't let him find me."

The black pressed his ears back as Frank unleashed another round of gunfire. Startling sideways, he turned from the noise and dashed down a narrow alley into the fog. "Stay where the crowds are thickest."

"That's only going to slow us down."

"It might also throw off his heat sensors." Jàden had no idea how to explain that to Jon or if she was even accurate. It wasn't like she spent her life in the cockpit—that was Kale's forte.

"Get in front of me and take the reins." Jon stood in the saddle then stepped one foot behind her.

"I can't—"

"Just do it!"

Damn dress. She pulled herself forward and grabbed the bolts of material, yanking them against her waist. As Jon dropped behind her, she grabbed the reins and delved into a merchant crowd.

But if she pushed the black like a mad woman, Frank would spot them for sure. She slowed the horse's pace to blend into the thick mass of wagon carts and merchant stalls.

"Is that Frank? The giant metal beast?" Jon unsnapped his weapons from the saddle and strapped them to his back. Except for his bow. He fit an arrow to the string.

The gunfire ceased, and the ship's engines roared.

Snow glowed orange as the scout craft lifted over the buildings and slid across the sky.

Jon pulled the tension on an arrow and aimed it at the ship.

"You won't hurt him that way. Frank's human— he's inside it." She clenched the reins and tugged her hood lower. "There's so much you don't know."

Soldiers poured onto the avenue from the adjoining alleys, tall riders in black uniforms with silver swords strapped to their backs.

Jon's black dead-stopped, his ears laid flat.

A tall, slender man nudged his horse forward, two silver bands beneath the Guild-like Rakir symbol on his left shoulder. His eyes fixed on her, black and cold and ruthless. "How's the family, Jon?"

Jàden shrank under the man's intense gaze, but a familiar ring to his voice nagged her instincts. She'd heard it before.

The black riders drew their circle tighter. But Thomas and Malcolm appeared to either side, both with their weapons drawn. Jon fired his arrow, the shaft grazing the black-eyed man's neck and plunging into the rider behind him.

The familiarity of the man's voice suddenly sparked, coupled with the horrible crunch of bone. Éli.

"Fuck." Jon dug his heels into the stallion and reined them around. "Split up!"

They crashed between two of the black riders, and Jàden crouched over the stallion's neck, clenching the reins with a handful of mane hairs.

A *whoosh* over her head curled her up tighter as the horses to either side reared up, their riders screaming in pain. Something wet dripped on her cheek as Jon's horse broke through and bolted into the nearest alley.

"Ayers!" Shouts erupted as the black-clad soldiers thundered after them.

Jàden wiped her cheek, crimson on her gloves. Blood, more death following her every step through this world. She tried to sit up, her body half-frozen with fear as arrows brushed past her head to the riders on their trail.

Theryn knelt on the rooftop, another arrow on his string as he pulled the tension.

The black dodged into the next alley, this one narrower and filled with crates and barrels. Jon grabbed his quiver then squeezed Jàden's waist and leaned toward her ear, his beard tickling her cheek.

"Head toward the bay and find Malcolm. Don't stop until you're on that ship." He pulled his feet from the stirrups. "I'll see you soon."

"Wait! What are you doing?" She glanced over her shoulder.

"Don't you dare stop fighting." Jon touched her cheek then leapt up to a low-hanging signpost.

"No!" Jàden grabbed for his leg, but the horse charged ahead. She tried to turn around, but the walls were so close she could reach out and touch each one. "Jon!"

Thomas was right behind her, waving her on. "Keep going!"

"Get the woman!" someone roared behind them. Jàden's hands shook. *Please don't leave me.*

Silver and orange slid across the top of the buildings. The ship's engines rumbled, and she hunched her shoulders up tight, fear crashing into her as the black dashed across the next road. *Kale, what do I do?*

He'd know how to handle his father or at least have some idea how to ground the scout craft and give them a fighting chance. His voice slid into her head like a warm breeze. *Have courage, Jàden.*

Yet, the words were tainted with the heat of Jon's mouth brushing across hers. She bit down on her lower lip, Jon's gentle command in her head this time. *Never stop fighting.*

She turned onto another side street, the salty ocean air washing over her. An icy wind blew through the city, two-story wood-and-mortar buildings blocking most of the chill. Fog banks hovered, obscuring the wharf.

"Get her to the ship!" Thomas yanked his horse around and drew his sword, half a dozen Rakir crashing into him.

"Thomas!" Jàden called. Chaos and fear pounded in her skull. All of Jon's men were gone, replaced by fog and scrambling citizens as black and gold soldiers raced toward her.

Something heavy landed on the back of Jon's horse.

"Keep going!" Theryn dug his heels into the stallion and fired an arrow behind them. "Move!"

She tightened her grip and leaned close to the stallion's mane, one of Theryn's arrows flying over her head into a warden's chest.

The black lowered his head, charging through the streets and sweating foam along his neck. White fog swirled, so thick she could barely see the outlines of the buildings.

Frank's ship hovered overhead, only a scout craft, but the wingspan was nearly the length of a full city block. Jàden turned them into an alley, then another, lost in a sea of white.

Her shoulders twitched at the memory of two years in the white.

The endless nothing.

Jon's horse panted as foam licked up the sides of his neck. She needed to slow him down before he strained himself.

The sound of riders faded as they plunged into bustling crowds again. Wooden carts lined a wide avenue, the stench of rotting fish nearly gagging her. She slowed the horse and searched the shadows in the heavy mist.

"Over there." Theryn tapped her shoulder and pointed to a stone block painted with bright orange flames and a black creature standing on top. The leathery canine was long dead, its hide stuffed tight as the hollow eyes stared toward the bay.

Beneath the hairless wolf-like creature, black letters were painted across orange flames: *The Fiery Shàden.*

Frank's ship hovered two blocks away, arrows pinging off the hull. People needed to stop doing that before he gunned them all down.

A loud whistle caught her attention.

Malcolm stood on the wharf, gesturing to a moored barge.

Jàden nudged the stallion to the far side of the wide avenue and trotted onto the dock.

"Jon's coming, right?" She clenched the reins as the stallion's hooves pounded against the weathered wood.

"He'll be here." Theryn clenched his jaw as he nocked an arrow and watched the streets behind them.

A shadowy barge loomed at the end of the dock, creaking each time the tide rolled in and out.

Theryn eased the tension on his bow and hopped down. "We leave as soon as the others get here."

Malcolm threw back his hood. "Go on, Jàden. Get the captain's horse tied up."

She nudged Jon's black up the ramp. The wooden planks creaked beneath her as they trotted onto the ship. Worry clutched her chest for Jon's safety as she dismounted and tied the stallion to the rail.

"Stay here," she muttered. "No running off this time."

The black grunted, his ears perked toward the city as if searching for Jon. Agnar raced up with Dusty and Theryn's horses tied to his saddle. He pressed his nose into her.

"Did you see him?" Jàden searched the road along the wharf as she tied off the rest of the horses and chided them with the same lecture. No showing off how they could untie their ropes. But she couldn't ease the worry in her heart as the seconds ticked by and the others still didn't appear.

Orange and silver slid over the cityscape, the ship's seams illuminating the clouds. She lowered her head, peeking out through the top edge of her cowl. *Please don't find me.* Wood creaked against wood with each roll of the waves. Jàden kept close to the horses, but knots twisted in the pit of her stomach. The ramp clattered along the pier then dropped into the bay. Theryn dove for the deck, clutching onto the side as he pulled himself up.

"What the fuck happened?" He nocked an arrow and scanned the deck as if Theryn expected an enemy.

Malcolm stood on the pier, an ax buried in a Rakir's skull. "They're on the ship!"

A strong hand clamped around Jàden's mouth and ripped her from the rail.

"Theryn!" Her scream muffled behind her captor's sausage-like fingers as she twisted and squirmed. Jàden clawed at the beefy hand.

The attacker tightened his grip and laughed from deep in his belly, hastening toward the far side of the deck. "Looks like I got me a wildcat here. Commander Hareth's gonna love you."

## CHAPTER 19
*Nelórath*

Éli wrangled his horse around, clenching the reins so tight his fingers hurt. "I know you're here, Jon!"

He signaled the rest of his men: *search everywhere.*

They'd have to rely on silent gestures for now as the sky beast roared louder. Sleek gray slid over the top of the towers, lines between its skin bright orange against the storm as if the creature's blood glowed from within.

He'd had everything planned meticulously, from his soldiers waiting in the mountains to the wardens who'd spied Jon and his men entering the city. But nothing could have prepared Éli for the fiery sky beast, and he was quickly losing control of the situation.

His men scrambled from their horses, kicking in doors and overrunning shops and taverns.

Or maybe the chaos would drive Jon's next move.

Éli circled the plaza, scanning all the rooftops, the stone and mortar slick with ice. Bright banners whipped in the harbor breeze, but nothing stirred over their heads, only chaos and screams in the streets as Nelórath citizens raced to safety.

The sky beast spit bolts of light from its belly, ripping a hole into a tower wall before it turned toward the harbor, heat bursting from its back end and momentarily warming the air.

"Of course." He'd ordered Granger and a squad of soldiers to wait by the docks in case Jon and his men tried to slip away by sea. Snowflakes glistened and melted to rain as he bolted down the nearby alley. If that was indeed their plan, Jon would head straight to the wharf.

A shadow leapt from one rooftop to the next, a flash of red beneath the cowl.

Inman. He'd know that freckle-faced bastard's bright hair anywhere.

"Split up," Éli shouted, pointing toward the roof. "And somebody kill that red-haired fuck."

He charged to the next corner. There weren't enough of them to cover the block, even with wardens attempting to barricade everyone. But with the sky beast roaring, most of the wardens were giving up the chase and retreating to help their own kin.

*Cowards.* He raced to the end of the block, the newly forged faux pendant hung around his neck, its metal cold against his chest. Éli would trade it for Connor and keep the real key, but Jon was proving to be a slippery bastard.

Fog rolled in from the coast, obscuring the bay. Éli whistled for his men and stormed onto the next street, bright merchant carts and colorful fruits on display. His stomach growled as a whiff of fresh-baked bread entwined with the salty air.

"This isn't over! I'm going to find that woman." Éli cursed as soon as the words came out. The woman, he wanted—if only because Jon was protecting her—but the key, he needed.

Another shadow raced by on the rooftops, this one with two swords strapped to his back.

"Up there," someone yelled.

"Don't kill him!" Éli seethed as an arrow whizzed past Jon's head.

He clenched the reins until his knuckles were white. His men had orders to hit him in the leg, something to slow him down. But with no one listening, maybe he could trigger Jon's anger. Get him to drop to Éli's level before he lost Jon to the rooftops again.

"Your sister begged me to bed her, Jon. Every night until I lit the stick that set her on fire."

Fighting Jon never gave Éli the peace he needed after the Tower stole the last shard of his soul, so he'd tried seducing Jon's sisters. The oldest spurned him, already happily bonded with her new wife, and the youngest no more than a child. But the third sister had fallen victim to his false charms. Éli bedded her with a single purpose: to produce an heir to both the Hareth and Ayers bloodlines.

And Connor was now trapped on the high council barge just beyond the horizon and in danger of getting branded to the Tower's will.

Éli clenched his jaw. They would not turn his son into a mercenary. When Jon didn't show his face, he bolted toward the harbor, trying to cut off his path.

The beast lifted one wing and turned away. A building exploded, rock and wood shooting into the sky. Éli's horse whinnied, and they both slammed to the ground.

Pain shot up his arm, rocks and debris raining down.

Shaking off the ringing in his ears, Éli stumbled to his feet, coughing through the cloud of dust.

"Horse!" Damn thing better be alive. He gritted his teeth, agonizing pain throbbing from his fingers to his collarbone.

The excruciating sizzle in his arm eased after a few moments, but his shoulder ached. Unwilling to lose one more second, he stumbled through the fog. His horse trotted toward him, a jagged shard of wood lodged in its shoulder. It looked to be a shallow wound and wouldn't lame his companion. He'd deal with it later. Right now, he needed to catch Jon.

Grabbing the reins, Éli swung into the saddle. "To the harbor. Let's move!"

Shadows followed him through the dust, keening wails high on the air a block over. Another explosion ripped apart the building behind him. Rocks clattered to the cobbles beneath. Orange fire burst from the sky beast, cutting a swath of flames across buildings. Citizens screamed and ran in a dozen directions. People burned to ash in the span of a heartbeat.

Éli cursed. Heat rolled through the icy air as he dodged through streets and alleys, getting as far away from the creature as he could. The wharf came into view through the fog and snow, rotten fish wafting through the air.

Ships broke free of their moorings as waves crashed against the wharf. One drifted several spans off the pier, black horses loose on the deck.

As the second sun lightened the sky, fog rolled apart, revealing a giant barge with the Tower and two moons on its sails. The high council vessel. A warning prickled the hairs on the back of his neck. His son was on that ship.

"There," he shouted to the few men still at his back.

Jon stood on the edge of the docks, a dagger gripped in each hand. He paced the wharf, dark eyes fixed on each of the soldiers. His hair and beard had grown long, creating the image of a half-crazed woodsman.

Éli stopped his horse a few spans back, the remainder of his men circling Jon in a half moon on the edge. He had to tread carefully. He wasn't above swimming after the bastard but he would rather fight Jon on dry land.

"Did Mather cry for his woman when he died? A brother for a brother, eh, Jon?"

The air seemed to grow more frigid as Jon shifted his weight onto his back foot. He slammed the twin daggers into their sheaths and drew a long, silver sword, the hilt bound with white cloth.

"Stay away from me and stay away from my men." Jon's voice held a deadly calm, sharper than a razor's edge.

Now he was finally getting angry.

The Rakir drew their swords, but Éli nudged his horse forward. He considered telling Jon that Connor was alive, but he wasn't ready to play that card yet.

Instead, Éli did what always forced the anger out of Jon.

"Do you know"—he slid to the ground and unsheathed his sword—"I could smell your woman's hair through that soldier's nose? I wonder if it's as soft against my own fingertips."

"You'll never touch her." Fury bled into Jon's eyes.

Bullseye. She meant something to him. Though Jon always did have a soft spot for weak females.

The roar of the sky beast grew louder. He charged Jon, swiping aside the white-bound blade with his sword as they hit the sea together, the icy cold seawater snapping him alert.

Explosions thundered along the dock, spitting fire and wood over their heads through the shimmering surface water. He slammed his elbow across Jon's jaw.

Jon kicked him in the gut, pushing them apart.

Whipping his sword around, Éli sliced the blade across Jon's shin. But Éli was running out of air. He swam for the surface for a breath, searching the choppy gray waters. "Jon!"

The bastard had to come up for air soon. Wreckage floated on the small swells, the Tower barge looming beyond the harbor.

Jon wasn't anywhere.

Éli slapped the water. "Mother fucking horse shitter."

Rage burned in his chest as he slid beneath the waves again. It couldn't be over this quick. Where was that fucking bastard?

Dust and debris littered the tide, making everything murky. Jon was nowhere to be seen.

He climbed onto the dock, the wharf-side street scattered with rock and wood, a wide crack running along the cobbles. Dust and smoke swirled around him. His eyes burned as he turned toward the sea, searching for a bobbing head.

"I'll find you, Jon Ayers. I haven't finished yet."

He wasn't even close to done.

Neither was the sky beast. It slid along the shoreline inland, almost as if it hunted something. Or someone.

Sheathing his sword, Éli whistled for his horse. The black limped toward him, blood dripping down from the chunk of wood buried in his shoulder.

"I'll get that trembling oaf to stitch you up. Can't have me a lame horse." Not all the men in his regiment took proper care of their mounts, but Éli was meticulous about his. The temperamental stallion had gotten him out of more scrapes than he liked to admit, and someday the two of them would find a way to disappear, far away from any Tower laws.

But not until Jon suffered enough pain to satisfy the rage in his heart.

Fucking Jon. Fucking sky beast.

Éli grabbed the reins and clutched the faux bloodflower. He would not be thwarted again.

If Granger had been successful capturing the woman, Jon would come to him. But for today, he had another duty. He had to get Connor away from those old pricks.

"To the barge," he shouted to his men and turned toward the far dock, where his own ship was moored.

## CHAPTER 20

*Nelórath Harbor*

Only Jàden mattered now.

Jon swam through the icy waters, trying to shake off Éli's words. He clenched his sword until his fingers hurt. Just his presence at her side put Jàden in more danger than she deserved.

But the sky beast worried him the most. Frank. Another man he'd have to kill to keep her safe.

Saltwater stung deep in the cut on his leg and forced him to the surface. Smoke plumes obscured the city as he gasped for air then dove under again before anyone could spot him.

When he surfaced a second time, Jon was beyond the moored ships, surrounded by swells. He turned about to get his bearings, fog wrapping the Guardian towers and most of the city. Smoke hovered along the waterfront, gold-armored and black-clad soldiers darting in and out of the adjacent roads.

Rakir and wardens had been enemies for hundreds of years, each sticking to their own side of the Forbidden Mountains. Watching them side by side unsettled his already turbulent thoughts.

"Captain!" A rope slapped the water next to him. Malcolm stood on the deck of a large ship, wine-colored sails flapping in the breeze.

Jon sheathed his sword and grabbed the mooring rope. He pulled himself out of the water, his leg killing him each time he put pressure on it.

Canon fire exploded, a column of water soaring into the sky. He gripped the weathered wood and pulled himself over the rail as the spray hit him and the boat lurched under the force of the waves.

"Where's Jàden?" Jon asked. "We got separated."

"We all got separated." Malcolm clasped his forearm, hauling Jon to his feet.

"Thomas and the twins are missing, I ain't seen Dusty yet, and that woman of yours..." Malcolm pointed toward the far side of the harbor where a black and silver Tower barge sat shrouded in a thin veil of mist. "She and Theryn got taken."

"Fuck!" He paced along the rail, gritting his teeth each time he stepped on his injured leg. The ship's crew shouted across the deck with strong female voices. Women clad in soft dresses and low hemlines tugged on the ropes to open a sail, while others—dressed as men in wine-colored breeches—tugged their hats low and climbed the masts.

He needed to get to that barge. The high council might keep Jàden alive, but Theryn was in serious trouble. Leaving his men behind wasn't an option.

Jon shouted in frustration.

Malcolm gestured to the ship's hevkor—a prestigious command title only given to merchant trade captains—as the ship's aft drifted toward the wharf. "Ain't never been terrified of a woman, but that one frightens me. Whatever you do, Captain, don't go pickin' a fight with her."

It was as if Malcolm didn't know him. Jon was already itching for a fight. Dusty raced along the exploded wharf. "Get a ramp down!"

The crew was already in motion. Several women shoved Jon aside and slid a rail from the top deck toward the pier. More than a dozen riders trailed Dusty.

Jon grabbed an arrow and sighted the tip as he pulled back the tension on his bow. The damn thing zipped past the warden's shoulder. He cursed under his breath and grabbed another as horses thundered onto the ship.

A small knife plunged into one warden's throat.

*Twins are here,* Jon thought, slipping another arrow onto his string. He released it into the last man's throat, but loud shouts erupted in the distance. Dozens of wardens poured out of a nearby cross-street.

"Shit, out of time, boys," Jon said.

Dusty and the twins bolted onto the ship, the latter with blood splattered across their cheeks.

"Toss the ramp," Dusty shouted to the crew.

"No, wait." Ashe pointed toward a knot of soldiers as Thomas burst through.

"Get your arrows." Jon grabbed two more then tossed his quiver to Dusty, who only had one left. Jon pulled the fletchings against his cheek and fired his arrow, piercing a warden in the knee.

"Open the lower doors!" one of the crew shouted.

Thomas laid low against his horse and bolted for the ship. The crew hauled up the ramp and dropped it onto the deck. The rusted black raced to the end of the pier and leapt, barely clearing the gap as both the stallion and Thomas disappeared into the lower deck.

Jon sneered at the soldiers racing along the wharf. "Let's go. And someone check on Thomas."

Guardians be damned, he needed a cigarette. His were soaking wet. Without a care for the women on deck, Jon stripped off his shirts and squeezed out as much of the moisture as he could while the ship slid away from the city toward the harbor.

His thoughts were on Jàden.

He'd damn near kissed her and only barely held himself back. Her gentleness breathed in his skin, but it was his mouth that burned with the desire to feel her lips against his.

Jon pulled on dry clothes and his leather armor, buckling on his weapons last. He was still freezing his ass off, but it would have to do. He needed to get to Jàden and Theryn before it was too late.

"Head for the Tower barge."

## CHAPTER 21
*The Tower Barge*

Sweat from cold fingers slid across Jàden's mouth, soiling the remnants of Jon's breath with the scent of sex and blood. She yanked her head away from the wretched man's beefy fingers.

Abducted again.

But fear's vice-like grip on her heart couldn't close the distance back to the wharf and the plumes of smoke along the cityscape.

Frank's ship disappeared into the fog as he retreated toward the heart of the city. He hadn't found her.

But everything was a mess again. She just wanted to get back to Jon.

Harbor waves rocked the longboat as Theryn crashed to his knees, a cut along his cheek streaking blood down his jaw. "Let her go, Granger!"

Jàden tried to twist out of the brawny man's grip, but he had the strength of an ox. Granger grabbed her jaw, pulling her cheek close to his mouth. "Jon Ayers ain't gonna save you. He's already in irons."

His putrid breath rolled across her nose, and she turned away, bile in her throat.

"He'll come," she whispered, the familiar words dropping from her mouth as if she'd never left the cage. She'd waited two long years for Kale to rescue her, clinging obsessively to the idea of a him as the hero so she didn't have to be one.

Tears slid down her cheeks.

Maybe Granger was right. Kale was the love of her life, and he never did save her. Jon held no love for her. He'd save his men before giving her a thought. "Don't listen to him, Jàden." Theryn spat blood onto the boat's wooden bench. "Granger's scared of the captain. It's why he's been cozying up to Hareth for years."

Granger shoved her face against the icy bench and kicked Theryn across the jaw. "Watch it, Blakewood. There ain't no orders to keep you alive."

A large ship loomed ahead as they sailed further away from the wharf. Lights flickered high on the deck of a midnight black barge, black sails bearing a silver tower image with two moons—Shelora and Maori—near the left apex. The same emblem she'd seen on the Rakir.

These were the ones trying to kill Jon for the bloodflower.

"He can't come here," she whispered. Jon would be a fool to try and save her when he carried one of *Hàlon's* most precious gate keys.

Granger grabbed her scruff and hauled her to her feet.

"I can walk." She tried to shove him away, but he tightened his grip as a scream tore through the air. Jàden froze, her eyes on Theryn. "That sounded like a child."

"Impossible." He spat at Granger's feet, but a shadow lingered in his eyes as if he wasn't entirely certain of his own words.

As they slid alongside the larger vessel, armored men hooked the longboat to a pulley system and hauled them from the sea to the top deck. Theryn struggled against his bonds, Granger's men gripping each of his arms.

The Rakir ship rocked in the gusty seas, creaking like an old door. More than fifty black-clad soldiers stood on the deck, the Rakir emblem on their shoulders and a silver sword strapped to their backs. Near the larger central mast, two cloaked figures were flanked on either side by soldiers covered head to foot in metal armor, the silver tower emblazoned across their breastplates. Each one carried a heavy iron pike. Behind them, a tall metal canister burned bright to fend off the frigid air.

Jàden's heart hammered as Granger shoved her onto the deck. If she couldn't get away from Frank and Bradshaw, she'd certainly never find a way to leave this ship.

Ice-blue eyes leered at her from beneath each shadowed cowl like glowing orbs. Both spoke at the same time, their voices interwoven. "Where is Jon Ayers?"

"He's busy blowing up the city. But I can take him a message—" Theryn started, but one of the men holding him punched him across the jaw, silencing his snarky tone. Blood dripped from the corner of his lip.

Granger tightened his grip on her scruff. "She's the bait. Ayers wants to protect this little lovely."

Jàden nearly gagged on the stench of his breath, turning away from the poisoned heat.

"Come here, woman," an old man's raspy, snake-like voice slithered.

Clamping down stubbornly on her jaw, Jàden refused to budge.

The cloaked figures raised their hands, darkness whispering along the fringes of her mind. Power surged, tightening its web of air and forcing her to step forward.

But this was something new, a slick hiss crawling along her skin.

She dug her heels into the deck's weathered wood, her weak muscles straining against the unfamiliar magic. "Theryn?"

"Working on it." He tugged at his bonds, a grim expression on his face.

Energy, dark and slick as oil, slithered over her like a serpent.

*They'll kill anyone with a hint of magic,* Jon's voice whispered in her head. Because these men wanted it for themselves. To be the power in this world when no one else could.

This wasn't magic. It was some type of energy manipulating the elements, just as the Violet Flame did when it burst from her hands. Compelling her toward the hooded figures until she was barely an arm's length away, their power's dark tendrils poked along her arms. Jàden shuddered under the slimy, alien brush of energy.

"I can feel your power." Their blue eyes fixed on her, and they gasped. "Herana. So it's true."

A pale, withered hand shot out from the dark robes and grasped her wrist, a surprisingly strong grip for an old man. He turned over her hand, flecks of light and shadow lifting from her skin. "It's been nearly three thousand years since I last saw this. The threads are incomplete."

"What are you talking about?" She tried to wrench away, but the bastard had an iron grip.

Three thousand, almost a full millennium after she fell asleep. No way could these withered crusts of men be three thousand years old, unless they weren't human.

"Who are you?" she asked.

The Flame flowed into her veins, crackling from its invisible well of power as tendrils of white light circled her forearms. She clenched her hands, torn between unleashing it to erase the guilt of Mather's death and fear she'd not be able to hold the Flame's power back next time.

"Feel her strength." Their blue eyes widened, and the old man gripped her arm tighter, the other fumbling inside his robes. "Get the iron ready."

Theryn shouted at her from across the deck. "Don't let him touch you, Jàden."

Before his words fully registered, the cloaked figure slapped a stone circlet onto her wrist. The gentle whisper of Jon's strength disappeared along with the Flame, leaving her alone, hollow and cold.

"No!" She clawed at the old man's hand, still too weak to peel back his fingers. Jàden reached for the Flame, no longer caring if it pushed her power too far, but an invisible barrier buzzed along her arms, just like when she'd first woken from hypersleep. "Theryn!"

The cloaked figures threw back their hoods, revealing long, white hair and pale, wrinkled features. Glowing blue eyes fixed on her. "Your lives belong to us until Captain Ayers brings us that key."

"No!" She understood now why Jon didn't want them to have it. The energy they wielded felt like drowning in oil, and she would not subject the citizens of *Hàlon* to it. "I'll die before I let you have that key."

An old man nodded toward his guards. "Stoke the fires and hang the traitor."

Armored soldiers grabbed her arms.

"Leave me alone." Jàden dug her heels into the deck.

"Let her go!" Theryn's voice was strained.

A scuffle broke out behind Jàden as the guards slammed her head against the mast. They wrapped her arms around the wooden pillar, tying her wrists to the far side.

Her vision blurred, pain shooting into her skull. Jàden's pulse raced as hands grabbed her skirt and ripped it off, peeling her breeches away from her waist.

"No, no! What are you doing?" She yanked against her restraints.

Theryn jumped in front of her, his face bloodied and beaten, but the guards caught him again. They wrapped a rope around his neck and pulled the noose tight before he could squirm away.

"Listen to me." His eyes locked onto hers, a grim determination in their depths. "Ignore the captain's order, or we both die."

Fire seared into her hip. Jàden screamed, hands clenched into a tight knot. The pressure released, and a red-hot branding iron was tossed into the burning metal container.

"Jon!" She tugged against the ropes, drool sliding from the side of her mouth. Where was he? Where was Kale? She tried to cling to both men, but she knew in her heart no one would save her again.

Kale was nothing but ash, and these men would kill Jon on sight.

*No one's gonna save you, darlin'.* Frank's voice seeped into her memories.

The storm clouds brightened as the insidious starship roared over the harbor. Almost as if his ship's tracking system could somehow read her thoughts.

"I know you're out there, darlin'." Frank's voice filled the air. "Ol' Doc's waitin'."

Jàden gripped the leather bindings and screamed at the storm. "Fuck you, Frank!"

"Herana." Blood dripped into Theryn's eye, and for the first time she saw an uneasiness there. But his voice was as calm as a placid sea. "The captain told us about the day he found you. Show these fuckers what happens if they mess with a Guardian."

Her hands trembled as someone dusted powder across her burned hip. She tried to reach for Theryn—*Save me, please.*

"I'm no Guardian," she whispered. Why did no one understand this? She was weak, broken, and holding tight to a dream that would never come to pass.

The armored guard pulled the brand out of the fires, the iron glowing a brilliant orange.

Theryn was yanked up the mast, hanging by his neck with his hands bound behind his back.

"No no no!" All the pain and fear of her captivity slamming into her. "Let him go!"

"If you think you're in pain now," the guard said, tracing a clammy finger across her cheek. "The second brand always hurts worse."

"What?" Jàden struggled against her restraints, reaching toward the Flame. "No, please."

Iron burned into her flesh as the brand pressed the same spot on her hip. Jàden screamed, pain ripping through her whole body until its fire consumed her senses. A pulse of white light thrummed across a web of voices.

*Help us.*

*Save us.*

The whispered voices twisted into Mather's, as if he bore witness to her anguish, even between lives. *Theryn's coming with me. Give up now and accept your fate.*

"Never!" Jàden slammed her mind outward to throw the voices back to the abyss. She'd heard enough screams during her years in captivity, and she could bear no more.

The cuffs around her wrist shattered, and white fire surged in her veins. Jon's strength followed on its heels and she clung to the sensation.

"I won't lose another one of Jon's friends." Jàden slapped her hands against the mast, light pulsing along the weathered timber toward the sky and deep into the hull.

Wood exploded skyward, ripping the ship apart at the keel.

Orange and silver roared across the bay, spraying water behind the ship in a city-high rooster tail.

Her heart beat faster. "I'm not going back!"

The Flame's power ripped through her mind. She reached through the threads of light, searching for the singular pulse of Theryn's energy. Frustration rippled back from far below her feet. He was already underwater.

Frank's ship zoomed straight toward her.

Jàden drew the Flame's crackling light into her body and stretched her hands toward the sea.

A column of water burst through the steel ship and tore it out of the sky. Metal exploded outward, and the wood deck cracked beneath her feet, plunging her into the harbor's icy depths.

Saltwater seared into her burn, shooting pain through her bones. Brilliant orange illuminated the sea, waves surging and bodies grasping for the surface.

And amid the chaos, the heart of Sandaris beat louder. Its threads of energy tugged her down, almost begging her to open herself up to more of the Flame's power. Her thoughts shifted to the moon's vision, a trail of giant bones illuminating toward the alien starship buried deep in the moon's core.

She would never go to that horrible place again.

Jàden kicked away from the sinking steel beast, gasping for air when she broke the surface. The icy wind filled her lungs.

"Theryn!" she called.

Ruptured down to the keel, the black ship's decks lay open to the air. She swam toward the lower level of the stern and grasped onto a beam.

"Theryn!"

*He must still be underwater.*

Stretching along the threads of light with her mind, she searched for him again. Anger and determination rippled back, and she couldn't tell one water-soaked head from another.

If Theryn died, Jon would never forgive her. "Please still be alive."

"Where are you, Ravenscraft?" Frank's voice sliced through the air.

Shit. Waves crashed over her as she scrambled for the stairwell and raced toward the next level. Her hip screamed in pain, heat pulsing from her chest to her knees beneath the burned skin. "Theryn!"

Granger kneeled on the far deck, hands over his eye with blood dripping through his fingers.

Theryn stood over him, the wind whipping his voice toward her. "You tell that fuck Hareth if he so much as looks at the captain or any of us again, I'll rip both his eyes out and stuff his own prick down his throat."

He kicked Granger in the chest, knocking him into the sea. Theryn held up the arrow in his hand, Granger's eye skewered on the shaft.

Jàden slapped a hand over her mouth and forced back vomit.

A raspy voice slithered from the stairwell above. Icy blue orbs peeked out from the old man's white hair slicked against his wrinkled features. He seemed to be enjoying himself as shadowy threads from his body whispered against her. "Oh, the power we will wield together."

"Fuck you." She bolted for an open doorway and slammed the door, shoving a bolt into place.

What am I doing? She'd left Theryn out there alone. He didn't have her power, but maybe he was strong enough to—

No, she had to get hold of herself.

But the fear tightened her chest as she retreated several slow steps backward.

The old man breathed heavy outside the door, his power sliding through the air and across her arms. "You cannot escape me, Guardian. Come out or your companion dies."

"Shit, shit, shit." She couldn't think straight.

Jàden scanned the small, luxurious room for a weapon. Layers of thick blankets covered the bed against one wall. On the other, a wooden chest sat open, stuffed with wires and hunks of metal. The hilt of a gun lay stuffed between a table leg and a cracked piece of shield panel.

"*Hàlon* technology." She dropped to her knees and dug through the scattered items. A hair dryer with missing coils. Cracked coffee pots. The panel to a replicator. Someone had collected broken junk from her world.

A heavy body slammed the door.

Then Theryn's muffled voice squeaked through the cracks. "You're a Guardian, Jàden. Fight!"

"I'm trying!" She grabbed the gun hilt and pressed it between her knees. Her finger traced across an old datapad, and she stuffed that next to the hilt.

Her people had created everything to last millennia. If she could find enough pieces, maybe something would work.

The bolt slid back, and the door creaked open.

The white-haired figure leered at her from the entry. "You killed Rian, and you must pay."

Theryn crashed into the old man. As they hit the floor, Theryn's body slammed into the far wall.

Energy thrummed into the room, an oppressive, slick mire crawling up the walls and over her skin. The old man wheezed and glared at the dark-skinned bowman.

"Use your magic!" Theryn clawed at his neck as if something invisible choked him.

She tossed items behind her as she dug deeper into the chest, the Flame's power pulsing so hard through her veins it threatened to consume her.

But she couldn't lose control, not again.

Besides, Kale had taught her a thing or two about shooting. She yanked a small handgun free. "Theryn, firemark!"

"Little. Busy." He kicked out his legs, the old man's power squeezing the air out of him.

She slammed the chest shut and climbed on top. Jàden scrambled for his pockets, but Theryn was quicker, clutching her hand with a firemark between their palms.

His eyes said everything his mouth couldn't: *kill that bastard.*

Jàden slapped the firemark into the hilt and swept her thumb across the transparent orb until it glowed. Red light bled through the etched steel lines to the tip of the barrel.

"Now I'm a fucking Guardian." She aimed the gun at the old man and fired.

The bastard howled and stumbled back, gripping his shoulder.

Jàden fired two more shots into his chest.

Red light burned a hole through the old man's heart, the light fading from his vivid blue eyes. He crumpled to the ground, the air in the room retreating to frigid ice.

Theryn crashed to the floor, rubbing his throat. His nose was broken and bleeding, the swelling around his eye darkening. Blood dripped from a dozen cuts as he gasped for breath.

"What the fuck is that thing, and where do I get one?" he said.

"Is he..." She couldn't even finish the words. Didn't want to know.

Her hands shook violently, the gun slipping from her fingers. She'd never intentionally killed another human. Jàden slid to the ground. She nudged the gun with her toe, the dead man's empty blue eyes staring through her. "I'm sorry."

Two beefy hands grabbed either side of the door frame, Frank's bulk filling up the space between. His hazel eyes pinned her, full of rage and the promise to make her suffer.

Mohawk slick against his head, a sinister grin curled the corner of his mouth. "Miss me, darlin'?"

# CHAPTER 22
*The Tower Barge*

"Who the fuck is this prick?" Theryn grabbed a dagger from his waist, his thick clothing soaked against the lean lines of his arms.

"Frank." Jàden scrambled for the gun.

In one swift move, Frank had a weapon in each hand.

He fired, several glowing wires wrapping Jàden's arms and pinning them to her body. Her connection to the Flame dampened, but this time it didn't disappear. Her power was too strong now. "Theryn, don't move!"

Frank pointed the handgun at Theryn's forehead. "You heard her, boy."

*Not again, not again.*

Jàden dropped sideways, slamming her palm to the floor. The Flame crackled through her arms, ripping the ground upward and tossing both men against the walls.

As the wires around her body shorted out, she unraveled enough to get her arm free and grabbed her discarded handgun.

Jàden squeezed the trigger, firing off a single shot.

"You fucking bitch." Fury in his eyes, Frank clutched his stomach. Crimson bled through his fingers, but he kept his handgun pointed at Theryn's head. "How the fuck did you get out of hypersleep?"

Her hands shook as she inched backward. "Where is he? Where's Kale?"

A sneer curved the corner of Frank's mouth. "He's dead, darlin'. It's just you and me and that glass cage you love so much."

"He was your son!" Tears spilled onto her cheeks. A raw pain ripped open her chest, widening the hollow gap. Tendrils of white light circled around her arms, the Flame's energy whispering against her senses. "I'm not going back, and we both know you'll never kill me."

"How right you are, darlin'." He fired at Theryn.

Jàden squeezed the trigger, wood shattering behind Frank's head.

A red-haired blur slammed into Frank, the two crashing into the wall.

"Dusty!" Theryn howled, clutching his arm and cursing as he raced across the room.

Jàden aimed her gun at the wrestling men then dropped her arm. She didn't want to accidentally hit the wrong person. "Pop the firemark out! He can't shoot if his weapon has no power."

A large swell crashed against the ship's hull, flipping the boat sideways and knocking her across the room. Her back slammed against the ceiling, pain shooting along her spine.

"Jàden!" Jon shouted from somewhere outside as seawater swelled into the room.

"In here!" She scrambled to her feet, fire digging into her hip as the saltwater soaked her burn. Jàden spied the datapad and shoved the thin tablet inside her bodice.

Seawater rose to her waist, a tangle of bodies splashing in the center of the room.

They had to get out, but the doorway was already flooding.

The hull ripped open, the ship groaned as wood shards burst into the air.

Jàden covered her head. Splinters sliced across her hand as Frank and the two bowmen fell through the submerged wall into the sea. She clutched the weathered wood, holding onto the edge. She tried to pull herself toward the orange-and-gray clouding but didn't have the strength.

The ship groaned again.

"Jon!" she called.

"I gotcha." Jon's face appeared over the torn wall. He grabbed her wrists and pulled her up beside him.

Relief flooded through her. As soon as he pulled loose the last wires wrapping her body, she threw her arms around him, burying her face in his neck. "You came."

"I'll always come," he whispered.

The storm had cooled his skin, but his deeper warmth pressed through the prickles of his beard.

Jon held her tight and buried his chin in her neck. "We gotta get out of here. This ship's sinking."

"The others—"

"Let's get you to safety first."

Jàden grasped Jon's arm as he helped her climb across the corridor wall to the edge of the sinking hull. His breath on her skin wound tightly to the Flame's power, and a sense of peace whispered through her.

This felt like home.

Waves crashed against the hull, the stormy seas gray and dreary. With some of the fog burned off, the city's stark white towers stood tall among rows of tight buildings.

Frank's scout craft flickered with orange light as one wing lay high in the air, a giant hole torn into the blast shielding.

"Shit, I did that," she whispered. Sparking wires and pipes dangled along the side. "I should detonate the ship."

She hesitated, glancing between the city and the storm waves crashing around the sleek craft. Citizens would come poking inside, or maybe merchants would tear it apart and sell off the pieces.

"Leave it." Jon clasped her hand. "We have to get away from this city."

A smaller vessel with wine-colored sails slid alongside them.

Jon pointed to where the others waited. "Go."

"You'd better be right behind me." She hastened for the edge and leapt across the gap.

Jàden crashed onto the deck, agony screaming through her hip and shoulder. She bit back a cry of pain and stumbled to her knees, the gun skidding across the deck.

Jon cursed as he crashed to the deck beside her, clenching his fist. Blood soaked his lower leg.

"You're hurt," she said.

"I'm fine." He clasped her arm and helped her up.

She doused the firemark and slid the gun into her waistband as dozens of women in wine-colored bodices and breeches swarmed the deck.

"Ship's going down quick, Hevkor," an umber-skinned woman with sleek, black hair shouted.

Someone replied from the stern, but it was garbled under Thomas's shouting. "There they are."

A dozen women raced to the rail, several tossing ropes over the side.

Jàden stumbled over and pulled the gun from her waistband, swiping her thumb across the firemark until it glowed, afraid that Frank would be trying to climb aboard.

Dusty and Theryn clung to a knotted rope and climbed up the side.

But she was searching for a third head.

For Frank's defining mohawk among the swells or another of those white-haired bastards. Dozens of Rakir cursed them, clinging to wood planks or swimming toward the orange flickers.

Frank was nowhere to be seen.

"That bastard disappeared," Theryn muttered as he pulled himself over the rail. He grabbed the gun from her hand, inspecting the weapon. Blood soaked his shoulder where a gunshot hadn't quite missed his arm. "You are one terrifying Guardian. Remind me never to piss you off."

Jàden swept her fingers across the firemark, dousing its power before the bowman accidentally shot himself, but she kept searching the sea. Frank would find a way to survive—he always did.

"I'll never go back, Frank," she shouted to the wind as snow scattered snow across the deck. "You come after me, and I'll shoot you again, this time between the eyes."

Jon laid a hand on her shoulder and pulled her away from the rail. "Is everyone here?"

She never wanted to see this city again. Tears burned in her eyes.

Two years she'd waited for Kale to come, only to watch him die. Jon found her in less than a day. She clutched his hand and leaned against his shoulder as wine-colored sails unfurled to catch the wind.

"So, the rumors are true." A short, stocky woman with black hair pulled back from her face strode up to them, dressed in a long wine-and-gold tunic. Salty air weathered her plain features, placing the woman's age somewhere near her eighties, just closing in on mid-life.

"What rumors?" Jàden tightened her grip on Jon's hand as women in dresses discarded their skirts, deck-hand uniforms the same deep burgundy as the ship's sails. They let their hair down to catch the wind, grabbing ropes and climbing tall masts like they'd lived all their lives on the sea.

"Herana, the moonless Guardian has returned." The shorter woman narrowed her eyes, almost as if she were displeased to see Jàden. "I'm Hevkor Naréa. Welcome to the *Darius*."

## CHAPTER 23
*The Lonely Sea*

Éli pressed a dagger against the trembling figure's throat. Wreckage floated across the harbor, upended chunks of wooden hull sinking beneath the stormy waves. The great silver beast lay dying on its side near the harbor wall. Life must still pulse through its veins, but he only had one thing on his mind.

"Can you find the boy or not?" he asked.

He'd never had a chance to get to the high council and exchange the faux-key for Connor. With the ship in pieces, he needed to know his son still lived.

"I-If..." Their lower lip trembled as they pulled their spindly knees to their chest.

They swallowed against the blade, blood beading along the sharp edge. The rail-thin dreamwalker tried to speak again, their lips and tongue stuttering without sound, but they nodded to show Éli what they couldn't speak.

"Try anything, and I'll make your former master look like a lapdog." Éli sheathed the dagger and tossed over the cuff keys. Who knew how many soldiers were left in the wake of devastation or if Connor's small body already lay at the bottom of the harbor. The thought of anyone killing his son drove a spike through the center of his chest. "Find my son."

The dreamwalker's hands shook as they inserted the flat slip of marble into the stone circlet until it clicked open and the cuffs fell away. They pushed their hands through their mousy brown hair.

Éli searched the sea, clenching his dagger hilt until his knuckles were white.

A soft voice whispered at the fringes of his mind, the tone surprisingly gentle and reserved. *I ask permission to see a memory of your son.*

Éli nodded, the dagger's hilt digging into his palm. The dreamwalker's whisper of power slipped between his thoughts and retreated almost as quickly, leaving in its wake a single name: Evardo.

Not like Éli cared, but he supposed he couldn't call the bastard Hey You. "If my son's alive, he'll be among the debris."

Evardo closed their eyes then pointed across the harbor toward the silver beast. *He's frightened.*

Éli's gaze slipped from the gray swells to the wine-colored sails disappearing into the storm. Jon and his men were gone again, leaving him behind to clean up their mess. He clenched his jaw to hold back the anger gripping his senses.

"Commander." A young soldier with sandy brown hair saluted him. "We're ready to go."

"Head for the sky beast." Golden sails with a black sun whipped in the storm. The smooth vessel slid away from the dock, the burly hevkor shouting at his men.

But dark power thrummed below the deck, one of the high council, Kóranté Alken, who lurked in the hevkor's private quarters. His black threads of power rippled through the brand on Éli's shoulder, holding him bound to the ship. He'd give anything to be free of the old men, free of the Tower caging him in a web of lies.

Today, all he wanted was his son.

They sailed slowly through the wreckage, tossing ropes to any soldier still alive as thunder rumbled across iron gray clouds. The ship slowed close to the silver beast. Metallic entrails hung out of a hole in its chest.

"Stop the ship." Éli hastened to the rail, leaning far over as a shadow moved within. "Connor!"

A small face peeked around a jagged tear, black hair slicked against his head.

Éli climbed on the rail and leapt the gap between them, landing on the slippery interior. He grasped the edge to hold himself steady. Metal sliced open his palm, but he ignored the sting and crouched in front of the quivering boy.

"You're alive," he said, his tone neutral. "You're stronger than I thought."

Connor pressed his back against the side, water dripping from his clothes as he clutched his small arm. Tears reddened his eyes, his voice the merest whisper. "A Guardian tried to kill us."

One sleeve still intact, Connor's left arm was bare, obsidian burned into his bony shoulder. The Tower and two moons emblem with a thread of Alken's power touching the surface.

Rage ignited in the pit of Éli's stomach. "Who branded you?"

His brother Sebastian had fought for years to keep them well fed so Éli never had to know the pain of being a soldier. So he would always be a free man, until Jon Ayers destroyed everything by digging a knife into his brother's spine.

History was repeating itself as Connor clutched his arm, hiccupping between sobs. Unless he lopped the boy's arm off, his son was bound to the Tower now.

Éli punched the sky beast in frustration.

Every man needed two good sword arms. He would find a way to keep the boy from becoming a soldier, but he wouldn't toss his arm away—not yet.

"Guardians ain't real, boy. What's that damn mother of yours teaching you?" But with the urge to smack the nonsense out of the kid, even Éli had witnessed the high council's barge explode down to the keel. If Jon protected a Guardian and felt something for the woman...

A faint smile pulled at the corner of his mouth.

"S-Someone lives here." Connor lifted a shaking hand, pointing over Éli's shoulder.

Éli unsheathed the dagger and whipped around, the blade held high.

A burly man in loose, gray clothing lay against the beast's innards, one hand pressed against his stomach with blood leaking between his fingers. Several deep cuts lined his arms and cheek, bruised skin circled his eyes. One of his legs bent at an odd angle as if broken.

Someone had beat the hell out of him. The stranger clasped a glowing metal object in his hand and aimed it at Éli. "Kóro."

The urge to kill the dying fucker grasped Éli by the throat, but he didn't know if the man held part of the beast or some type of weapon. A glass window next to him illuminated with a figure's head, his hair glowing green like the dalanath and slicked to his head. "Oné Frank."

"The fuck is this thing?" Éli stepped between Connor and man moving on the glass. "Get to the ship, boy."

But the injured man started screaming at the glass and pounding his fist against small lights. "Bradshaw, bareh ró!"

Evardo whispered against Éli's thoughts, a vague image of Jon's woman screaming in pain. *Don't let him find the Guardian. Kill him.*

Éli's shoulders wound tight. "Who the fuck are you?"

The glass turned smoky black and the face disappeared, but the injured man with the shaved head shifted his hand to the side, a loud pop as the metal object in his hand burned a hole in the beast. "Kóro!"

Éli wasn't sticking around long enough for the bastard to use that weapon on him, and he wasn't certain he could get his knife in the man's throat fast enough. He yanked Connor to his feet. "Jump to the ship, or I throw you across."

"Who—" Connor glanced at the waiting vessel then back at Éli with eyes as black as his. "Who are you?"

Éli pressed his mouth into a thin line. Tightening his grip on Connor's arm, he threw the kid over his shoulder and leapt off the beast onto the ship's deck, dropping his son next to Evardo. "I'm your real father, boy. You're lucky that bitch mother of yours is dead or I'd kill her myself."

He snapped his fingers at Evardo. "You, take care of the boy and finish stitching up my horse."

Power thrummed against his skin, a distant tug calling to him. Éli could sense the rest of the high council beyond the harbor, waiting like locusts. Most Rakir wouldn't feel more than an urge to head to sea, but the dark threads of power tugged him toward the fleet of ships beyond the horizon.

Éli ignored their pull and tossed the cuffs toward Evardo. "Put those on, or the high council will figure out what you are."

And he'd never see his new servant again. That still left the half-alive high councilman below decks to deal with.

Hands shaking around the cuffs, Evardo tried to hide their tears as they cuffed themself with the stone, keeping the unlocking slip of marble clutched in their hands.

Éli grabbed Connor's shoulder, the skinny runt barely coming halfway up his chest. "How old are you now, boy?"

"Seven." His wide eyes glanced around at the other soldiers. "Sir."

"Good, old enough to be a man. Get to the rail and search for anyone in a uniform like mine. We'll need more soldiers where we're going."

*To destroy your uncle.* The boy might never forgive him, but he didn't care. Jon deserved to suffer—for Sebastian, for Connor and for the pain in Éli's heart that hadn't eased once since his tenth naming day.

## CHAPTER 24

*The Lonely Sea*

Jàden shivered and leaned her forehead against Agnar's nose. The soft, velvety fur warmed her skin as the stallion grunted and closed his eyes. They were tired—the horses, Jon and his men and she could barely keep her legs straight enough to stand.

Cold to the bone, she needed to find dry clothes, but her body was so stiff she could barely move.

Letting go of the stallion, she turned about the large room nestled inside the prow of the ship. Arced in a half-circle, the ungated stalls held harnesses for the horses. Each one could walk a step forward and back, but if the ship rocked too much, the hammock-like restraints would keep the animals upright and steady. Such a smart setup for transporting livestock between the landmasses.

Two empty stalls at the back were stacked with the horses' gear and most of their supplies. Jon sat next to the saddles, a small needle in his hand as he sewed up his injury.

She stepped toward him, intent on helping.

But Thomas cut her off, vivid blue eyes looking her up and down. "You tired?"

She nodded. "Exhausted."

"Put on dry clothes and weave your hair into a single braid. You have three minutes." He retreated toward Jon to speak in hushed tones.

Great. Barely twenty minutes below deck and already he made demands. She needed sleep, and curling up in Jon's arms to do it sounded just fine to her.

Jàden crouched near her saddle bags and pulled out a set of clothes. All were soaked through except a pair of breeches and a single over-shirt. She pulled them on, along with a pair of dry socks, shoving the data pad under a blanket. The rest of her clothes she tacked to the wall, hoping they'd leach out the moisture.

"Let's go," Thomas said.

She followed, untangling her wet hair with her fingers. The others ignored her. Jàden glanced back at the entry, hoping Jon might meet her eyes for some small measure of comfort, but he was hunched over his ankle, stitching his wound.

The loneliness crept in, widening the hole in her chest. She wove her hair into a loose braid and tied off the end, every inch of her body screaming in pain. Fire burned in her hip as they entered the midship galley.

A box built into the middle of the floor held sand around an iron pot. Flames crackled from the burning wood inside, the fire's orange tongues reaching through the grate to a pot chained over the top.

Thomas dished a bowl of gruel and shoved it in her hands. He nodded toward the table. "Eat."

"I'm not..." She pressed her mouth closed under his intense gaze. *Hungry.*

Jàden grabbed a spoon and sat at the table, curling her legs tight around the bench so she didn't fall backward each time the ship rocked. She shoved her spoon into the steaming blob of food, pushing it around to release the heat against her face.

Thomas tossed a second bowl onto the table and sat across from her. "You'll eat what I put in front of you, every meal."

She tightened her fingers around the spoon and opened her mouth to speak.

"You've got no strength and no fire in your eyes. Ain't been a female Rakir in more than a thousand years, but Captain says you need to fight like one. So for now, I have two rules: stay dry and stay alive." He nodded at her food. "The sooner you eat, the sooner you sleep."

Jàden stared hard at the food in her bowl. Two bowls. She'd never be able to force it down without throwing half of it back up.

She never should have made that deal. Though, the moment she thought it, Kale's voice burrowed into her head, whispering for her to be strong.

Determined to fight Thomas for sleep first, fatigue pulled at her senses, and she shoved the first spoonful into her mouth, followed by the second. The sooner she found Kale, the sooner they'd be off Sandaris. Off *Hàlon*. Maybe then she could control her connection to the Flame before it consumed her. Before she turned into a planet-eating monster.

An ache lanced across her stomach as she finished the first bowl. Barely two bites into the second and the pain grew sharper. She couldn't shove any more in, not without her stomach twisting it back up. She leaned her head against her hand, closing her eyes for a moment to rest.

Thomas slammed the table with his hand. "Wake up."

She jumped, meeting his intense gaze. A sparse blond beard grew along his jaw. Yet for the ferocity in his eyes, Thomas's features were surprisingly youthful. He massaged one of his arms but pinned her with his eyes.

"No sleep until you're done eating." He nodded toward her bowl.

"Could have waited until tomorrow." *Not like I didn't just save Theryn's life.* But it was Mather in her thoughts now as guilt pushed tears into her eyes.

"Yesterday is too soon, tomorrow is too late," he said.

Jàden had no idea what he meant, but she was too tired to care. She shoved her spoon into the gruel, side-eyeing Thomas's movements. "I can help with your pain."

"No one can help." Thomas stopped rubbing as if he was fine but still held tension in his arms.

Sighing deeply, she dropped her spoon and held out her hand. "Give me your arm."

"Eat, Jàden."

"Do you want to sleep tonight or be in pain?" Her grandfather's horses sometimes got muscle cramps, and she'd gotten pretty good at working out the aches.

Thomas laid his wrist in her hand and said nothing.

She untied the bracer on his arm and pushed up his sleeve. His pale skin was hairy and freckled, with a nasty scar near his elbow. Tracing her fingers along the inside of his arm, his skin hot to the touch, she massaged from his wrist to his elbow.

"What happened here?" She touched his scar.

"Just an old wound." His tone was biting and cold as the corded muscles in his forearm tightened.

*Must be a sore subject.* Jàden continued massaging, taking the occasional bite of gruel. But as she worked each of the aches out, Thomas visibly relaxed and even seemed to feel some relief from the pain.

It took nearly another hour for her to finish eating, woken three times by Thomas's slap against the weathered wood. When she finally scraped the last bite out, she shoved her bowl toward him and covered her mouth.

"Good, go take care of your wounds and get some rest." He pulled down his sleeve and tied the bracer back on. "We start training in a few hours."

*Oh goody.* The food burned in her throat. Jàden didn't argue, moving like molasses away from the table and down the narrow corridor. She kept one hand over her mouth as the ship rocked. Her shoulder slammed against the wall. Eyelids grew heavy.

How long since she'd slept? Nearly two days by her count.

She stumbled into the bow, the horses blanketed and resting with their heads hung low.

Theryn and Dusty curled up near Andrew, Ashe keeping watch and sharpening his knives. He glanced at her then went back to his work.

Jàden searched for Jon, her lifeline in this world, but wooden walls stared back amid the darkness and Andrew's loud snores. She grabbed a dry blanket and the data pad. The firemark she'd borrowed was still in the gun, and it was too dark to go searching for another.

She wrapped the blanket around her shoulders and clutched the pad to her chest. It was a link to her past. To Kale. She searched for the darkest corner to be alone and curled up in the blackness, an arm under her head. Jàden pulled the blanket tight, wishing for Jon's warmth at her back.

Red light sparked, illuminating scruff across a strong jaw in the far corner of the stall.

She tensed and scrambled back, her burn pressing against the stall planks. Heat seared into her leg, and Jàden bit back a scream.

The stranger lit a cigarette, his features illuminated behind the smoldering tip. "You get those injuries taken care of?"

Except that voice was no stranger.

"Jon?" Heat blossomed in her cheeks as he lit a small lantern.

He'd shaved his beard down to a few days' growth and cut his long hair to shorter locks, spiked and shaggy atop his head. Underneath all the mountain shag, he was one of the handsomest men she'd ever seen, and her body responded with an ache for his arms around her. But his eyes were the same soil brown, deep and thoughtful with an intensity that pierced straight through the loneliest part of her heart.

"I'll do it after I rest," she said.

"Thomas tell you to do it now?" He blew out a stream of smoke, but the tension in his shoulders didn't add to the illusion of relaxation. "I'll assume your silence means yes. No sleep until your wounds are cared for. Don't want to risk infection."

Did these men never sleep? She sighed and dropped her head into her hands. If she was on *Hàlon*, she could slap a medpatch on her wrist and never worry about infection. She set the datapad aside and unwound the blanket from her shoulders.

Jon shifted next to her. "Lay flat. I'll help you."

Curling the blanket like a pillow, she lay on her stomach and stretched out her legs, biting back a scream when he pulled aside her breeches. Branded skin clung to the fabric, the fiery burn slicing like razors down to the bone.

Jon laid a wet cloth over her hip to soothe the wound. Waves of pain throbbed through her flesh. "It's their emblem, isn't it? Like yours. The tower and moons."

"No." Deep anger edged his voice. "Our brands are for soldiers. You've been marked as a servant."

Lower than a soldier, owned by a withered old white-haired man with a hole in his chest. Dread clutched her stomach. "He doesn't own me now. I shot that bastard."

"No one will ever own you, Jàden."

She breathed deep of the comforting smell of his cigarette smoke, a reminder of her grandfather and all the quiet moments they'd spent together.

"It'll be a few weeks before you're comfortable."

"There is no comfort in this world," she said. Yet Jon's was what she craved as she grabbed his wrist. "You're one of them, aren't you? Those soldiers."

Jon took a long drag on his cigarette. He stripped from the waist up and twisted his left shoulder toward her. Branded into his skin was the Rakir's tower and two moons emblem wrapped in the infinite circle. "Since I was fifteen years old."

She traced her fingers over the obsidian melted into his arm, trying very hard not to notice the thick, corded muscles rippling his tawny skin. "They brand as if you were livestock."

"And add the metallic obsidian before the second burn." He scratched his chin. "The throbbing you feel is the high council's imposed will. Even now, we all sense the pull to return north."

Power wielded through metal, just as the Alliance had been doing for thousands of years. It was how firemarks powered everything from a clock to a datapad to a starship—theric energy from the glowing bacterium in a focused beam.

"The old men showed their power before they branded me." She swallowed the lump in her throat, tracing her finger along the black shimmer. "Like oil. Suffocating. It was horrible."

She'd give anything to erase the unease the old man's power left behind. After such an encounter, Kale would have held her in his arms and whispered strength against her cheek. The hole left by his passing refused to close as she caressed Jon's arm down to his bloodflower tattoo.

"How many of the old men did you see?" Jon dipped the rag in cool water and pressed it against her wound again before he leaned on his elbow and met her gaze.

"Two. One is for sure dead." Would Jon hate her if she pulled him onto the blanket? Could she live with herself knowing it was to satisfy a hunger to feel loved? She'd already forced his energy to bind with hers, a criminal act in the eyes of *Hàlon's* Enforcers.

Exhausted beyond reason, she wanted to feel more than the pain in her body and the loneliness in her heart. She ached for softness, intimacy. Something good she could clasp onto in this cold, wretched world. His strength in her veins tugged at a deep longing as he brushed back a few strands of her hair.

"Thank you," she whispered, her eyelids growing heavy. "For saving me."

"You saved yourself. And Theryn." He caressed his fingers along her temple, his voice no more than a soft whisper. "Rest, Jàden."

She traced her thumb along his arm, the gentle heat lulling her senses. "I'd be lost without you."

## CHAPTER 25
*The Lonely Sea*

A staff plunked onto the wooden planking, barely an inch from Jàden's nose. She gasped and scrambled away, her mind and body sludging through half-sleep.

"Morning." Thomas crouched next to the staff, a mischievous gleam in his blue eyes. "Ready to feel some pain?"

Her stomach squeezed tight. Too tight. Jàden slapped a hand to her mouth as last night's dinner pushed into her throat. She scrambled to her feet and raced past Thomas. Twice she tried to swallow everything back, but as soon as the icy air hit her face, it was a losing battle. She grabbed the deck rail and leaned over the side, throwing up everything in her stomach. This time because she'd eaten too much and her body couldn't process it fast enough.

Jàden leaned her head against the weathered wood and breathed in the frigid air until her stomach settled.

Theryn yelled across the deck. "Ready for breakfast, Jàden? Dusty and I just caught some fresh fish."

She glared at the splintered rail, flecks of paint still buried deep in the cracks. Jàden may have saved his life, but now she wanted to punch the laughter right out of his throat.

Gray swells rocked the *Darius*. Snowflakes fell in a quiet haze, the wind gusting them every so often into dancing swirls. A wall of mist surrounded the ship, making it impossible to see further than a few hundred spans. Jàden lifted her head, breathing in the icy storm.

"If you're done throwing up, let's get started." Thomas. His voice needled at her senses as he waited behind her like a heavy boulder about to squash her flat.

*For Kale,* she told herself.

Jàden sighed and turned away from the gentle beauty of the mist.

Thomas led her below deck, away from the laughter of those who had witnessed her weak stomach. Back to the enclosure where he grabbed a bucket and shoved it in her hands. "The horses get taken care of first. This is your duty now. Food, water, clean stalls and brush them down. If they aren't well and healthy, we don't ride."

A small sense of relief flowed into her. This, at least, was something she could do. She'd spent years taking care of her grandfather's horses, mucking out stalls, feeding, training, and even taking notes on his research while he had his eye to a microscope.

She moved slow, her skin still burning around the embedded metal, but one horse at a time, she brought them fresh water. Then grain. While they ate, she brushed Agnar from head to tail, checked his hooves for stray pebbles, then cleaned out his stall and tossed the muck over the side of the ship.

Next was Jon's black. She greeted the stallion with her palm out. He huffed against her hand, then turned away and grunted.

*So, you're ignoring me now.* At least this was an improvement. Jàden brushed the black, though he did not offer the same affectionate nips as Agnar.

One by one, she went to each horse, noting how they all seemed to have similar quirks to their companion riders. Ashe and Theryn's horses greeted her, pushing their noses against her pockets in search of treats. Dusty and Andrew's horses showed curiosity but shied away and let her work. Malcolm's horse seemed to know his business, stretching his neck for a brushing or picking up his feet when she inspected his hooves.

But Thomas's horse snorted at her hand and reared up before she even had a chance to say hello. Bright red fur grew through the black, making the stallion's hide a speckled mess of color.

She'd dealt with strong-willed horses all her life. Holding out her palm, she kept still until the fiery beast exhausted himself trying to scare her off. He snorted a warning as she pressed the soft brush along his nose then his cheek. Soon, the horse settled, grunting his displeasure as he leaned into the brush.

"I've never seen horses like these," she said. For weeks she'd been with Jon and Mather but never really took notice of the finer points of their mounts. "The lines are different, and stallions never get along this well."

"They're norshads. Tower-bred stallions. Somewhere in the past, strong mountain horses were mixed with notharen blood. These hybrids are stronger, smarter and faster than the average equine." Thomas patted his horse on the shoulder. "You won't find better mounts anywhere in the world."

"Notharen." Jàden sized up each horse again, recalling her grandfather's research on the horse-like notharens. Stallions herded together. They roamed prairie lands and marsh lands and were extremely territorial.

But the notharen had more in common with an octopus than a horse. Their fur could change color as part of a camouflage defense, and they grazed in shallow tidepools, pulling urchins and small creatures off coral reefs when the prairies were flooded.

"Twice a day. Fed, watered, stalls cleaned. Brushed every morning, walked in the evenings on the top deck to keep them active." Thomas grabbed the bucket from her hand. "Now, we have fun."

Every morning over the next few weeks, Jàden could barely move. Pain shot through every part of her body. She ate, held heavy rocks, scrubbed floors, polished saddles, tended her wounds and cared for the horses when she wasn't training. All part of Thomas's torture to "build her strength."

When she did have a few moments of silence, she was so exhausted she fell asleep wherever she curled up.

Storms across the sea grew darker, fiercer, and every time Jàden pulled a horse on deck for some air, she kept one eye on the sky and her hood pulled low.

Frank was still out there. She knew it in the deepest part of her gut. If he followed the ship, she'd have nowhere left to run but the bottom of the sea.

Jon strolled over, a cigarette hanging out of his mouth. "You two ready? I want to see what she's got."

He'd barely said two words to her since that first night. Jàden forced back her frustration as the faintest hint of a smile touched the side of Thomas's mouth. "You heard the captain. Let's go."

Jàden handed Agnar's lead line to Dusty to return to his stall. As she breathed the cool afternoon air, Thomas pressed a staff into her hand.

Waves crashed against the hull as the women running the ship stopped their duties and edged toward Jon's men to watch, leaning against the rail and whispering with their heads together.

Hiding in the stall with Agnar sounded like a good idea right about now.

Except Thomas stood in front of the door to the lower deck. "The captain has two rules of fighting. One, everything's a weapon. Two, don't die." He crossed his arms and stepped close, lowering his voice so only she could hear. "Every Rakir spends years in training. You will need to learn everything twice as fast if you're going to survive."

Jon pulled the half-spent cigarette out of his mouth. "We have enemies hunting us on the ground and in the sky. That means we have to be stronger, faster and smarter. There are no secrets between me and these men. We stay alive because we know one another's strengths and weaknesses, and there is a bond of trust between us. You will have to earn our trust, just as each of us will need to earn yours."

"Part of earning that trust," Thomas said, "means you don't stand idly by while others fight. You have a duty to protect your own life, and I expect you to fulfill it."

She gripped the staff close to her chest. Hadn't she just protected herself and Theryn?

Something else burned beneath Thomas's warning. A deep anger edging his tone. When she met his eyes, their depths sliced her to the core. He blamed her for Mather's death. If Theryn had died, she doubted even Jon could have stopped Thomas from pitching her overboard.

"Time to work." Thomas placed his feet shoulder-width apart. "Hit me as hard as you can."

She clenched the staff, a deep ache burning in her chest.

"Come on, Jàden," Theryn shouted. "Kick his ass."

The others laughed at the words and added their jeers.

Releasing a held breath, she closed her eyes and swung the stick, hitting his solid form. She froze on contact and cracked an eye open. The tip of the staff pressed against his shoulder.

"I said hit me." Thomas' voice grew sharper.

"You feel anything, Thomas? I sure didn't see anything." Theryn leaned against the rail, a woman to either side of him.

Jàden hunched her shoulders and pulled the staff back then swung it again, hitting further down his arm.

"I said hit me!"

She jumped then swung as hard as she could, the wild movement slamming the staff across Thomas' jaw. Her mouth fell open. "I'm sorry! I—"

"About damn time." Thomas ripped the staff from her hands and swung.

Jàden flinched and shielded her head.

He stopped a hair's breadth from her neck. "That's how you fight. All your strength into every hit because you never know which one's going to be the last." He smacked the staff against her burn. "Again."

She seethed under the fiery sting in her hip. He'd smacked it dozens of times over the past few weeks, always saying the same thing over and over.

"You fight with the pain, or you die."

The crew laughed. Made fun of her. Shouted comments to both her and Thomas as he put her through an excruciating training regime.

Every inch of her body burned, ached and throbbed. Sweat poured down her neck, under her arms. All the while, Jon watched, never speaking a word. The jeers were easy to ignore; she'd spent two years taunted by Frank. But Jon's silence was getting under her skin.

"Pay attention." Thomas stripped the staff from her hand and slapped it against her shoulder.

The hit stung.

"Sorry," she muttered when he handed it back. She wiped a hand across her brow, sweat and cold drizzle making her palms slick. Her eyelids were heavy and her stomach growled, but she held the staff tight. She pulled back to swing.

But Jon caught her wrist. "Not like that."

He moved directly behind her, sliding her hands along the staff until she held a wider grip. Jon pressed her shoulders down, moved her arms into a stronger alignment, then grabbed her hips and shifted her stance.

Fire ached in her gut from the intimacy of his touch. She held her breath, barely able to focus with Jon standing so close.

"Like this." His breath blew across her ear, raising bumps on her skin. "Don't swing with your arms. Use the power within your body." He laid his hands over hers and slammed the staff forward, straight into Thomas' jaw.

Thomas stumbled away, holding his cheek. "You fucking ass."

Laughter erupted across the deck.

Jàden clenched the staff, Jon's warmth enveloping her hands.

"Feel the speed," Jon said. "The power coiled in the movement, not in your grip."

But the only power she craved in that moment was Jon's mouth against hers. She dropped her eyes, biting down on her lower lip so no one could see her longing.

"That's enough for tonight." Jon released her and stepped away. "Get the other horses handled. Then go rest."

And like that he ignored her again.

The horses were already bedded for the night, so that was one thing she didn't need to do. Clenching her jaw in frustration, she handed the staff to Thomas before disappearing below deck. Dressing her wounds, she dug into her gear for a fresh blanket and retreated to her sleeping space. Picking up the thin wool coverlet, she frowned at the datapad nestled beneath. Exhausted by Thomas's aggressive training schedule, she'd forgotten all about it.

Jàden rifled through Jon's saddle bags for a firemark. Curling up with the blanket around her shoulders, she pushed away thoughts of returning to Jon's side. Maybe a woman would seek out his company, though that needled a jealous pang into Jàden's heart.

But Kale always had a way of making her smile, and tonight she needed to see his face. Jàden pressed the glass orb into the small indention on the front of the datapad.

Violet light traced across the seams and lit the screen. She pressed her thumb to the bottom corner so it could read her biometrics.

"All right, Kale. I need a little help here."

## CHAPTER 26
*The Lonely Sea*

Pain shot into Jon's leg as the ship crashed over a swell. Éli's sword had cut deep, and the sting lingered long after he'd sewn the opening back together. He considered heating his knife to burn the wound closed, but he welcomed the ache to distract him from thoughts of Jàden.

Jon smoked the last of his cigarette and tossed it over the side as laughter erupted from the women near Theryn.

He was in no mood for it, mostly because he so desperately wanted his wife tonight. To pull Jàden into his arms and smell the sweetness of her skin against his. He still hadn't told her the truth about their bond, but she seemed persistent that their connection was only shared energy.

Jon sighed and ran a hand through his hair. He should be resting too, but Jàden's steady breath on his skin about drove him mad. If he went below deck now, he may not be able to resist his desperate need to kiss her. Guardians be damned, he hadn't had a woman affect him so much in years. Maybe ever.

"You're different." Snow scattered across Malcolm's beard as he lit up a pipe and leaned against the rail. Mist rose off the barren, watery landscape that stretched to darkness in every direction. "I thought it was the mountains at first, but now I'm not so sure."

"Nothing's changed." Jon breathed in the frigid sea air. It kept him sharp. Kept him from hastening below deck and doing something stupid. He popped the firemark out of the strange black weapon Jàden found, the seams of color going dark.

Malcolm chewed on the stem of his pipe. "Known you far too many years, son. I daresay your mind is more occupied these days with that woman."

The wind blew flurries across each swelling wave. Jon scratched his chin, a rock in his chest hardening. As much as he wanted to deny it, Malcolm wasn't wrong. "We need to find this Kale fellow quick. He and I have a few things to sort out."

A scream ripped across the night.

Jon whipped around to Jàden shouting at the sky with a slim silver block in her hand. Whatever had triggered her this time ripped through their bond, a wave of rage speeding up the rhythm of his heart.

"You fucking bastard, Frank!" She scrambled for the rail and chucked the silver item into the sea. Jàden climbed the wood planking as if she planned to jump over.

Jon pocketed the items in his hand and raced across the deck. Fire surged in his veins, a sharp indicator that she was about to release her magic, as he grabbed her around the waist to pull her back. The last thing he needed was his men and horses dead at the bottom of the sea.

"Leave me alone!" She twisted in his arms like a terrified child.

"Relax," Jon whispered in her ear.

"I saw him." She tried to squirm away. "Let me go."

"You're safe, Jàden." The smell of the sea clung to her hair, but beneath that lay a hint of fresh flowers after a fall rain, a scent Jon identified as solely hers. His chest tightened at the strong warmth in her frail body—he didn't want to let her go.

"I'll never be safe." Jàden screamed the words, but she had no fight left. She collapsed against his chest as sobs wracked her. "I saw them. They're going to find us."

Jon held her tight against his chest. Only one thing made Jàden lose control of herself: the men who tortured her. Flashes of her screams from the glass sheets rippled through his thoughts. He was going to kill those men.

He leaned his cheek against her head. "Come with me."

Away from the eyes of Naréa and her crew. They'd already witnessed too much of Jàden's eccentric behavior, and the whispers about it only increased with each passing day. Some of the women wanted to pitch Jàden overboard and let her drown—they didn't like unpredictable passengers.

Jon guided her down the stairs and back to her sleeping spot. As he passed Thomas, he gestured a few silent commands with his hand. *Wake everyone. Be alert.*

Thomas nodded and quietly began waking the others.

Each time Jàden went into a panic, something bad happened. Jon leaned against the wall and pulled her to his chest, gently soothing her hair away from her temple.

"He knew," she whispered. Jàden curled her arms over her head and sobbed against him. "Kale knew he was going to die."

Jon closed his eyes, the ache to protect her so strong he had an itch to draw his sword. Instead, he slid his hand into the hair curling her neck.

Jàden was his, not Kale's.

With that thought, he embraced her tighter. He had to tell her the truth about their bond, that the day she tied her magic to him, she'd made him a husband. All his life he craved what his parents had, a strong connection with a lover. Jon craved intimate moments of peace, no matter how the world swirled its anger. He wanted a life away from the Tower, a family of his own, and yet people treated him the same—as if he were a terrifying predator.

But Jàden wasn't afraid of him.

He spoke softly to her again, hoping to ease some of her pain. "We'll be at the boundary soon."

"Kale said it wasn't my fault, but it was. So many people died because of me—Kale, my grandparents, the other experiments. Some of them at least."

She had to stop beating herself up. Jon had seen her on the glass sheets, the torture and the cages. How she screamed and doubled over, unable to move, as if some invisible force held her pinned to the ground. A sea of white, just like she'd yelled about in the mountains.

Yet as he tried to comfort her, he listened for any off sound—anything to alert him to danger.

Andrew edged into sight and gestured silently: *two below, others on deck.*

He nodded and ticked his head to tell Andrew to go. With his men awake and alert, he could relax a few more minutes.

Jon slid his hand along her jaw and tilted her head toward him. "None of this is your fault. Put the past behind you and focus on what's in your life right now."

It was the only way to live, in the present, especially with enemies tracking their every move. Guardians knew, Jon was calling the kettle black— he still couldn't stop blaming himself for what happened to his family or for Mather's death, but he couldn't bear the sorrow etched in her dark eyes.

"You're not alone, Jàden." Jon traced his thumb down to the corner of her mouth and leaned in, aching to show Jàden she had him, and not just as a protector.

Tears flooded her eyes again as she tightened her grip on his shirt. "Always alone. Isn't that what you said?"

As her stinging words rolled over him, he froze barely a breath from her mouth. Jon sighed, the hurt in her voice touching the ache he carried with him through each day of his life: refusal.

She was still in love with a dead man, and he would never be more than second best. He pulled back a fraction, his muscles taut to hide the pain. If only he could make her see how much she still clung to that dead lover of hers, a man who would never again exist the way he did in her head. Maybe she needed more time to grieve, or she might never let him go.

But Jon wasn't ready to give up just yet.

Clenching his jaw to find the right words, a soft noise bumped the outer hull of the barge. He snapped to alertness, lifting his head away from Jàden and cocking it toward the outer wall. The merest hint of a voice caught his attention, and he reluctantly released her and put his ear to the wood.

Another bump—this one louder. There should be nothing but sea to the horizon. He pulled Jàden toward the other end of the stall and peeked around the corner.

"What's happening?" she whispered, clinging tighter to him.

The corridor beyond their sleeping space was too quiet, but the horses were alert, their ears forward.

"Son of a..." Jon slipped the metal weapon from his waistband and pressed it into her hands. "Someone's boarding us. Take this and stay near the horses. You're the only one who knows how to use it anyway."

She reached into his pocket for the firemark, her fingers brushing his leg.

Jon barely stifled a groan as he unsheathed his daggers. "Stay here. I'm going to pitch these assholes overboard." He grabbed her chin. "No magic. Unless you have no other choice."

No way was he going to stop her from saving his men again, but this time Jon was determined to get rid of the problem himself.

He leaned in close to her ear. "Always alone. I was talking about me."

# CHAPTER 27

*The Lonely Sea*

Jàden's gut ignited with heat as Jon's beard prickled against her cheek. By the light of the Guardians, she needed to feel this man's kiss, and she'd just had to open her big mouth when he'd tried. The change in his demeanor was instantaneous, from gentle and intimate to steel in his eyes and body coiled like a viper.

Something knocked again on the ship's outer hull, and Jon disappeared to the inner corridor.

She cursed under her breath and slammed the firemark into the gun. Violet light bled through the seams from the butt to the tip of the barrel, powering up her shots. She pressed her head to the gun, another wave of fresh sobs gripping her chest.

Kale was really gone, and there wasn't a damn thing she could do to bring him back. She'd only wanted to see his face and feel like she wasn't fighting for a dead dream.

But Jàden would never be able to erase the video of Frank Kale in full Guild Command regalia speaking at his son's funeral, talking about how Kale's urn only held a piece of the ship as there was nothing left of his body. As if he actually cared about his son.

"Fucking traitor," she muttered, jabbing the rear sight repeatedly against her forehead.

"Oh, little darlin'." Frank's deep voice reverberated from the top deck. "Three warm bodies inside the hull. Do I shoot one down or start with these bastards on their knees?"

A shudder raced from the top of her head to the burning ache inside her gut.

Frank would keep coming after her, and she had no one left.

Kale wasn't able to protect her anymore, and she couldn't hide under the covers and hope the bad man went away. She pressed a hand to her mouth to suppress a scream of frustration.

*Courage cannot awaken without fear, Jàden,* Kale's voice whispered in her thoughts.

Terror squeezed her throat like a vice. He'd always wanted her to understand that it was okay to be afraid, but now that fear was all she knew.

*I have two rules: stay dry and stay alive.* This time it was Thomas in her head, his sharp tone needling her body to move. To fight. But she didn't want to be alive anymore, not if her future lay trapped between glass walls. She should tell Thomas to fuck off and just drown herself beneath the waves, cradled in the embrace of her bonded moon.

But a hint of Jon's scent filled her nose, his heat clinging to her cheeks. *Put the past behind you and focus on what's in your life right now.*

Jon. She had her protector. The strength in his blood rippled through their tied energy. He was up there somewhere with Frank, except Jon wouldn't have a gun. As strong as he and his men were, they only had their smarts and steel weapons while Frank had an arsenal of firepower at his disposal.

Without Jon, she really would be better off dead. She couldn't lose him too.

But as the heat from his embrace, the closeness of his mouth, washed over her again, Jàden lowered the gun to her side and peeked around the stall. Time to show her courage.

As the large object bumped the hull again, a scuffle broke out on deck, followed by gunfire.

Her shoulders bunched up tight, but she had to protect Jon.

Theryn's muffled voice filtered below, and by his cocky tone, he was probably going to get everyone killed.

A single shot fired, and tears slid down her cheeks.

She couldn't be responsible for another death. Jàden held the sight to her eye the way Kale showed her years ago, but nothing moved in the outer corridor. If Frank really was monitoring heat signatures, he'd be able to see by her stance exactly where she was.

His voice washed over her from the deck again, loud and clear. "I have a secret, darlin'. Wanna know where he is?"

Pain stabbed through her heart. Kale.

"That boy used to look too much like his mother, but now he's got my features. My grit. Maybe I should brainwash this bastard and turn him into the son he should have been."

"Fucking..." She slammed the butt of the gun against the stall, her hatred producing a fresh round of tears. Her hands shook so hard she had to clench the gun tight to hold on. Frank had taunted her like this for years, and there was always a truth to everything he said. She had no doubt he'd found Kale and would hurt him just to torture her.

Jon first.

The horses were restless now. If she crept to the deck with the horses, Frank wouldn't be able to isolate her heat signature, and he wouldn't shoot. Not until he was certain the target wasn't her.

With the gun pointed at the door, Jàden went to each stall and untied the harness ropes with one hand. The norshads were smart enough to untangle themselves from the restraint cloth, and within minutes, all eight stallions surrounded her. Agnar stayed close to her shoulder, but Jon's black wanted his rider. He trotted to the outer corridor, his ears laid flat.

Andrew squeezed in next to her, a small silver dagger gripped in each hand. "The fuck are you doing?"

"Frank can't find me next to the horses." She couldn't really explain to him how heat tracking worked, but with one hand against Dusty's horse, she followed the herd toward the deck.

"Smart girl," Frank muttered. "Gonna be fun breaking you again."

Jon's black stopped at the top of the ramp, his ears laid so flat they practically disappeared into his head. Something was definitely wrong. The other horses bunched up behind him, neighing for their riders.

Crouching low, Jàden edged between two legs and put the sight to her eye. One of Naréa's crew lay sprawled across their path, a hole in her head. Vacant eyes stared at Jàden, but beyond the body, several people in full Enforcer battle gear lined the deck, their black armor glistening in the early morning storm light.

At least, they stood like Enforcers, but the emblems on their shoulders were wrong. Some had a silver flame wrapped in the infinite circle just like Bradshaw's lab. But one had a strange green orb that didn't quite close, and something about that symbol sent a shudder to the deepest part of her psyche, though she couldn't say why.

Jon and the others were on their knees, electrical taser wires pinning their arms to their bodies. One press of a button and they'd either be shocked into submission or die by electrocution.

"Who the fuck are these assholes?" Andrew whispered in her ear.

"Dead, if they dare hurt Jon." She bit her lip against another sob, wracking her brain for any idea to short out the wires.

"Yes, sir," shouted an Enforcer, who raised his rifle, pointing it at Malcolm's head. "They're at midship, and the place is empty."

Andrew nudged her shoulder. "What'd he say?"

"They're behind us." Before she could say more, Andrew retreated to the back of the herd, no doubt intent on killing Frank's men. If she tried to warn him, it would give her away.

"I see you, darlin'." Except every soldier with a rifle in their hands had the wrong build. Short, tall, bald, blond.

Where was Frank?

Gray light streaked across the dawn skies as a loud *rhuum* broke the morning silence. Jàden unbunched her shoulders. She'd heard that sound before as a child and again during her later years when she'd entered the Bioengineering Guild.

The atmosphere processor.

She found Jon in the lineup, fury in his eyes as he stared down the barrel of a rifle.

There was nothing left to do—it was her or Jon.

Closing her eyes, she pressed the barrel of the handgun against her temple. "All right, Frank. You win."

Jàden pushed past Jon's black and stepped onto the deck, her hand shaking so hard she could barely hold her weapon.

"Let them go, or I squeeze the trigger," she said.

"Nice to see you again, darlin'." Frank's voice echoed from a small device in the middle of the deck.

That bastard. He wasn't even here.

She met Jon's gaze, silently screaming at him that she had no idea what she was doing. Edging toward the rail, she peeked over the side to a sleek black submersible clamped to the hull.

"What are the orders, sir?" one soldier asked into a headset.

The device on the deck illuminated to a floating holoscreen, Frank in the center with crutches under his arms. "You may think you found yourself some muscle, darlin', but I know where my son is. If you ever want to see him alive again, drop the gun."

Pain gripped her chest so tight she could barely breathe.

"Should we shoot, sir?" an Enforcer asked.

"You fucking do, and I'll pull the trigger!" Jàden screamed. "Put your weapons down!"

"Oh, darlin', I forgot how fun you are when you're angry." Frank chuckled, limping toward the console with a cast on his leg.

That was why he wasn't there—Theryn and Dusty must have broken his leg. Jàden searched for their faces, both bowmen on their knees with cold anger etched into their features.

"Fourteen new lives that boy lived without you. Shall we go for fifteen?" Frank hovered his palm over the console. "Got a ship targeting him now."

"Don't hurt him!" Jàden clenched the gun tighter, sliding the barrel down until it touched her ear.

Someone was going to die today if she couldn't find a way out. The Flame's power burned in her veins at the temptation to blow Frank's soldiers off the deck. But one click of a button, one pull of the trigger, and Jon along with the others would be just as dead.

She'd have to sacrifice them for Kale or sacrifice Kale for them.

"Jon," she whispered as several swallows landed on the ship's rail behind Bradshaw's Enforcers. Coastal birds who made their homes out of hard-packed mud.

A steel column from the atmosphere processor slid into the corner of her eye, the northern half of it covered with earth and grass. The birds must have perched somewhere on that rocky spire, but Jàden couldn't ignore the glowing firemarks embedded along its southern side, the steel lines of technology showing that power still flowed through its machinery.

She loved Kale, a certainty gripping her thoughts as Jon stood up, his men mirroring the action as if they refused to die on their knees.

But she needed Jon, and she wasn't about to let Frank hurt him.

Another small flock of birds landed on a soldier, creating a trail along his arm to the glowing firemark in his rifle.

There was something creepy about how calm the birds were. The one near the firemark scraped its claw across the glass orb, dousing its glow and the gun's power.

Jon must have caught it too as he pressed his chest against the barrel. "You gonna kill me now?"

Hundreds more birds descended to the deck like something out of a nightmare. Jàden edged back against the rail as Naréa and her crew stood too.

Something was happening she didn't understand, but it made every inch of her skin crawl.

More birds circled the sky like a dark swarm as Jàden gripped the rail, unease twisting her gut.

Everyone on deck had gone quiet except for Frank. "Last chance, darlin'."

She couldn't take his taunting anymore. Jàden pointed the gun at the device and fired, crushed metal sparking as it skittered across the deck into the sea. Now she wouldn't have to hear his voice or how he was going to kill the man she loved—again. *I'm sorry, baby.*

The deck erupted in chaos, Jon and his men ducking the rifle barrels and charging Bradshaw's Enforcers.

Jàden froze when a dozen birds melted together into a man with bright blue paint on his cheek.

The bird man grabbed an Enforcer by the back of the head and broke her neck over his shoulder. Her gun fired an arc into the sky as her eyes glazed over.

Jon and the others dropped to the deck, electricity through the taser wires jolting their bodies. The man with the button reached for the dial to turn up the juice, and Jàden fired on the device, shattering metal bits into his palm.

"Jon!" She raced across the deck and slid next to him, trying to untangle the wires pinning his arms. "I'm so sorry—"

A shot fired between them, barely missing her head and scraping across Jon's. Someone threw a spear from the other direction, slamming into the Enforcer's neck where the seams were weakest.

A dozen more people surrounded them, small blue feathers woven into their hair. Gripping long spears painted with bright blue swirls, they jabbed their points at Jàden. "You drop or we kill."

Jàden released the gun as irritation burned in her chest. "Please, just let them go."

## CHAPTER 28

*The Dark Isle*

Éli put the spyglass to his eye, tracing the outline of the smaller corsair ship shrouded in a thin veil of fog. The brand on his shoulder pulsed, the high council's magic pushing the fleet further away from the north and toward the most dreaded land on Sandaris.

The Dark Isle.

A realm of shifters, death dealers and deep magic. No one ever returned from the Dark Isle.

The high council reinforced the belief in Ìdolön that all shifters and forms of magic were inhuman and must be eradicated. Only in the prisons did Éli learn a much darker truth.

Magic wielders were tortured so their power could be siphoned away by the old men.

It was the main reason he held onto his own magic so tightly, so he wouldn't end up dead behind bars. And why he kept a tight leash on Evardo. If Kóranté Alken knew the breadth of the dreamwalker's power, he'd have Evardo branded and in chains. So far, his servant had escaped the iron fires, but his son had not been so lucky.

Éli lowered the spyglass.

Granger leaned on the rail beside him. "Forty-seven men plus the boy and the servant."

"And how many still loyal to the old man?" He tightened his grip on the spyglass as the skies darkened toward night.

"Thirteen." Granger kept his voice low and crossed his arms, his one good eye watching the activities on deck. Two young soldiers sparred near the prow while others walked their horses near the stern. "Night could give us the advantage."

It still wasn't enough. The thirteen Rakir still loyal to the high council were older soldiers, well-seasoned and still in their prime, including General Tyken, who had tossed the hevkor overboard nearly a week ago and taken command of the ship.

If it wasn't for the kóranté in the hold and the magic he wielded through their brands, Éli would have already tried to kill Tyken. Even then, one false move and he'd have the rest of the army to contend with. More than thirty ships followed the corsair carrying horses and soldiers, yet his gut told him something else was in play beyond the bloodflower key.

Éli had never reached for the full breadth of his own power before, but after two seasons outside prison walls, he ached for the freedom his brother always promised. To feel the Flame's smooth silk in his veins like a forbidden mistress and to finally be the master of his own life.

"Stay ready. We'll figure a way out of this mess." Then he was going to head straight for Jon. To steal his woman while Granger ripped Theryn Blakewood's eyes out of his skull.

The corsair blended into the fog with the rest of the fleet, unfurling the last of its sails and breaking harder south.

"Wait a minute. Something's happening," Éli said.

Before he could lift the spyglass to his eye, a zankata soared across the ship's bow, its gray under-feathers blending into the storm. The crow-like bird settled on a nearby crate and squawked at Éli.

A high council messenger bird—probably for Tyken, but the bastard slept below deck with his own personal guards watching his back.

Éli unrolled the small strip of parchment. *Take your men west to Hezérin. Kóranté Dràven will meet you there. He has a surprise to bait Ayers.*

Crushing the parchment, Éli glanced at Granger. He wasn't going anywhere near Dràven. The old bastard had more strength in his magic than the other five high councilmen combined. Besides, nothing would bait Jon Ayers into a trap more than a woman in distress. Especially one he cared for. "Fleet's breaking off. It's now or never."

A sinister grin curled the edge of Granger's lip. "Let me kill Tyken."

"Do it." Éli stormed across the deck toward his son and servant.

Connor was teaching Evardo how to tie a sail closed, showing them how to grip the rope and which knot to use.

Éli clapped Evardo on the scrawny shoulder, and they hunched under his grip. "Take the boy below and tend to my horse. I don't want to see your faces until dawn."

"Y-Yes, sir." Evardo seemed to have the mind of a child when they replied to any of Éli's orders, and yet in his head, they held a strong, sensible voice as if more certain of their abilities than their hands. The servant grabbed Connor's hand, and both hastened downstairs, either to avoid his anger or finally have a reason to hide out he couldn't be certain.

Neither of them belonged among the ranks of a militant army, but they kept their heads down and did exactly what they were told.

"You, Hareth. Get up on that sail. The men say the fleet turned south," Tyken shouted from across the deck, his hair amess as if he'd just awoken.

"Follow your own orders." Éli shoved the high council note in his pocket and gestured a silent command to his team: *Kill them.*

Like Granger, his team had always been loyal, and they were desperate to cut the north away from their lives. He stomped down the stairs toward the stern cabins. Granger would either be dead within the hour or Tyken would, but he had to take this chance or his revenge might be lost before he ever set foot on land again.

Alken's dark power beckoned as if the old man had sensed the message. "Come, commander."

His stomach knotted at the raspy voice, so like a snake slithering among soggy reeds. He shuddered at the disgust of it and shoved open the door.

The hevkor's cabin held a single table, a firemark lantern glowing from the center and cots with heavy, soft blankets. Two women huddled together in the corner, half naked and clinging to each other for warmth. The brands on their hips marked them as sex slaves to the high council.

Granger had forgotten to tell him that small detail, no doubt intent on using both women to warm his own bed.

Kóranté Alken stood next to the table, his long hair silvery white against pale, wrinkled faces. The old man's eyes went straight to his chest, leering like a hungry wolf.

"You have something for me," Alken whispered, reaching out his hand. White hairs sprouted from his graying knuckles, the wrinkles deeper than those trailing from his nose to his mouth.

Éli had to strike now before he missed his chance. He unsheathed his dagger and closed the distance between them, slicing across Alken's throat. His arm froze in midair as the high councilman's eyes grew dark, black smoke swirling in their blue depths.

"Betrayer," Alken whispered.

Éli tried to pull his arm back, but the air pressed against him like a heavy blanket. Black power slammed him into the wall, pain shooting up his spine.

The air grew thicker. Stifling.

Éli roared as the old man's magic pressed him to his knees, twisting his arm as the sharp end of his blade inched closer to his throat. "I. Will. Not—"

The young orphan in Éli slid into his mind, a child who feared every ounce of pain and beat of his lonely heart. Forcing the familiar terror into submission, his muscles tightened as he fought the old man's power, his own magic sliding into his veins like silk. He'd never reached for his power before in their presence, but he was desperate to break the Tower's will over him.

Alken stumbled back then slammed his hand against the table as if a bull squaring off to charge. He sliced his hand across the air, the motion cutting a deep gouge into Éli's back. "You are a soldier no more but mine to wield."

Too many years he'd endured this kind of pain. The cuts across his back, the shame of subservience when his magic whispered through his body. Éli suspected they'd always known what he was, but he'd never openly rebelled. He'd only hoped to one day secure a future of higher status within the ranks so he'd never be forced to serve under Jon's command.

Alken made a ripping motion with his hand. The blade tore from Éli's fingers and slammed into one woman's chest. The other screamed.

Silk slid into his veins as Alken sliced the air again, over and over until Éli's power faltered, suppressed under the weight of the old man's strength.

He dropped to his hands and knees, sweat beading along his temple as his back screamed in agony.

Twelve. Thirteen.

Each one stung like the cut of a blade, but the old man's magic forced the pain to burrow deep into his bones.

This was Connor's fate unless Éli could put a stop to it.

## CHAPTER 29
*The Dark Isle*

Something about Frank's taunting voice grated on Jon's every nerve, but as the anger threatened to burst out of him, he clenched his jaw and glared at the man with a spear pointed at Jàden's throat, calculating how fast he could have the bastard on his back.

Recognition burned in the leader's eyes. "Humans go back. You do not belong here."

This guy was starting to piss him off too. Jon glanced around the deck to make sure his men were still alive. Blue-painted warriors with long spears pinned nearly everyone, including the crew. Only Naréa still walked free. With hands behind her back, she sized up the damage to her vessel and the women under her command.

"Horses loose on my ship and three of my crew dead." Naréa stopped in front of Jon, a murderous rage in the taut lines of her face. "You owe me three strong men, Captain."

"Not a chance, Naréa." He'd throw the woman off her own ship before he'd give any of his men into her service. "Tell these fuckers to back off before I start breaking arms."

And their skulls. Except his sword was buried in some bastard's chest, and his knives were in a midship wall.

Naréa snorted. "Since your men don't know how to keep their pants on, this is where you get off."

Jon tightened his jaw. "It's the middle of the ocean—"

"You leave, or you die." Naréa stalked off, shouting something in a language he didn't understand. The bird shifters disappeared into a large flock, circling high into the storm.

Jàden rolled to her side and grabbed the gun, dousing the firemark and stuffing it into her waistband, probably before anyone could take it from her.

But Jon wasn't finished with Naréa. He rolled to his feet and grabbed his sword out of the dead soldier's chest. He sure as hell was going to pick a fight with her now. "Naréa!"

The crew spread across the deck, weapons in their hands, blocking him from the hevkor. "You promised me a village. There's nothing here."

"You're at the boundary, Captain, as requested."

As the *Darius* entered the wall of water, Jàden reached across the rail. Small droplets slid along her skin and rose toward the sky. "This is *Hàlon* technology."

A loud *rhuum* blasted through the air, reverberating through the mountainous spire. The same sound he'd heard when Frank's people attacked.

Jon didn't understand much of what Jàden saw in those Guardian structures, but he sure as shit knew how to deal with the people in his world.

"Land, Naréa, or we'll see who swims first."

Jàden grabbed his wrist and lowered her voice. "We're here."

The muscles along his arm tightened as he followed her gaze to the prow. The ship surged and fell with each crashing wave, snow beating down across the deck. As they slid out of the barrier, choppy swells smoothed out to a glassy surface. Storm clouds lowered, icy flakes melting to a cool drizzle.

Thick fog clung to the sea's eerily calm surface. The icy chill warmed to sticky, humid air, sails flapping once before they stilled. Wine-colored canvas rippled, bleeding across each surface until each showed a green orb with trailing arms over a field of black.

Jàden squeezed his arm, dread in her voice. "Jon."

"I see it." They didn't need any more magic digging through their lives.

He sheathed his sword, his instincts screaming a warning he couldn't ignore, as deep water on one side of the ship became a shallow reef on the other. Giant trees grew along the shore, dozens of roots twisting into the shallows.

He didn't know these woods, but at least it was dry land and would get his team the fuck off this ship. It would be a cold walk in the sea, but he no longer cared. "Load up!"

Shoving between Naréa's crew, Jon retrieved his daggers from the wall and slammed them into their sheaths. They'd had their asses kicked today, but Jon wouldn't let that happen again. Every one of his men was lucky to be alive, himself included.

"Grab one of those weapons, Jàden. I think it's time we all trained again." As cadets, he and his team learned how to fight against anything from a fork to a longsword but never a metal weapon that could burn a hole in a man's skull. The next time Frank's soldiers found them, Jon would not have his ass handed to him.

She furrowed her brow, scanning the sky once more. "I don't think that's a good idea."

His men retrieved their gear from below deck as the *Darius* slowed, but Jon touched the small of Jàden's back as she secured her horse's bridle, lowering his mouth to her ear. "That's an order."

Her shoulders stiffened.

It was hard to keep the biting edge out of his tone as he saddled her horse, yanking the girth hard enough that Agnar tried to bite him.

"You know your world. I know mine." She pointed toward the dead soldiers as Naréa's crew pulled each one to the edge of the deck and tossed them overboard. "They all have tracking beacons, and so do their weapons."

She grabbed Agnar's bridle, anger in the way she tightened her shoulders, and both leapt into the sea.

Jon clenched his jaw so tight the pain throbbed into his neck. The damn stubborn woman wasn't listening. He needed one of those weapons to understand how to fight such an opponent. But as he crouched next to a dead soldier, her soft magic wove deeper meaning into his senses. A hunter tracking a bird, able to see its path without line of sight.

They couldn't take the risk.

Taking another count of his men to make sure they were all present and ready, he gestured after Jàden. Naréa obviously didn't plan to stop.

So Jon shouted orders to his men to get their horses into the water. "Let's move."

It would be a long walk in the cold surf, but at least the tides were low. They'd sustained no injuries, but the heavy silence meant his men were all probably as angry as he was. A few hours more and they would have had to swim—or kill Naréa.

When he was the last one left on deck, Jon turned toward the hevkor, meeting the hardness in her eyes. She'd gotten them across the sea, and her crew helped keep them alive when Frank's men attacked. But he still wanted to strangle the woman. He sure as shit hoped they'd never cross paths again.

Without a parting word, he slapped the backside of his horse. The black leapt into the sea, and Jon jumped in after.

Icy water slammed into his senses, chills running straight up his spine as he broke the surface. He swam toward his horse and grabbed the reins, the two angling for the shore until soft dirt brushed against the bottom of his boots.

The stallion found his footing and snorted his displeasure, ears pricked toward the thinning mist along the shore.

"I know, buddy," he muttered, clapping his companion on the shoulder.

The spectral silence broke every few seconds with a low, moaning creak of Naréa's ship as it turned once more toward deeper waters, the strange black-and-green sails the last to disappear into the fog.

He couldn't feel his body anymore as the water dropped to his chest and finally his waist.

A long wharf jutted into the placid sea. Its empty, wooden planks stretched to a cluster of small wooden shacks, strings of threaded shells hanging off the eaves. In the faint breeze, they clattered a hollow, mournful sound.

Jàden held tight to Agnar's bridle as she waited for him beneath a web of twisted roots, her eyes on the sky. Her shoulders hunched again as if hiding something from him. "Frank will send more soldiers."

The water dropped to his ankles, and his horse pushed his nose into the water, yanking a clump of sea grass out of the sand.

"Then we keep fighting." Jon pulled her forehead against his. Even through his chilled skin, her warmth heated his insides. He sighed and closed his eyes. "We don't stop until Frank's dead, got it?"

His men already on dry sand and settling the horses, he only had a few moments of privacy left with Jàden, and she had him so twisted up right now he couldn't think straight.

One question burned his insides. "Why didn't you take Frank's offer?"

## CHAPTER 30
*The Lonely Sea*

Blood soaked Éli's uniform, his body tensing with each slice across his back. At twelve years old, he'd tried to run away from the other orphans. When the Rakir returned him to the Tower, Kóranté Dràven had given him his first lesson in submission.

The scars from that first encounter still lined his back, just as the brand on his shoulder had destroyed the last remnants of his birthmark. His Guardian had marked him from birth with a rearing horse wreathed in flames.

"You're going to do great things, little brother," Sebastian had said to him every night before bed. "A few more years and we can leave this place. You'll never have to endure the shame I feel every day of my life."

Clenching his fist until his knuckles were white, Éli tried to block out the nerve-shattering pain. He had to be stronger to honor his brother's memory. Stronger than his son.

And he couldn't let Jon's betrayals be what bound him to this fate.

His vision blurred as Alken grabbed his hair and yanked his head back. "You can no longer be trusted, Commander. Unless you find me the bloodflower, I will slice open your son's throat and leave him to die at the bottom of the sea."

Alken's head straightened as a strong, sure voice whispered into Éli's thoughts. *Don't feed him your power. You're stronger than him.*

Evardo.

The air lightened, small flecks of dark dust lifting away from the chained woman's skin and flowing toward the old man. The same dusty flecks lifted away from his hand and twisted toward the old man. Alken was siphoning power.

These women weren't sex slaves—they were magic wielders.

*Herana needs you. Save her,* Evardo's voice whispered.

What in all of Sandaris would Jon's woman need him for? But in his blinding pain, he latched on to Evardo's voice.

The Guardian needed Éli, not Jon.

Not Jon.

This thought was like music to his ears. The idea that he could make Jon feel the full weight of his pain and humiliation drove him to push back. He needed someone to take his pain, to free him from the anguish of Sebastian's death.

Éli punched the floor, his magic flowing like silk through his veins. He ached to unleash it, but Alken must have been using his own strength against him.

Sweat beaded across his brow as he focused on Alken's face, holding tight to the Dark Flame's silken power and pulling it deeper inside himself.

"No!" Alken released Éli's hair and slapped him hard across the cheek. "You serve me."

"Not anymore, old man." Éli pulled harder, siphoning pain and fear and desperation until the air snapped. The flow of power reversed, the weight on his body unburdening.

"Give it back!" Alken bolted across the room and yanked the dagger out of the dead woman in a desperate attempt to protect himself.

Éli stumbled to his feet and ripped his sword from its sheath, slicing the old man's head off his shoulders.

Long, white strands tumbled across the room, and the head hit the wall, dropping into the corner with the light gone from his vivid blue eyes.

"Mother fucking prick."

The pressure eased on Éli's back, pain still screaming from the cutting gouges. But the bone-deep anguish had withered away with the old man's power.

Éli retrieved his dagger and wiped both blades clean, returning them to their sheaths.

"Please," the woman whispered, lifting her chained arms. "Help me."

He stormed out of the room and slammed the door behind him. Wiping the sweat from his neck, he trudged back on deck to a heavy silence. Tyken lay dead with a sword in his spine, the last three loyal soldiers surrounded by Éli's men.

"Everyone on deck," Éli shouted above the gathering storm. "This ship belongs to me now, and we do not serve those white-haired bastards. You follow my orders or get the fuck off my ship."

A shadow moved near midship, the half-naked woman with her chains gone and murderous hate in her eyes. She spread her arms to the sky and burst into a flock of gold-and-black finches, disappearing into the fog. Granger would be pissed, but it was one less mouth to feed.

"You heard the commander." Granger walked along the line of soldiers, pointing the tip of his sword toward them. "He is the law now."

Anger burned in the last three loyal soldiers, but the others lined up in front of Éli and pressed their fists to their left shoulders. "We follow you, Commander."

Evardo lingered at the fringes of his mind, his silent way of asking for entry. As quick as a silver fish, he had the names of four soldiers who were already plotting Éli's murder.

*Tell Granger,* Éli snarled.

One by one, Granger drove his sword into each of the four men's chests and tossed their bodies overboard.

Éli strode across the wood planking, his boots ringing a hollow sound. "Someone bring me a map."

As his men scurried to carry out his command, Connor crept up on deck with Evardo at his side.

Éli crouched in front of his son and fixed his gaze on the boy. "Are you willing to do anything to find your uncle?"

A streak of hesitation blazed across Connor's eyes as they welled up with tears. But he lifted his chin and wrung his fingers together. "Yes, sir."

Éli wasn't certain if he despised his son because he carried Ayers blood in his veins or if he was jealous of him. The boy was the endeavor of trying to find a weakness in Jon, and he wasn't about to let that go to waste.

"Good. Then you do exactly as I say." He signaled Evardo over.

"Yes, sir." Connor lowered his head, tears sliding down his cheeks.

"And don't cry, or I'll pitch you over the rail." He stood tall when his men brought out a map and unrolled it across a stack of crates.

Evardo followed, shoulders hunched inside the makeshift uniform, pieced together from what was left of the dead Rakir they'd found in the harbor. Their rail-thin body swam inside the clothing.

"Find the woman." Éli gestured toward the sea. "She can't be more than a day ahead of us."

Evardo seemed to hesitate as they eased their mind toward Éli's. *You and the Guardian burn with the fires at the heart of Sandaris. She needs you, and one day, you may need her.*

Leaning his hands against the table, Éli sized Evardo up once more. He ought to punch the bastard for daring to make any form of a demand, but the scrawny dreamwalker kept his head down in deference.

"I'll do what I damn well please with that woman. Her only value is in her ability to hurt Jon." Éli slapped the table, startling Evardo. "Are we clear?"

Their body tightened, and they bowed low. "Y-Yes."

"What are we looking for?" Granger, his brawny second in command, scratched his thick beard. He wore a patch over the hole where his eye had been, his good blue one hard as flint.

"Change of plans." Éli scanned the coastlines, poking his finger on several cities along the northern shore. Hezérin was on the northwest corner of the Dark Isle and in the opposite direction of the fleet but much too far for anyone to travel without a ship full of goods.

The wheels in Éli's mind turned. Take the bait the high council offered or follow Jon. Connor could be of use, but the biggest payoff now was the woman: both a Guardian and someone Jon showed clear feelings for. Just the thought of such a volatile combination in a woman made Éli ache for vindication.

Yet he still couldn't ignore his own curiosity. What had Dràven found that could bait Jon Ayers? Perhaps another family relic, but it had to be something more precious than his own nephew.

Dràven couldn't possibly have anything Jon wanted more. Éli leaned over the map and tapped his finger against the two most likely cities, trying to guess where the other ship would land. Jon and his men would need supplies, and that meant they'd want to slip in and out of any city unnoticed.

Something roared in the sky, and Éli's head jerked toward the clouds. Several sky beasts, their skin lit up with different colored lights, blazed through the storm—gone in a matter of seconds.

*They're searching for her,* Evardo spoke into his mind. *They will tear her apart until there is nothing left.*

Not when I have her, he snapped back.

Another glance at the map and Éli chose the nearest city, right in the path of the sky beasts. "We sail to Felaren and slip into the city at night. You two"—he pointed a pair of younger soldiers—"sell off whatever we don't need to resupply our stock."

"Yes, Commander," they said in unison.

Éli had nearly thirty men at his command now, not including the boy or his new servant.

"And what about the high council, sir?" a younger soldier asked.

For the first time in his life, he could not feel the high council's power thrumming through his brand. He never wanted to be within a thousand spans of them again.

"They sail for the darkness." His men didn't need to know any truth other than what he told them. "We follow Jon Ayers."

# CHAPTER 31
## *The Dark Isle*

The atmosphere processor blasted vapor into the clouds. A wall of seawater stretched to either side, the boundary fueled by a subsurface filtering system that split oxygen and hydrogen atoms and fed them back to the processor.

Jàden had learned the engineering side years ago before she'd entered the Guild program, but right now Jon held all of her focus. His forehead warm against hers, his breath rolled across her mouth, triggering a burning desire she could not ignore.

"I worked in the prisons a long time, and I know when a man is telling the truth. Frank knows where Kale is." Jon's thumb caressed her cheek, but a dark anger hardened his features.

"Two lies and a truth," Frank always used to say, long before he knew about her connection to the Flame. "Give a man the truth he wants and two lies to trap him with. You'll always get what you want."

And she'd done the same damn thing to herself. The truth that she needed to find Kale. A lie that Kale would fix everything wrong in her life.

And the trap of an energy tie binding Jon to her side.

Except it bound Jàden to him, and as she traced her fingers down his prickly jawline, the atmosphere processor blasted again. "This is why Frank's taunting is so effective. Bird in a cage, that's what Kale used to call it. You give a bird exactly what it wants, and it doesn't see the bars of its cage until it's too late."

"What does he want, Jàden? This isn't about power. It's about something bigger, or Frank wouldn't be hunting you this way." The way Jon swallowed the lump in his throat and tightened his jaw against her hand told Jàden he would keep digging until he found the answer he wanted. "I need to know everything." He lifted her chin. "I won't lose you, but I can't protect you when everything you do is so damn unpredictable."

He pulled her into a tight hug.

She gripped his shirt, thankful for the seawater to hide her tears. Giant firemarks lit the unmuddied side of the atmosphere processor, all the power and computer systems she'd need to search for Kale, if she could get past the security locks.

But Frank had found her today because of the datapad. He'd tracked her location the moment she accessed her account, Kale's horrible funeral ending with a single nightmare word across her screen: *Gotcha.*

"How do you do it?" she whispered. "How can you live every day with this constant barrage of death and fear?"

Jàden wanted so desperately to return to her old life, but all roads led to death or a cage. Kale's zankata, with its promise of safety, had ended in a graveyard. Using the Flame had resulted in waking Frank from hypersleep. And now she couldn't even use a computer without him sourcing her location.

"I can't do it anymore," she said.

"You have to, or today means nothing." Jon leaned his cheek against her head. "Look for the things that matter and hold on tight."

"I had someone who mattered, and now he's gone." Bitter anger flowed through her veins. Kale was too young to die.

He stepped back, his eyes unreadable and anger etched into his features. "You didn't answer my questions. What does Frank want with you, and why didn't you take his offer? I want the whole truth."

Agnar grunted, and she leaned against the stallion's shoulder, though more for her own comfort than his. "Frank wants the Flame, but he can't wield it without me."

"Why? For what purpose, Jàden?" Even Jon's blade couldn't hold a candle to the sharpness in his words as his demeanor transformed from gentle protector to tense soldier. "What will he do with this power?"

She shied away, one hand over her ears as if that would quiet his tone. This was the secret she couldn't tell anyone, not in her world and definitely not in Jon's.

Below the sand and the sea, deep in the hollow caverns of the moon's interior beat the heart of something else. An alien technology whose builders died to protect it. A gateway that sparked the technology for *Hàlon's* tower gates and the key Jon carried around his neck.

She'd only seen it once, and the secret had nearly gotten her and Kale both killed. It was where she'd first met Bradshaw, a brilliant biotheric surgeon with the charm of a playboy and the heart of a rabid hound.

He'd changed after her capture—cold, distant, eccentric. He didn't see humans anymore; he only saw test subjects.

That horrible place filled with monstrous creatures was something she wanted to forget. And by the look in Jon's eyes, she had to tell him at least some part of what she'd seen.

"Frank won't do anything, not until he finds the other Flame." The heart of Sandaris had its own energy stream weighing her down, blending into her senses as if it ached for the Flame's power.

Jon pulled out his cigarettes, cursing that they were soaked. "What other Flame?"

"An opposite from me, different as day and night. When power from both Flames unite, it creates a reaction, a fusion of energy that doesn't exist anywhere else." She couldn't explain it without delving deep into physics and scientific principles Jon most certainly had never learned.

He laid his hands on her shoulders. "But why? What does he want?"

*To power the inner gate.* Words she couldn't say without putting Jon in even greater danger, and she'd already torn apart his life enough. "I don't know."

The lie wedged into her chest. She had to let him go, cut him loose. Because next time Frank attacked, they wouldn't be so lucky. Someone was bound to die, and as Jon's strength flowed through her veins, it pulled with it the guilt of forcing him to be her bodyguard.

"You don't deserve any of this." If she continued trying to find Kale, she would get them all killed. And her feelings for Jon were becoming more complicated by the day. She wanted him in her arms, in her bed, and every day she rode beside him pushed Kale into faded memory. "I don't know what to do anymore except find a way off Sandaris before I get everyone killed."

Before Frank and Sandaris pulled the Flame's power out of her and opened the gate inside the moon. No one knew what lay on the other side, but the creatures they'd found near it were a nightmare Sandaris didn't need. Thank the Guardians they'd never made it to the surface.

Jàden tightened her fist, hating that the only thing keeping her from a lonely insanity was Jon's energy, but she had to let him go. She had to stop the lie. She'd kept Jon bound to her out of fear for her own life, but he deserved the freedom he and his men had worked so hard for.

A thread of light pulled away from her wrist as Jon stepped closer. He towered nearly a span over her head. "Then I'm coming with—"

Engines roared high in the clouds, and three silver scout craft raced by. Jàden pressed closer to

Agnar, hiding behind his bulk until the craft were out of sight.

"The tracking beacons."

Sure enough, they disappeared in the same direction as Naréa's ship. Frank wasn't messing around anymore. He'd expected her to be a broken blob of a woman, but she'd gotten away from him twice. He would use every soldier and every tracking program to find her.

"He'll be angry now," she muttered.

The gun pressed against her stomach like lead. If Frank could track his soldiers and monitor heat signatures, what else could he do that she didn't know about?

She pulled the gun from her waistband and popped the firemark. "I have to get rid of this."

She hated to let go of her gun, but its metal alloy would stand apart from the forged steel of the others' weapons, and she didn't trust that they could elude Frank a third time.

Jon grabbed the gun and lobbed it into the trees. "Every day, from now on, we learn to fight against those weapons. Including you."

He grabbed his stallion's reins and nudged her forward, but she already led Agnar toward the others. She still needed to untie her energy from Jon, but as they angled deeper under the canopy, any exertion of power might alert Frank to their exact location.

And they needed to get dry before they did anything.

But as the waves crashed over their feet, Jon threw his arm in front of Jàden and froze where he was, the horses tossing their heads in irritation.

A long, shimmering thread stretched across their path between two mangrove roots. They followed the thread's trail through a cluster of branches to vivid green leaves with bright orange flowers. Dewdrops glistened along the petals, attaching to several more threads that stretched high in the trees to a giant white web nearly as tall as the Ironstar Tower.

"Fuck me," Jon said.

"Sahirä." Lead dropped into Jàden's gut. "There must be millions of them. Billions."

The feathered sahirä spider, never larger than the palm of Jàden's hand, carried a neurotoxin in its body that could knock out a grown man. But they were nomadic creatures that lived alone until mating season. The males never lived longer than a year, but the females could live more than a decade.

"Not millions." Jon edged backwards, pushing into her so she and Agnar were forced to retreat. "These are shifters, Jàden, not animals. Sahiranath are cannibals."

Dread fell into her gut. Spider shifters, just like the bird men. What the fuck had happened to this world? The others had all frozen, edging away from other web threads, but the only safe place now was the sea.

"What do we do?" she asked. They had no chance against that many spiders if they released their toxin into the air, and turning around wasn't an option.

She wanted so desperately to climb on Agnar's back and keep running until all her terrors disappeared with the tides. Everyone on *Hàlon* was human, or so the Guilds would have them believe.

"I don't understand. Where did they come from?"

Maybe they'd come across another ship while she'd been in hypersleep, a parasitic sentient that could mimic human physiognomy, though even that seemed a little far-fetched.

"There are more shifters on Sandaris than humans." Jon wrapped an arm around her shoulders, edging them backwards until the water was to their ankles again.

But even Jon's warmth wasn't enough to push away the ice in her skin. Her clothing and hair were soaked, and cold rain drizzled the landscape. She needed to get dry before hypothermia set in.

Plus, Frank could be anywhere now.

She tightened her grip on Agnar's bridle and followed Jon away from the giant web. It stretched at least a league down the shore.

"We're safe as long as we don't touch any of the threads," Jon muttered, but by the look on the others' faces, even skirting the sahiranath would take hours.

The rain turned to a heavy drizzle, adding to her misery.

If Frank turned back, maybe he'd see more heat signatures in that tower of web than a small cluster of horsemen, but it was a very thin shot.

"I think I have an idea," she whispered.

Death in a cage, drown in the shallows if a sahirä toxin hit her or be fed to a horde of spiders. She may have nowhere left to go, but she didn't want to die yet.

If her idea worked, she might stay alive long enough to figure out a way off the moon's surface. "We're going to need some blankets and a really hot fire."

# CHAPTER 31

*The Dark Isle*

Jàden had no idea if her plan would work. She only hoped that the creatures within that massive tower put off enough heat that Frank wouldn't be able to source which signature was hers. While she helped Ashe start a fire, the others strung up blankets to form an enclosed space between the mangrove trunks, creating a shelter large enough for the horses to fit inside.

Three more times the engines roared, and Jàden hated that she had to give up her gun. Twice it had saved her, but if she really wanted to appear Sandarin and ride under Frank's radar, she had to be one. At least until his ships no longer patrolled the sky.

Soon the fire was so hot sweat poured down her neck. Jàden stripped down to her underthings and wrenched the extra water out of her clothes.

"Got this from one of Naréa's crew." Thomas unwrapped a thick bundle. A set of dark gray clothes lay inside. She pulled the breeches and hooded shirt on, grateful they were only mildly damp.

Black leather wrapped the hilts of twin daggers beneath, a green orb with trailing legs imprinted onto the bindings. Something about that symbol creeped her out. She slid each knife from its sheath—one crafted with silver steel, the other obsidian steel. Each blade was also stamped with the orb and trailing legs symbol.

"You'll wear these from now on," Thomas said, fatigue in his voice as he rubbed muscle pain out of his arm.

She slid the weapons back in their sheaths.

Jon grabbed the bundle and unrolled the attached strips of leather, the sharp edge still heavy in his tone. "These blades will help keep you alive."

He looped the straps around her shoulders until they crisscrossed her chest, buckling between her breasts. The daggers nestled against her back, one hilt poking over each shoulder. Once the unit was tight against her, Jon laid his hands on her shoulders. "And we have a deal—you learn to fight without magic. I help you find Kale."

Except if she continued the search for Kale, someone was going to get killed.

An engine roared above the canopy, blue lights twinkling through the high branches.

Jàden instinctively ducked. Dropping her gaze to the ground, she grabbed a damp undershirt and wrapped it around the lower half of her face, tying it off at the back of her head.

Frank would use every tracking system he had and might even go so far as to send in drone cameras. She couldn't leave any part of her body exposed. Pulling her hood up, she stayed close to the fire, hoping its heat would mask her own.

"I know you're out there, darlin'." Frank sounded furious this time, the playful taunt gone from his voice.

The others didn't draw their weapons, though their fingers itched toward their arrows.

"Doesn't feel right hiding like this," Ashe muttered.

Jàden dug her fingers into the sand to hide her fear. These men at least listened to her plan, but if they took the fight head on, it could be the end of their road. "The alternative is he shoots all of you and I'm in a cage."

Ashe clenched his jaw, clearly unhappy with her biting words. These men didn't understand how powerful Frank was in the cockpit of his ship. One flip of a switch and he could kill them all.

She gripped the sand so tight she was certain the others could see the fear hammering her heart.

For nearly an hour, the ships hovered above the canopy. Why wouldn't they leave? Perhaps Frank saw through her ruse and was just waiting for something.

Jàden was certain at any second that Enforcers would rappel through the trees. Keeping her hood low over her eyes, she peeked through the hole above the blankets. Shimmering gossamer threads glistened in the late morning light. "The spiders."

"They're after the sky beast," Andrew muttered, sliding in close beside her. He and Ashe were so identical she could barely tell them apart, except that Andrew was far more serious than his twin. He pointed to a hole in the canopy where a silken thread attached to one wing.

"How big are those things?" A chill crawled along her skin at the idea of giant spiders.

"In many ways, they're human, but a single thread of their web is strong enough to hold a full-grown buck in place." Andrew gestured toward the captain. "We should get out of here."

"Agreed." Jon picked up one of his now-dry cigarettes from near the fire and lit it. "Pack everything except the blankets. If the webbing holds that ship when it tries to leave, that's our signal to get out of here, nice and slow."

Jàden quickly packed all her belongings and stuffed them inside Agnar's saddle bag, sparing the stallion a moment to scratch his cheek. But he flattened his ears and snorted at her. Something was bothering him, probably because he was stuffed into another stall when he wanted to ride.

"That web won't hold those ships." Not if the pilot pushes the thrust. But then, she'd also never seen a web as tall as a gateway tower. All the things she'd learned in her biology classes might be useless knowledge now.

Peeking out between the blankets, she searched the mangroves rooted along the shore for any sign of more web. If the sahirana surrounded them with the same silken threads, they might never escape.

"We should leave now," Jon said beside her. "Nice and slow while the shifters are distracted."

"We'll be exposed." She pointed toward the ships. "Those webs won't hold—"

"Do you trust me, Jàden?" His dark brown eyes pinned her in place, a strong intensity burning in their depths. As if to punctuate his words, a surge of strength breathed into her skin from their bond.

"Yes, of course I do."

Jon touched her chin, tilting her head to meet his. "Then trust my instincts. If we don't leave this place now, we never will."

Fire burned in her gut at his closeness, at the edged expression daring her to fight him on this. But she didn't want to fight. She ached to pull him close and feel the softness of his mouth against hers.

By the Guardians, she wanted this man.

But she couldn't give in to the energy tangling them together. One intimate kiss could forge their energy as one, and she'd never be able to free him.

She bit down on her lip and turned away, grabbing Agnar's saddle and pulling herself up, something she didn't have the strength for a few weeks ago.

They pulled down the blankets, and Jàden rolled hers into a bundle as she followed Thomas into the labyrinth of tree roots.

Jon stayed behind, getting everyone else out before he climbed onto his stallion, holding a lit stick like a torch. Sahirä web was flammable, and one touch of the fire might set the whole tower ablaze. Trusting Jon's instincts should have been easy.

Except now they were exposed to heat signature tracking, camera drones and anything else Frank might throw at them.

Jàden had to bite down hard on her lip to keep from bolting through the high roots. Fear pounded in her ears as she clutched Agnar's reins, white fire surging through her veins. She couldn't lose control of her power, not with Frank looming overhead.

"Sit up, Jàden. Act Sandarin." Thomas nudged his horse beside her. "This is your training until we're out of this place. Act like you belong here."

As he trotted ahead again to guide them around stray web threads, she wove her fingers through Agnar's mane hairs and sat up straighter, trying to emulate the others. Twice she had to duck under a stray thread. Even one brush against it would have her trapped by its sticky fibers, at least according to the others.

An engine roared, and a ship veered off into the jungle.

Maybe they weren't watching her like she'd thought and something else had their attention. Anything could lurk in the trees. The spiders had to feed on something, and she hoped it wasn't only humans.

"Let's pick up the pace," Jon shouted.

She followed his gaze to the sea, a small dark blot on the horizon. At first, it seemed Naréa might have turned the *Darius* back, but a ripple of power whispered through the burned skin on Jàden's hip.

The Rakir followed them.

"One more problem we don't need," she said.

Another of Frank's ships roared louder and veered off toward the sea, but halfway through its turn, it hovered in the same spot. The pilot gunned the engines, blue fire cutting a swath into the trees as it shot over Jàden, smoke billowing out of its wing.

The top of the web tower burst into an inferno, the merest whisper of screams on the air. She nudged Agnar to a trot as they stumbled onto a muddy road winding through large rubber trees with strangler figs wrapping trunks and branches in a thicket of vines.

"Keep a steady pace," Thomas hissed at her. "Slow and steady."

One ship remained overhead, its engines whining as if something stalled them out. An explosion rocked the upper canopy, the force of the blast so strong it startled the horses.

Agnar bolted.

Jàden tightened her legs to hang on. She tried pulling on the reins, but he dropped his head and charged.

Fire and metal rained down behind them, igniting the web threads. Shadows scuttled everywhere she turned, and her heart pounded so hard she had to bite back a scream of terror.

Jon's instincts were right.

If they'd waited, they'd all be buried under raining metal and a blaze quickly spreading from one tree to another.

"Slow down, Agnar!" She tried to watch for more webbing as she gripped the reins and leaned all her weight backwards, but he shook his head and reared, hopping sideways before all four hooves hit the sand and he bolted.

He was going to get them both killed if he didn't slow down.

Agnar raced under a large branch, and she threw herself against his neck, the foliage scraping along her back.

"Dammit, Agnar!" She glanced behind her, but the others were scattered, wrangling their horses around the roots with their weapons out. She had to get back and help, but the Flame's white light surged in her veins.

She couldn't unleash it. Not without condemning them all.

Agnar plunged around a curve in the road and ran until his sides heaved and foam licked up his neck. Cut off from the others, she dropped the reins and gripped her fists tight to force back the Flame's consuming power.

The stallion hopped sideways several times to slow himself then dead-stopped in the middle of the road.

Jàden leaned her head against his neck as they both panted heavily. "I thought nothing spooked you."

Yet as soon as she said it, she stretched to the side, a long string of drool hanging out of Agnar's mouth.

*Shit.*

He was in pain. The stallion had been a little moody the last few days on the ship, and she'd figured it had to do with being cooped up. "That bit must be hurting you."

*He's your horse now,* Mather's voice whispered into her thoughts.

She was all alone, cut off from the others, though their shouts filtered through the trees.

Jàden dropped to the ground, grabbed Agnar's bridle and trotted him off the road, the trees so silent it sent a warning straight up her spine. Hiding just out of sight, she untied the blanket and wrapped the rope around Agnar's neck.

"No more running. Let's get this thing off you." She unbuckled the bridle and pulled it off his head, fiddling with the bit to unhook it.

A family of otters poked their heads out of the brush, watching her intently. Or maybe they were shifters too. She edged back, wrapping her hands around the leather strips to hold them like a weapon. Could be just animals, but she'd done enough animal behavior classes to sense that something was off.

The otters melted together into a man with muddy blond hair and a bow strung across his back. His clothes the same brown as his otter fur, intent gray eyes held her in place. He stood from the brush, his words in perfect common speech. "I won't harm you."

*Hàlon's* language from the mouth of a Sandarin. He said the same words again in the local tongue and stepped closer.

Agnar laid his ears flat and tossed his head at the stranger as she gripped the bridle tighter. As the man stepped closer, she swung the metal bit, but the stranger caught her wrist.

He tugged down the make-shift mask across her face, his eyes tracing over her features. "Jàden. You're alive."

"You know me." Her chest tightened, the man's words in flawless common as if he'd grown up on *Hàlon*. No, this couldn't be right. It had to be another one of Frank's ploys. "Who are you?"

Jon and the others' shouts drew closer.

"I'll find you again," he whispered so close to her ear that the hair on his chin prickled her skin. Releasing her wrist, he melted into a pile of otters and scurried into the bushes.

Every hair on Jàden's neck stood straight as a presence whispered across her shoulder.

Theryn's usually jovial features were hard and focused as he stepped beside her, a cut across his eye. He pulled a feathered arrow shaft next to his cheek, tightening the tension on his bow. "Back to your horse."

"Don't shoot him." The man hadn't tried to harm her and he'd known her real name and language. Maybe another hypersleeper like her.

"We'd be dead if I did." Theryn glanced around the trees then eased the tension on his arrow. "He's not alone."

The stranger emerged deeper in the trees and climbed to a low branch covered in ivy. The vines slid together until a blond woman crouched beside him, whispering in his ear.

"See?" Theryn muttered. "Not alone."

"Let's get moving," Jon barked as the others caught up.

Jàden tugged the strip of cloth back over her mouth. Looping the bridle on her arm, she climbed in the saddle and gripped Agnar's mane hairs.

"You don't stop. Keep riding." Blood splattered Jon's cheek, and the anger in his voice gutted her. Kale had spoken to her like that once, as if she were under his command and better start following orders.

She hated it then, and she hated it now. Not even the fire in her gut could quench her irritation. "Yes, *Captain.*"

Jàden didn't care if he caught the heavy sarcasm in her voice. She wasn't a child and wasn't about to be ordered around like one.

Clenching her fists, she tried her best to keep from cursing up a storm. She needed to put up a wall between them anyway before she did something really stupid that couldn't be undone. And she might as well do it now, while he was angry anyways.

Ignoring his glare, she nudged Agnar around him and trotted after Thomas.

## CHAPTER 32
### *The Dark Isle*

Jon turned toward the towering inferno, thousands of lives now in peril because of Frank's sky beasts. Only one remained overhead, keeping its distance as it hovered over the sea. Screams blew across the wind and faded to silence, the shifters moving east as they tried to escape the blaze.

He tossed the torch into the sea, thankful he hadn't been forced to use it. Even with the rain cascading over the land, the shifters would lose half their homes, or if they were lucky, the fires would extinguish before any more lives were lost.

This was not the entrance he wanted to a new land.

Nudging his horse closer to Malcolm, he pressed two fingers against the old man's neck. His pulse still beat strong as he lay unconscious over his horse. He'd accidentally run into a teenage shifter hiding from the ships, and the boy was so scared he'd released all his venom into Malcolm's face.

The old man should wake up soon. Jon grabbed the lead line and trotted after the others, anger burning in his heart. Not because of the fires or the man who was like a second father to him.

All because Jàden called him captain.

Once they found a safe spot to bed down for the night, he would have a few words with her. No wife of his would call him captain, and he sure as shit wasn't going to let her push him away anymore.

He was her husband, and it was about time she learned the truth.

They rode until afternoon when thick fog rolled in from the coast. He could barely see a dozen spans into the foliage.

Frogs chirruped loud enough to mask the crashing waves as they followed the muddy road along the shore, crossing a tributary from the sea that turned into a wide river flowing straight into the heart of the Dark Isle.

Jon wrangled his horse alongside Theryn. "What happened earlier with Jàden?"

"Shifter," Theryn muttered. "The guy saw her face, Captain. And he called her Jàden. The man *knew* her."

Jon clenched his jaw. "Which means he'll be following us. We need to know more about this place." If traders like Naréa always dumped their human cargo near the sahiranath web, chances were few escaped with their lives. "You and Dusty see if you can create a projectile launcher similar to those weapons. Everyone learns how to use them and how to avoid them."

"Yes, sir." Theryn rode ahead to catch up with Dusty.

"Th'fuck happing." Malcolm groaned and wove his fingers into his stallion's mane. "Cap'n?"

"Right here." He lit one of his nearly dry cigarettes. "Rest, old man. We're safe for now."

Malcolm sat up, stiffness in his movements. Not much changed over the next few hours except they had new shadows tracking them. Likely the ones who saw Jàden's face, but Jon was so exhausted he could barely keep his eyes open.

Jàden held her shoulders hunched. *Still hiding something.* He didn't like unknown variables or how unpredictable she was in a fight. No doubt Jàden was smart, but she always seemed to react by her own fears. He had to figure out a way to understand her moves.

"Last web I saw was hours ago. I think we're out of sahiranath territory, but I don't want to take any chances. We keep riding until dark," Jon said. Fog became trapped between the barrier and the shore while the rain remained a constant cold drizzle.

"And hope those shifters don't blame us for what happened." Malcolm pulled out his pipe, improving back to his cranky self by the time the last sun set.

Jon scanned the sky for any sign of Frank's ships as he dismounted and tied off his horse. The sky turned full dark, a hint of illumination in the west as if a large city lay nearby. In any normal circumstance, he would have ordered his men to check it out, but he couldn't risk an encounter with another web. Nor could he risk sleeping on the beach with Frank's ships in the sky. Only Jàden's shelter idea seemed to be the trick.

"Same as this morning," Jon said. "Blankets up, everyone inside for sleep. Three watches set."

"Yes, Captain." His men went about their duties.

Thomas was the exception. "We should let her rest, Captain. She won't be any good to us sick."

Anyone else and he might have agreed, but it was time he cracked Jàden open. He needed to get to the truth of everything—her truth. Jon didn't like the idea of another Flame, another variable that could cause more problems. "No, push her harder. Do it now."

## CHAPTER 33
*The Dark Isle*

Jàden searched the sky for any of Frank's ships. They'd disappeared hours ago, but a very bad feeling settled in her gut. "He must be furious."

The only thing likely saving her ass right now was his leg injury. But with every day that passed, he'd heal, just as her shoulder had healed to no more than a deep ache in the joint.

As she finished brushing Agnar, Thomas shoved a staff in her hand. "Time for some fun."

Sparring with Thomas was never fun.

Jàden leaned her head against the stallion's shoulder, her thoughts in turmoil. The ache to be in Jon's arms was so strong, even sensing his gaze on her back caused her stomach to twist into knots.

Exhaustion tugging at her senses, Jàden moved onto the sand opposite Thomas.

Always wound tight with anger, Thomas's movements were fast and precise, and the bastard never broke a sweat. It was only after their sparring she ever saw him rubbing his arms as if he'd been hiding some injury.

She missed a hit, and he smacked her brand again, a fiery sting shooting into her hip.

Jàden clenched her jaw to bite back the pain. Sweat dripped along her face and neck as she finally had enough and shouted at him. "I'm never going to heal if you keep hitting my injury."

"So, stop me." Thomas circled her with the staff tucked behind his forearm. The longer she sparred with him, the bigger an asshole he became. His light taps in the beginning had turned to solid hits. "Again."

She circled once more, her palms slick with sweat. Her body resisted each movement, as if she couldn't get the right leverage. She aimed for Thomas and swung.

He dodged her blow then swept her feet.

Jàden hit the ground hard. She grabbed her hip, barely biting back another cry.

"You're distracted tonight." Thomas pressed the staff against her neck and lifted her chin. "Is this about Kale?"

"None of your business." She shoved it away and rolled to her feet. The last thing Thomas needed to know was how much she wanted to kiss Jon and the guilt that came with it.

Thomas laid the staff across his shoulders, draping his arms over as if he didn't have a care in the world. "Everything's my business."

She swung the staff across his gut, relishing a small victory when he stumbled back out of breath. *Stupid bastard.*

But an amused light touched his eyes as he stood up straight again. "Or maybe this isn't about Kale at all."

"Shut up, Thomas," she muttered.

Whatever this new dirty tactic was, she didn't like it. The last thing she wanted to talk about tonight was Kale or how much he was fading to a distant memory.

"You're keeping secrets from us." His staff slammed into her burn, causing her to cry out in pain before she could block the hit. "Where's the other Flame?"

"I don't know!" She stumbled out of his reach and kept her weapon up. "Frank never found the other one."

Fire burned in her hip as she took a step back, the twins circling behind her. Ashe held up two smaller bamboo staffs tied together and tossed them toward her. "These might be more your size."

One wary eye on Thomas, she untied the sparring sticks and held one in each hand. Smaller and lighter. She stretched out her arms, noting a broader range of movement without her grip tied to a single weapon.

"You spar with two sticks," Ashe said. "You spar with two fighters."

Thomas grabbed her staff and stepped aside, while Ashe and Andrew circled around her. Yet something in the set of Thomas's jaw told Jàden he hadn't finished with her.

"What will Frank do when he puts the Flames together?" he asked.

Jàden protected her hip as the twins circled. Identical faces, one on each side. She had to keep moving. Keep turning.

But Jon was always there in the back, watching like a hawk.

Thomas crossed his arms. "Get the truth out of her."

"Dammit—"

Before she could say more, Andrew attacked, Ashe sneaking a hit across her shoulder. In and out, when one lunged, the other swooped in for a hit.

She raised her arm to block, a stick hit her thigh. Jàden attempted to keep pace with the twins but soon doubled over, fighting for breath. Her heart pounded so hard her chest spasmed with a deep ache.

Thomas lifted her chin, forcing her to look at him. "What will Frank do?"

Tears burned in her eyes as she tried to look away. She wanted to keep the knowledge clamped down tight, but the ice in Thomas's tone pulled her words out. "He'll open the other gate."

"What gate?" He tightened his fingers, but like Jon, his grip was both gentle and strong, commanding her attention. "You're playing with our lives, Jàden. We need the whole truth."

Something that nearly got her and Kale killed, so they opted to keep their silence. To run far away from both Sandaris and *Hàlon* where they'd be safe and no one could ever exploit her powers. A space where she could live her life until the Flame consumed her, without risking death to all the *Hàlon* citizens who had no clue what really lurked beneath the moon's surface.

"The one below," she whispered, "in the moon's core."

Thomas frowned and glanced at Jon as if waiting for his next order.

"Enough." Jon's single word held the command of a Guild general, and both Thomas and the twins backed away. His shoulders still held the tension of a coiled viper as he walked toward her. "You're on watch tonight, with me."

Her chest tightened. Of course she wouldn't get to sleep. He'd want to know more, and Jàden couldn't tell him everything, though she'd already said too much. "Yes, Captain."

His gaze lingered on her for a long moment, his jaw growing tighter by the second. Jon finally grabbed his bow and quiver, retreating to the trees along the shore.

Thomas waved the twins off. "You're still hunching your shoulders. Focus on the fight, not the fear."

Jàden clenched the sticks, tempted to throw them at Thomas's head. She'd rather be focused on sleep, but she retreated to her saddle bags and wiped the grime from her face.

"Aren't you the favorite." Theryn grinned as he ran a blade over a piece of wood, carving it to look like a handgun. Likely to help them all train for different types of weapons.

"Oh, shut up." The muscles in her arms burned as she pulled on her thicker hooded shirt.

She was honestly a bit jealous he could laugh so easily in the face of danger when her only coping tactics were to run and hide like a child. The last thing she needed was to sit in uncomfortable silence when she could barely keep her eyes open.

"The captain's in a foul mood tonight. Whatever you do, don't lie to him. That'll piss him off faster than a knife to the gut."

"It's just the rain making him grouchy," she muttered. Jàden wanted to tell Jon the whole truth about everything, but as his strength flowed into her veins, so did her guilt.

Every day, she dragged Jon deeper into her mess.

"Hear that, Dusty? Genius here thinks the weather's souring the captain's mood." Both men chuckled. Then Theryn leaned close and lowered his voice. "Just bed the man and save us all a headache."

She punched him hard in the arm and stormed off, cursing under her breath while his laughter followed. Of all Jon's men, he was the most opinionated and loud-mouthed.

And the last thing she needed was anyone to see how hard his words hit her gut.

The idea of intimacy with Jon heated up every inch of her body. She craved the gentleness of his strong arms holding her tight. But tonight she'd have to deal with the angry captain, and she doubted anything she said could flip his switch back to the softer man who'd comforted her tears.

*Jon's a good man with a kind heart, and he'll always have your back in a fight.* Mather's voice slipped into her thoughts. *When I'm gone, it'll be up to you to take care of him.*

She wished she'd known what the future held and could have forced Mather to go home before they ever found Kale's graveyard ship. But Mather was wrong—Jon didn't need anyone to care for him. Despite his mood swings, Jon was strong, smart and sure of himself, and she envied him for it.

He leaned against a tall palm near the edge of the surf. Smoke rose from the ember on his cigarette as he drove three arrows into the sand and crouched next to them, a bow across his knees. "You never answered my question."

"Dammit, Captain, I have answered every single one, and yet you keep digging. Leave it alone." She moved to a palm a few feet away and sulked against it.

"Cut the shit. I ain't your captain." He drove the end of his bow into the sand, his jaw so tight it was practically forged in steel. "You had a choice on that deck, Jàden. Kill me, or kill *him*."

The venom in Jon's tone stabbed her heart.

*Him*. As if Kale was the problem.

She hated how much it stung to have his anger turned on her. "Leave Kale out of this. Frank would have killed him no matter what I did."

That was the horrible truth. Even if she'd gone with Frank, the bastard would have shown her Kale in his new life then gunned him down before she could turn away. Frank would do it to break her spirit and any hope she had left.

"Why would Frank care about some old lover of yours?" Jon wouldn't even look at her. "He had you, Jàden, your little bird-in-a-cage theory. But a man like Frank wouldn't give two shits about some ex-lover. There are other ways to break a mind."

She kicked at the sand, trying to ignore Jon's penetrating anger. "His real name is Command General Frank Kale, one of the highest Guild Council members and a tracker from the Alliance rim worlds. Jason Kale, the man I've been searching for, is his son."

If Jon's silence before had been a minor irritation, this time it was a punch to the throat. She could almost sense his fury through their tied energy, and the longer he said nothing, the more her body tightened.

Jàden couldn't bear the quiet any longer. "Frank doesn't give two shits about his son. He only wants the Flame. I spent years in a cage while he killed my dog, my grandparents and eventually the man I love, just to watch me break under the grief."

Tears burned in her eyes as she dropped to the ground, digging her fingers into the sand to fight off the urge to run.

Jon lit his third—or twelfth—cigarette. She'd lost count, but every time she glanced at him, another one was already in his hand.

"Then why the fuck are you searching for him if he's gonna end up dead again?" he asked. "Kale failed you once, Jàden, and there's no guarantee he'll protect you now."

Anger ripped through her chest as she stumbled to her feet, fury boiling her blood. She threw a handful of sand at him. "Fuck you."

His accusation cut straight to the heart of her deepest shame. She'd waited two years, and the moment she understood he'd only broken through the lab's defenses to say goodbye, bitterness had seeped into her psyche. Why come at all if he couldn't save her?

"Kale didn't fail anybody." She hated herself for needing a rescuer, that she couldn't save her own ass against a bastard like Frank.

But she couldn't let Jon see this side of her, the lonely coward who was desperate to put the fight in someone else's hands.

Fuck Jon and fuck being on watch.

"I'm still alive because of Kale," she said. "But you can't say the same for your sisters."

She stormed down the beach, not caring who saw her right now.

"Get the fuck back here. We're not finished." Jon chased after her, fury deepening his voice.

"Yes we are!" The Flame crashed into her veins, crackling white light across her fingers. "You can't keep pushing—"

"The fuck I can't." Jon grabbed her arm and pulled her back until she stood face to face with him. "I did everything to save my sisters. Everything!"

"Then stop blaming Kale. He died trying to save me." Still, she painted him the hero, the lie in her own words like a bitter plague. And now she so desperately needed Jon to fill the same role and hated herself for it.

"Kale's dead. I don't care how many lives the bastard lived. He ain't the same man, Jàden."

"He *is* the same! He'll always be Kale." Wrenching herself free, she tried to shove him away, but Mr. Muscular didn't budge.

"Then why did you save my life?" Jon tossed his half-spent cigarette away and grabbed her shoulders. "He's gone. My sisters are gone. You can't bring him back, no matter how much it hurts. So why, Jàden?"

"Because *I* failed *him*!" She shoved Jon's hands away, her heart hurting so much she would have given anything to rip it out of her chest. "I needed him to save me, and it broke him."

"You can't blame yourself for what happened—"

"Yes I can! Every day of my life until I can make it right. But if I climb aboard Frank's ship, he'll kill Kale, whether he's a child or an old man. I can't put him through it again—I can't. And I can't fail you again." Tears streamed down her cheeks as she pressed her hands against her forehead, pain throbbing across her skull.

"What the fuck are you talking about?" Jon paced in front of her like a caged bear.

"This power I carry is like a parasite that will never go away."

Jon held up his hand, two threads of light twisting away from his palm. "You mean what *we* carry."

"That's where I've failed you, Captain."

"Dammit, Jàden, I ain't your captain." He practically growled at her as he grabbed her cheeks. "You've never failed me, not once, but this power you carry isn't just about you anymore. I carry it too, and you need to get that straight in your head."

"Don't you tell me what I need." Tying Jon's energy had been a terrible mistake. "If I don't leave Sandaris, this power will become so strong I won't be able to control it."

"How strong?" He caressed his thumb along her jaw.

The heat from his touch sent an ache to her heart. White light burned in her veins as she leaned her forehead against his chin. "Strong enough to kill everything on this moon."

As the Flame whispered out of her, every fish and crab under the water lit up for a single beat of Sandaris's heart then faded to darkness. A single flash of millions of creatures beneath the waves and gone the next second as if she'd never touched their hearts.

"Guardians be damned." Jon stared at the sea in shock as she turned over his hand and traced her thumb across his palm.

"And I won't let anyone hurt you, not even me." He deserved better, someone who wouldn't get him killed. She had to protect him from her, from the Flame. As the tears slid down her cheeks, Jàden pulled the Flame back into her, slowly untying the threads of energy binding her to Jon.

"Hey, what are you doing?" Jon yanked his hand away and stumbled backwards. "Jàden."

A cold, lonely ache soured her heart as the whispers of strength disappeared. Guilt spread through her chest that she'd put all of them in so much danger. That her tie with Jon led Mather to his death. "I shouldn't have gotten you involved. I'm sorry, Captain."

"Jon." He stepped close and held her cheeks, leaning his forehead against hers. "My name is Jon. Please don't do this."

"You're free now. One day you'll thank me—"

"Not for this." He pressed his thumb against her mouth to stop the flow of words. "Jàden, please."

She couldn't bear the pain in his eyes or the hollow ache gutting her soul. Everything in her screamed to pull him back into her, to hold him close and never let go.

Jàden kissed his palm, breathing in his masculine scent of mountain pine, and pulled away. It was the right thing to do, giving Jon back his life and freedom, but she hadn't expected the regret that burned in her senses. She still wanted him, needed him, ached to curl up in his arms and cry out all her pain.

He wrapped an arm around her, leaning his head against hers. "Bonded or not, you will always have me at your side. But please, don't leave me so empty."

# CHAPTER 34
*The Dark Isle*

The emptiness, a hollow hole in his heart so wide it threatened to swallow him, lodged in Jon's chest worse than the day his parents died. He crouched in front of the stone ruins, a zankata freshly painted on the pillar. Pressing his fingers to the damp ochre, he clenched his fist, numb to the anger that should have burned through him.

He couldn't forgive Jàden for stripping her magic away and tearing his soul to shreds. His family dead, his best friend killed and now a wife that didn't want him. No matter how far he rode across this world, he'd never be able to outrun the pain.

Dusty and Thomas crouched beside him, but when neither one spoke, he growled at them. "What is it?"

"You ain't gonna fix nothing by ignoring her, Captain." Dusty's sharp green eyes searched the woods for the smallest movement.

"I agree with Dusty." Thomas ran a whetstone along his blade, something others might consider a threat. But the younger man was meticulous about caring for his weapons. "You two need to finish fighting it out. Or *something*."

Jon wanted to punch them both, especially Thomas for the way he muttered that last phrase. Jàden had made her intent clear the moment she'd ripped her magic out of him.

"Not this time. That symbol she's been looking for, they're here. We'll find her lover and let her go." Jon lit a cigarette and scanned the woods, nothing but foliage and tall trees rising to a thick green canopy.

Whoever had painted the zankatas the last few days were leading them toward the light haze on the nighttime horizon, and it had to be straight into the heart of a city.

Jon returned to his horse and climbed in the saddle. He shouted to his men, "We ride until dark."

His gaze lingered on Jàden as she searched the sky for the hundredth time that day. It was time to find that lover of hers and punch him so hard the bastard never looked at her again.

Wrangling his horse around, Jon trotted ahead of the others. Shallow reef stretched in all directions, islands and waterways broken up by large, spherical rocks with eroded carvings covered in lichen. Ruins from a civilization long dead.

He kicked his horse ahead, but Dusty and Thomas cut him off, forcing the black to rear up.

"Don't lie to yourself, Jon." Thomas rarely used his name, always preferring the deferential Captain. "Jàden belongs with us."

"She belongs with that lover of hers." Even his own words stung as she disappeared ahead, Theryn antagonizing her like an irritating sibling. Jon backed his horse up to move around them.

But Thomas grabbed the black's bridle. "You're scared of her because she *sees* you. It was in your eyes the night Mather died."

"You told us outside Nelórath that her life matters more than yours. It got me thinking—if she ain't your sister, there's only one other reason you'd risk your life to protect her." Dusty nudged his horse closer. "Jàden saved Theryn's life. She's family now. So fix it before you lose what's really precious."

As the two men wrangled their horses around and trotted toward the others, Jon dug his heels in and charged past them all, anger and hurt tightening his heart like a vice.

She may have been his wife for a whole season, but with the bond gone, years of loneliness swallowed him whole.

He couldn't fix this, not without magic of his own. But even if he held the power to bind them again, it didn't change the fact that she was in love with another man.

Jon followed the road for several days, the heavy rain souring his mood as he kept his anguish wound tight around his heart. He and Jàden barely spoke two words to one another, and he insisted Thomas keep pushing her harder. Maybe he just wanted her to break down in his arms again so he could comfort her, or maybe without him, she'd never be strong enough to face the shadows haunting her footsteps.

As they neared the city lights, the road ascended to a low cliff. White spires peeked through the jungle canopy between two giant mountain precipices. A maze of waterways wound through the landscape, cascading over a series of falls at the edge of a giant river storming toward the harbor. Ships moored below, a few of them with insignias he recognized from the Ìdolön shipping docks, but most were unfamiliar. The only one he cared about, though, was any black sail bearing the Tower and two moons emblem—and there were none.

"Guardians be damned," Andrew muttered, nudging his horse alongside. "The city's as big as Ìdolön."

Jon lit a cigarette and dropped to the ground. "We should go in now, before it gets dark."

He didn't care about sleeping in the mud again, but a city could mean an inn, fresh supplies and maybe some real food for a change. Plus, with Frank's ships still in the sky, the city could offer a better way to disappear.

Eventually, they'd need to ride inland to get far enough south to find the Ironstar Tower, and civilization might give him a chance to observe the true nature of Dark Isle inhabitants.

"These ain't our kind of folks, so I want weapons hidden," Jon said. "Don't need any of them to think we're a threat."

As Jàden stopped her horse beside him, Jon grabbed the stallion's bridle. Agnar had shed much of his black fur for a clouded gray, though Jon didn't think he was more than twelve years old. Too young to be turning gray.

"Hood up, cover the lower half of your face," he told her. "You ride with me."

"I can ride my own horse, Captain." She slid to the ground, avoiding eye contact with him despite her stinging tone.

But Jon wanted her near him in case something went wrong. He tugged the reins over the gray's head and stepped close to her. But instead of her sweet breath on his skin tugging at the ache in his heart, cold emptiness slapped him with the gentle scent of rainfall.

"No arguments. I'm the captain." The words tasted like bitter ash on his tongue.

Jon unbuckled his larger weapons and wrapped them in a blanket, tying them to her saddle. Only the daggers stayed at his back, hidden beneath his outer tunic.

Growling her contempt, Jàden unbuckled her own daggers.

But he grabbed them out of her hand. Adjusting the leather straps, he wrapped them around her waist like his, one hilt pointed at each hand. "I said weapons hidden, not off."

"Yes, *sir*." She barely kept the poison from her words as he tightened the buckle at her waist, his mouth dangerously close to hers.

He desperately wanted to kiss her and end this stubborn bitterness, but surrounded by his men was not the place to do it.

"Don't reach for them unless you have to." Though right now he'd welcome a stab in the back to stifle the pain in his heart. He grabbed her waist and lifted her onto his horse.

"I can only think of one person I'd use them on," she muttered under her breath.

Jon climbed in the saddle, his jaw so tight his head throbbed. "Ashe, take her horse."

Gathering the black's reins in his hand, Jon led them along the cliff as the road widened onto hard-packed dirt. A ship with orange light flew over the city and disappeared into the jungle.

Fuck, the last thing he needed right now was Frank.

Jàden slipped her arms around his waist. She must have seen the ship, and no doubt her fear overrode her anger.

Jon nudged his horse into a trot. They needed to get inside the city crowds before the ship doubled back. Even as angry as he was right now, she mattered more to him than anything else.

They wound along the cliffs and beyond the muddy road to a narrow street. Zankata lined the walls, ruffling their feathers or watching them with sharp eyes. Several blue-feathered zankata flew down, melting together into a single, uniformed figure in the middle of the path, her black tunic emblazoned across the chest with a blue feather.

The guard held up her hand. "You shifter?"

Something about the woman's rigid demeanor reminded him of Naréa—someone who'd spot a lie in two seconds.

Jàden hunched against Jon, but he stopped far enough away that the guard couldn't reach him or his horse with a weapon and said, "No, ma'am. Human. My brothers and I were shipwrecked, lost nearly everything. We'd like passage into the city for supplies."

The birds along the wall were still as statues, turning their heads to size up Jon and his men.

"Where you comin' from?" The woman walked a circle around him, lifting the blankets on Agnar's back. She was looking for something, but the truth was they didn't have more than their clothes and weapons. Even last night's meager stew had been gone by morning.

"Forbidden Mountains. Them Ìdolön bastards been killin' families and burning farms." He really hoped news of the soldiers had already spread this far south. It might help his words have a bit more weight. "We're just looking for a fresh start."

"You'd be safer up north." She stepped next to him, one hand on the dagger hilt at her waist. "Though I can't say I'm surprised. We get a lot of folks escaping those northern soldiers. Usually the deserters."

She fixed her gaze on him, the sharpness of her words revealing that she knew he and his men were soldiers. Likely by the branded emblem on their horses. The guard would be well within her rights to have them all jailed and sent back north, but Jon would kill her and every shifter on the wall if they tried.

"Try Riven Mountain Inn near the broken bell tower. Mostly humans there to help get you settled. No hunting within a day's ride of the city—all meat must be purchased at the markets where it's one hundred percent animal." She pointed toward a section of the city where two smaller rivers merged into one.

But his stomach was already growling at the thought of hot meat.

"City gates close at sundown. Welcome to Felaren." Her body exploded in a burst of feathers, a dozen zankata returning to perch on the wall's apex.

"Thank you." Jon nudged his horse forward, but the hairs along the back of his neck rose as half a dozen people crouched in the trees, barely visible except for the bows on their backs.

Those same folks had been following them since the sahiranath and could even be the ones who'd painted the zankata symbol for Jàden. Maybe they were leading her toward Kale. Or maybe back to another grave like what happened in the north.

## CHAPTER 35
*Felaren*

Jàden brushed the fur along Agnar's neck, her horse the only comfort she had left. She leaned against him, a whisper of breath on her cheek as he softly nipped at her, but he could barely keep his eyes open.

"I hate that Jon's angry with me," she whispered, the unbearable emptiness eating her insides. Her gentle warrior had disappeared since that night on the beach, replaced by a cold, moody captain who barely spoke two words to anyone.

Agnar grunted, dozing against the warmth of his brother-herd. Even he couldn't offer the comfort she needed.

"I don't know what to do anymore."

She stuffed the brush into her bag and closed the gate. Barely more than a circled fence with a roof, the pen was just large enough for all eight horses to fit comfortably and keep off the wind.

As she secured the latch, a herd of deer plodded along the road, a buck in the lead with a fifteen-point rack and a dozen does trailing behind. The buck turned toward her, staring hard as if to penetrate the shadows within her cowl.

Jàden turned away, rubbing the ache in her chest.

She'd made a horrible mistake, pulling her energy out of Jon, even if it was morally the right thing to do. Certain it would cut off her growing desire toward him, the severed tie had only strengthened her need to be near him. Day and night as they rode, she'd kept her head down, silently begging for a kind word or his soft touch on her cheek. She still needed to find Ironstar Tower and go back to the beginning, but that path was starting to feel more like a dream.

The human quarter settled on a marshy spit of land stretched between two wide rivers. A cool breeze blew in from the twilight harbor, and she wanted to tear off her cloak and turn her face to the last of the sunlight. But she held her hood tight against her cheek and scanned the skies for any sign of a ship.

Jon had set them up in an inn for the night, a celebration of their freedom from the Rakir and surviving their first days in a new land. Most of the others went out drinking at the local tavern, but she suspected their ploy was to learn about the Dark Isle and what lurked beyond the city's trees.

It would have been nice to drown herself in a bottle of réva, but with her rotten luck that would be the moment Frank showed up.

Toppled stone spires jutted out from dark green waters, one with an old bell nearly rusted through inside its apex. She searched for Jon but instead found Thomas leaning against the bathhouse, clean-shaved and dressed in fresh clothing.

She trudged toward the low, stone building, ready for a hot bath and a few moments to nurse the lonely ache in her soul. "Anyone in there?"

"You're the last." Thomas ran a hand over his fresh-shaved hair. "You've got the night off. We start fresh in the morning."

It was more than she could have hoped for. She hadn't had a hot bath or a soft bed in years, if she didn't count her time in hypersleep.

She pushed open the wooden door, steam lifting off a bathing pool in the center. Heat pressed against her skin, filled with the scents of lavender and hickory. She breathed them all in, a beautiful blend of fragrance, and yet it wasn't the mountain pine smell she craved.

"Just make sure no one comes in," she said.

Thomas chuckled and shut the door as if he had some secret amusement.

Steam frizzed out the hairs around her neck as she dropped her bag near the side. She pushed back her hood, glad she didn't have to cover her face anymore. With Thomas standing guard, there was no need to worry about unwanted visitors.

Tugging off her boots and breeches, Jàden settled on the side of the basin and dipped her bare feet into the heated water. Candles flickered along the walls, the low light fueling a sense of relaxation as she breathed a sigh of relief in the silence. Here was the only place she could be alone with her thoughts—and her tears—as she tugged off her hooded outer shirt.

Water splashed upward from the center of the pool, followed by a low sputtering.

Jon rubbed the water out of his eyes, a silver and ruby pendant glistening against his chest. Fire burned in her cheeks as his dark eyes found hers, water droplets sliding down his muscular arms from soldier brand to bloodflower tattoo.

"I'm sorry. Thomas said it was..." Empty.

Except he hadn't. The bastard must have known Jon was in here. The last thing she wanted right now was another confrontation.

"Not like you ain't seen me every day for an entire season." Jon forged to the edge of the basin, only the water covering his nakedness from the waist down.

She tried to avert her eyes.

But he laid a hand on either side of her legs. "Besides, you and I ain't finished. We need to get a few things sorted—without the others."

"I'm not going to fight you, Captain." She pulled her knees to her chest to stand up.

Jon grabbed her thighs and yanked her back down, her backside hitting the ground hard. "You might once I speak my mind."

Heat blazed up the inside of her thighs as he wedged his body between her legs. She wanted to scream at him to stop touching her like that—she belonged to Kale.

Except every time he stood so close, Jàden's heart split in two.

She ached for Jon with a burning desire in the deepest part of her gut, but her heart still grieved for Kale and the love they'd once shared. Even after watching Kale's funeral, she wanted him back. *Her* Kale.

But she would never get that chance, a hard truth she still struggled to accept even as an intense ache for Jon's affections clutched her heart. She loved him, wanted him. He deserved so much better than a broken woman like her, but damn if she didn't harbor a selfish desire to feel the heat of his lovemaking.

"This is the last time I'm going to say this." Frustration edged his voice. "I want you to call me Jon. You and I are in this together. Equals, got it?"

"We've never been equals. I can't wield a sword the way you do." She pressed against his chest to push him back as he caressed her thighs. By the Guardians she wanted him to kiss her. "Do you have to stand so close?"

"Damn right I do. You gutted me, Jàden. Ripped the best part of me away and left me cold and empty." He tightened his grip and pressed closer, leaning his forehead against hers. "I want it back. I can't bear this hole you left behind."

Why did he have to make everything so difficult? She tried to hide her own frustration, telling herself the hole in his heart would heal with time. Except she didn't believe it. She'd been gutted too and ached to have that tie to his energy again. But she couldn't rely on Jon forever and needed to find her own strength.

Jàden grabbed his cheeks, his fresh-shaved beard prickling her fingers. Caressing his jaw, each of the fine, dark hairs glistening in the low light, fueled her need for intimacy. "I told you, I have to leave Sandaris."

"Not without me." He slid his hands along her legs. "This is as far away as I ever want to be again."

Her body ignited like an inferno as his soil-brown eyes pinned her in place.

"I made up my mind before we ever left the north. My place is by your side, whether that's here in this city or wherever you Guardians come from." His fingers trailed up her side, tugging at the hem of her lighter undershirt. "I know you're in love with another man, but you ain't gonna get rid of me that easy."

"You misunderstand me." She didn't want to get rid of Jon; she loved him. And yet the intensity of his words left a trail of tingles up her neck.

Except here they were, over a thousand leagues from his home. He and his men had given up so much for her already. Jàden caressed her thumb over his lower lip. Whispers of Kale faded to the back of her mind. She'd been so cold and miserable without Jon's energy woven into her senses. She could kiss him now with no fear of their combined energy forging together, but one taste of him and she'd never be able to let go.

She couldn't put him in danger anymore. "Jon, I can't. If I lose control of my power, you'll die."

"Let me make that choice." His hand slid beneath her shirt as he pulled her closer. "I'd rather die by your hand than live another day without your soft breath on my skin."

He was killing her. She'd never once flinched when Kale decided to follow her off *Hàlon*, but Jon was like a wild stallion and a ship in deep space would surely be a cage he couldn't bear. "You have no idea what you're asking me to do."

"I know exactly what I'm asking." Jon lifted the silver chain over his head and laid the pendant in her hand. "It's been in my family for generations. I want you to have it."

A large red ruby sat in the middle of her palm, cradled by four silver petals. The bloodflower key.

"Is this real?" She turned it back and forth, candlelight glinting off the jeweled surface. Embedded in the gemstone's matrix were millions of lines of code. Instructions for the gates to open and ignite the theric fires between the ship and the moon's surface.

A single energy source to power the gates, but in her mind lurked the one she'd seen years ago buried in the moon's core.

The one that could get them all killed.

She sighed and pressed the bloodflower into Jon's hand. "You can't give this to me. You're a gatekeeper. This key—"

"Is yours." He slipped the chain over her head. "This pendant is my family's legacy, Jàden, and you're the only woman I'd ever let touch it."

A hole opened in her chest as Jon ran his fingers through a lock of hair against her left temple, then wove it into a three-strand braid with a fourth, twisted lock looping in and out of the weave. He tugged a wet thread off her breeches and tied off the end. "My sister taught me how to do that. It means you're part of a family."

"Jon." His words warmed her heart, but they were not enough to fill the hole his strength left behind.

"You're part of our family now. Me and these men," he whispered, the edge gone from his voice.

He slid his hands inside her shirt again and pulled her tight against him. The heat burned along her thighs as she tightened her legs. Letting the bloodflower fall against her chest, she gripped his arms.

His lips brushed against hers and the fire surged in her gut. "I want you to bond with me again so neither one of us is ever alone."

"Jon—" Between the softness of his voice and his mouth so close to hers, she could barely breathe.

"I need you."

Jàden bit down on her lip as the Flame crackled in her veins. She wanted this so much, but the thought of accidentally hurting him stabbed at her heart. He had a raging fire in his soul and the stubbornness of an ox, and she loved him for it.

"You don't understand. I won't be able to reverse it again. We'll be bound until death." Unless they never kissed, but with his breath on her lips, Jàden already knew that argument was useless.

"No, you don't understand. I want this. I want you, my beautiful kóna," he whispered against her neck, trailing his mouth across her skin. "Nakshirnén. Until death."

Without the bond, Jàden could not feel the meaning of the two northern words. Jon had not spoken them before now, and with the fire raging in her soul to feel every piece of this man, how could she refuse? She never wanted him to leave her side.

Tendrils of light lifted away from her arms and dug into Jon's chest until the strength of his energy surged into her once more. She breathed him in, pine and mountain and sea whispering into her essence. "I missed you."

Jon pressed his mouth against hers.

Tugging her shirt into his fist, he pulled her tight against his chest.

As his tongue brushed hers, the fire in her veins wove their combined energy as one, sealing Jon to her as a bonded soul. She wrapped her arms around his neck, pulling him into a deeper kiss.

Jon slid his hands along her back and into her hair. "Don't ever gut me like that again. I'm yours, Jàden, body and soul."

Clutching him tight, guilt tugged her heart. What would she say to Kale if she ever found him? She was family now, but did Jon understand that they could never be too far apart, or their combined energy would stretch to the point of pain? "There's something I need to tell you."

"About the bond," he muttered, capturing her mouth again and kissing her deeply. "It means you're my—"

"Captain." Ashe appeared at the door, graciously keeping his back to them. "It's the old man."

Jon tightened his jaw and groaned against her mouth. "He shouldn't be drunk for at least another hour. What happened?"

Her heart pounded, silently willing Ashe to disappear and Jon to finish his earlier words. It meant she was his what?

"Not sure, Captain. He's on the warpath tonight. Worse than usual."

"You can't fix it?" Jon's voice took on a biting tone, but his eyes burned with desire, all the anger of the past few days gone. He caressed her lip as if he'd rather be kissing her again, and finally shook his head. "Never mind. I'll go shove Malcolm's head in a water barrel." Jon leaned toward her ear, warm breath whispering across her skin. "I won't be long."

She wanted to cling to him, beg him to stay, but something in his voice warned her that Malcolm might be in trouble. Releasing her grip, his strength flowed through her veins once more, strong and sure and bound to her now.

Jàden gripped the edge of the basin.

Jon climbed out, quickly pulled on dry clothing and grabbed his weapons with a lingering glance at her.

"I'll be back."

Then he retreated into the evening air.

## CHAPTER 36

*Felaren*

Jon cursed under his breath as he stormed toward the tavern, the heat of Jàden's kiss like fire against his mouth.

All he wanted was a night alone with her and was determined to give her every reason to stay with him instead of leaving. To stop hunting a dead man she'd never be able to reclaim.

But first he had to take care of the old man. Jon hurried down a series of wooden steps buried in the hillside.

He tugged his collar open, sensing the missing weight of the bloodflower. Maybe giving it to her tonight had been a bad idea, but he'd been trying to work up the nerve to tell her she was an Ayers.

At least she didn't rip the bond out of him again.

The steps ended at a gravel lane winding along the river. At the far end of the rolling lawns, a small tavern nestled beneath a large willow. Amber light glowed from the windows, but no laughter reached his ears. If anything, he should have heard Theryn spouting poetry or some horse shit to the crowd.

Jon threw open the door. Half a dozen patrons were pinned against the wall, Malcolm's daggers sticking through a sleeve or a pant leg. Malcolm leaned back in a chair, a pint in his hands. By the glassy gaze in his eyes, he'd been drinking long before he ever set foot in the building.

The Felaren citizens glared at Malcolm.

"Here to talk, old man." Jon stepped inside the tavern and kicked the door shut. He raised his hands to the side but didn't dare light a cigarette. Not yet, and especially not with Jàden's intoxicating scent still clinging to him.

Every time Malcolm got drunk, his mind blacked out while his body kept on fighting the enemies that killed his wife, children and grandchildren, wiping out his entire bloodline. Any minute he'd start talking about the past. About why he had no one left. Jon had heard the same story for the last twenty years.

"He's my grandson. Did you know that?" Malcolm finished off his pint of réva and slammed it on the table. He stood and kicked the table across the room. "Did you know that?!"

Jon's other men circled the tavern's central area, standing protectively in front of the other patrons and staff. Their expressions were hard. They'd all seen Malcolm crack before, and it was why the old man rarely drank. Something in the last few days must have pulled his past tragedy to the surface— likely the gutting fight between him and Jàden.

"Family's dead, Malcolm." Jon shuffled closer. *He had to pick tonight.* "They died more than twenty years ago. You have no enemies here."

Malcolm threw an ax at him.

Jon shifted aside and caught the handle before easing it down on the table, never taking his eyes off the old man.

"It wasn't right what they did to your family." His chest tightened at the thought of anyone harming Jàden or any of his men.

"Him." Malcolm slammed his other ax into the chair, the wood splitting apart. "What *he* did to my wife. My children. My grandchildren. I only have one left." There were tears in his stormy gray eyes. "One grandson, and if I don't protect him..."

Jon furrowed his brow, edging around the table until they were no more than a dozen spans apart. This was new information to him. "Who's still alive? You never told me."

There was shuffling behind him, the others getting the patrons outside until Jon could get the old man under control.

"One grandson. He doesn't know. Thinks he's alone." Malcolm gripped the ax handle and shook his head. "That boy is never alone."

"Why didn't you tell us?" An uneasy feeling settled into Jon's chest as he inched closer.

"Wherever he is—" Malcolm started.

But Jon clocked him across the jaw, knocking him out cold.

As the old man collapsed, he turned and glared at his men. "What the fuck happened? I told you to find him a companion, not a barrel of réva to drown in." He cursed under his breath and yanked the ax out of the chair. They'd be lucky if the tavern owners didn't have them all arrested. "Get him back to the inn."

As he searched the remaining faces for who might be the angriest—no doubt the owners—his vision blurred. He shook his head, a strange sensation needling his senses.

The room tilted sideways, and he grabbed the chair, crashing to the ground.

"What the fuck is wrong with me?" The ax slipped out of his hand as black oil slid along his veins, covering up Jàden's light.

It doused her breath until all he could feel was anger. Betrayal. Hatred.

"Jàden," he whispered as his head hit the ground. "Someone find Jàden."

## CHAPTER 37

*Felaren*

Jon's kiss burned through Jàden's senses as she scrubbed herself clean and dried off. She should stay and wait for him to return while she relaxed in the heated pool, but the inferno burning through her wanted to tear off his clothes and wrap herself in his heat.

Nakshirnén.

Kóna.

With the bond sealed now, she still didn't quite understand their meaning. Maybe she needed Jon to say them with their energy tied.

The last threads of Kale were slipping away, and she needed to let him go.

No matter how many times she tried to believe he was still out there waiting for her to find him, it simply wasn't possible anymore. She'd seen his ship explode with her own eyes, and these past few weeks, her grief hadn't been nearly as strong.

But that didn't mean she'd ever stop searching for him.

She dressed in clean clothes, let her hair hang loose and stepped outside onto the path, her dirty items stuffed in her bag.

Ashe leaned against a nearby tree, his stance rigid. Even in his most relaxed state, the man always looked ready to tackle a shàden to the ground. He whistled nonchalantly, raising his brows at her as a grin spread across his face. "Fun night."

"Shut up, Ashe." Certain her cheeks were red from embarrassment, Jàden slipped the bloodflower inside her shirt. She was tempted to tell him to shove off, but no way would Jon let her out of sight—not even for a second. Heading toward the horses, she needed to gather her gear and get everything cleaned and ready for morning.

A shadow stepped onto the path, cutting her off.

Jàden hesitated, her eyes lifting from black boots firm against the ground to even blacker eyes in a tanned face. "Éli."

"Run!" Ashe shouted, a knife sailing past her head.

Éli shifted aside, the blade barely missing his shoulder.

Black-clad men melted from the shadows, but even without the tower and two moons emblem on their shoulders, Jàden easily identified their silver weapons.

Rakir.

She inched back, hearing a scuffle behind her. "Ashe?"

But only Éli stood there, tall and thin, with a single sword strapped to his back. His obsidian eyes bored into hers.

She tried to bolt, but he grasped her neck in an iron grip, shoving her against a nearby tree. When she tried to punch him, he grabbed her wrist, stretching her arm to the side and forcing her fingers open.

"No!" She struggled against him, but he tightened his grip on her neck.

Flecks of light and shadow lifted away from her skin.

"You're not one of Jon's sisters. I want to know who you are." A smirk tugged the corner of his lip. "I hear you have the power of a Guardian."

"Get off me." Jàden clawed his hand, trying to peel his fingers away from her neck.

Éli curled his fingers into her hair and pulled until she cried out. He barked a loud laugh. "I've been searching for you a long time, woman."

He pressed his mouth against hers.

Jàden shuddered, shoving against his chest as his hard and demanding kiss stole the fire in her skin. She kicked his legs, but he pressed closer. Her stomach twisted into her throat as she dug her nails into his arm.

Nothing had any effect.

Grasping along his waist for a weapon, her fingers wrapped around a dagger hilt.

Éli groaned, his mouth caressing her cheek to her ear as he spoke in a low, sensual tone. "You must be Jon's woman."

Ice gripped her stomach at the idea of Jon with a lover still in the north.

Jàden yanked the dagger out of its sheath.

He grabbed her wrists and slammed them over her head, the blade cluttering to her feet. Éli breathed in deeply and groaned against her cheek. "Feisty too. I knew Jon wouldn't disappoint me."

"Get off me, shàden breath." She struggled against his grip. "You have the wrong person."

Éli laughed a deep, sinister chuckle from the pit of his chest. The same laugh of her attacker the night Mather died.

He leaned in, crushing her between his chest and the trunk as his mouth lingered close to hers. "We are like brothers, Jon and I. Everything that's his belongs to me."

"I'm not..." Her throat closed around Jon's earlier words.

*You're part of our family now. Me and these men.* He'd been trying to tell her. First in the mountains before Mather died then again tonight. *This pendant is my family's legacy.*

But how?

As if in answer, the moon's heart thrummed against her as the Flame's fire slid into her veins.

"Nakshirnén," she whispered. As soon as her mouth formed the words, the full meaning slammed into her.

Bond of the Flame. Twin souls.

Spouse.

The Sandarin word slid into her thoughts. Its meaning flowed through her skin, a word that didn't exist in her language, but the energy pulled Jon's understanding of the bond into her. She'd not tied their energy together. She'd bound herself as his wife from that first day in the mountains. "Shit."

"Commander Hareth," someone shouted behind her.

Jàden twisted her head so she could see what was happening.

Dozens of black-clad men lined the path with their weapons out.

One said, "Kill this asshole or keep him alive?"

Ashe was on his knees, arms pinned back with their swords at his throat. The humor was gone from his eyes as he locked his gaze onto her. "Run, Jàden. Never stop fighting."

"No." She struggled again, trying to shove Éli away. Fuck everyone else. She wasn't going to let someone else die. She lifted her knee toward Éli's crotch.

But he sidestepped and pulled her away from the tree, pinning her wrists behind her back. "Kill him."

"No, let him go." Her heart raced as fire crackled in her veins.

Ashe struggled, trying to fight off the other men, but the Rakir forced his head back, pouring a milky liquid down his throat. He sputtered and spit, choking on whatever they were shoving into him.

"Ashe!" Tears spilled down her cheeks. She slammed her head forward.

Grabbing her neck before she could break his nose, Éli dropped his mouth next to her ear. "I know Jon better than anyone alive. Now that I have you—"

"Fuck you!" Jàden cried out, struggling as Ashe fought to push the liquid out of his throat.

"Can't be." Éli's hand closed on her throat, his voice growing darker. His finger slipped beneath the bloodflower's chain. He tugged the pendant toward the top of her bodice.

Fuck Frank and anyone hunting her.

She dug her fingers into Éli's hand to focus her power, the Flame's white light burning through her senses.

But it stalled, almost as if an energy barrier protected him.

An oily feeling oozed over her skin, the same icky substance from the withered old man on the ship. Éli must possess the same power they'd wielded.

She cried out, the Flame's power blazing along her arms into him as a seed of darkness thrust into her chest. Anger and vengeance, hatred so twisted it masqueraded desperation turned obsession. Buried under it all, a void dark and wide, empty and hollow.

Jàden tried to push it away—the horrible emptiness that once lurked deep in her own soul, but it kept growing wider, sucking all the light from inside her heart. "Get it out!"

"What did you do?" Hatred burned in Éli's eyes as he stumbled back and lifted his hands. Blackness oozed around his forearms, a touch of light threading through like the rogue lock of hair in her braid.

"What did *I* do? You fucking bastard, Éli, make it stop!" She scratched her arms, trying to get rid of the slimy feeling. When that didn't work, Jàden reached for the Flame and a terrifying amount of power to blast him away from her.

Shadow and light, dark flame and bright, pulled into her.

Ambition flowed through her veins. Obsession. An oily black slick wrapping light and shadow. Her hands shook so hard her wrist hit something solid against her waist.

The daggers. Of course—Jon had her keep them hidden.

She unsheathed a dagger.

An arrow slammed into one Rakir, green feathers shuddering along a pale wood shaft. A dozen more plunged into the soldiers.

"Protect Herana," someone shouted as green-cloaked figures scrambled onto the path.

Éli pulled her mouth to his, kissing her so deep he cut off her breath.

The dark seed sprouted, digging roots deep into her soul and forging a second bond.

Jon and Éli—both whispered through her skin now.

She shoved her dagger into Éli's side. "Stay away from Jon Ayers."

Pain bled into his eyes, and he stumbled back, half the dagger blade still showing. He yanked the weapon out and pointed the tip toward her, blood dripping off glittering silver.

Whatever he was about to say, two green-clad figures crashed into him, knocking him and her blade to the ground.

"Ashe." Jàden ducked a soldier's sword and raced to his side. "Ashe. Look at me."

His body shuddered, spittle foaming at the corner of his mouth.

She slid her arm beneath his shoulder and pulled him upright. "Don't you dare die on me."

A man with a sandy blond beard crouched beside her, his forest green clothing muddied and soaked. "What happened to him?"

"We have to get the poison out." Jàden slammed her elbow into Ashe's gut. When nothing came out, she leaned him forward and shoved her fingers into his throat.

Ashe seized then heaved onto the path.

"That's it." She knelt at his side, forcing him again and again to unload the contents of his stomach as she tried not to gag at the smell.

Ashe shuddered then dropped his head and didn't move.

"No no no." She pressed two fingers to his throat, a faint pulse thrumming against her. "He's still alive."

The blond man rolled Ashe onto his back and pressed an ear to his chest. "The poison's got him now. It must have gotten into his lungs too."

There was something familiar about him. Jàden couldn't put her finger on it, but she could almost swear she'd seen his face before. "Why do I know you?"

He glanced around the path then grabbed a small vial and held it up to the lantern light. "Sejhna. Dammit. You won't find any cure in Felaren."

"I can't let him die." She felt again for a pulse. "Where do I find the cure?"

"Only in the jungle. The fungus must be plucked straight from the earth, or it will have no effect." He pushed back his hood and shouted to his companions, using a language she'd never heard before.

"You." She grabbed his jaw, the same stormy gray eyes locking onto hers like they had days ago. "I saw you, in sahiranath territory."

A woman with platinum blond hair dropped from a high tree branch onto a soldier. She grabbed his head with her thighs and dropped backward to her hands, pulling him down and snapping his neck.

The Rakir retreated. Éli wasn't anywhere to be seen.

The blond stranger grabbed Jàden's shoulder, something deep inside her sensing a long, lost instinct. Some piece of her she never knew existed seemed to slide into place.

"If we can get to the jungle fast enough, we can save him," he said.

She ignored the alien sensation and shoved his hand off. "I have no reason to trust you."

All that mattered now was getting the poison out of Ashe, but as she glanced around the grassy spit of land, Jon and the others were nowhere in sight. They had to know how to help him, but she had no idea where they'd gone drinking.

"We must hurry." The blond man stripped off his shirt, winding it into a thick rope, which he slung beneath Ashe's shoulders. Black lines were inked along his side, an image of a zankata with its wings spread wide and feathers wrapped around his neck.

*Look for this symbol,* Kale whispered into her thoughts.

Jàden grabbed the man's arm, turning him around so she could see a full view of the tattoo. "You have Kale's zankata."

"Yes. We're part of the Tahiró. We serve you, Jàden." He gestured toward the others. Each of the forest figures tugged open a collar or pushed up a sleeve.

They all bore the same tattoo—Kale's zankata.

There was no question in her mind what to do. She had to save Ashe, and she trusted Kale with her whole heart.

"I'll get my horse." Racing to the enclosure, she threw open the fence, startling the horses awake. "Let's go. Ashe needs you."

She slapped Ashe's horse, Hena, on the backside to chase him out of the pen. Grabbing Agnar by his bridle, she tugged him out too and didn't bother closing the door.

"Go find the captain!" she shouted.

The horses raced onto the rolling lawns as she bolted back toward Ashe with his horse and hers. Hena nudged his companion and whinnied.

This was her fault, just like Mather.

She should have used her power, or had she? Jàden clenched her hand, the slick black obsession breathing through her skin.

No, she *had* used her power, but something in Éli doused it—that same kind of power the high council men wielded but stronger.

"I won't let you die." Jàden pulled up her hood then grasped Ashe's hand as several men pushed him onto his horse. She squeezed gently then wrapped her fingers in Agnar's mane and swung onto his back.

They hurried down a dirt path as it wound around the hillock then into a reedy marsh near a river. The swift current drowned out the shouts and noise of the city. Horses picketed near the bank raised their heads and pressed their ears forward. With slender legs and long necks, they were smaller than the norshads.

The sandy-haired man held Hena's mane in one hand, the twisted shirt holding Ashe upright against his chest. They stopped long enough to toss the stranger's saddle on Hena and tie Ashe properly to his horse.

Jàden knotted a lead rope and put it around Hena's neck. "You follow. We're going to save him."

"We'll make sure he doesn't fall." The woman who'd snapped a soldier's neck rode alongside on a short mare, branching brown lines like a birthmark across her pale skin. She shoved something in Ashe's mouth then gestured to several of her companions. "Go find the fungus."

They burst into flocks of birds and disappeared into the trees.

The blond man grabbed the reins and mounted his tawny mare. "Let's ride."

They raced along the ravine. Grassy strips of lawn mingled with reedy marshes and low-hanging willow. Jàden gripped Hena's lead tight, watching Ashe for any signs of seizing again. His breath was shallow, sometimes jerking him when he gasped for air.

She followed the others into the swift-moving waters under a mass of tangled vines and branches. As the river widened, they climbed the bank on the far side and wound deeper into the trees.

Jàden glanced back once, a deep ache stabbing at her chest. *I won't let him die like Mather.*

Lights flashed to the north.

A black splotch flew over the harbor, barely the size of a thumbnail to her eyes. Blue light glowed against the hull as a ship disappeared beyond the sea.

Frank. He was no longer in a scout craft but a Raith fighter, just like the ship Kale had died in.

The blond man doubled back, circling his horse in front of her. His stormy gray eyes were curious. Gentle. "We should go."

Jàden nodded and wrangled Agnar alongside his mare.

She didn't care who the man was or where he came from. His tattoo would lead her to Kale.

# CHAPTER 38
*Gulséa Prison*

The iron bars slammed shut, and Jon dropped his head back against the wall. "Someone get that old man sobered up so I can beat the shit out of him."

Of all the stupid things for Malcolm to do, this was possibly the worst.

Jon's thoughts were all scattered now. Jàden's gentle sweetness was barely a thread of breath whispering through his skin. Something else slid through his senses, a dark, devouring wave of nothingness that threatened to swallow her light.

*Please be safe.* He pulled himself to stand again and pressed his head against the cool iron door. Her kiss still burned on his lips, and Jon ached to rip the bars off their hinges and fight his way back to her, but he barely had the strength to stand. It was hard to breathe too deep without the darkness sliding through every inch of his body.

Whatever had happened to her, it was affecting him too.

Frank must have found her, and Jon sure as shit wasn't going to leave her to suffer like that damn lover of hers. "Hey, guard!"

Several of the prison guards glanced in his direction, but none of them budged. Jon clenched the bars, all too familiar with their behavior. Twenty years of his life spent on the other side meant he knew one wrong word could mean the difference between freedom and execution.

Malcolm groaned from the corner. "Where's my boy?"

Clenching his jaw, Jon turned to glare at the older man. "Ashe ain't here, and he ain't your grandson."

Ashe and Andrew had grown up inside the Colony, a gated community of wealthy families within Ìdolön that never had to live by the rules of the rest of the city. They threw parties, maneuvered marriage alliances and generally congratulated themselves on the wealth they hoarded that kept most citizens on the brink of starvation.

"I ain't talking about Ashe." Malcolm rubbed his head as if he were in pain then skillfully tried to change the subject. "Where are we?"

But Jon didn't miss a beat as he counted all of his men except Ashe and Thomas. The latter had grown up a Tower orphan since he was only a few months old.

*Of course.* Jon groaned inwardly.

Thomas's birth year was the same as when he first stumbled across Malcolm drunk and almost dead in the gutter. Jon clenched his jaw, kicking himself that he hadn't realized sooner.

"Let's just figure a way out of this place." Half a dozen veteran prison guards should have enough smarts to plot an escape.

A group of city guards laughed out loud as they emerged from deeper inside the prison.

Jon couldn't think straight, but the moment he recognized the shorter, more muscular woman, he called out to her. "Guess we're acing this 'fresh start.'"

The woman barely gave him a glance. Then recognition seemed to hit her as she stopped and faced him fully. "From shipwreck to prison cell. I see we've made quite the impression on you boys."

He tried hard to force a smile to his face or at least appear somewhat relaxed. He still had no doubt this woman could see through a lie, so he had to frame his words just right. Maybe if he played off that it was nothing but a drunken brawl, she'd take pity. After all, humans had no abilities like shifters did, so maybe they would be less of a threat.

"Réva's a bit stronger here in the south," he said.

"Where's the woman? She cleaning up after your mess?" The guard narrowed her eyes, glancing at each of them before her gaze met Jon's again.

He had to lie at least a little. Or at least stretch the truth. "She's my wife. We were only trying to protect her."

One of the guards who ignored him before stepped up behind the woman and whispered in her ear.

"Captain, is it?" she asked.

Something in her tone pulled at the hairs on the back of his neck. Jon had good instincts with most people, but this woman's shift in demeanor had just pushed her into dangerous territory. He fought to keep himself upright as sweat beaded along his brow and the ice in his instincts warned him again to watch his words.

"I need to find her," Jon said. "She's in danger."

That at least was the full truth, and thankfully Thomas and Ashe would be with her now. Any real danger and they'd keep her safe, but Jon didn't trust whatever was happening to his body. Almost like an interference with their bond had twisted it up and made him feel like shit.

Whatever was happening, he couldn't fix it behind these bars. "Just tell me what I need to do to get us out of here."

"Serve your time." She turned away and hastened down the hall, calling out over her shoulder. "And next time maybe that old man will think twice before attacking people."

Fuck. Jon cursed under his breath, a dark anger gripping his chest.

Malcolm sat up, groaning again as he clutched his jaw. "I get in a fight or something?"

Jon charged across the cell—he was gonna punch the old man again—but Dusty and Theryn forced him back.

"Not yet, Captain." Dusty's calm tone was about to piss Jon off. "Wait until we're out of here."

Theryn clapped Jon's chest. "Let's just get free. Then you can beat the fuck out of him. And when you're done, I'm gonna strangle him for losing me a shot with that raven-haired temptress."

Jon tried to untangle himself, but as the obsessive darkness pressed in on him again, he glared at Malcolm. The old man had been like a second father to him, but tonight he'd fucked up in a bad way.

"Jàden better be safe, or it's on you."

## CHAPTER 39
*The Jungle*

*The others will find us*, Jàden told herself.

Ashe's life was the only thing that mattered now. She tightened her grip on Agnar's mane, Hena's lead rope rough against her fingers. The narrow path widened onto a road, hard-packed dirt softened to churned mud by weeks of never-ending rain. She touched Ashe's cheek. He was still warm. Still alive, his breathing shallow.

She followed the blond man and his companions deeper into the jungle. Rubber trees and strangler vines clustered together, their roots digging deep into the earth to line each side of the road like a low barricade.

They kept the horses to a fast trot to cover ground, but every second fell like a hammer against her chest. She raced to the front of the line and cut off the leader. "I've studied plants all my life. Tell me what to look for."

He waved the others ahead, bringing his horse alongside hers. His expression softened. "It's called the violet star, a mushroom barely the size of a single firemark."

Violet star. Jàden wracked her brain, pulling forth more than a decade of knowledge. She'd studied some fungi but mostly the species slotted for terraforming projects. "Where do I find—"

"Braygen." He held out his forearm. "Our people will take good care of your friend. I give you my word, Jàden."

"I don't know you enough to trust it," she blurted out before she could stop herself.

But he'd done it again, used her real name though she'd never introduced herself. Perhaps it had something to do with the tattoo across his chest, but it was a mystery she couldn't dive into yet.

Ignoring his offered arm, she turned a circle to search for anything glowing violet. "He has to live."

"Then my life is yours. Until you and your companion are safe." Braygen wrangled his horse around and raced after the others. "Come. We need onions and nettles to help with the broth."

Jàden pushed Agnar to catch up then handed Hena's lead rope to the blond woman. "Take him—"

"Alida." Her hair had been plaited with what looked like vine leaves.

Nettles and onions Jàden knew how to find— especially with onions she could usually follow the scent. But the last sun was already below the horizon, leaving the jungle much darker than their coastal road. If any spider shifters lurked here, she'd never be able to spot their webs. "What of the sahiranath?"

Alida pressed a small leaf into Ashe's mouth. "You won't find them on this road. Not anymore. And Braygen has excellent sight."

Of course, otters were nocturnal.

Though the thought of him breaking apart into a pack of weasels sent a chill up her spine.

Ashe vomited again, brown ooze sliding down his chin onto his clothes. As Jàden sniffed the air for any trace of onion, all she could smell was vomit and mud.

They rode until the sister moons were high in the sky, casting their silvery light through the branches. Soft green glowed high in the trees, foxfire fungi scattering bioluminescence through the jungle.

She searched the brush along the road for any signs of onion, sniffing the air for traces of its strong odor, and finally caught a whiff of a strong sweetness.

Braygen must have caught it too as he wrangled his horse around. "This way."

"Don't let anything happen to him," Jàden muttered, uneasy leaving Ashe. But desperation was slowly turning to panic as she bolted after Braygen.

"He'll be fine, ya," Alida shouted after them, her voice between teasing and somber.

Jàden tried to ignore it as the surefooted horses leapt over felled bracken and raced around large boulders.

Braygen pulled on the reins. "Onion's over there. Nettle leaves should be down the path."

Jàden dropped to the ground, alone once more as Braygen disappeared into the trees. Alone and just left by strangers in a strange land.

*I sure hope you trust these people, Kale.*

The onion scent lured her in like her grandmother's cooking used to. She pulled off her cloak and crawled beneath a large fern into a dark hollow. Patches of long green stems grew among lighter grasses. She dug into the muddy earth, ripping out several bulbs. Unsure which part of the onion was needed—roots, bulbs or stems—she grabbed everything and tied up the bundle.

The jungle went silent, the creepy quiet raising the hairs on her neck.

Jàden scurried back to Agnar's side, scanning the skies for any flash of light. *Please don't find me. Not yet.*

A ship rumbled above the canopy, the sound so low it could be directly overhead. Frank must have turned off its exterior lights.

Jàden ducked her head and leaned against Agnar's neck. She'd forgotten the covering for her mouth, plus everything she and Agnar owned. Her saddle, clothes—everything was still back in Felaren.

"Thomas said we have to act Sindarin." She rubbed the stallion's nose then grabbed a handful of his mane and swung onto his back. "Can you find your way back to Ashe?"

Braygen trotted out of the trees, followed by a dozen small parrots coalescing together into a single man. Parrot-man raced toward Braygen and whispered in his ear then broke apart again and flew into the canopy.

"Another hour. Hurry," Braygen said. A cluster of nettles stuck out of his saddle bags.

They raced to catch up with the others, the ship's engines growing louder. Every nerve in her body on edge, Jàden silently wished she had Jon at her side. By now, he should have found the loose horses and her stuff scattered across the path. Hopefully, he was no more than an hour's ride away because right now she could really use his strength.

Braygen searched the sky, a tightness in his jaw as they caught up with the others, almost as if he recognized the sound. But Jàden pushed that thought aside and pressed a hand to Ashe's forehead. Sweat dripped from his skin, his shorter dark hair soaked.

"Tell me we're close," she said.

Braygen jutted his chin out. "Straight ahead."

"Hang on, brother," she whispered, using the endearment she'd heard from the others. She clasped Ashe's hand and squeezed it tight until they angled off the road into the deeper woods. "Not gonna let him get us, okay?"

The ship's roar dulled to a soft rumble as they stepped into a muddy clearing, a tiny violet light glowing from a shallow puddle.

"The violet star. We're here." Braygen yanked dried branches off the thick underbrush. The Tahiró shoved a bowl in her hand. "We need water."

She dropped off Agnar's back and rooted around for bromeliads, tipping their leaves until the pools of water rushed into the bowl and hoping no small frogs came tumbling out. Agnar followed her around like a stray dog.

"Rest," she whispered, caressing his nose. "Ashe first. Then I'll get you taken care of."

He grunted and dropped his nose to a patch of grass, keeping close to Hena.

Jàden retreated to a smoking fire as two Tahiró tried to feed a small flame. She dropped her bundle beside them and hastened to Ashe's side, laying a hand on his neck.

His skin was hot to the touch, and he kept mumbling incoherent words.

"Stay strong. The others are coming," she said.

"Put his head in your lap, ya?" Alida sliced open the onions, yanking out the interior core of each and pounding them to a pulp with the hilt of her dagger.

Ashe lay stretched out on the ground, the blanket beneath him half soaked with mud. Crossing her legs, Jàden lifted his head into her lap and wiped the sweat from his brow. The fire grew brighter, its warmth radiating. Rain fell heavy on the higher canopy, but by the time it reached her cheek, it was no more than a light drizzle.

Braygen steeped the nettles and onion into a broth, adding in bits of pine bark and an herb Jàden didn't recognize. "Once we put the fungus in him, our men will keep him clean. It is a matter of honor with our warriors."

She frowned then the underlying intent hit her. "The broth will push the poison out. Oh, he'd never forgive me if I had to wipe him clean."

The Tahiró folk laughed, but the sound was hollow.

Alida crouched near the tiny mushroom no larger than her fingernail. It glowed a deep indigo. She pulled out a dagger then nodded to Braygen. "When you're ready."

He ladled some of the broth into a bowl and nodded. "Go now."

Digging the fungus out of the ground, Alida shoved it in Ashe's mouth. Indigo sap bled from the stump and glowed from between his teeth.

Braygen lifted Ashe's head and poured the broth into his mouth, massaging his neck so he would swallow, then poured more down his throat until the bowl was empty. Ashe coughed and spasmed as Braygen pressed a hand over his mouth. "Hold his shoulders and watch your head."

She nodded, laying a hand on each of Ashe's shoulders. "Stay strong. Andrew's coming."

Ashe's stomach gurgled loudly. His eyes popped open, and he sucked a lungful of air. He arced back, coughing and sputtering, shaking his head side to side.

"Let him go," Braygen said.

Jàden released him, laying her hands on Ashe's cheeks. "Braygen, let him—"

Ashe shot up, slamming his head against hers and punching Braygen in the jaw. Pain ripped through her forehead as the men shoved him back down. Ashe coughed again, indigo light sliding into his mouth. He tried to spit it out.

Jàden pressed her hand over his mouth. "Shh. You're safe. Captain's coming."

Ashe's strong hand gripped her wrist as he swallowed the liquid in his throat. "An-Andrew."

"He's right behind us. I got you, brother." Her voice remained soothing as she caressed his hair back, her chest so tight she could barely breathe.

Ashe's grip on her loosened, and his hand fell to the mud.

Jàden gestured toward the few remnants of the broth. "Soak the rest up into a cloth so he can breathe it in. Might help the fungus get into his blood faster."

Braygen nodded and gestured to Alida.

She yanked up the root of the fungus as he soaked the broth up and then smeared any remnants on the rag until small patches glowed.

Jàden grabbed the rag from them and, ignoring the screaming pain in her head, pressed the cloth over Ashe's nose and mouth. "Breathe deep if you can."

Not that he could hear her—he was already unconscious, cheek against her knee.

She closed her eyes and held him tight. "Please, stay with me. Jon can't lose another one."

## CHAPTER 40
*Felaren*

Éli punched the wall again, blood leaking from his torn knuckles as pain from his stab wound doubled him over. "Fuck, fuck, fuck! Who were those bastards?" He kicked a chair across the room, cursing under his breath. "Is anyone following them?"

A dozen men stood at attention, all staring at the far wall. They'd lost three more soldiers tonight, but none in front of him had the audacity to show grief in their hardened expressions. They were as angry as he was.

"We put two men on their trail, Commander." Sweat beaded across the brow of the graying man who spoke. Blood stained his cheeks. "We can have the horses ready to ride in—"

"Then go!" Éli clenched his fists so tight the knuckles turned white around the bloody scrapes. "When Granger returns, we find the woman and kill those green-hooded bastards."

His men saluted and hurried out the door, slamming it behind them.

He hated waiting. Hated not knowing his field of action. Those green-clad bastards had come out of nowhere and stolen his prize. His only consolation was the warm, sensual burning of her kiss on his lips, something he knew would piss Jon off.

At times, he could still remember the rain-slicked alley. The smell of fresh-baked bread wafting from a nearby eatery. Sebastian's last glance as he tried to pull the dagger from his back. Then it was over. He'd crashed into the gutter, lifeless eyes staring at nothing while Éli screamed from the shadows.

He'd been just a kid, but he'd wanted to kill Ayers that night. The Rakir had come and taken him to the Tower, stolen his life before he had a chance to bury Sebastian's body.

"I will not let him win, brother," he growled, punching the wall again. Jon had won too many times, cleverly evading the full wrath of Éli's vengeance.

Now the whisper of soothing rain on his skin was going to drive him mad. Whatever she'd done to him tonight, he could feel her now, a bright light shining on the darkest parts of his heart. In that moment, he both needed her and wanted to kill her.

"Evardo!" Éli righted the chair and plopped down in front of the fire, his injury stinging deep into his side. He stripped off his uniform shirt and leather breastplate then winced as he inspected the stab wound.

His son and servant slipped silently into the room, evading his gaze and likely his anger.

"Stitch this up," Éli said, "and I want to know who the fuck those people were."

Connor seemed to hesitate, too young to really do more than try not to become the focus of his wrath.

But Evardo dropped to their knees with a satchel clasped in their hands. *Would you like me to dull the pain first?*

"No!" he barked much harsher than he should have.

Evardo's shoulders hunched tight.

"I don't care if it stings. I need to be ready to ride ten minutes ago."

He flexed his fingers, softness breathing in his skin. Jon's wife now bonded to him. She was his ticket to freedom from the pain that burned like iron in his heart. *And a Guardian too.*

*They call themselves Tahiró, the future. They're believers of—*

Evardo frowned as if trying to understand something or maybe picking over their words.

"Just spit it out." Éli waved Evardo away and grabbed his dagger from the fire, the blade hot in the embers. He really had no time for a healer tonight. Éli pressed the hot blade against his wound, seething under the burning pain.

*They follow the Guardian. Protect her. One of them is a strange sort of—*

Someone knocked at the door, cutting off Evardo's words. Éli had heard enough anyway. Just a few more assholes in the way of his prize.

"Come." Éli set the dagger aside to cool.

Granger stepped into the room, dripping water across the floor.

"You'd better have good news," Éli muttered.

"The old man was at it again tonight." A grin spread across Granger's face. "Scared them tavern folks half to death with his sob stories."

"I said *good* news, not the insane ramblings of an old man." He flexed and unflexed his fingers again, breathing in the Guardian's softness. "You kill those bowmen yet?"

The smile slid off Granger's face, his one eye hardening. "City guard arrested them before we could move in."

"Are you fucking kidding me?" Éli stood and grabbed the chair, flinging it against the wall. Wood shattered in a dozen directions as Connor ducked and covered his head. "You were supposed to kill those bastards! Not let the city guard have them. Fuck!" He seethed. "Get everyone into woodsman clothing. We're going after the woman."

"Yes, Commander." Granger pressed a fist to his shoulder and exited the room.

Flames crackled in the hearth. Éli opened his hand, black and white flecks drifting away from his palm. The black ones seemed to suck the light from the room, while the softer ones brightened.

"I've got you now," he whispered, groaning at the recollection of her mouth against his. He wanted to drag her to Jon's cell so that bastard could see what he'd lost, but he'd have to find her first.

Éli pulled on a fresh shirt and grabbed his weapons. Kicking open the door, he barked orders at his men and headed to the stables. Time to find the woman before Jon did and make his brother proud.

# CHAPTER 41
*The Jungle*

Jàden leaned against a tree trunk, Ashe's head in her lap as the sky turned gray in anticipation of dawn's first sun. Any moment, Jon and the others would ride through the trees to find them, and yet the past lay heavy on her shoulders.

Two years in a cage waiting for Kale when she should have done more to free herself.

"Maybe we should get you back to the city and a soft bed to help you recover." She traced her fingers across Ashe's forehead, sweat fevering his brow. Breathing shallow and skin pale, Ashe's condition hadn't changed as he fought the effects of the poison. Jàden tucked a blanket around his shoulders to keep him warm. "Hang on a little longer."

Braygen crouched next to her, his stormy eyes flickering with sympathy in the gray dawn light. His chest was bare and his beard freshly trimmed. He must have been cleaning up down by the river. "You need to rest."

"Not until he's out of danger." Picking up a small cloth, she dipped it into the bowl of water and laid it across Ashe's forehead. Yet the zankata inked onto Braygen's chest stayed in her line of sight. Part of her so desperately wanted to learn everything these people knew about Kale, but she'd already spent two seasons trying find him and everything backfired. "I need to return Ashe to Felaren and find his brother."

"Oi, them fucking bastards!" Alida stumbled into the clearing covered in mud, two of her Tahiró companions flowing together from birds to human. "Rakir from Felaren found our tracks, but I killed two more of 'em. Fucking bastards tried to rip my shirt off." She clutched a torn bonding cloth in her hand. "My wife is gonna be pissed."

"When is Sumaha not pissed?" Braygen chuckled as if the situation were amusing, but his features turned serious. "How far back are they?"

"Maybe an hour, but they're ridin' like they got a fire up their asses." She pointed at Jàden. "The skinny one's lookin' for her."

"How many?" he asked, already moving toward his horse as he spoke quietly with Alida.

Éli. It had to be him. Jon and his men would never assault a woman like that. She ignored whatever Braygen and Alida were saying and laid Ashe's head against the ground. "I'll get you back to Andrew, but we gotta hide from Éli."

She wasn't going to let Éli's men finish killing Ashe. Jàden gathered the horses.

"We kept the trail fresh for your friends, but no more. Come, we disappear with the wind." Braygen helped her clear all trace of their passage.

"Can you send someone back to Felaren? I need to get a message to Jon." She clutched the bloodflower's chain then thought better of it.

This was Jon's legacy and the key to the Bloodflower Gate. She couldn't put it in the hands of a stranger.

She cut off a corner of her shirt, dipped her finger in the mud and drew the bloodflower on one side then wrote *sanda ven* on the other. "It will be only six horses like these and their male riders. Jon will have a cigarette in his mouth—that's how you'll know."

Braygen nodded and slipped her message to one of his companions. As they worked the rest of the small camp and lifted Ashe onto a makeshift litter between two of the smaller horses, Jàden needed to be sure Jon found them, even if the message never got delivered.

Only one way she could leave a marker for Jon and not Éli, whose power slid through her veins like rotten slime. She'd give anything to untie herself. His energy was so different. Like a cloud of death and terror on a bright spring day, and she couldn't help but wonder if Jon sensed it too.

Jàden grabbed a handful of mud and drew Kale's zankata on a rubber tree trunk. The Rakir shouldn't have any clue what it was, but if Jon or the others were close, they'd know she'd passed through here.

She was almost done when Braygen grabbed her arm and tugged her to the far side of the trunk.

"I'm not finished."

He pressed a hand over her mouth, his gaze fixed down the path. "An hour my ass."

Back pressed against the tree, she couldn't see anything as hooves thundered against the ground. She closed her eyes, listening to the horses and how the jungle silenced with their presence.

Ten...twelve...

This wasn't the sound of eight riders like she'd grown accustomed to but a distinctly harder rhythm with more tangled beats.

Braygen pulled his hand away from her mouth. When she opened her eyes again, he was watching her. The fine hairs of his sparse beard glistened in the pre-dawn light, nearly the same shade of dusty blond as Kale.

Jàden's heart ached as she traced her fingers along the black lines inked on Braygen's chest as if they would show her Kale's face.

Looking for him again would put Jon at risk, and she couldn't bear if anything happened to him. And now, as Braygen lowered his hand to caress her jaw, she couldn't shake the ease and warmth his presence commanded. Nor the stirring of a buried instinct that he was the key to her past and her future.

Harnesses jingled along the road, and a horse whinnied, shaking her from Braygen's spell.

The Rakir slowed, many of them circling back into the clearing.

"Prints stop here, Commander," one called.

She knew that voice. Twisting around, she pressed her chest against the trunk and peeked out.

Granger, the beefy soldier who'd abducted her in Nelórath, crossed back and forth over the muddy ground. His beard was thicker now, and Jàden couldn't help a faint smile at the patch over his eye.

"They didn't just disappear. Find them!" The shout came from Éli this time, his anger easy to see with the way his jerked his horse around.

His bonded magic slid through her veins as dawn's gray light brought out the deeper shadows in the woods, each branch a little more twisted. Lurking behind a tree wouldn't hide them for long.

She glanced around to see where Alida and Ashe were, but they'd disappeared. Everyone had.

"Spread out into the trees." Éli was practically looking right at her.

The urge to run was so strong she clenched her fists. One little movement and he'd spot her for sure. Or maybe he'd seen the zankata symbol she'd painted.

Something whispered up the back of her spine, the same presence she'd sensed just before Mather died. It seemed to hang like a ghost between her and Braygen as he laid a hand on her waist.

"Keep perfectly still," he breathed.

A horse plodded onto the road just in her line of sight, a young boy clutching the reins with a tall, slender figure holding onto him as if for dear life. Their face turned toward her, a thousand years of anguish etched into their features. They couldn't have been more than twenty and yet wore the fear of heavy abuse in their eyes. A terror she knew all too well.

But it was the young boy sitting in front who held her attention. Hair as black as midnight, this kid couldn't have been more than eight or nine. She recalled the scream she'd heard on the Tower barge only moments before she boarded.

"What are Rakir doing with a child?" Braygen whispered softly, a rigidness to his tone.

"I don't know." She kept her voice low.

The boy sat tall in the saddle, white-knuckling the reins and giving off a vibe of both confidence and terror.

An arrow whizzed by Éli's head from across the road and sailed off into the brush.

Braygen leaned close to her ear. "That's our cue."

As Éli and his men drew their weapons and stalked toward the far trees, she and Braygen crept backward into the brush. He moved as silently as a soft breeze, while she was about as graceful as a shàden climbing a tree.

"Come, Guardian." Braygen untied the horses from a dense thicket of tall ferns.

She nodded as the Tahiró ushered her aside and lifted Ashe onto a makeshift litter between two of the smaller horses, heavy blankets stretched over his chest to keep him warm. One man grabbed the reins and guided the horses.

The thick foliage blocked them from the Rakir, but still the presence lingered over her shoulder as if waiting for something. It had to be the dreamwalker from the north, but why did they not tell Éli where their group was?

*Who are you?* she whispered into their mind, hoping they'd hear.

*I can't hold him off long. You need each other.*

As she followed Braygen, the presence lingered for several long minutes then slipped away as if letting her go.

"Need him, my ass," she muttered under her breath. They hadn't answered her question and Éli terrified her. She scratched her arms as if she could dig out his power and get rid of him for good.

"What is it?" Braygen asked as she turned back.

"Nothing." She had no choice but to move forward and keep Ashe alive. As the Tahiró wiped their trail clean, she climbed on Agnar's back and grabbed Hena's lead line.

Frank's ships crossed over the canopy. She glanced again at the black ink crossing Braygen's chest.

Kale needed her to find him.

To set him free or maybe to erase her guilt that she'd expected him to be her savior. Maybe it was time to save him and follow the trail of life she now had in front of her.

As she nudged Agnar alongside Braygen, she nodded at his chest. "I need you to tell me everything. Take me back to the beginning."

## CHAPTER 42
*The Jungle*

Jàden rode close to Braygen. Exhaustion pulled at her eyelids, but she refused to sleep until Ashe was out of danger. She could do nothing but wait for him to wake up, and she needed answers. "How did you know my real name?"

"I wondered when we'd get around to that." Braygen chuckled. Guiding his horse around a fallen branch, he waited for her to catch up again and moved close enough that their knees nearly touched. "I was born on *Hàlon*, a few years before the war. Everyone knew your name."

"What war? What happened to *Hàlon*?" When he didn't answer right away, she nudged Agnar ahead and cut him off, meeting his stormy gaze. That was when his words clicked. "You're a sleeper."

"Like you." His expression grew somber as the others forged ahead, leaving them alone on the empty road. "I was barely a toddler when the war started. My parents were botanists and trying to earn their Guild badges. They wanted to work on the moon's surface and study all the new flora once terraforming took off."

Jàden's stomach twisted into a knot. Her last day on the surface, when she'd tried to say goodbye to Sandaris, the Guild scientists were still scratching their heads because nothing would grow.

His voice broke her reverie. "My father wanted to fight the Enforcers to free you of all charges that your connection to the Flame put everyone's life in danger. Most of *Hàlon* called you the moon's savior, but Enforcers arrested anyone with even a hint of your power. Protests turned to riots, and riots turned to death squads."

"I don't understand."

Even after her and Kale escaped the moon's core all those years ago, they were still pursued. Barely able to get to the Sandaris surface, they were heading toward the Ironstar Gate when Frank caught up. She knew nothing about a war or any rioting, only that the Guild Council closely guarded the secret truth of *Hàlon's* technology. The firemark bacterium hadn't come from a rim world but directly from the alien starship buried in Sandaris's core.

The one that tethered her and the Flame's power.

She needed to escape Sandaris but couldn't do so without a pilot. And the only one she trusted was Kale.

Braygen grabbed her hand and gently squeezed as if trying to comfort her, despite his words. "Your connection to the Flame, once it came to light, started a war between the Guild Council and *Hàlon's* citizens. They wielded Enforcers to suppress the knowledge that Jason Kale brought to light, but the Enforcers took it too far. Thousands of people got spaced out the docking bays, millions more locked in hypersleep."

"Locked in hypersleep," she murmured. Forced like her. Millions. Jàden was going to be sick, recalling the high numbers on the hypersleep pods the day she'd awoken. As her heart filled with grief, she clutched Braygen's hand.

A hidden instinct pushed to the surface of her senses.

A completeness, peace. As if she'd been searching for Braygen her whole life instead of Kale. His pale, freckled skin seemed to glow with some hidden fire deep beneath the surface.

She yanked her hand back, some small part of her aching to grab his hand again as rain drizzled on her cold palm.

He fiddled with his bow as the flicker dimmed.

She must have been hallucinating from fatigue. Braygen traced his thumb across the polished wood where her zankata was etched. Carved below it was another creature, something she'd seen only once in her life.

The terrifying monster with giant wings and a long tail from inside the moon.

Jàden turned her horse away and nudged him after the others. She didn't want to see that *thing* ever again and definitely not tied to her mark.

But Braygen's words took hold of her gut.

If millions of people had been locked in hypersleep, did it mean they were still on *Hàlon* or scattered across Sandaris like her?

Braygen stayed alongside her for the next few hours while she digested every piece of information from the war after Kale's death to hypersleep. There were so many unknowns, and she couldn't quite put the pieces together.

"Why would Enforcers do such a terrible thing?" She'd met many of them over the years, and despite their duties to follow the chain of command, Jàden had found many of them to be kind, generous souls when they weren't ordered to aim a weapon.

"That part is still unclear." He patted his mare on the shoulder as she shied away from Agnar's nipping. "All I've learned for certain is the Enforcers believed they were under attack and kidnapped all the gatekeepers. They opened the gates and forced a mass exodus to the surface by gunpoint to protect *Hàlon*. Then they sealed the gates and trapped everyone on the surface."

Her fingers itched toward the bloodflower pendant as tears slid down her cheeks. Never could she have imagined a war because of her and the power she wielded or the hypocrisy of the Guild Commanders.

She couldn't shake the memory of the emptiness she'd seen in the Enforcer control room. Guild citizens barely made up a tenth of the population, but they were the ship leaders, scientists, medics and military. All other citizens worked the pipeworks, sewage and water and other essential duties to keep the ship running smoothly.

"The Enforcers control *Hàlon* now?" Even as the question floated off her tongue, it didn't make sense.

Braygen shrugged. "No one knows anymore. But they have the keys, and we can't get back."

Millions of Enforcers plus nearly four thousand years of time would have swelled their numbers to fill the ship with life again. There was a piece of the story missing, but she didn't want to hear any more. Not until she could process what Braygen had already told her.

"So how are you awake?" she asked. Maybe his story would be brighter than the horrors of what happened during hypersleep.

"I was five years old when the Enforcers found us. My mother tried to protect us while my father shouted opposition. The last thing I heard him say was 'Free the Flame wielders' before his head exploded."

"Shit," Jàden breathed, trying to settle Agnar so he'd stop being such a nuisance to the mare.

"I was shoved into hypersleep alongside dozens of other children. When my pod failed, I woke up to my parents' bones scattered across the substation floor."

"I'm so sorry," she whispered, the bloodflower key heavy against her chest. If it was held captive on *Hàlon*, how had it come to be part of Jon's legacy?

Another piece of the story she couldn't yet grasp.

She lifted her gaze toward the storm, the ship far beyond the clouds now and still running on full power.

"Kale and I tried to leave so no one's life would be at risk because of me." The clusterfuck of energy under her skin made her sick. Éli's Flame suffocated everything, rotten oil she couldn't rip out of her veins no matter how much she hated it. "But it didn't matter, I guess."

"You asked how I knew your name." Braygen touched a stray hair, caressing it back from her head. "I've known your face since before I could walk, the woman who healed Sandaris. Your image was in every hall, every library and on every screen."

"And now I'm a Guardian statue in practically every city," she muttered and pulled away.

The fire of Jon's kiss whispered across her mouth. She needed Kale in the cockpit, Jon by her side—and yet Braygen was another link to the life she'd once cherished.

*What a fucking mess.*

The horses trotted through deep puddles, mud splashing up their legs and onto her boots. She needed time to heal from the lonely ache in her heart, not feel the fire of intimacy from every man who touched her like it was her last breath.

She nudged Agnar faster to get away from Braygen and breathe the fresh jungle air. Like with Jon, Braygen's touch elicited a gentle heat that was hard to ignore, and she didn't need to complicate her life any further.

As they broke through the tree line, a triangulation sensor stood in their path, gleaming silver in the storm.

A blue light flashed on top.

"Shit." She ducked her head. This was why Frank's ships kept flying back and forth. His men were setting up sensors to locate her. "Frank has no idea where I am."

Braygen dropped from his horse and flipped open a panel on the sensor pole. He pulled out a wire, shoving it into a datapad he slid from his tunic.

"You have a datapad?" The sight of it straightened all the hairs on her neck.

These people saved Ashe's life, but was it all a ruse to get her closer to Frank? Using the zankata to lure her in was definitely a dirty enough trick for Frank to orchestrate.

After several minutes, Braygen closed the panel and returned to her side. "Someone's sectioned off parts of the coast. Whoever's in the sky, they're looking for something."

He handed her the datapad. The screen showed a half-formed map of the jungle with a honeycomb of triangulated sections. She could almost see their route from Naréa's ship to Felaren, but the map was far from complete. And if she was reading it right, beyond the tower was out of range, until Frank's men planted more sensors.

"We have to get beyond that line of bushes." She handed the datapad back to Braygen, thankful she had gloves on so the system didn't try to read her biometrics.

They rode past the sensor tower and into a muddy field. Jon and the others were still back there, somewhere on Frank's map.

She glanced at the trail behind her. *Come on, Jon. Where are you?*

Eventually Frank would map all of the Dark Isle. But that could take him years, and he certainly didn't have such patience. She imagined him yelling at his pilots and threatening their families if they didn't find her soon.

She searched the sky for starship light, but only low storm clouds greeted her. "Braygen, how did you even find me? It can't be a coincidence."

"A rumor from the north. A Tahiró sent a message claiming the Guardian Herana lit up the harbor and killed a silver sky beast. Our brothers and sisters fled to the coast to find you. One spotted you on a barge two days before I found you near sahirana territory."

"The silver sky beast was a scout craft, and the asshole flying it is the one who started this whole mess we're in."

They rode in silence until the others were in sight.

Braygen's features softened. "We are like the wind now. You will not be seen unless you wish him to find you."

If only she could believe that.

## CHAPTER 43

*Felaren*

Jon clutched his side, stumbling down the long, stone hallway. Guards dressed in black uniforms with bright feathers painted on their breastplates pressed themselves against the wall so Jon and his crew didn't touch them. They all believed he had some kind of plague, and none of them wanted a human in their prison anyway.

"You're a damn genius, Thomas." Jon leaned heavily on the younger man.

"We can't ever return to this city, Captain." Thomas kicked open the door to find rainy drizzle over the foggy metropolis. "Took selling nearly everything we had to bribe that idiot."

"At least it worked. We have to find Jàden." Jon couldn't feel more than a hint of her now, only anger and bitterness suffocating everything within him.

"Found this near the bathhouse." Thomas held out one of her daggers, blood dried against the blade. "I'm sorry, Captain. Couldn't find her or Ashe anywhere."

Jon picked up the dagger, the pain in his heart echoing the day he'd seen his family's ashes. No matter how hard he tried, he couldn't protect his family. Not his sisters, not Mather.

And now Jàden was missing.

"She better be alive." He growled and flung the knife, the blade slamming into a nearby tree. This was Malcolm's fault, and the anger ripped through his chest as he tackled the old man to the ground and clutched his neck.

Tears burned in his eyes, but the merest whisper of her soft breath wove through his skin. It had to mean she wasn't gone yet, but that didn't explain the swallowing darkness unless Frank had done something to her.

The pain in Malcolm's eyes reflected his own. "Forgive me, son. I didn't know she was your wife."

"No one knew!" Jon clenched his jaw to rein in his anger.

"Those two better be alive, or you and I have a real problem." As much as Jon wanted to beat the shit out of him, Malcolm was a damn good tracker. If anyone could find Jàden, he could.

He retrieved Jàden's knife as the prison guards lined up behind them, likely to usher them out of the city.

His horse pressed a soft nose against his cheek and snorted his displeasure. No more familiar saddle on his back, just a blanket and Jon's bags laid on top with Jàden's. "Sorry, buddy. Wasn't my fault this time."

Jon climbed onto the stallion's back and shoved her knife into her bags where it wouldn't accidentally cut him. His fingers traced across her clothing, and the pain of loss tightened his heart again. Whatever had a hold of him was like a bad sickness sucking the light from his body.

"Let's get the fuck out of here."

With no idea where to go, they returned to the bathhouse.

Malcolm hadn't said a word, the root of his silent brooding likely his guilt. It took him damn near an hour, but he finally found norshad hoof prints that led to the river.

"Two sets of prints," he muttered as they reached the other side. "Lotta smaller horses here, leading the way, looks like."

Jon's conscious thoughts slipped in and out as they followed the tracks. He jolted awake hours later, no idea where he was except somewhere deep in the jungle. Flames crackled from a nearby fire, root potatoes roasting on a set of skewers.

"Cigarette," he muttered, trying to sit up.

"Rest, Captain." Theryn laid a hand on his shoulder and tried to keep him down. "You can't keep pushing yourself."

"Give me a damn cigarette!" He tried to swat Theryn's hand away.

Someone stuck a cigarette in his mouth, and he sucked in a lungful of smoke, the pain in his chest easing.

"Jàden." He forced himself upright, leaning against a large boulder. "Where is she?"

"Has he asked about Ashe, yet?" Andrew paced on the far side of the fire, fists clenched around a set of daggers so tight the deep brown of his skin turned pale. "My brother is missing too."

Theryn rolled his eyes. "We found two of Éli's men dead. They're over by that tree, weapons stripped and left where they fell."

The air went out of Jon's lungs. He couldn't seem to get a single thought straight in his head. If Éli had her, she was in far more danger than she might be with Frank. He grabbed Theryn's shirt and pulled him close enough that he could see the rain misting across his umber cheeks.

"Tell me Éli doesn't have my wife." He was going to kill that mother fucker.

"Captain!" Thomas drew his sword as several bright blue birds flew together and melted into the shape of a short, bald man with a long beard.

Jon stumbled to his feet and gripped his daggers, the trees spinning as he tried to focus. The rest of his men circled around the stranger, his bowmen with arrows ready to fire.

The shifter held up his hand, a piece of cloth between his fingers. "I bring you a message from the Guardian Herana."

"Where is she?" Jon growled then bit his tongue. He didn't need to scare the man off before he spoke, but Andrew and Malcolm disappeared, likely to find any other shifters lurking in the trees.

"You are Jon," the bald man said and pushed up his sleeve, a zankata inked into his skin.

"Mother fucker." He let go of his daggers. "Where the fuck is she?"

The man held out his hand, revealing a piece of her shirt with the bloodflower on it.

Jon turned it over, bloodflower on one side, "We're safe" on the other. It definitely belonged to Jàden. "You still ain't answered my question."

"The man was poisoned by Rakir and fights to stay alive. Alida is taking them all to Veradóra, three days' ride if you follow the wind." He crouched next to the fire and drew a makeshift map in the mud. "You are here. The Rakir are here. You must travel the flooded plains to here—Veradóra."

Jon crouched beside the man to study the map as it related to the road. Éli had tried to kill another of his brothers, and the anger burned black inside his heart. He was going to have to put that bastard in the grave if he ever hoped to have a moment of peace.

"Jàden and Ashe weren't kidnapped." Theryn tightened his jaw and eased the tension on his arrow.

"They followed," the bald man said. "She is Herana, always safe with the Tahiró. Follow the wind. You will find her." He broke apart into a flock of birds and disappeared into the trees.

But Jon clenched his fist, and the slick magic flowed like oil in his veins.

"He was telling the truth." Thomas cursed under his breath and sheathed his sword. "If Éli's ahead of us, he might find them first."

Jon tossed his spent cigarette aside and followed the lines of the map. The alternate route would take them several days to find Jàden. But with Éli ahead, they could run into trouble. And damn if Granger wasn't nearly as good a tracker as Malcolm.

"By her own hand, she's safe for now," Jon muttered. "Keep on Éli's ass. Time to pay him back for what he did to Mather and Ashe."

A wave of dizziness crashed over him as he fell to his knees, darkness sliding through his veins on a wave of rage.

"What the fuck is happening to me?" he said.

"We don't know, Captain." Theryn poked the ground with one of his arrows, a rare serious expression on his face. "We thought it might be poison, but then Dusty spotted this."

"Think this might have something to do with it." Dusty forced open Jon's fingers.

Black and smoky flecks drifted away from Jon's palm. A single white spark twisted upward then dissolved into the afternoon air.

Another bond—not his. Was it possible?

He cursed under his breath. He'd never known Éli to possess power like the high council, so it must have been whoever Jàden was with now.

"Someone else bonded her." Or as she would say, tied their energy.

An engine roared in the sky as orange light filtered through the canopy. One of Frank's ships still searching for her, about the only good news he had right now. If she got trapped in a sky beast, he might never find her. Plus, he wasn't sure how to kill Frank yet without learning how to use one of those weapons.

Jon closed his hand and leaned his head back. His chest tightened like a vice.

The blackness gripped his senses as he closed his eyes, trying to hold on to that single spark of light and Jàden's soft, sweet breath on his skin.

Jàden's voice came back to him from the bathhouse, adding a layer of clarity. *If I lose control of my power, you'll die.*

Maybe this wasn't a bond but a loss of control.

"Jàden's in trouble," he whispered, his cheek hitting the mud.

## CHAPTER 44
*Dreamwalker*

*Herana.*

A soft voice whispered in Jàden's thoughts. Pain pounded against her temple, but each time she tried to open her eyes, heavy darkness sucked her back down.

*They're coming for us. We can't hide any longer.* A gentle hand pulled her from sleep into a vivid green meadow filled with bright sunshine and tall màvon trees. Her hair ruffled in the breeze as a pale entity with brown eyes watched her.

Panic squeezed her chest. She recognized the slender figure who rode with Éli. She tried to step back, but the wind only blew harder, curbing her to the meadow. *Who are you?*

*Evardo.* Their eyes filled with tears, mouth unmoving as they spoke with a gentle mind voice. *I have heard your screams my whole life, Herana. You and thousands of others who cannot escape the sleep between one life and the next.*

Jàden's heart hammered with fear as she tried to piece together their words. *You mean those still in hypersleep.*

But that couldn't be. Stasis was supposed to be dreamless.

And yet Evardo nodded affirmation, heavy grief etched into a face far too young to carry such weight.

There was a gentleness about them, a longing so deep she almost expected Evardo to break down into sobs. But still as a companion of Éli, she didn't trust them.

*You're the dreamwalker.* A snarl curled her lip as she thought about Mather.

Sunny trees faded to thin lines of light, a thousand colorful threads webbed together. Soft whispers pulsed along each thread, voices of all the people who had once suffered in Bradshaw's cages.

Jàden could hear them—whispers, screams, aching hearts for all they'd lost. *They're still alive.*

She'd spent two years trying to block out their screams. The pain and loneliness they'd all endured for the sake of Bradshaw's 'science' still stabbed at the deepest part of her heart. *Where are they?*

*Safe, sleeping. They will wake soon enough, and it will begin again.*

The words hit her sharp as a blade. *No!*

*I need to show you something.* Evardo's gentle voice filled with pain as the webbed lines melted away to steel walls.

Jàden hunched as if the walls would crush her, but slowly the truth set in. This was a dream or, at best, some unconscious space inside her head. Evardo was the dreamwalker from the north, and they'd pulled Éli into that young warden's head.

*You killed Mather.*

*I didn't want to.* Evardo squeezed her hand, so much pain and fear in their eyes she thought they might crumble. *My owner made me do it. I am so afraid, Herana, that you will abandon us. If you do, I will be forced to do so much worse.*

*Nobody's forcing you!* She pulled her hand away from him. *What Frank and Bradshaw have done is vile and fractures the essence.*

Evardo stifled a sob as blue light traced through the seams in the steel walls. Jàden followed their path to the cockpit of a small cruiser, large enough to comfortably transport six people from one star system to the next.

"You ready, baby?" Kale sat in the pilot's seat, a headset over his ear.

She settled into the navigator's chair and clutched his hand. Lucie, her black-and-white collie, curled up on the floor between them, panting happily. "I'm with you until the end."

It was the ship she and Kale prepped to leave Sandaris, but they'd never made it further than the Ironstar Tower. *Wait, Evardo. This never happened.*

*No.* Evardo hung their head as the cockpit melted away. *That is the moment that nearly doomed us all.*

Jàden rubbed a hand across her chest to dull the ache in her heart. She'd wished so many times for that moment, just the three of them together. But the dread in Evardo's words gripped her. *I don't understand. This should be a happy moment.*

The vision changed again, showing Sandaris after they'd disappeared from *Hàlon's* radar. Without her, the moon started to die. Small seedlings carpeted the plains then withered once more as her tether with the moon stretched to the point of pain.

*Its agony isn't on the surface but deep within the core,* Evardo whispered as the anguish of a dying, sentient technology withered away, its last breath slowing the flow of power through *Hàlon's* core. The bionet generators exploded, and the Sandarin atmosphere disappeared, spacing thousands of citizens from the surface.

As if in fast motion, *Hàlon* became a graveyard. The cold black seeped through steel welds. The ship drifted slowly away from Sandaris until a fleet of Alliance ships dropped out of lightspeed. Their engineers dismantled the starship and mined the moon until they found their prize.

The gateway core wrapped in a vessel Jàden couldn't put words to.

The shape and color was so alien, and she'd never forget her time inside that awful place and the thousands of chrysalis-like pods clinging to every wall—and still occupied.

*That's their starship, isn't it?*

Evardo only nodded. The ship or creature—she couldn't honestly say which—disappeared into a station built from *Hàlon's* gutted remains. The station and the last of the fleet disappeared until nothing remained but a graveyard of bone drifting in the black.

*This is our future if you leave,* Evardo whispered. *They were right to keep you here. You should have opened the gate the first time.*

Jàden stared at the emptiness, seething anger at Evardo's last words. *You weren't there, and you know nothing.*

Her words came out much sharper than intended, but she refused to take them back. Evardo killed Mather, sided with Frank and Bradshaw. They may have had the gentleness of a lost child, but if she could see inside their head, what would she really find?

Evardo stepped in front of her, a raw terror stark in their eyes. *Please, Herana. You must stay, or both halves of your life-essence will be lost. The one from before and the one you seek now.*

Evardo's mind retreated abruptly as raindrops fell on her face. Jàden jolted awake, her cheek pressed against a soft warmth. Groaning with heavy fatigue, she lifted her head from someone's shoulder, the jungle alive with frog chirrups.

The horrors of her dream lodged deep inside her chest, stirring up that unknown instinct deep in her bones.

Beside her, Braygen leaned against the tree trunk, tracing his thumb across the hilt of her dagger and the strange orb with trailing legs. "You okay?"

"Bad dream." She sat up straighter, gripped her head in both hands and leaned against her knees, trying to shake away the anger.

"Where did you get this?" He gripped the obsidian blade and offered her the hilt. Something in his voice had become guarded.

"From the crew on the *Darius*." She sheathed the dagger and leapt down from the low branch. An engine rumbled overhead, its gray hull practically invisible against the clouds.

But Evardo's words hit her again. *They're coming for us.*

Us. As if Evardo was somehow involved in all of this. Though with their strong dreamwalker abilities, Bradshaw would scoop them up in seconds.

"Tell me what you saw." Braygen placed his hands on her shoulders to stop her pacing, his eyes a gray storm of emotions.

"No." She ached to hug him. To hold on tight as if he might shield her from what Evardo had shown her. She clenched her hands to keep herself rooted in place. "I don't know. But the man from Felaren who held me pinned, he's got a dreamwalker with him. A powerful one."

Someone who could show her whatever they wanted her to see. Maybe Éli forced their hand now, furious that she'd disappeared with the wind. Or maybe he'd found Jon instead.

Jàden pulled away and resumed her pacing.

*This is our future if you leave. They were right to keep you here. You should have opened the gate the first time.*

She cried out in frustration. Frank had never been in the right. Opening that gate was too unpredictable and could easily make things a lot worse.

*You must stay, or both halves of your life-essence will be lost. The one from before and the one you seek now.*

This one hit her chest hard. The one she sought now was easy to figure out—Kale. But another half of herself, another soul mate.

Maybe that was Jon. Except she'd met him after Kale, not before.

Braygen leaned his shoulder against the tree and watched her calmly, only his eyes in turmoil. She couldn't say if it was about the symbol on her dagger, her anger or something that happened while she slept.

"We need to get out of here." She couldn't stay all day fretting about Evardo or whatever they had planned with Éli.

The ship roared again and lifted skyward, zipping away into the storm. At least that was one problem gone, and yet she still couldn't shake Evardo's vision. She had no reason to trust them, but there was no way they could have known about the inner gate and the moon's sentience. No one knew except her and Frank and a few dozen others who could be dead or in hypersleep.

She crossed the small clearing to check on Ashe, his eyes open and staring at the sky.

Relief washed through her, sweeping away her anger. "You're awake."

Ashe groaned and rolled to a crouch. "Where's Andrew?"

She pressed a hand to his forehead to check for any lingering fever, but he batted her away. "Andrew's with the captain," she said. "They should catch up tomorrow."

Still pale and weak, his gaze darted between the Tahiró. Ashe grabbed her dagger and slid it out of its sheath. "Where the fuck are we?"

"Peace." Jàden lowered his hand. "These people saved your life."

He grunted and flipped the blade against the flat of his arm, his dark eyes boring into hers. He shoved past her and climbed onto Hena's back. "Shouldn't have left the captain."

"What was I supposed to do, let you die?" she said. The others were waking up as she grabbed Hena's bridle. "It's been three days since Felaren. Just listen and don't charge off like a stubborn ox."

If a glare could kill, Ashe's would have sent a dozen spears straight into her heart.

Letting go of Hena, she placed a blanket on Agnar and climbed onto his back. "The captain knows we're safe."

"Not likely," he muttered, glaring at Braygen. He coughed a deep hack strong enough to make him grip his chest. "I don't like that guy. He's keeping too close a watch on you."

*Aren't you a ray of sunshine.*

"You've been awake all of ten minutes." Jàden nudged Agnar between the two men while the others packed up. She tried to tell Ashe everything that happened since Felaren. "Éli's here with thirty Rakir and a child."

"A child?" This seemed to snap his attention back to her. He practically barked his words at her. The poison must have erased any sense of humor he once owned. "That bastard cares as little for a child as he would a dead whore. Boy or girl?"

"Boy, seven or eight. Why?"

Clenching his jaw, he kept opening his mouth as if to say something then shutting it again. "We need to find the captain."

"Good to see you alive, soldier." Alida nudged her horse alongside, grinning at Ashe. The dark branch-like birthmarks against her pale skin seemed to stretch with her smile. "Come, we ride for Veradóra. If you're nice, I'll let you sleep with me and my wife tonight."

That seemed to get his attention. Ashe turned his horse around and followed. Jàden rolled her eyes and patted Agnar's shoulder. They trotted along a narrow trail through the trees, the ferns so tall they stretched over her head.

For the next few hours, Alida led them through thickets of wood and over large, fallen trees while Braygen stayed close to her side. The invisible trail became more defined as a dirt path, tiny glowing lanterns along one side. The pathway curved along the cliff, opening into a wide meadow filled with horses. Several women stepped from the trees, orange-fletched arrows nocked in their bows.

A woman with umber skin and black hair curled tight against her scalp stood ahead of the others, tiny leaves and flowers growing along her arms. "Rakir are not allowed in Veradóra."

"Do you see a Rakir uniform?" Braygen's voice was laced with a hard edge as he trotted ahead. "You do not rule this land, Sumaha. Not yet."

Jàden grasped the dagger from Ashe's hand and returned it to its sheath so he'd be a bit less threatening.

"Northmen do nothing but destroy." Sumaha eased the tension on her arrow. "You are a fool to bring him here."

Alida dropped from her horse and raced to Sumaha, pressing her forehead against the dark-skinned woman. She whispered something in a language Jàden didn't understand, but the sentiment was clear.

This must be Alida's wife.

"Not Rakir." Ashe's deep voice sliced through the air. "Hunted by Rakir because my brothers and I protect Herana."

Sumaha cursed under her breath and wrapped an arm around Alida. "You leave at dawn. We do not want your hunters in our land."

"Guess that means I ain't sleeping with them," Ashe muttered.

Jàden scanned the others, all women, and each one looked ready to put an arrow in Ashe. Yet they welcomed Braygen with open arms, hugging him like a long-lost brother or punching him playfully on the shoulder. They were wary of her though, even when she dropped her face covering. The branches were so thick overhead she doubted Frank could get more than a heat signature off anyone.

She slid off Agnar's back and scratched his cheek, watching the trail behind them as if Jon would ride around the bend at any moment.

Ashe held Hena's reins as he stepped close to her. "Be careful what you say. I don't trust these people, and neither should you."

"They killed Éli's men and kept you alive." Jàden unclipped the reins from Agnar's bridle as his ears practically zeroed in on a herd of short horses at the far end of the field.

"You trust too easy," Ashe muttered. "Have you learned nothing?"

She unbuckled the twin dagger sheaths and handed them to Ashe. "Then here. Take it."

"The captain would murder me." He shoved them back. "Rule number one, Jàden: I am your weapon."

She bit back a harsh reply as Braygen clapped her on the shoulder. "Come, I will get you both settled. Alida already has scouts searching for your friends."

## CHAPTER 45

*Veradóra*

"I promise I'll get you back to Andrew." She leaned against the rail, overlooking a large valley illuminated with glittering silver light.

Pain etched across Ashe's dark eyes with each breath, but he squared his shoulders and stood beside Jàden as if he was fully armed. Sick or not, he wasn't about to let anyone harm her.

Kóra trees, each with trunks wider than a cottage, were connected by a labyrinth of hanging wooden bridges. In the middle of the web of walkways was the largest tree Jàden had ever seen. As wide and tall as any of the Sefirön towers, its branches spread a canopy over the entire valley.

But unease tugged at her gut. The walkways were eerily quiet when they should have been full of life.

Ashe seemed to sense it too. He nudged her shoulder and pointed up. Giant nest huts hung in the high branches, built with mud and sticks that made their shadows eerily spider-like.

"You should sleep." Exhausted as she was, Jàden's mind raced with thoughts of Jon as the last sun set, the lanterns in the village brighter than an hour ago. The lake below shimmered each light's reflection, like a sea of stars below her feet that stretched the length of the valley.

Ashe opened his mouth as if to fight her on it but doubled over and hacked again, a dryness to the wretched sound. The poison still had the last few tenuous claws in him.

Jàden helped him into the small cottage inside the kóra trunk. "I mean it. Rest. We can't do anything until Jon's here."

Or Éli found them.

But she didn't want to bring that stressor bearing down on Ashe's shoulders. As he finally relinquished and crawled into bed, she closed his door and leaned her back against the solid wood.

Braygen waited for her, dressed in fresh clothing with his beard neatly trimmed. "Coffee?"

"Yes, please."

He pressed a cup into her hand, warmth seeping through to her palms.

"Any news yet?" Her stomach knotted at the idea that Éli could be lurking at the borders of Veradóra when Jon and the others arrived.

Braygen shook his head, a shadow in his eyes. "No word yet."

She leaned against the rail, soft laughter echoing from high in the canopy. "How long have you been awake?"

"Two hundred and thirty-seven years."

Her hands froze halfway to her mouth as she tried to sip her coffee. "Impossible."

"Hypersleep slows the aging process." He leaned on the rail, watching her closely as if trying to work something out.

Her cheeks warmed in embarrassment as she studied the dark liquid, wishing it could unlock all the truths she so desperately sought.

"You asked me to take you back to the beginning. What did you mean by this?"

"I don't know anymore." Jàden clenched her cup tighter. Kale's words seemed like they were spoken a lifetime ago. The first time they met was on *Hàlon*, their first dance at one of her grandparents' parties. And the first time they kissed was during a dust storm. "There's someone I need to find, but every time I try, death follows."

She clenched the coffee cup, Evardo's words still brewing turmoil in her thoughts. Kale was her pilot, the love of her heart. And she had to get away from Sandaris and the *thing* buried in the core.

Yet all she could think of was Jon. His kiss no longer lingered on her lips in the cold rain, but the fire in her heart still burned for him.

Except it shouldn't.

She hadn't seen him for days and ached for his presence. But *the one from before and the one you seek now* wouldn't leave her thoughts. Evardo's words rang with a truth she didn't want to believe.

"I don't know what you learned of me as a child, Braygen, but—"

"It doesn't matter what I knew. I learned the truth when I took the Tahiró ink." He leaned his elbow against the rail as he faced her fully now. "I see the truth now with my own eyes, Jàden Ravenscraft."

The bloodflower seemed to get heavier the moment he spoke her true name. She'd wanted to thank him for what he'd done for Ashe and set him straight on the whole Guardian thing, but it didn't seem to matter.

She was Herana in his eyes, no matter which name he used.

"You don't know anything, Braygen. No one does." Bitter frustration welled in her chest that she couldn't tell him everything, not without putting him at risk too. He and Alida has shown her nothing but kindness, and the thought of hurting them tugged at her heart.

"I see loneliness." His voice softened. "The deep ache that comes from too many years of loneliness. Of a burden so heavy it threatens to crush your soul."

"You're wrong," she whispered, the tremor in her voice betraying the lie. Every word hit like a hammer as she shoved the coffee aside and turned away. She couldn't let him see her tears. Or the weight of the inner gate, Bradshaw's lab full of innocent, tortured lives or that all she ever wanted was a quiet, monotonous life without the Flame ripping through her senses.

"Then offer me one night," Braygen said. "Prove me wrong or let me help drive away the emptiness for a time."

Jàden's heart skipped as she faced him again. She ached for touch, for the warmth of intimacy so she could pretend the pain in her heart didn't exist. A chance to escape the lonely grief—something she desperately ached for with Jon.

Braygen stepped closer and touched her cheek, thumbing away a stray tear. "You wear no bonding cloth. I have no wife. Let me dry your tears for a night and put your heart at ease."

She swallowed the lump in her throat, his fingers warming her cheek.

There was gentleness in his gaze. A promise that he could make her forget all her troubles until the cold and bitter Sandarin world ceased to exist.

But she loved Jon. She loved Kale.

She was a walking disaster of emotions that none of them deserved.

"I can't."

"This pain will not go away. It will only fester." He caressed a lock of hair away from her neck. "What can I do?"

Despite the things he'd told her, she knew almost nothing about him, and yet the warmth of his fingers against her skin seemed to dig deep into her soul, tugging at something dark and angry far beneath the years of pain and loneliness. Almost as if they had a connection from another life.

"No." Jàden stepped back, pushing his arm away.

Bitterness welled in her as she thought of Frank. Of two years stripped of her dignity and senses to become this creature who needed to be touched, desperate for intimacy and a hero to save her.

"Guardian." A strong, feminine voice sliced through her thoughts. Alida's wife—Sumaha—stood behind Braygen. "We must speak."

A chill crept up Jàden's spine. She met Braygen's gaze, the storms back in his eyes, but she could not see past his shields. "Will you keep an eye on Ashe?"

His expression softened as he tugged aside his collar to show his tattoo. "By this ink, my life is yours. The offer stands for whenever you need it most."

"Thank you." She pushed past him but didn't look back.

Braygen had no idea how tempting his offer was. Kale would never have to know, or Jon, about how much she burned with the idea of intimate heat against her skin.

But the bloodflower hung around her neck like lead, and Jon's words whispered through her thoughts. *I know you're in love with another man, but you ain't gonna get rid of me that easy.*

If he only knew the truth.

She was in love with him too.

The wind blew a chill across her cheek, as she followed Sumaha onto a well-packed path that rose along the cliff. Birds called from high in the canopy, verdant leaves dark against the evening sky and ominous thunderheads. Jàden pushed aside stray branches, fingers scraping over sharp thorns, velvety flower petals and prickly leaves.

Energy pulsed into her fingertips. Jàden sensed the mark of the Flame as she pulled back, inspecting her hand. "What is this place?"

"Where no man can tread." Sumaha's curt response sent another chill through Jàden. "You do not protect this world, Herana. We do. You protect the northman, whose existence stains this world."

Jàden's hands clenched as they stepped into a clearing. Water rushed over a large boulder into a pool of crystalline purity. Shelora's moon was already above the horizon, its full phase casting a bright glow upon the land.

"He's a good man," Jàden said. "Only the poison seems to have erased his sense of humor."

Sumaha rounded on her. "He is a northman. And you are protecting him. They steal and rape and burn anyone in their path."

So this was why Suhama wished to speak with her.

Jàden clenched her jaw, fighting back a scathing remark. This woman judged her, the light of doom flickering across her eyes.

Sumaha had no right to be angry at her.

"Ashe and his brothers saved my life, and I will be forever grateful. These men are not villains. They protect me, and I'm trying my hardest to protect *your* world," Jàden said. Ashe was alive, but all the anxiety of his brush with death, coupled with Evardo's dooming dream, boiled to the surface. "So don't any of you dare tell me I'm a destroyer or that the *outlawed* Rakir I call brothers are. You know nothing, Sumaha."

"I still do not trust them."

Jàden clenched her fist to hold back her irritation as Sumaha regarded her with a stony gaze.

"Come." Sumaha trudged deeper into the field.

Soon they were surrounded by tall grasses forming a barrier around a large willow. Sumaha pressed aside the curtain of leaves, gnarled branches twisting away from the trunk in a dozen directions.

The air cooled beneath the willow's shadows. Trying not to shiver, Jàden stepped through the far branches, hanging in a curtain of leaves.

Low ultraviolet light blazed across a second clearing, this one larger than the first. Rows of corn and tomato, leek and gourd, filled every inch of the wide-open space. Tall willows and almond trees arched high overhead, the canopy of branches like a dome keeping the light inside.

Jàden walked along a row of tomatoes, touching the soft fruit with her fingertips. Peppers grew on the other side, green and purple, red and yellow, balls and long, curled arcs. She breathed in the heavy aroma, a blend of flavor and a symphony of color. She ached to pull off a smaller tomato and pop it in her mouth, but she refrained under Sumaha's hawkish gaze.

"I do not believe you are the Guardian," Sumaha said abruptly.

Light pulsed along the ground, catching Jàden's eye and disappearing into the dirt. Ignoring Sumaha's comment, she crouched over a plastic tube and traced her fingers on the arced section looping above the ground. The light flashed again, power surging in waves from one end to the other.

This was *Hàlon* technology.

She followed the line of plants. Several more tubes arced above the ground, no more than a zip of light from one patch of muddy soil to the next. They pulsed in the same direction. As Jàden passed rows of pumpkin and patches of herbs, the light converged into a pattern. Rock rose ahead, a sharp plymouth covered in lichen and soaring into the high canopy.

*It's a starship.*

Except this one didn't have her zankata painted on the side but the orb and trailing legs like her dagger hilt. Jàden tugged her shirt over the knife sheaths as if they somehow cursed her.

The top of the tail fin was nearly invisible, black shield plating and sharp edges burrowing down into the rock. She followed the line of the craft, guessing it to be a small cruiser with the nose buried far beneath the high meadow.

Unease tugged at her gut. A war, the gates shut down. *Hàlon.*

"What's inside that ship?" Jàden asked.

Sumaha waited for her by a large sheet of glass standing upright in the dirt. Rocks and flowers lined the base, bright yellow blossoms unfolding between the tight spaces. "You will show me what's inside. Put your hand here."

Biting down on her lower lip, Jàden stepped to the shield glass and held her hand up. A pang of guilt thrummed through her chest. She so desperately wanted to see Kale again, but she definitely did not want to call Frank to her location.

She let her arm fall to her side. "No."

"Open the ship, *Guardian*." Sumaha nocked an arrow onto her bowstring and aimed at Jàden. "You are a Guardian. You must know how to open it. I do not want that shadow"—she gestured to the orb symbol—"over Veradóran lands."

"You'll die if I touch that screen." Jàden glared at her, almost daring Sumaha to try and shoot her. "I won't—"

"Sumaha!" Alida's loud shriek reverberated across the garden as a dagger slashed through Sumaha's arrow. "How dare you threaten Herana."

Jàden eased back, happy to let Sumaha take the brunt of Alida's fury.

"She is not to be trusted." Sumaha had a fire all her own as the two went head to head. "A woman who rides with northmen and brings their hunters to our land. Why do you believe in this legend?"

Their argument escalated, and both fell into the soft rhythm of a language Braygen had spoken earlier in their travels.

Jàden eased back until they no longer noticed her. But she couldn't keep her eyes off the ship and the strange painted marking. Someday, she'd need to understand where it came from, but today it only seemed to present danger.

And the last thing she needed in her life.

It was time to find Kale. Find the beginning and put an end to her journey.

## CHAPTER 46

*East of Veradóra*

Éli seethed. He wanted Jon's woman, but the sky beasts were making a mess of everything. The nearest one opened its belly, dimming its fires.

Granger put the spyglass to his eye. "What are you thinking, Commander?"

His men spread out across the ledge, uncertainty in their eyes. They'd lost five soldiers to those shifter bastards in the last two days, and the Guardian's trail had disappeared. Now more sky beasts were following, but this was the first time he'd spotted one on the ground.

Several figures emerged from its underside and spread out across the field. One kept poking something on his wrist while others set up a tall silver tower.

"They look human, sir," one of his men said. "How is that possible?"

From what he'd seen in Nelórath's harbor, humans controlled the creatures from the inside.

Éli wanted one for himself.

If he could figure out how to control it in the sky, he could capture his woman and be halfway across the sea before Jon could blink.

A figure removed his helm—*her* helm. Bright red curls tumbled past her shoulders, but the woman pulled her hair back in a knot and shouted orders at her companions. The woman was too far away to hear her words, but the body language was clear. She was in charge.

"They're looking for the Guardian," Éli muttered, anger gripping his chest. Another question among thousands burned through his thoughts. It was time he learned where the Guardian came from and why Jon protected her. And he sure wasn't going to let these bastards get to her first.

"I'll be back." He clapped Granger on the shoulder. "Kill them all."

Slipping away from the others, Éli circled quietly through the woods until one figure was no more than a dozen yards away, pressing his back to a tree. The helmed figure wore bizarre gray clothing, a flame inside a circle on his shoulder. He wasn't Sandarin and, by the black weapon slung over his arm, would likely go on alert with any small sound.

Crouching on his hands and feet, Éli crept into the overgrown grass, careful not to rustle even a single blade.

Easing close to the figure's feet, he rolled onto his back and swept the man's ankles. The bastard slammed onto Éli's chest, hands already on the weapon.

Grabbing the figure's neck, Éli twisted until it snapped.

Éli yanked the glass helm off the dead man and stripped away the gray uniform before elbow-crawling back to the tree line. He pulled the gray uniform on, hiding his clothes and sword deep under a knot of thick foliage.

Lighter than his uniform, the gray material was loose and warm, but the smell was terrible. Éli tugged the helm over his head. Strange symbols illuminated the bottom corner, but he could see perfectly through the glass front as if the sun shone brightly.

Voices spoke in his ear, but he ignored them and grabbed the weapon, blue light glowing from its embedded firemark.

Everything had gone to shit again and again.

This time he wasn't going to lose.

As if Sebastian watched from the grave with his approval, Éli kept his eyes on the beast as he stepped into sight of the others. Someone shouted in his helm, and he hit the side. Now was not the time to be hearing voices.

"Tower assembly complete," a woman said in the Guardian language. Her voice was sharp and rough. Pain throbbed in his skull. Éli shouldn't be understanding her words, but each phrase melted into the silk of his power, leaning him into comprehension.

"Rogers?" Her voice came through his helm again. "Quit playing with your bugs and help us get this thing working."

Laying the weapon across his shoulders, Éli raced toward the sky beast and into its belly. Metal lined its insides, threads of light weaving patterns toward its main intestinal system.

There must be a way to control it, maybe near the head. Tossing the strange weapon aside, he unsheathed his dagger and pressed his back against the wall, peeking into the intestinal hall.

Lights glowed along metal seams in a narrow corridor filled with curved, alien lines that made his head pound.

Éli crept along the smooth walls, overhead squares glowing with a soft light. Sebastian had told him once about bugs that lit up inside their bodies and the jungle filled with bioluminescent fungus. But this place gave him the creeps.

A door slid open at the end of the corridor.

Two figures sat side by side, a man and a woman bound to their seats.

The man turned around, anger etched into his features. "The fuck are you doing, Rogers? General Ka—"

Éli drove his blade into the man's neck and grabbed the woman's throat. "How the fuck does this thing work?"

She pressed a patch of light.

He yanked the dagger out of the man's neck and slammed it through her hand. "Where's the Guardian?"

The female screamed, tears forming at the corner of her eyes. Blood leaked from her hand into the lights. She started to speak, but Éli tightened his grip on her throat.

Glass spread over the front of the three-seat room, small symbols scrolling across the bottom in a series of boxes.

Éli pulled her face close, practically smelling the fear roll off her in waves. "You're going to help me find her."

A noise echoed his words, speaking in the language of the Guardians.

The woman seemed to respond to the voice, tears leaking onto her cheeks. "Wh-Who are you looking for?"

He narrowed his eyes, taking in the lights and symbols on the glass, almost grasping their meaning. "Guardian Herana, my wife."

A strange ache pressed on his chest.

Jon's wife—his wife. He hadn't really thought about it before, but what if Jon had bound the Guardian too? The idea of his enemy possessing magic set Éli's nerves on edge.

The woman panted in her seat, her pained features tight from the knife buried in her hand. Rapid-fire noises came from somewhere outside the beast.

She showed Éli her other palm then slowly lowered her hand to press a lit circle. "General, we have a—"

"You'd better have good news." A face appeared on the glass, sandy brown mohawk crowning an older face with a thick beard. Ink lines tattooed the man's neck, which stretched tight as he pulled a cigarette out of his mouth. "You. The one with the small boy."

Éli growled.

The bastard from the first sky beast whose leg had been twisted the wrong way. He'd recognize the man anywhere by the steel flint etched into his wrinkles. "Who the fuck are you, and why are you chasing *my* Guardian?"

The older man slammed the glass. "Costa, get that fucker in a cage and bring him back to the lab. He knows something."

*Get out of there,* Evardo screamed into Éli's thoughts, voice panicked. *They want to hurt you.*

Images flashed in his head. The Guardian screaming inside a glass cage. Her body deteriorating until she was skin and bone.

The pain and tears ripped into the blackest part of his soul.

Éli had spent his life suffering that kind of anguish. Watching the light fade from Sebastian's eyes and screaming as the Rakir dragged him away. He'd never buried his brother, the body discarded with hundreds of others inside a giant kiln.

His eyes stung as he clutched the woman's throat tighter. "How do I fly this thing?"

*Commander, run!*

The woman's hand shook as the translation reached her ears. She closed her eyes, tears sliding down her cheeks. "I'll never tell."

He slammed his hand on the lighted symbols, black fire burning through his senses as he unleased the Flame's power building inside him. "Get this thing in the sky!"

Something solid pressed against the back of his head. "Step aside, asshole."

Releasing the dagger, Éli dodged to the side and slammed his elbow into a glass helm. Loud noise screamed into his ears as he twisted around the second figure and snapped her neck, the woman dropping to the ground. He ripped off her helm, red curls spilling onto the corrugated metal.

He grabbed his dagger and shoved it into the seated woman's throat, blood spilling down the front of her uniform.

The man in the glass shouted a string of obscenities. "When I find Jàden, I'm going to hunt you down and put a dozen holes in your head."

Éli wiped his blade clean. "Stay the fuck away from my wife."

A loud noise rattled his ears, the beast's belly starting to close.

*Run! More are coming.*

Ignoring Evardo's cries, Éli bolted down the corridor and leapt out of the beast. His men circled the field, but the other armored soldiers had disappeared. Probably dead on the ground.

Éli ripped the helm off and threw it at the sky beast, roaring in frustration.

Evardo sat astride their own horse now, thanks to the men they'd lost, but Éli grabbed their shirt and threw them to the ground. "I told you to stay the fuck out of my head."

Curling up into a tight ball, the servant covered themself and tried to stutter out an apology.

"Shut the fuck up." Éli grabbed Evardo's scruff and dragged them to their feet. "Tell me where she is!"

The idiot wiped an arm across their tear-stained cheek and pointed south, an entirely different direction than they'd been traveling all morning.

"Stop crying like a blubbering idiot and be a man." Éli shoved his servant aside in disgust. If it wasn't for Evardo's ability to see through the eyes of others, Éli probably would have killed the bastard weeks ago. "She'd better be in my grasp in the next forty-eight hours, or you can say goodbye to that head of yours."

Seething with fury and certain the mohawked man would have another sky beast on their ass, Éli gathered his clothing and weapons and climbed on his horse. "We don't stop until I find my prize."

## CHAPTER 47

*Veradóra*

Jàden's thoughts raced as Ashe paced back and forth, both of them worried that Jon and the others still hadn't arrived.

"You shouldn't have slept so long," he growled at her. "We should leave this place."

"I'm not going anywhere." She wove her hair into a single braid.

She'd made up her mind on the verge of sleep that the Tahiró hadn't inked their skin to be part of a club. They knew something—she just didn't know what yet. She and Ashe needed to get back to Jon and the others, but maybe here she had a real shot at finding Kale and figuring out what to do next.

"Where's Braygen?" she asked.

Before Ashe could answer, she spotted Braygen on a high bridge and trudged toward him.

A life on the run was something she couldn't continue, and fear lurked in the back of her thoughts that maybe something bad happened to the others.

Braygen met her halfway.

"You said you learned the truth when you took your ink," she said. "Where's Kale?"

He tightened his jaw and glanced around the village as if trying to decide what to say. Finally, his stormy eyes found hers. "Commander Jason Kale entrusted the Tahiró with a secret. I know who you are, Jàden, but some of the others aren't so sure."

"Commander?" Last time she'd seen Kale he'd been a sergeant. He must have been promoted during her absence. But before she could dwell on that, she needed to know what this big secret was. "Show me."

He nodded once. "Come."

Several villagers crept onto the walkways. They did not draw their arrows but watched with an eerie anticipation. Alida and Sumaha stood together on a higher path, arms around one another, appearing to have resolved their argument.

Ashe stuck like glue to her shoulder as they followed. "What's with them?"

"They want to know if she is the one." Braygen led them across several wooden bridges, though he held tension in his hands as he opened and closed his fist.

Jàden wasn't certain if it had to do with Ashe or something else, but it reminded her of Thomas when he was fighting pain in his muscles.

"The one what?" Ashe asked.

"You will see." The bridge led to a muddy path along the valley wall. Roots and brush dug into the mud, clumped together to form a narrow alley between the leaves. Thorns pulled at her clothing, but she slid through the brush and stopped next to Braygen.

Jàden's heart raced at the steel door closed within airtight seams.

Etched into the brushed metal, a tree with branches reached skyward, its roots digging toward the earth below her feet.

Three symbols stood out along the trunk. A zankata at the top, a wolf in the middle and a horse near the base.

She swallowed a lump in her throat—her zankata. "Kale."

Bits of wire dangled from a steel wall, clinging to a frosted plexiglass plate. Jàden gripped the smashed light pad. Lichen grew along the surrounding cliff face, dusting the components with verdant green life. Her fingers slipped between the panel's loose wires. The circular fitting was still snug in its stone fixture.

"Someone give me a firemark," she said.

Braygen pressed a glass orb into her palm.

Cupping her hands around the firemark, she blew until it glowed and then pressed it into the holder. The orb pulsed once, and the light box illuminated.

"The Temple of the Three Moons," Braygen said. "This is the place most fiercely protected by the Tahiró."

"Sandaris has no third moon," Ashe muttered. "It was lost. Right, Jàden?"

"Sandaris *is* the third moon," she whispered. Her moon, and one she still needed to abandon.

Disbelief flashed across Ashe's eyes as she laid her hand over the panel, then hesitated. Frank had found her when she used the datapad. She searched the sky, unable to see much through the thick canopy.

She shouldn't, but she had to know. Jàden pressed her palm to the panel and held her breath.

The light pad flashed blue.

She dropped the smashed unit and stepped back, searching the sky for any of Frank's ships. The door shifted, air hissing at the seams, and slid silently open. Thin lines of white light traced along dusty stone walls, weaving across the glass-like surface.

She trailed her fingers over the smoothness, stopping shy of the threaded web. "Maybe this is a bad idea."

"Don't tell me you're afraid of spiders." Braygen stepped into the corridor beside her, brushing his gloved hand across the wall to clear the surface.

"Spiders. Sahiranath." Ashe muttered under his breath, obviously still not over their near miss with the shifters.

Light flicked on overhead, firemarks aglow inside hanging crescent lanterns. Energy flowed through the corridor, illuminating sections divided by stone columns arched high overhead.

Jàden breathed in the smell of sterile dust.

She'd waited so long to find Kale that stepping through the door from soft earth to stone floors seemed like entering an alien world.

She traced the thin lines of power woven through walls built to last several millennia. Her fingers stopped on illuminated words etched among the lines of power. *Laoné lenä freon và naréa. Naréathana freon amshe farioné. San 'endlan và drér fré. Vó e vastana ara zenathar o.*

"This can't be right." She brushed dust from the etchings, her brows pulled together in concentration. "Light does not exist without darkness. Darkness cannot breathe without light. Bond them to create shadow, who both divides and unites." She shook her head. "It uses two different meanings for light. The first refers to sunlight and moonlight, but the second—"

"Darkness cannot breathe without magic." Braygen stepped close and leaned his forearm against the wall, reading over her shoulder.

Her cheeks warmed at his close proximity. "Even darkness is energy and fuels life."

"The Tahiró believe it can be combined, bonded together from one person to another. They were the first to discover this place when they went hunting for the lost Guardian." He met her gaze. "They were looking for you."

"I'd love one day where someone's not searching for me." Jàden stepped away, pressing aside a curtain of web now that she knew it wouldn't stick to her hand. Dust floated into the air. She stripped one web after another, clearing the enclosed space.

At the end of the hall, she brushed her fingers over a second steel door. To the left, a square of frosted plexiglass glowed against the wall.

"The last Tahiró to open this door died three hundred years ago." Braygen laid his hand against the glowing panel. It buzzed red, and the door remained shut.

Jàden swallowed a lump in her throat.

Ashe unsheathed her dagger and nodded. "Do it. Let's get this shit over with. I'm tired of searching for this asshole."

She placed her palm against the light pad. White turned blue, and the door slid into the wall.

"I knew you were the one," Braygen said.

"All right, Kale. Show me the way home." She slipped inside, heart racing.

Illumination bled through the floor along trails of light like the gate rooms, curving in long arcs toward the center of the large chamber as she stepped inside.

Dozens of statues circled the outer wall, backlit to cast their features in stark relief.

"It's a Guardian temple from the world before mine." Jàden frowned at the statues. She'd never believed in such deification, and Kale knew this. "Few sing to the old Guardians anymore, even in my world."

"Why would someone build statues to the old Guardians?" Braygen asked.

"Someone must sing to them." Her grandmother had, but only a few people she knew held onto the old beliefs.

"Ain't nothin' here but dusty old statues," Ashe muttered. "Guardians abandoned Sandaris long ago."

"The Guardians aren't divine. They're ordinary, terrified people who stood out against their nature in one courageous act that defined history." But Jàden tracked the light through the floor as if a fiery gate orb might suddenly appear.

The energy came together as a large circle with flames around the edges.

"Stay back." She held her arm out to keep them at bay.

Rock burst through the center, building itself like nanotech into a tree trunk as branches stretched toward a high, domed ceiling. Three symbols glowed against the trunk: the horse, the wolf and the zankata.

Jàden shuddered. That kind of tech could only be found in one place.

As if Sandaris heard her, its gentle heart thrummed alongside hers. How had Kale gotten hold of alien tech?

Flecks of dust shook from the ceiling as the walls groaned with the grinding of internal mechanics. Three pillars rose in a circle around the trunk, two of the stones crude and rugged, waiting for a sculptor to chisel them to perfection.

The third lifted in front of Jàden, ground stretching into a long body covered by a Guild uniform, a zankata surrounded by flames on her left shoulder. One arm reached forward, palm turned skyward as three swirls of light lifted away.

"Oh, shit," Ashe said. "It's—"

"Me," she whispered.

The statue's long hair pulled back in a single tail. The Guardian statue's narrow features and thin nose were unmistakable, bangs fringed across the forehead in a style Jàden hadn't worn for nearly four thousand years.

"Herana," Braygen said. "Guardian of Lost Souls."

Ashe touched her shoulder, turning Jàden so she had to meet his gaze. "We need the captain here. Don't you dare leave this village until I find him. Understand?"

It was crazy for him to leave. "You're still sick, and you have no weapons."

"I am the weapon." He slapped his chest. "And this is not my world, Jàden. This is yours."

Ashe had never shown an ounce of fear in all the time she'd known him, but something about this place left a deep worry in his eyes. Maybe he felt safer with Jon and his brothers around, she couldn't honestly say. Only that the set of his jaw told her one thing—he wouldn't change his mind.

"Be safe." Hugging him tight, she kissed his cheek. "I'm staying. I have to find Kale and finish this."

Braygen stripped the bow and quiver from his back and tossed them to Ashe. "Take my saddle and any supplies you need. Tell Alida what you've seen. She'll go with you."

Ashe slung the quiver on his shoulder and leaned his forehead against hers. "As a brother to his sister, I will come back."

Jàden swallowed a lump in her throat as he stormed out of the room. "Can I see your datapad?"

As Braygen handed her the device, she zoomed out the map to try to get a better view of her location. Northern side of the Dark Isle while the Ironstar Tower—the beginning of her nightmare—was still far to the south.

"This isn't the beginning," she muttered. "It can't be."

She glanced at the other two unformed rocks—two more Guardians. Frank and Bradshaw searched for another Flame while they held her captive, but they never found anyone like her.

Except who was the third rock?

Shield glass stretched across the front of each. She pressed her palm against the screen embedded in her statue. If Frank already knew where she was from touching the light pad, she didn't have much time left.

"Here goes nothing," she said.

A trail of light bled across the screen, illuminating Kale as he rubbed his short hair. He'd lost weight, his cheeks hollow. A cigarette smoldered between his lips, the smoke curling across his cheek.

"Kale." She traced the worry lines on his face. "What happened to you?"

He'd searched for her, that much she knew, but this man was broken, devastated. When he finally met her gaze, there were tears in his eyes.

"I'm going to die, Jàden. I don't want to, but it's the only way. "Enforcers are closing in. I've lost everything—my command, my home. But losing you, that's the pain that eats away at me every day."

Grieving him and letting go had been hard, but seeing him now, so broken, sliced her to the core.

"Do you remember what I told you? About courage and fear?" He shifted to the side to reveal large statues circling the chamber behind him. "This is where we started. Do you remember?"

"No, I..." Jàden glanced around the cavern. She'd never seen this place.

But one look at the datapad's map, and it all came rushing back.

They'd been caught in a dust storm in this area, Kale's ship grounded for fear the sand would clog the turbines. He'd kissed her for the first time that day.

She pressed a hand to her mouth. "I remember."

"Everything you see in this place I built for you. It's a safe house, with enough food, water and power inside to keep you alive for three years. This bunker is secure. My father can't trace you here. Time enough for you to learn how to fly."

"No, Kale." She passed the datapad back to Braygen. "Don't say goodbye."

"I have no doubt hypersleep fucked your head up really bad." His expression flickered between pain, distress and anger, but beneath it all, a hollowness lurked. As if he'd lost hope.

She caressed her thumb across Kale's digital cheek.

The way he held his cigarette reminded her so much of Jon her chest ached. *You've never smoked a day in your life.*

"I want you off this ship. Off Sandaris, just like we always talked about. Even if you have to leave me behind." Uncertainty flickered across his distraught hazel eyes.

"My father"—Kale lit a second cigarette, the first one still smoldering in his grasp—"he had the answer all along. There's a way to survive, to balance your power. I should have seen it sooner."

Pain pulled at his features as he tried to hold himself together. "There's another Flame. He and Bradshaw want to unite you and the other. But he's not really after you."

For a moment, she thought Kale might break down into tears, something she'd never seen him do. Some of this she already knew, but a sense lingered in her gut that he was circling around to something worse.

"The spark he seeks isn't what's generated by this union. It's what the spark creates—a third Flame so strong this person can draw from both energy sources as one."

"A third Flame." Jàden didn't like the sound of this at all, and by the distress in Kale's body language, he hadn't finished.

"You have to unite the Flames, or you'll die. But if you do, who knows where you'll end up. My father's planning to go through the moon's gate into the otherspace, and you can't let him."

Jàden shook her head, desperate to turn away and cover her ears. This is what they all feared, her and the others who had seen the moon's inner gate.

"There isn't much time." He wiped a tear from his cheek. "I'm sorry I wasn't there for you, baby. I knew my father was a cold-hearted asshole, but I had no idea what a monster lived inside him."

Regret lay raw in his eyes. "I love you with every piece of my heart. Stay alive, and we'll be together soon."

The bands of light disappeared, and the glass smoked over.

Jàden stared at the empty transmission panel. "Kale? No no no. Come back!"

His brokenness cut her to the core.

Braygen wrapped his arms around her.

"I'm not leaving you." Anger flowed into her veins at what Frank had done. Kale might as well have been in a cage for all the horrors etched on his face. Her hands shook harder as she curled them into fists.

She shrugged off Braygen and punched the glass, pain shooting up her arm. Blood beaded on her scraped knuckles as she stormed toward the door.

Braygen caught her arm. "Where are you going?"

Shoving him away, she slapped her palm against the lightpad. "I'm going to kill Frank Kale."

No matter what Evardo said, Frank wasn't in the right to keep her here. And she wasn't going to let anyone else suffer.

She would find Frank.

And then unleash the Flame's fury until all that remained of him was ash.

Late afternoon turned to evening as she closed the outer door to the Temple of the Three Moons. "What I wouldn't give for a gun right now."

The gentleness in Braygen's eyes turned sharp. "I meant what I said before. My life is yours. Tell me what to do."

"But why? You know nothing about me."

He sighed deeply, almost as if choosing his words. "That man you saw in there—the day he died is the same day I was born. When I woke from hypersleep, I was still clutching a picture of you."

Braygen touched her cheek. "I wanted to be the hero that found you and stopped the war."

Jàden's chest gripped so tight she couldn't breathe as she noted just how much Braygen looked like Kale. His hair was darker and his eyes gray, but he had the same gentleness and tall, lean build.

Tears burned down her cheek as she grabbed his wrist, desperate to know the truth. "Are you Kale?"

An engine boomed past the village so low it rattled the Veradóran's central mother tree. Branches cracked and shook, leaves raining over the valley.

Between slots in the canopy, an obsidian ship zipped toward the eastern horizon. It could only be one thing—a Raith fighter. And she knew without question who sat in the cockpit. "Frank."

# CHAPTER 48

*The Jungle*

"Captain, over here!"

Jon wrangled his horse around, the devouring darkness a heavy shadow looming over his shoulders. The closer he got to Jàden, the stronger her energy flowed through him, but he still couldn't shake the nausea as the invader's magic. He trotted through the flooded woods to a mud-churned road.

Malcolm picked up a broken arrow shaft, green feathers on the end. "Someone took a hit."

Jon growled and forced himself to focus on the trail. They'd trusted Jàden's messenger hoping to catch up to her before Éli did, but this was the first sign of anything beyond wild jungle. He couldn't be sure anymore Jàden had gone in this direction. "Come on, Ashe. Show us where you are."

As a wave of dizziness hit him again, Jon rubbed his eyes to force back the blurriness. If he could just get close to her again, maybe her softness would breathe so strong through his skin again that he could fight off this other power.

Opening his mouth to shout an order toward his men, his eye caught another zankata painting, this one streaked with rain and losing form.

"Kale," he muttered, clenching his fist around the reins. Wherever that asshole was, Jàden was sure to follow. "This way!"

"Son, you sure about this?" Malcolm followed but kept glancing over his shoulder as if he wasn't certain. It made the most sense. Jàden had been bent on following that lover of hers since day one.

Jon's instincts told him to follow. "Them shifters have her, the ones from the coast."

They tracked for more than an hour before Andrew shouted ahead.

"Here, Captain."

Tracks appeared in the mud as if horses rose from nothing.

Jon dropped to the ground, tracing his fingers across a set of larger hoofprints surrounded by smaller ones. "It's them. Maybe a day."

Ashe and Jàden shouldn't be so far ahead, but as he climbed onto his horse, Jon dug his heels in. "We ride hard."

Pushing the horses as hard as he dared, they rode until Shelora's bright moon was high in the sky. They stopped long enough to let the horses rest, but Jon could barely sleep, his mind racing. He wasn't giving up his wife without a fight, but the darkness seeped into his bones, oily and rotten, making his body ache all over.

Andrew crouched in front of him, his features rigid. "Tell me you'd fight this hard to find Ashe."

"Every damn time." He lit a cigarette, sweat beading along his brow. "For you, for Ashe, for any one of you boys. You're all the family I got."

He'd craved a companion like Jàden his whole life though. Someone gentle and warm who could take away the world's cold cruelty just by slipping their hand in his. Jon would never tell his men, but given the choice, he'd choose her every time. He only hoped it never came to that.

"We'll find him," Jon said.

Jon led his men down a narrow path that looked more like a game trail, but it was getting harder to follow in the growing storm.

He turned to Malcolm. "Get up here, old man."

Malcolm would have to discern the rest, but before the old man reached his side, a figure crouched on the path ahead, an arrow pointed in their direction.

Jon held up a hand to stop his men.

"Shifters," Malcolm muttered. He'd barely said more than a few words since Felaren, but the guilt lay stark in his eyes.

"No sudden movements." Jon kept his hands where they could be seen. If one shifter was on the path, half a dozen likely followed in the trees. He didn't want any trouble, he just needed to find his wife.

The figure's head lifted. "Andrew?"

"Ashe." Digging his heels into his horse, mania gripped Jon with a desperate need to find Jàden. If Ashe was here, she had to be close. "Jàden!"

Grabbing him by the shirt, Ashe yanked him off his horse, Jon hitting the ground hard. Pain shot into Jon's shoulder.

Ashe pressed a hand to his mouth. "Are you trying to get her killed?"

Mud covered his aching back as Jon followed Ashe's gaze to a tall, silver pole. Blue light flashed at the top. "What the fuck is that thing?"

"Frank is watching her," Ashe whispered harshly.

Andrew crashed into his brother, hugging him tight as Jon rolled to a crouch. Fury gripped his chest, followed by a wave of dark obsession. The invader magic fueled his need to kill Frank as he gestured to Ashe: *where?*

*With her lover*, Ashe gestured.

"Kale." Jon clenched his fist and climbed onto his horse. He'd had enough of that asshole for one lifetime, and he wasn't about to lose Jàden without a fight. He signaled Ashe: *show me.*

It was about time he had it out with that bastard. Jon sure as shit wasn't going to leave her in the hands of her ex.

Ashe had paled and thinned in the past few days, dark rings around his eyes as if he hadn't slept. Something in him was different, darker.

A woman with silver-blond hair stepped onto the path, dark brown lines across her features like tree branches. "You comin' or what? I still ain't had my dinner."

Ashe retreated toward her. "Shut your damn mouth, woman, and go kill something. You've been moaning the whole way here."

"Then quit layin' around being lazy." The woman punched him so hard Ashe fell flat on his back. "I got a wife to get home to." Dusty and Theryn had their arrows strung and tight, but the woman laughed them off. "Oh your man ain't hurt. You kill me, and there ain't gonna be no gator stew for you bastards."

Ashe groaned and stumbled to his feet, mumbling curses.

Jon and his men followed in silence, keeping their heads down and their faces covered. They trotted past the silver, metallic object, and Jon itched to draw his sword and rip it all down. But if anyone was watching, it could give them away.

Once the silver object was out of sight, Ashe wrangled his horse alongside, telling Jon everything that had happened from Éli's men to the poison to the buried temple. "Them shifters were following us from sahiranath territory. They may have saved my life, but I still don't trust 'em."

"Then why the fuck did you leave her?" As relived as Jon was to see Ashe alive, his anger burned deep and hot. And the stronger it got, the harder it was to feel Jàden's soft breath weaving through him.

"Because at least two of them assholes are trying to protect her. Including that piece of work." He gestured toward the blond woman.

"I don't like the other guy, but he sticks close to her the way you do. They all got that bird thing of hers inked into their bodies, like they know her or something."

Ashe slowed his horse as they ducked under thick kóra trees. "These people are ruled by women who hate Rakir. Keep your weapons sheathed."

Clenching the reins, Jon nudged his horse ahead of the others as women in drab browns and bright feathers materialized from the grass.

"You are not welcome here," a dark-skinned woman shouted, tiny orange blossoms in a line across her forehead.

The twins stopped at either side of Jon, Ashe holding out the bow he'd been using. "We're here for our Guardian. Tell Braygen."

"Jon!"

The unmistakable sound of Jàden's voice sent Jon's heart pounding.

"Jàden!" He tried to wrangle his horse toward her.

But the shifter women bunched together in a long line, forcing the black to rear up.

"First one to fire an arrow will become denerada." An older woman with deep wrinkles in her skin shuffled through the line of women. Leaning heavily on a thick cane, her long, gray hair shed dry leaves with each step. Yet her voice commanded authority.

The women eased the tension on their arrows and stepped aside, showing deference to the older woman.

Dropping the reins, Jon slid to the ground, fighting to hold back the nausea. If that bastard Kale was here, Jon wanted him to understand right away that he wasn't about to give up Jàden without a fight. "I'm here for my wife."

"We will not give up our women for your kind." The orange-flowered woman spat at the ground.

Jàden pushed through the crowd, her eyes wild with anger. He could almost sense her frustration as she raced to his side and shoved him backward. "Why didn't you tell me?"

Grabbing his horse's mane to steady himself, Jon tried to blink away the dizziness. "Jàden—"

"No." She shoved him again. "'You and I are equals.' Isn't that what you said?"

Fuck, he could barely see straight. He was the captain here and needed to get this situation under control. "I was angry."

"Well, now I'm *furious*. You should have told me about the bond, Jon. I can't be—"

"You gutted me, Jàden. You ripped everything out of me without so much as a warning." This was not the place to have this fight. Jon could practically feel the eyes of every woman boring into him.

Grabbing the back of Jàden's neck, he pulled her close, her magic surging brighter the moment his skin touched hers.

"I know the bond doesn't mean the same thing to you, but I don't care. Call me your husband or your bodyguard. As long as I can be near you." Guardians be damned, he wanted to kiss her again.

But the old woman was standing so close she was breathing on him. Clenching his jaw, it took every ounce of restraint Jon had not to yell at her.

"I am Ìana, daughter of the great wind and ruler of Veradóra," the old woman said.

He didn't honestly care who she was. Jon would take his men and leave—but not without Jàden, whose brown eyes filled with angry tears. She'd still said nothing, hadn't even touched him.

Jon dropped his hand, and the bright spark that was her essence dimmed, leaving him dizzy and nauseated.

Ìana laid a hand on each of Jàden's cheeks. "So the rumors are true. Our Herana lives."

Jàden kept her gaze fixed on him, but her words were for Ìana. "If you allow us one more night of rest in your fields, we'll be gone by morning. I found what I was looking for."

As the tears slid down her cheeks, Jon ached to pull her into his arms.

And yet the sting of her words stabbed his heart. She'd found Kale, and he had every intention of sorting this whole mess out before the next dawn. No way would he lose her to a dead man. Nor would he stay with the certainty that Éli and his men would circle back and find their trail.

Jàden pulled Ìana's hands away from her cheeks and stepped back, her eyes now on a man speaking quietly with Ashe.

"Let Herana's companions rest, Ìana," the sandy-haired man said. "At dawn, they will be gone, and so will I."

## CHAPTER 49
*Veradóra*

Jàden could barely hold herself together as she leaned against the door inside her hut. She was so happy to see Jon and the others, but her anger toward Frank erupted in harsh words she desperately wanted to take back.

*I love you, with every piece of my heart,* Kale's voice whispered through her thoughts. Pressing her hands to her eyes, she tried to stop the tears, but they kept coming. She wanted to hold onto Kale's heart-wrenching words. But Braygen's revelation had her torn apart inside. *I wanted to be the hero that found you.*

"Kale." Similar physique, same color hair, but all the broken pieces of the man she loved were gone. If it was him, Kale had been born where he could live two lives—disappear with the wind and smile like he held some secret happiness in this world. No Frank, no broken dreams. Just a gentle man with a kind heart.

She couldn't let him be broken again. Not because of her. She'd finish this mess first and then either tell him who he was or let him continue his life of peace. All the pieces still didn't quite fit together in her head, but she was an emotional wreck of anger and desperation.

Jàden yanked open the door and stormed onto the bridge.

"Training in one hour," Thomas shouted after her.

"Fuck off, Thomas."

He could live another night without smacking a stick against her brand. There was only one way to stop this pain in her heart, to let go of the urge to hide all the anguish while it festered.

Without bothering to knock, she shoved open the door to the next hut and slammed it behind her. "This argument isn't over."

As long as she'd known him, Jon was like a stallion, charging into everything head on until he was satisfied with the outcome. Jàden wasn't sure yet what she wanted at the end of this argument, but Jon had seen her at her worst and nothing seemed to shake him.

As he gripped a nearby chair, his skin paler than usual, it seemed as if he struggled to stand.

"Why didn't you tell me? I would have never bonded you if I'd known. I was desperate—"

Jon crossed the floor in two strides and pressed his mouth against hers.

Heat ignited in her gut. Jàden shoved his shoulders, but her back hit the door and his tongue brushed across hers.

She wrapped her arms around his neck and pulled him into a deeper kiss. The Flame's power brightened a little more each time her fingers brushed his skin, pushing back the dark oil of Éli's suffocating power.

Jàden was forever cursed to be in love with two men. With Kale happy and free, she couldn't drag him back into the nightmare of her life. Not until Frank and Bradshaw were dead.

"Why didn't you tell me about the bond?" she whispered against his mouth.

Apparently this was going to be how they argued tonight.

And her body didn't complain one bit.

"I wanted to so many times." Jon leaned his forehead against hers. He caressed his thumb across her cheek, tracing back a lock of stray hair. His calloused hand was gentle against her skin. "I've never wanted any woman so much in my damn life. You are *everything* to me."

She breathed in his earthy scent as she traced the scruffy beard along his jaw. "I'm sorry I got you into this whole mess."

"Ain't any bigger than my own." He slipped an arm around her waist and pulled her against his chest. "It's you and me now, and I ain't never letting you go."

Jon tossed her on the bed. His hands lost contact, and his strength in her skin dimmed until she couldn't feel him anymore. The cold empty void of darkness slid through her as he pulled off his shirt, his branded shoulder glistening obsidian in the hearth firelight.

"What are you doing?" she asked.

"Making love to my wife." He dropped on top of her and trapped her against the blankets, fierce desire bleeding into his kiss. Tendrils of shadow wrapped around his forearms as he slid his hand beneath her bodice.

The ache in her heart wouldn't go away.

She needed more and wrapped one leg around his, the darker magic absorbing into her. Jàden caressed his arms, the corded muscle tight as his calloused hands wove a gentle spell along her skin.

As he kissed along her neck and down to her hip, Jàden groaned.

Two long years she'd withered in the empty cold of her cage, and Jon's mouth against her stomach filled her with an intoxicating need that burned between her thighs.

Jon kissed and caressed her until he'd practically torn her bodice off. As he moved up her body again, Jàden curled her fingers in his hair and pulled him into a deep kiss, brushing her tongue along his.

She needed this, needed him, absorbing his warmth as he slid his hand along her thigh.

He tugged her breeches, kissing down to her hips again until he had her pants off. The energy between them burned brighter with each new connection, each caress of his mouth against her skin.

Jon kissed along the inside of her thigh.

She gripped the blankets tight, years and decades and millennia of loneliness peeling away with each intimate caress. With years of pain shedding through her tears, Jàden grabbed his arms and pulled him up so she could see his eyes. "I want to feel you inside me."

She tugged the leather belt holding up his breeches, but Jon pulled her hands back to his cheeks. His beard prickled against her fingertips.

He kissed her palm, closing his eyes and inhaling deeply of her scent. His hands deft and fast, he shed the last of his clothing within seconds. Jon caressed her thigh, sliding his hand between her legs before he pushed two fingers inside her.

Jàden arched back, a soft moan escaping her lips. A shiver traveled from her thighs up her spine, a faint tingle blossoming in her skull. She kissed his upper arm, lips moving across the strong, muscular definition.

Her mouth found his again, and she wrapped her legs around him.

"I can't live without you," she whispered.

The words had slipped out without thought, and yet truth blossomed. She needed Jon, and the thought of dividing herself from him nearly brought a sob to the surface.

He pushed his hardness inside her, his groan fanning the fire in her belly.

Jàden tightened her legs and pulled him deeper. She wrapped her tongue around his, the emotional aches and pains bubbling up to the surface.

As the fire dimmed in the hearth, his intimacy washed away the loneliness she'd endured for too many years. The Flame's power fed the forged energy tangling them together, breathing his strength into her until the swallowing darkness retreated to the corners of her mind.

Tendrils of light and shadow circled around them. Binding them.

The blended magic fueled her desire until sweat covered her body. She leaned her forehead against Jon's shoulder, feeling him shudder beneath her.

He pulled her close.

Caressing a lock of hair, he slid his fingers along the back of her head.

She stretched out across his chest. Jàden pressed her forehead against his neck and closed her eyes. The steady thumping in his chest lulled her senses. They stayed that way until the fire died down, Jàden more content than she'd been in years.

"Why does Éli hate you so much?" Jàden traced the scars on Jon's chest, each one a roadmap to a rough life in the north.

"I killed his brother." The ember on the end of Jon's cigarette glowed brightly, smoke curling from his lips. "I was nine when it happened. My father took my sisters into the city, and before he left, he gave me my first real dagger. Told me I was in charge and needed to protect my mother."

She caressed his chest, small rough spots on his skin giving her a glimpse of Jon's past.

"A Rakir named Sebastian Hareth came on the farm and demanded my mother make him a hot meal. When she refused, he punched her so hard she flew into the wall." His hand tightened against her head. "He beat and raped my mother, and I couldn't stop him. I knew I'd never be able to look my father in the eye again, so I stole his horse and followed Sebastian into the city.

"I found him in an alley beating an old man, with my mother's blood still on his knuckles. When he wasn't looking, I crept up behind him and stabbed him in the back, right where I knew he'd bleed out the fastest."

Jon's fingers traced through her hair, caressing gently as if giving himself comfort from the intimate touch.

"Years later, I found out Sebastian was Éli's only remaining family. Éli was taken to the Tower with the other orphans and branded a Rakir." His hand stopped again, and he flicked his spent cigarette into the hearth. "I stole his life, Jàden. Stole his family. But avenging my mother never erased the memory of what Sebastian did to her."

He wrapped his arms around her, pulling her forehead against his cheek.

"I couldn't live with the guilt of what I'd done, so I left home and joined the Rakir, hoping to shoulder the injustice I'd done to Éli."

"But you probably saved so many other lives." Tears burned on her cheeks at the guilt in his words. "This is his revenge, to make you suffer for it?"

Flames crackled in the hearth, burning low on the stack of logs. The hushed whispers outside had ceased, wrapping the world in silence.

"He wants me to feel his pain. Éli thought I was taunting him when I joined the Rakir. His anger turned to obsession, and for the last twenty years, he's become darker and crueler."

"On my life, I'll never let him hurt you," he said. Jon laid his hands on her cheeks and pulled her mouth against his, kissing her deeply.

Jàden breathed deep of sweat and mountain and sea. This had become her home—her safe space. "I love you, Jon."

"You're all I've ever wanted," he whispered, gently kissing her forehead. "This life, next life, it doesn't matter. I love you with every piece of my heart."

# CHAPTER 50
*Veradóra*

*Be strong, Jàden.*

She jolted awake, Kale's whispered voice echoing across her sleepy thoughts. Frogs chirruped along the outer banks of the quiet village, only the faintest whisper of voices on the bridge.

She curled into Jon's side, his skin cool and clammy.

Jàden lifted her head. His breath was raspy, and he muttered incoherently.

She traced her mouth across his, hoping to rekindle the fire in their bond, but her own body had a strange heaviness, as if thick tar covered her arms and legs. "Jon?"

He didn't stir.

Jàden shifted to her elbow and kissed his forehead, but something slick thrummed along her skin. An oily ooze dancing through the lines of theric energy.

Éli's power was growing.

"Hey, wake up," she said.

*Find the other Flame,* Kale's voice whispered into her thoughts.

Jàden uncurled Jon's fingers, black flecks drifting away from his skin as she recalled the words etched on the temple wall. *Light cannot exist without darkness.*

She lifted her hand, darkness and light lifting from her palm. She'd bonded with Éli, but even her power hadn't been right since then. Doing the math in her head, they would need three bonds to create the 'spark.'

*A third Flame so strong this person can draw from both energy sources as one.*

Jon needed to connect with the darkness.

*You have to unite the Flames, or you'll die. But if you do, who knows where you'll end up.*

Jon and Éli never bonded one another to tie Jon to the Dark Flame.

Her power was killing Jon.

She scrambled off the bed and dressed quickly, an awful dread sinking into her gut. "Thomas!"

Thomas crashed through the door. "What's wrong?"

"When did this start?" Jàden spied the dagger she'd lost in Felaren sitting on the table and sheathed it alongside its twin. "How long has Jon been sick?"

"Since Malcolm..." He glared at the open door.

"I need to speak with Braygen." Jàden pressed her mouth against Jon's, the scent of pine and mountain warming her skin. "I know how to save him."

Thomas caught her arm. "How?"

She needed to tell him, but Thomas would never let her leave without one of Jon's men at her side.

And Éli's Rakir would certainly try to kill them.

If she'd done the math right in her head, Éli's power was using her bond with Jon to get to him. Whether by intent or because of the vengeance he craved, Éli's Flame viewed Jon's energy as an invader.

"The Flames are hurting him, but I know how to fix it." By leaving him again. Which was the last thing she wanted to do.

The Flame's white fire slid into her veins, diminished under all the heavy darkness. Maybe she didn't have the risk of losing control of her power anymore, but without Jon sealed to both energies, she and Éli might spend an eternity ebbing and flowing between each other, one always consuming the other.

She bolted out of the room as a ship rumbled high in the clouds. Frank would find her soon if she didn't fix this and get them all on the road again.

Tugging up her hood to hide her face, Jàden trotted over the bridges until she spied Braygen in a hushed conversation with Alida. "I need your help," she said. "When the captain wakes, take him to the Temple of the Three Moons. He'll be able to open the doors."

At least she hoped so. But he may not be able to open them until the final energy tie was complete.

Braygen opened his mouth to say something.

But before he could answer, Jàden raced toward the high meadow.

It only took a moment for him to catch up with her. "Whatever you're doing, I'm going with you."

"This isn't your fight," she said. Braygen had to be Kale, which explained the strong connection with him from his first appearance on the coast, and she wasn't about to drag him into this. She searched for Agnar. "Besides, the Rakir will kill you."

"Rakir?" He caught her wrist. "Do you know what they do to women? You can't go there alone."

"And you can't come with me. Not anymore." She laid a hand on his cheek, a sharp pain stabbing her heart. This man was her everything and still held such a tight grip on her heart.

"What are you talking about?" He grabbed her wrist and stepped closer, towering over her. "My life is yours, Jàden. Where you go, I go."

Storms brewed in his eyes and she ached to tell him, but it was time to let him live free. Of her, of Frank, of all the pain he'd once suffered.

Besides, she loved Jon so much it hurt. He'd kept her alive and safe since she woke up, and it was time for her to set things right.

"I have to do this." She stepped away, wishing she could numb the pain in her chest. Someday she'd tell him, but not until Frank was long dead.

Sumaha and half a dozen women trudged along the path, Alida grinning with a mischievous twinkle in her eyes. "We spotted Rakir last night on the next ridge. If she's going to that nest of vipers, we're coming too."

Jàden clenched her fists, glaring at the other women. "No, you're not coming. They won't hurt me."

Well, Éli wouldn't. She was counting on him to want to rub his bond with her in Jon's face.

"Try and stop us." Sumaha swung her bow against Jàden's cheek.

"Sumaha!" Alida grabbed Jàden's shoulders to help right her.

Sharp pain throbbed along her skull as Jàden glared at the orange-flower woman. "What is her fucking problem? I'm trying to save Jon so we can get out of your hair."

Alida's grin disappeared, her vivid green eyes angry. "She is next in line to rule Veradóra, and she's afraid a Guardian will take command of our kin. Sumaha has a kind heart, but her fear is always shielded by anger."

"She's got no need to worry," Jàden muttered. "All I want is to set things right and be gone."

Dozens of other women followed in Sumaha's wake, armed with bows and arrows and small vials of green liquid.

"Poison." Alida grinned.

One woman had jagged green lines across her skin. Jàden had seen something similar on bright-colored frogs. Their bodies secreted a mucus that could kill a human in a matter of minutes.

Maybe she needed these women after all.

As Alida raced after Sumaha, Jàden shifted her gaze back to Braygen. "Promise me you won't tell anyone where I've gone."

He clutched her hands and sighed as if she'd placed the whole world on his shoulders. "I will only keep my silence until Jon has seen the temple. That's all I can promise."

His words stung, but she kissed his cheek, lingering a moment longer than she should. The smell of the rain and trees clung to him. She ached to tell him who he really was and kiss him until she couldn't breathe, but she wouldn't be responsible for killing him again.

Kale was free now, and she would never take that away from him.

"Thank you," she said. "And search for any other doors or storage in there. Kale loved his weapons, so there has to be a gun."

The Veradórans called their horses with a series of tongue clicks. Agnar was easy to find, trotting up to Jàden, his ears pricked forward. He shoved his nose against her shoulder.

"Come on, let's do Mather proud," she said. "We're going to save the captain."

Agnar tossed his head as if he understood.

She grabbed his mane and pulled herself onto his back.

The other women trotted toward her, Sumaha in the lead. "I take you to the Rakir."

They raced away from Veradóra, through thickets and vines, along narrow paths and muddy roads. Sleet turned to heavy rain as storm clouds gathered overhead. They followed a narrow game trail south of the village as it slowly angled east.

Malcolm appeared at her side, a grim determination set in his jaw. "Didn't think you were going anywhere without me, did you?"

Jàden cursed under her breath.

Sumaha slowed her horse, nudging Malcolm backwards until she rode alongside Jàden. "You are going to kill Rakir, right?"

"They're hard to kill," Jàden said. But then, Alida had snapped one's neck with her thighs in Felaren, so what did she know. "If they move the way Jon and his men do, they'll have scouts at least a league out."

"I do not fear the Rakir." Sumaha scanned the woods, but deep shadows lurked in her eyes, as if she feared something Jàden couldn't see. "Alida has pledged her loyalty to you, Guardian, and you will protect her when I cannot."

Except Jàden could barely protect herself without a burst of power.

"Alida's a strong fighter, but I'll do my best." Jàden bit her tongue before she made a promise she couldn't keep.

Besides, as soon as Jon was well, she had every intention of returning to her bunker and going underground. Whether she decided to leave this world or not, she would finally learn how to pilot a ship.

"Don't harm their leader," she said. "Or the boy and the skinny one who follows him. I don't care about the rest, but those three have to survive." Maybe she shouldn't have included Evardo, but Jàden needed to understand how they knew about the starship at the moon's core.

Gray gloom pressed through the trees as another storm rolled in.

She kept a loose cloth over her features as they passed a triangulation sensor. Frank and his soldiers would be watching her now, even if the sky was strangely quiet.

Tethering the horses at the bottom of the ridge, Jàden climbed with the others.

"I'm sorry," Malcolm said as he caught up to her again. The Veradórans melted into the trees and disappeared. "When I drink, I black out."

"Now's really not the time." She grabbed another branch to help steady herself as she climbed the sharp incline.

He grabbed her arm and turned her to face him. "You saved Ashe where I fucked up and nearly cost everyone their lives. I'm indebted to you, Jàden."

She hated seeing the guilt in Malcolm's eyes, but between worry about Jon and fear that Frank would find her before she could save him, she didn't have time to console Malcolm's guilt.

"Then help me save Jon," she said. "He and Éli need to tie their energy into a bond. Jon once told you all that my life was more important than his, but now that's changed. He's the key. To everything."

Alida's pale hair flashed further up the incline before she disappeared behind a tree trunk. By the time Jàden caught up, the jungle was dead silent.

Laughter echoed ahead, along with horse whinnies. She crawled onto the ledge and under a thick bush, a cluster of orange flowers on one side that could only be Sumaha, and parted the branches toward a line of picketed horses.

A young boy brushed a stallion which had turned a dark chestnut.

"Connor," the old man whispered. "He's alive."

"Who is he?" Jàden searched the other faces, spotting Evardo when they stood up between two horses.

"The captain's nephew. He's supposed to be dead." Malcolm tightened his fist. "Fucking Hareth."

Fucking Hareth indeed, but where was he? Two dozen horses were picketed between the trees, but only three men sat near the fire sharpening their weapons.

Steel touched the back of her neck. "The commander said we might have a visitor or two. Guess we've got us a pretty prize today and a dead man who ain't in his grave yet."

# CHAPTER 51

*Temple of the Three Moons*

Jon shivered in the morning chill. Bumps rose along his arms. He'd passed out after making love to Jàden and forgot to keep the hearth lit. Rolling onto his side, he reached across the bed for his wife's gentle warmth, but all he found was cold sheets as the wind howled through the trees.

"Where are you, baby?" Pushing onto his elbow, every muscle in his body dragged like they were stuffed with lead. His head pounded, a slick oily energy threatening to suffocate his senses.

Thomas shoved open the door and stormed in. "Jàden's gone again. Dusty and Theryn are shadowing her." He nodded toward the open door. "And this guy out here needs to speak with you. Says it's important."

"What do you mean she's gone?" Jon tried to stand, but his knees hit the ground. He grabbed the edge of the bed and pushed to his feet, as naked as the day his mother gave birth to him. "Maybe I should find my pants."

He fumbled for his clothes, trying to will the leaded weight in his veins away. Belting his weapons on, Jon stumbled to the door.

Fuck, he felt like shit.

"What do you want?" Jon muttered as he stepped outside. The fresh rain sharpened his senses, but damn if he didn't want to crawl back into bed with his wife.

"Braygen." The man ran a hand through his shaggy blond hair. "Herana asked me to show you something."

That guy. Jon grabbed him by the shirt and slammed him against the hut wall. "I hear you've been sniffing around my wife."

This had to be him, her new lover or whatever he was. Ashe had told him how close he was sticking, even curled up with her a few nights ago in a larger tree. Jon wasn't about to put her life in the hands of the prick who left her to rot.

A grin spread across Braygen's features, no fear in his eyes. "Should I make you the same offer as well? To push back that lonely grief clutching you tight."

Jon had no idea what offer Braygen had made to Jàden, but as soon as he got his bearings he'd have words about it. A wave of vertigo washed over him. He leaned his forehead against Braygen's shoulder so he didn't fall again.

The man untangled Jon's hands and gently shoved him upright.

Braygen pulled back his collar, exposing part of a tattoo. "I have sworn an oath by my skin to protect the Guardian, and she has given me an order to show you the temple."

Ashe's hand rested on his shoulder. "You need to see for yourself, Captain."

Clenching his jaw, Jon wanted to sort this business out right now, but with Jàden running off again, he had to get her back before anything else. He stepped away and lit a cigarette, grateful for Ashe's strong grip. "I need my horse."

"Jàden found what she was looking for." Braygen stepped onto the bridge, gesturing for him to follow. "She insisted I show you."

"Always about fucking Kale." That bastard was going to be the death of him.

Jon pointed at the twins and gestured: *Find her*.

They didn't budge as Ashe gestured back: *After*.

Jon grunted and glared at him. He wanted to go back to bed and sleep for a week, but he nodded at Braygen. "Fine. Lead the way."

What a fucking miserable mess. One day was all he asked, to be with Jàden and let the rest of the world disappear. He followed the Veradóran to the far side of the village, holding the rail at times when the dizziness hit. The twins stayed back as if they didn't trust these strangers to remain peaceful. Not that Jon did either.

He tossed the cigarette aside, stopping in front of a steel door. "What is this?"

Braygen held up the frosted square. "She says you can open this."

White light faded to blue when he slapped his hand against the smooth material. The steel door slid open, revealing a lit hallway beyond. Jon stepped inside to the same glassy smoothness as the old prison near Nelórath. He stopped in front of the carved script.

"Don't like this shit, Captain." Andrew's hand itched toward his sword. Ashe hung back.

"Light cannot exist without darkness," he muttered, but the harder he tried to concentrate, the more that devouring darkness ate through his senses.

Braygen gestured to the second door panel at the end of the hall. "Herana believes you will be able to open it."

"Woman's out of her damn mind." This place felt too much like the prison—too much like a trap. He pressed his palm to the second illuminated square.

The door slid open to a lit chamber.

Stale air greeted his nose, that same dusty, metallic scent he'd smelled long ago when he'd stepped through the red fires. His muscles tensed as he wrapped his hands around his daggers and stepped inside.

"You're one of the three," Braygen whispered.

"I ain't no such thing." Jon scanned the chamber, no clue what the hell that man was prattling on about.

Dozens of statues circled the outer wall. His gaze drew to the central stone tree circled by three additional monoliths. Jàden's sweet face stared back at him. He crept around the exterior, searching the deeper shadows for any movement.

The hairs on the back of his neck went up.

"There's no one here." Braygen circled the statues as if searching for something, but Jon couldn't imagine what.

Jon released his daggers and shuffled toward the two faceless rocks near the central tree, tracing his fingers along the glass of the first. "You said she found what she was looking for."

The ground shifted beneath his feet until his face rose from the rock, his body covered in a uniform like Jàden's with a wolf on his left shoulder surrounded by flames. He carried a sword in one hand and a gun in the other.

"Fuck me," Jon said.

"Captain, let's get the fuck out of this place." Andrew unsheathed two of his daggers, his body coiled tight like a viper.

Braygen gestured toward the statue. "Touch the screen, Jon. That is where you'll find your answers."

Jon pressed his hand to the glass as light flashed across the surface, illuminating symbols from the old world: *Begin transmission.*

He poked them with his finger. "What's this supposed to mean?"

The words swept away as he leaned against the statue, sweat beading along his neck. Bands of shadow filtered over a metal wall indented with long, hollow spaces stuffed with blankets. Orange light glowed across pale, hollow features.

A man in a strange gray shirt sat in a chair, the bloodflower emblem on each shoulder. Yet it was the anger and grief in his eyes that held Jon in place.

"Kale." Jon clenched his fist, dark jealousy bleeding into his senses. The first time he'd seen Kale on the glass, Jon thought him a man trapped inside. Now he understood—the magic glass showed him real people who once existed. Jon had more than a few words to say to this bastard. "You're Kale, aren't you?"

"If you're watching this video, I'm already dead." The man coughed, a bitter, hollow sound. "My name is Commander Jason Kale, Enforcer Second Class, and you used to be me."

Jon closed his mouth and bit back his words, his heart beating faster. "This can't be right."

"I'll soon be born into another body. Yours." Kale ran a hand over his buzz-cut hair, distress in the movement. "So first, let's cut the bullshit and get right to the truth."

A small image of Jàden appeared in the bottom corner. "Her name's Jàden Ravenscraft, and she's in a lot of trouble."

Kale leaned back in his chair, a gun gripped in his hand. He popped the glowing glass orb free from the hilt and pressed it back in. "Jàden touches the Violet Flame, an energy source generated by technology deep in the moon's core, and its power is waking up. Soon, she won't be able to control it. We made plans to leave this place and start over on another world, but my father abducted her. I've spent two years trying to find her again."

Kale grabbed a cigarette and lit it.

"What I didn't understand at the time is Jàden can't leave. She's tied to the moon the way some people get tangled and follow each other from one life to the next. It's a universal law that nobody talks about because most folks want to believe every life is a fresh start."

Kale set the gun aside and leaned forward.

"But Jàden's life has been tangled by another, an ex-lover obsessed with owning her. His obsession dug its claws in so deep it nearly killed her once."

Stepping back, Jon rubbed his hands over his face, trying to piece together the words. Obsession was something he knew all too well after years of dealing with Éli. Hopefully the prick was dead and would stay that way. One obsessive asshole was already too much of a pain in his ass.

Braygen laid a hand against his shoulder to steady him.

But Jon was too riveted to the screen to care.

He couldn't be Kale. No way would he have let those men viciously torture her for so long.

Kale continued, breaking into his thoughts. "There's a way to balance Jàden's power, something I didn't know about. A subtheric energy field called the Dark Flame. If you combine them..."

Jon rubbed his temples. "I can't be him."

"...the two substances ignite a spark. A person so strong they can draw power from both energy fields and open the moon's inner gate.

Freezing where he stood, Jon digested Kale's last words. Draw power from both Jàden and the other Flame. He hadn't seen another Flame, but he could feel it deep in his skin now.

Obsession, anger, a power so strong it stifled Jàden's sweet light.

The answer hit him hard.

Éli.

Jon lifted his hand, black flecks lifting away from his palm with Éli's poisoned power. It was trying to get to him, and he didn't have the magic like Jàden to fight it off.

"Éli bonded Jàden." Jon searched for the whisper of soft breath in his veins, but it was suffocating and he couldn't pull her power forth.

"You are the spark now, but you have to bond with both Jàden and Trevor. Love one, hate the other, the darkness and the light. This is the only way to save her." Kale's voice hitched as he fiddled with the glowing firemark, popping it free and slamming it repeatedly back into the gun's hilt.

Braygen seemed to stiffen at Trevor's name as Jon shook his head to clear some of the dizziness.

After a long silence, Kale leaned against his hand, fiercely rubbing the top of his head. His deep-set hazel eyes seemed to stare at nothing. "I wish I could have been her spark. I had my chance to be with Jàden, and I fucked everything up from day one."

Tears spilled onto Kale's cheeks as grief stabbed Jon's heart.

"Get this into your head right now, future me. It's your job to take care of her, so don't you dare fuck it up. You have one shot to set things right, or we all die and start again. I don't care what you have to do or who you have to kill. Tell Jàden I love her and I'd give up everything to hold her again."

The glass darkened.

## CHAPTER 52
*Veradóra*

Fog hung heavy in the morning drizzle as Éli crept through the trees, making as little noise as possible. His skin softened with the Guardian's breath. He pressed the sensation to the furthest corner of his mind and entered the trees, half his men dissolving into the shadows.

He'd left a few behind to look after Connor until the boy rejoined his uncle.

*"Get over here, boy." He tightened the girth on his horse as Connor edged over, trying to stand tall despite the fear in his eyes. Éli took the faux bloodflower and slipped it around Connor's neck. "Your uncle's coming to kill me. When he arrives, tell him everything."*

He'd almost discarded the pendant several times, but now he understood its purpose. To make Jon choose between his wife and his nephew.

Éli wasn't returning to his men. He would steal Jon's wife and disappear into the jungle. When Jon tried to 'save' Jàden from him, all he'd find is a nephew who was supposed to be dead.

The plan was perfect this time.

Jon would be happy to see Connor, angry that his Guardian had been abducted and slowly drive himself mad wondering if the rest of his family was still alive and who to rescue first.

Fucking bastard wouldn't beat him again, not this time.

Jàden was somewhere in this village, and according to his scouts, so was Jon. He and his men just needed to stay invisible to the Veradórans.

The chilly air was nothing like the icy cold of the north, but the constant dreary rain made him just as miserable. He only had one shot at this.

Granger dropped beside him between two large roots. "We've got a shadow, Commander. Ever since the sky beast."

"Then get rid of it." One of those damn figures must still be alive.

"Can't find him, sir." Granger spat at the ground. "Every time I get close, the fucker vanishes. Could be one of them bastards searching for the Guardian."

"Fuck." Like the mohawked man he'd enraged inside the sky beast. Éli clenched his fist. If their shadow was after his woman, he'd just led the bastard right to her. "Keep your eyes open. Kill the shadow first. Then Blakewood is yours."

Women's laughter rang out from the other side of the tree.

Cursing under his breath, Éli crept silently through the dense foliage. His eyes adjusted to the gloom as he searched the walkways and the few sentry birds on duty. Most were looking the other way. A knot of men trudged across a bridge, the one in the middle grasping the rail like he could barely stand.

One glance and Éli's lip curled into a sneer. Jon.

There he was, with *both* twins still alive. Éli clenched his jaw—he'd have to beat the shit out of someone for that mistake. Tracing his gaze back the way they'd come, he spied Thomas heading away from several clustered huts.

Éli waited for him to leave then slipped onto the landing and pushed open a door.

Easing it closed, he looked around the modest interior, a few chairs with a large bed in the middle, the blankets tossed about. Several saddle bags lay on the table, and he rifled quickly through them. The first held Jon's clothing, but the second had the Guardian's attire.

He picked up one of her shirts and sniffed deeply, her scent as gentle as her soft breath in his skin.

An ache clutched his chest. It had been months since he'd lain with a woman. But he couldn't linger here too long. Unable to find anything else of use, he stuffed the Guardian's shirt under his leather armor and slipped out of the hut, rejoining his men in the brush.

"Don't see her anywhere, Commander," a younger Rakir whispered. "She might be up in them bird huts."

Éli had a pretty good idea where she was—wherever Jon was headed. "I'm going to need a diversion. And put two men a few heartbeats behind me. I want that shadow dead."

Slipping through the brush, Éli couldn't get far without alerting nearby sentries to his presence.

One of his men raced onto the bridge and shouted, "Death to the Guardian."

As villagers swarmed out of their huts, he leapt over the rail into the valley's deep lake. Ashe raced past with several others.

Éli spied his opening.

He slipped through the shadows onto the path, retracing the steps to where Jon disappeared. If she wasn't in the village, she had to be with that pretentious prick.

The way narrowed to a thin trail barely wide enough for a single man, ending at a metal door buried in the cliff. He traced his fingers over the tree and crouched in front of the horse symbol, so similar to his birthmark.

No, identical to his birthmark. *What the fuck*?

Sebastian had always told Éli he was special, a Hareth marked for greatness by the Guardians themselves. But since his brother's death, Erisöl—the Guardian of Empty Dreams—was his only comfort.

Tracing his fingers along the symbol, Éli's chest tightened. Maybe he was a Guardian too.

And if that was the case, then nothing would stand in his way ever again. He poked along the door's seams for a release latch then grabbed the dangling light mechanism, gripping it against his palm.

The door slid open.

Éli pressed his back to the side and peered in. A stone hallway stretched into the rock. His muscles bunched as he stepped inside, silently creeping across the dusty floor. Muddy footprints led to a steel door at the end of the hall. Éli traced the lines of illumination, the same glow he'd seen in the sky beast, in the Tower of Idrér and in Jon's lighter.

"What are you hiding?" he muttered, his voice barely a soft breeze escaping his mouth. He stopped in front of the Guardian symbols, a faint tingle in his skull.

*Light does not exist without darkness. Darkness cannot breathe without light. Bond them to create shadow, who both divides and unites.*

He'd never been able to read the old Guardian language, and yet the meaning coiled around his thoughts. Éli lifted his hand. Darkness and illumination, the dual-colored flecks lifting away from his palm.

Light does not exist without darkness.

He could almost taste his Guardian's kiss again, that sweet fire with Jon's scent all over her. Evardo's words rolled back through his mind. *She needs you.*

A devious grin curled the corner of his lip as he crept toward the inner door, tracing his fingers along the seams. A small square of frosted glass lay to the left.

Éli brushed his hand over the surface, the light shifting from white to blue.

## CHAPTER 53

*Temple of the Three Moons*

"By the Guardians," Andrew muttered. "Jàden's been searching for you the whole time."

"I can't believe I'm Kale." Jon had wanted to kick that guy's ass so many times, and now the man's heavy grief settled in his heart.

*He* was the asshole that never saved her, never protected his family and could never take back Mather's death. All of it weighed on him now as he stumbled for the door.

"We find Jàden now," he said.

He had the power Frank needed. Almost. But Jon wasn't gonna let that stop him. He'd stack the whole world around Jàden to keep her safe, but first he had to find Éli and bond that fucker.

"She's gone after the Rakir," Braygen said. "The Veradóran women are with her."

"And you didn't stop her?" Jon tried to punch Braygen, but a wave of darkness washed over him, twisting his thoughts to the point of dizziness.

Andrew caught his fist. "You need to rest, Captain. Our brothers are with her too. Hareth won't touch her."

Jon clenched his jaw at the third stone, still unformed with no defining lines yet. He knew Andrew was right but would still feel safer if she was in sight. "Éli's the Dark Flame. I'm going to take his power, and then we're going to start tearing those beasts out of the sky."

If he could only walk straight.

The further away Jàden rode, the less her light shone, and right now the darkness suffocated him. He shoved both men away and stumbled toward the entry. The Guardian statues swam in his vision.

The door to the temple slid open, a silent swish of air against the vast chamber. Éli stepped through the entry, a sadistic twist to his features and punched Jon across the jaw.

Jon flew backward, and pain exploded across his cheek.

"Where is she?" Éli clutched Jon's shirt and pulled him to his feet. "You took my brother from me. I'm taking your woman."

Willing his body to fight back, Jon barely got his arm up to block a punch when Éli's iron fist hammered his jaw. His lip split open, blood trickling across his chin.

"Bond me." Spitting blood out, Jon groaned and signaled to Andrew: *find her*.

A shadow slipped through the open door and disappeared.

Jon shook the blurriness away, his vision sharpening on Andrew with a small knife in each hand, ready to throw.

"Have you tasted her yet? Soft and so full of fire." A sadistic smugness laced Éli's tone but didn't reach his eyes. Pain lurked there, beneath pools of obsidian blacker than the night sky. "Her sweet lavender scent will make my sleeping blankets so sweet."

Jon slammed his elbow into Éli's jaw and kicked him in the groin. "Don't you ever come near *my* wife." Fuck, it was hard to think. The leaded sensation in his muscles dragged him down as he grasped Éli's collar. "If you kill me, you kill her. And you still lose."

He had no idea if that was true, but he would never, ever let such a loathed man touch Jàden. Especially not after what the bastard had done to his sister.

Éli's jaw clenched so tight a vein pulsed through his thin beard. He growled and kicked Jon hard in the gut. "She's *my* wife now."

Doubling over, Jon fought to catch his breath as Andrew and Braygen disappeared, likely to secure

Jàden or ensure nobody interfered. But the door didn't close all the way. Jon leaned against his statue, stumbling around to the unhewn rock in the hopes Éli would follow.

"Give me your arm, brother," Jon said to Éli. His stomach twisted in loathing at the thought of bonding the man he despised most. Jon's sisters would roar with laughter at the thought of him as a husband to Éli, but he'd do anything to hear their teasing voices again.

Éli chuckled. "Ready to make peace now, are we? I can feel her breath deep in my veins. Her power weaving through mine." He grabbed Jon and slammed him against the rock. "But like the old men on the high council, you have no power of your own."

Blood dripped from his lip as Jon smiled. "Wrong again, brother." He slammed his head into Éli's and twisted around, grabbing his hand and slamming it against the glass. "I want to know who the fuck you are."

The ground rumbled again as dust shook off the third rock, slim lines tracing long grooves until Éli's features emerged. Garbed in the same uniform as him and Jàden, the statue clutched a sword in one hand, three spirals lifting from the palm of his other. His left shoulder bore a mark similar to his and Jàden's—a horse wreathed in flames.

"What the fuck is this?" Éli tried to pull back, but Jon held him firm.

Kale's face appeared, steel shelves lining the walls behind him. Something was odd about his expression. About the way he held his shoulders.

"Let go." Éli yanked his hand out and slammed Jon's head against the rock.

Jon hit the ground, pain ripping through his skull. His vision blurred as he lifted his head, trying to focus on Kale.

"Who is he?"

On the screen, Kale's jaw tightened. He lifted a weapon like the one Jàden had on the *Darius*, appearing to point it straight at Éli's head.

Cold steel pressed against the back of Jon's neck.

He should have shouted about that shadow, but something in his head told him it had to be Ashe. He should have known better.

"Frank fucking Kale." Jon cursed under his breath.

"Looks like someone beat the hell of you, boy," Frank said.

Éli whipped around with his sword unsheathed.

Frank lifted a second weapon and aimed at Éli. "You move, you die."

On the glass, Kale swept his thumb over his weapon's firemark, red light tracing along the brushed steel. His voice was eerily calm. "I know what you did, Trevor. You sold Jàden out to Doc Bradshaw. This isn't over." He fired and the screen went dark.

"You're the shadow following my men." Éli looked ready to murder Frank, but he eyed the weapon with caution.

Jon itched toward his daggers so he could rip Frank's throat out, but he'd already seen too many times how fast those black weapons killed a man. And with Frank here, Jàden *should* be safe for now.

Jon shook his head at Éli, silently urging him not to move.

"So, you're Trevor." Frank stepped back with his weapons pointed at both him and Éli. "You boys were always too obsessed with that woman."

Pain seized his muscles as Jon slowly pushed to his feet. If he was going to die, he would never do it on his knees.

"And she's useless to you now. Barely a half-magicked woman." Jon would do anything to save, Jàden, and all he needed was to prove to Frank that he was the spark—a wielder of two Flames so his wife and men would always be safe. He lifted his palm, black ash floating upward from his hand.

Frank laughed and shook his head. "Boy, you are stupider than a naïve whore. Think you got it all figured out, do you?"

He fired at Éli's statue, glass shattering outward.

Someone shouted in the outer corridor, feet pounding against the stone.

Frank cocked his head, a silver metal disc in his ear. "Get him in here."

A dozen figures in light-up armor scrambled into the room, dragging Andrew with them. They kicked him to his knees, each one pointing a long, black weapon at them.

Jon seethed as they shoved him and Éli to their knees. Something about Frank's words needled at him, a piece he was missing to this whole puzzle. Maybe he could get Frank to tell him what it was.

"I want to see this moon gate," Jon said.

"In time." Holstering his guns, Frank lit a cigarette, blue smoke swirling from the tip. "But first we're gonna capture that vixen of yours."

"Don't you fucking touch her." Jon tried to stand, only to have his knees kicked out again as a wave of dizziness crashed over him.

Éli's power surged with anger, but Jon tried to hold onto the last thread of Jàden's light.

"Touch her. Fuck her. I'll do whatever I want to my little darlin'." Frank lifted his eyebrows and pointed around the temple. "Who knew you'd make it so easy for me to find her."

"The fuck are you talking about?" Jon spat at his feet, eyeing the soldiers with their weapons trained on him.

Frank chuckled and pointed his gun at Andrew. "You're the one who made her a Guardian. And that spark bullshit still don't work without the key."

Éli's silence was unnerving him, and his power boiled with anger and obsession. If Frank didn't need him for the moon's inner gate, then Jàden was still in more danger than ever without him to protect her.

"You bastard! Do you know what you've done?" Scrambling to his feet, Jon grabbed Éli's head and slammed it into the shattered glass. He punched him and unsheathed his dagger, pressing it against Éli's throat. Gripping the back of Éli's neck, Jon tried to pull forth the darkness, the pain, the obsession. "Give it to me."

Jon pressed his mouth against Éli's scraggy cheek, hoping he'd never have to kiss the man on the mouth. Black oil burned in his senses.

Éli grabbed Jon's cheeks, the murderous rage of more than twenty years without Sebastian bleeding into his eyes. "Go fuck yourself."

Éli head-butted him so hard Jon hit the floor, black spots swimming in his vision.

Agony exploded across Jon's temple and a gunshot went off, echoing loud in the enclosed temple.

Andrew tumbled backwards.

A hole burned the middle of his forehead, his lifeless eyes staring at Jon as blood leaked across the floor.

"Andrew!" Jon scrambled painfully toward the younger twin and pulled him into a tight embrace. He roared his anguish at Frank, "You mother fucker! I will stick every blade I own in your skull."

Frank's fist slammed into his cheek, and Jon reeled onto his side, excruciating pain sizzling into his skull.

He spit up blood, trying to clear his blurred vision.

"Lock him up tight and get him to the cage." Frank nodded toward Éli. "That one too. If they try to resist, shoot their legs off."

# CHAPTER 54

*East of Veradóra*

Jàden raised her hands to the side to show she held no weapons, but the man behind her only laughed and pressed the tip of his sword deeper against her neck. "Now stand up, nice and slow. Both of you."

"Do what he says," Malcolm muttered, but he sounded half a heartbeat away from burying his ax in the guy's skull.

*Don't move.* Evardo whispered through her thoughts like a slippery eel. Whatever they were about to do, she closed her eyes as the man pulled his weapon away from her.

"No no no," the man behind them roared, and a soft squish hit her ears.

Afraid another had crept up on them, both she and Malcolm glanced over their shoulders. The Rakir held the hilt of his sword in both hands, the blade buried in his own throat.

*Go now.* Evardo screamed into her head. *More are coming.*

Jàden bolted over the ridge to a sharp incline and slid against a tall tree.

*What did you do to him?* she whispered harshly.

A sigh seemed to exhale in her head. *What I should have done in Felaren.*

*Where's Éli?* The moment her words landed, Éli's power disappeared from her veins. White fire crackled through her as pure as the day she rode into Felaren.

Jàden opened her palm, darkness and shadow no more than a single speck as the Flame glowed brightly. It surged within her, desperate for release, but she clenched her fists and leaned against the tree. *Evardo, what's happening?*

*Cages wrapped around them.* Evardo's palpable fear wove through their words as they crouched in the mud with their hands over their ears, rocking back and forth. *Find them. Find them. Find them.*

"Hey, you all right?" Malcolm grabbed her shoulder.

Jàden removed her hands from her ears—wait, had she done that? Glancing around the tree, she scoured the campsite for Evardo. They'd curled up on the ground like her while the boy tried to soothe them.

"Help them both," she whispered and pointed toward the camp. "Something's wrong." She didn't have time to explain to Malcolm, only to follow the cold dread in her gut.

Fighting back the Flame's insistence, she scrambled toward the horses and climbed on Agnar's back.

The sky was unnaturally quiet. She dug her heels into the stallion and bolted back the way she'd come. She couldn't sense Jon at all, and Éli's power was so weak inside her that he must be dying.

If Jon was already dead...

*No!* She wiped a stray tear and leaned low over Agnar's neck. Her mind raced with a dozen possibilities of what might have happened, but she couldn't put words to it, only sense something horrible.

Agnar reared up, and she hit the ground hard, pain searing into her shoulder.

Dusty dropped to her side. "Shit, you okay? I thought you heard me."

She groaned and rolled to her side, waiting for the pain to subside. "Jon—something's wrong. I can't feel him."

A shadow crossed his features.

"Nor Éli. The Flame is too..." She clawed the dirt as her power surged again in an attempt to break free. "Find them."

The muddy earth bubbled under her hands as Dusty shuffled back.

White light wove around her arms and dug into the soil. Jàden screamed through her teeth, pushing hard against the Flame's power, but it was like trying to force a falling building to stand back up.

"Get back!"

Worry stretched Dusty's features as he grabbed the horses and backed away. "Fight it, Jàden. You can do this."

No, she couldn't.

She'd never be strong like Dusty and the others, no matter how long she trained. As she curled her body tight to fight the rush of power, something Kale said came back to her.

*You have to unite the Flames, or you'll die.*

She needed Éli. As much as she hated that bastard, even a little bit of his power would suppress her own. Using the puddle water, she pressed outward with her mind, searching for a thread of darkness.

"Help me," she whispered to the moon and the terrifying alien starship at its core.

Sandaris was listening, and the Flame's power burrowed into the ground, giving her incremental control.

Jàden closed her eyes to use the moon's second sight.

*The bunker door open, several dozen Enforcers dragging two cuffed men into the mud.*

Jon. Éli.

*Both were enraged, bleeding from half a dozen different cuts, but Jon looked like he'd been beaten. He could barely stand. A static barrier buzzed around each man.*

Frank's tech from the cuffs must have been cutting off their power.

Darkness swirled just out of their reach.

"Help them." Pushing the Flame's power toward the barrier, she clenched the dirt so tight the granules dug into her palm. The static fractured, and a whisper of darkness bled through. Its rotten slime slid over her fire until it dimmed enough for her to breathe.

Releasing her hold on the Flame's power and the dirt, Jàden crumbled into the mud. The Flame swirled in her veins, but no longer strong enough to control her.

"Frank has him," she said. "He found the other Flame."

"That bastard has them both." Braygen dropped from his horse and he and Dusty helped her up. "Frank found us in the temple. He captured Jon and some Rakir asshole. One of the twins too. I had to shift into an otter just to scurry past his guards. Got one in the arm and I think he pissed himself."

She and Dusty might have laughed except his green eyes were hard as flint.

Jàden wiped her muddy hands on her breeches. "It's me or Frank. One of us has to die."

Dusty laid his hand on her shoulder. "And we ain't gonna let anything happen to you. We kill that bastard and get the captain out of there."

"No fear," she muttered.

She didn't need the bravery of a seasoned warrior to face off with Frank. Kale had taught her many things over the years. Time to start using her brain and not letting fear rule her decisions.

She could still see Jon's deep brown eyes from that first moment inside her hypersleep pod, feel the warmth of his hand when he stopped her from ripping the arrow out of her shoulder. But even as Braygen watched her, Kale's essence whispering through his eyes, it was the heat and comfort of Jon that she craved.

"We're going to save him," she said.

As they climbed on their horses, Braygen nudged his mare alongside hers. "It won't be easy. Frank's men have high-powered rifles and full armor."

"Then we find his ship and make sure it stays on the ground. As long as we stay far away from the lab, we have a fighting chance." She dug her heels into Agnar as they raced toward Veradóra, pushing the horses until sweat lathered up their necks.

The eerie quiet in the sky was compounded by the jungle, birds and frogs, now silent. As Jàden slowed Agnar past the last triangulation tower, traces of a strange smell touched her nose. One she recognized from the day of her abduction. Kale had used a smoke bomb to buy them time to escape the Enforcers, but Frank had been one step ahead.

"I smell knockout gas," she said.

Dread tightened her gut.

Wisps of white cloud lingered in the trees. Most Enforcers used the stuff in their training so they understood how to handle it against an invader. But it was lethal to people with specific DNA markers and highly flammable if Frank ignited the starship engines.

"He's going to kill everyone."

"I didn't see any ships as I raced here to find you," Braygen said. "He must have one grounded on the south side of Veradóra."

"Where the women keep the garden sanctuary," she said. Frank planned to erase Veradóra. He wasn't just a command general. He could be ridiculously petty when he forced his hand.

"If the ship isn't already gone, he'll know we're coming." Braygen stopped his horse and dropped to the ground. "There's a way to disappear beneath the village and come out the other side if you can hold your breath long enough. It might give us the chance to attack unseen."

"The others might be in there. I'm gonna circle south and find them. We'll need everyone's help." Dusty's eyes fixed on Braygen. "Jàden's got six brothers now with no morals if she gets kidnapped. See that she doesn't."

The not-so-subtle threat lingered in the air as he disappeared into the trees. Jàden slid off Agnar's back, both warmed that Dusty saw her as family and disturbed by his words.

*All right, Jon. Show me where you are.*

As she and Braygen crept through the trees, something else nudged at her thoughts. Frank claimed on the *Darius* he knew where Kale was, and both she and Jon believed him. Yet Braygen had been at her side for nearly a week.

Something about that small nuance continued to needle her as Braygen stopped near a kóra sapling. "Do you trust that I will do everything to keep you alive and safe, even give up my own life if I must?"

Trust didn't come easy, but this was no longer about her or Kale. "Jon's all that matters now. It's as much as I can give."

He tightened his jaw as if something in her words bothered him but nodded his assent. "Take a deep breath here then run until you hit air. Once you're in the water, follow me as fast as you can. It's a long way down."

She didn't like the sound of this, but she breathed in all the air she could and bolted into the gas cloud. Almost instantly, her eyes burned.

Then the ground fell away.

Jàden nearly screamed but pressed her hands over her mouth and hit the lake, icy water chilling her instantly.

She swam down, her lungs already desperate for another breath.

Opening her eyes, she spotted Braygen off to her right, swimming hard for a small light that looked about a million spans away.

She would never make that distance, and panic gripped her. She swam faster. For Jon and Éli. And because she needed one day where Frank wasn't looming over her life like the hand of doom.

Her lungs tightened, burning with the lack of oxygen. The light grew larger, but she still wasn't going to make it.

The Flame seemed to sense her danger and fire ripped through her veins, but Braygen pulled her to eye level.

*I have to go bac—*

He pulled her mouth against his. Gentle and warm, he parted his lips to breathe air into her lungs.

*Kale.* She clutched his shirt, allowing herself one moment of freedom to say goodbye as the pain in her chest dimmed.

An old sensation crept into her thoughts like something out of a past life memory. She touched bone, sensed energy so strong and alien it terrified her.

Braygen pulled back then turned and swam toward the circle of light, gesturing for her to follow. He made a wide stroke with his arms. Then his body slid apart into five dark brown river otters with white bellies.

Of course. His lung capacity must be at least three times hers. She swam after him, recalling that river otters could stay underwater a long time compared to humans.

But that didn't erase the gut-wrenching ache in her chest. She wanted to kiss him one more time. To say goodbye. Or maybe out of pure selfishness.

The light widened, and Braygen shifted back from otters to human. He grasped the edge and pulled his head through then turned and held out his arm for her.

She grabbed his offered hand and slid into the light, gasping for air as she leaned over the edge. The water rippled, held back by *Hàlon* shield technology inside a circular stone chamber. What else might he have in this place that could help her?

Braygen helped her through the opening to a stone floor, but he didn't let go. Conflict brewed in his stormy eyes as water slid from his hair to his jaw. He touched the side of her temple, his fingers tracing the side of her forehead. "You really love him, don't you?"

He should have shoved a spear into her chest—it would have been kinder. The pain in her heart was unbearable. "I waited for you, and you just gave up."

The words barely more than a whisper, she leaned her forehead against his chest. "Why did you leave me there?"

Braygen's hand slid down to her neck and he tilted her face up to meet his. "I've wished every day for the past two hundred years that I was Jason Kale."

Water slid from his hair to his jaw, deep grief in his stormy eyes. "My ink was not taken as part of any belief in Guardians but because I'm connected to you and this moon, and I don't understand why."

Jàden furrowed her brow, piecing together his words. "Wait, you're not Kale?"

He sighed and pulled the bow off his back, holding it out to her.

The zankata sat on top of the monster's wing as if about to fly off. "When I woke from hypersleep, I was no longer human. I learned to live as an animal first, but I dreamed every night about this."

He pointed to the monster.

"I know you're with Jon, and I will do whatever you ask of me to protect him too, but I don't regret my offer and it will always be open to you." He touched her cheek then turned away and grabbed boxes off his shelves, digging out a variety of items and trying to hide the pain in his eyes.

Jàden bent over, hands on her knees as she tried to process everything. He wasn't Kale, that's why Frank hadn't already captured him. So who was?

"I hope you're ready to use that power of yours. I can get rid of the pilots, but we need to make sure that ship stays on the ground," Braygen said.

Jàden touched his arm, freezing his movement. She didn't want to admit it, but she sensed it too. Some deep connection with Braygen she couldn't quite grasp.

"We protect the living," she whispered, repeating something Jon had told her long ago. "Then we can chase the past."

## CHAPTER 55
*Veradóra*

The steady *drip, drip* of water splashed against small puddles as Jàden crept after Braygen, a longsword strapped to her back between the twin daggers.

Both dressed in dry clothes Braygen had rummaged from the shelves. They trotted through underground tunnels to the far side of the village. Jàden tried to measure her steps but sensed that each split kept leading them more horizontal, as if avoiding something large buried in the ground.

*Everything in this place I built for you.* Kale's words followed her steps as the corridor ended in a wooden ladder climbing straight to the surface.

Power surged inside her, white fire crackling through her veins alongside the gentle beating heart of Sandaris. But she was all alone again, hollow and aching for Jon's gentle embrace.

"Surface is straight up. I'll check first to make sure we're clear of the gas." Braygen disappeared into the darkness above.

She grabbed onto the weathered wood and climbed behind him, stepping softly to muffle any sound. Someday she planned to figure out the enigma of Braygen and why they were so connected.

Light cracked the earth above then flooded the tunnel as Braygen opened a hatch and signaled that the air was clear.

Jàden took a deep breath and climbed out into the brush.

Nothing stirred or made a sound, not even the wind as rain showered over Veradóra. She turned back to ask Braygen a question, but he'd disappeared, the hatch underground already closed.

Softness pounced on her. One of Braygen's otters curled along her shoulders, whiskers tickling her cheek.

Of course.

The only way for him to get to the pilots unseen was to be invisible.

Light pulsed in thick tubes along the ground toward the crashed ship with the orb and trailing legs symbol. Jàden itched to head there first and search for weapons, but that would only give Frank more of a chance to hurt Jon.

She couldn't sense Jon anymore, and for all she knew, he might be laying in a pool of his own blood.

Forcing back the tears, she scurried to the underside of the angled ship and crouched down. Beyond the enclosed garden lay open meadow to a tree line on the horizon, but her eyes pinned to the midnight black shadowrunner, its boxy style so different from the Raith fighters. Its bolting claws curled beneath the hull's belly, the lights along the seams the only sign that anyone was aboard the ship.

"Even as an otter, they'll track your heat signature and know I'm not alone," she muttered.

Braygen leapt off her shoulder and melted together into his human form. "How many men do you think he has?"

"At least thirty, unless he crammed the ship full of Enforcers, then maybe a hundred. Kill the pilots, and I'll unleash the Flame on everyone else. If I have to, I'll rip that hull apart like I did in Nelórath." The Flame surged in her veins, but she had to hold it in just a little longer.

Lifting her hands in surrender, she stepped out of the brush as the back door to the cargo bay lowered. One of Braygen's otters clung to her back, masking itself behind her heat as the metal ramp thumped to the ground.

Jàden's heart pounded so hard she thought she might suffer a heart attack before she ever laid eyes on Jon again.

She stepped onto the ramp, only able to see the bay's ceiling from her lower vantage point. With each step, a little more came into view. Frank had installed more than a dozen glass cages, and it sent a shudder down her spine.

Braygen climbed to her neck and scurried under her shirt.

"The fuck are you doing?" she muttered.

Black figures melted out of the foliage, aiming their rifles at her as they boxed her in.

But her gaze found Jon, and panic tightened her chest. "Jon!"

He whipped his head around, shouting something and waving her back. The distress in his eyes mirrored her own as she bolted across the threshold into the bay.

The Flame disappeared from her veins.

"Oh, shit," she said. Frank had set the ship up as a barrier to her power. Electricity buzzed along her skin. "Go, Braygen."

As he slipped down her leg, she tried to bolt back outside, but several shots zipped by her head.

"Careful, darlin'. No turning back this time," Frank said over the loudspeaker.

She halted on the edge between the bay and the ramp, the armored Enforcers closing in. She tried again to step outside the barrier, and several shots barely missed her feet.

Fuck.

They'd shoot her if she tried to leave. And she wasn't sure the Flame's power would be faster than their shots.

*I'll teach you to fight,* Jon had told her the day she accidentally woke Frank from hypersleep. *In return, I'll help you find Kale.*

She'd found his bunker but not him.

Jon was all she had now, and as the tears burned in her eyes, she knew there was only one way out of this. Unite the Flames, unleash Jon and hope that Braygen disabled the pilots and kept the ship grounded.

Bolting from the edge to the cages, she ignored Éli and pressed her hand against Jon's release panel. It buzzed red.

Jon's soil-brown eyes found hers as he tried to say something to her.

But she couldn't hear him through the barrier. She pressed her hand to the glass, tears streaming down her cheeks. "I'm so sorry."

He looked torn between fury and worry. He gestured silently to her, and this time she understood the meaning. *Fight!*

"Get this ship in the air." Frank's voice and a whisper of wind on the back of her neck alerted her to danger as all the training with Thomas crashed into her.

Jàden dropped to the ground and unsheathed her dagger, slamming it into Frank's leg. She tried to roll away.

But Frank yanked her off the ground and slammed her face against the glass. "Do you know what a fucking pain in the ass you've been?"

She cried out as his fingers dug into her. Before she could answer, he pulled back and slammed her again. Pain lanced through her skull.

Jon relentlessly threw his body against the barrier, murder in his eyes. Even Éli tried to claw his way out of an adjacent cage as rage tightened his features.

Jàden would have given anything to hear their fury, but someone had shut off the sound, leaving her with silence and Frank's heavy breath. She grabbed his waist, hoping to find a holstered gun.

But as soon as her fingers brushed steel, Frank twisted her arm painfully behind her back. "My son went mad knowing how much you screamed and begged for him once."

The bay door shut. Overhead lights flooded on as Frank pressed against her, his eyes pinned on Jon.

"Medic," a women shouted and dropped beside Frank. "Get in here. Boss is injured."

Frank's taunting voice was back as he rubbed his beard along her cheek. "This time I'm going to bolt you to a chair and make you watch as I rip him apart, piece by piece.

"Please, no," she whispered, her cheek against the glass wet with tears. "You have me. Let Kale go."

Jon had stopped trying to rip down the glass and stood still as a statue in her line of sight, one hand pressed where her cheek touched the glass, the other held up two fingers and mouthed, "Never stop fighting."

Two fingers, two rules.

Frank yanked her away from the glass so she could no longer see Jon and shoved her down the aisle. "The last sound you'll ever hear is his screams."

She wasn't sure if he was talking about Jon or Kale, but she repeated Jon's rules in her head.

*Stay alive. Everything is a weapon.*

Jàden spied the panel on the next cage and the open door. The ship's engines ignited, the floor rumbling through pre-flight as the sound grew louder. Shaking her head, she tried to backpedal, but Frank grabbed her neck.

"I won't go back!" *Never stop fighting.*

She leaned against Frank and kicked her legs to either side of the door, propelling them both backwards until they slammed against the cages on the other side.

*Courage cannot awaken without fear.*

She unholstered Frank's gun and fired at the panel near Jon's cage to fry the circuits.

"You little bitch." Frank stripped the gun and threw her toward the open door. "I swear to—"

Jon crashed into Frank, the gun clattering to the ground.

Pain lanced through her shoulder, and she scrambled toward the door as gunfire blasted down the aisle. Jàden pulled back, hesitating for a moment, then dove for the gun and rolled to her side, firing toward the gunman. They wouldn't dare kill her if they knew Frank like she did.

"Lock down the bay," a woman shouted into the overhead speakers.

Jàden stumbled to her feet and hastened toward Éli's cage, shooting the control panel until the glass slid open.

He bolted across the aisle and slammed her against the glass, pressing his mouth to hers. "You're mine. Don't forget that, wife."

## CHAPTER 56
*Shadowrunner*

Jon grabbed Frank by the throat and shoved him against the wall. Rage burned in the deepest part of his soul. "Don't you ever fucking touch my wife."

The butt of a rifle slammed into the back of his head. Pain and nausea gripped him as Frank slipped out of his hands.

"No! Let me go!" Jàden's high-pitched scream grabbed his attention.

Éli had her pinned.

That fucking traitor. Jon was going to kill him too, but Éli unsheathed the sword at Jàden's back and stalked toward a knot of armored figures as Jàden fired at them.

Air whispered across the back of his neck.

Jon ducked another blow, ignoring the hollow emptiness inside him. Jàden had ripped her magic out of him again, but he didn't know how.

As Jon turned around, Frank's shoulder slammed into his gut, and they both hit the ground. Something roared louder and the ground vibrated. But Jon drove his elbow into Frank's shoulder. The bastard was strong as an ox and nearly as fast as Éli.

Letting go of all other thoughts, Jon tried to pull the captain back into himself as they rolled across the ground, Frank wrapping an arm around his neck.

"Don't think for a second I won't kill you." Frank's arm tightened.

Jon gasped for air and bucked his hips, slamming down onto Frank and ripping the dagger out of his leg.

Releasing his hold, Frank kicked him off and rolled away as he drove the knife into the waffled metal. "Come on, boy. Fight!"

Still clutching the dagger, Jon rolled to his feet, every muscle screaming in pain from Éli's earlier beating. Only his training and adrenaline kept him moving.

But at least for the moment, Éli's power wasn't suffocating him.

"Someone get this beast in the air." Frank charged him again.

Jon tried to drive the knife into Frank's gut, but the bastard blocked him and knocked the weapon away.

Instead, he cracked his elbow into Frank's nose.

"Pre-flight almost done, General," a woman's voice said over the air. "We've got a small prob—"

The voice cut out as Jon threw Frank into the glass, the black-armored figures like shadows on the far side of the cage walls. They were fanning out, and even if he killed Frank, they'd likely gun him down.

"Éli," Jon yelled, "kill those fuckers!"

Frank punched him hard across the jaw, and Jon reeled backwards, holding his chin through blinding pain. He tried to stand up, but Frank punched him again, this time blurring his vision.

Doubling over, Jon shook his head to clear the grogginess, but another hit dropped him flat on his back.

Frank put a foot on Jon's chest and pointed a longer weapon at his head. "You move and I will make that bitch bathe in your guts."

Jon couldn't move a muscle through the pain. He spat blood as his chest tightened. "Kill me, and she dies too."

## CHAPTER 57
*Shadowrunner*

Jàden couldn't shoot without hitting Jon as the two men slammed back and forth across the aisle between cages. She panicked about who to protect— Jon or Éli. One's death could kill the other, and without the Flame, she couldn't rip the ship apart.

As the engines grew louder, she had her answer.

If this ship got off the ground, they were all done for. Bradshaw would be waiting to put them on lockdown. But on the ground, they had a chance to fight their way out, no matter how slim.

She slipped in the narrow gap between cages and ducked low, inching toward the far side and trying not to be seen. Shadows moved beyond glass walls. She held her gun pointed in one direction, her dagger in the other.

Braygen should have had those pilots taken care of, but by the sound of the engines, they'd be in the air any minute.

At the far edge between two cages, she peeked out.

Half a dozen figures bunched together at one corner, their rifles aimed and ready to fire. They had to be hunting Éli.

"Pre-flight almost done, General," a pilot said over the loudspeaker.

Jàden glanced the other way, and several figures slipped between the cage walls like her. She held perfectly still, waiting for them to disappear. When only two were left, she spied the corridor to the cockpit open behind them.

When their attention was drawn by Frank's angry shouts, she slipped out and fired toward the knot of soldiers stalking Éli.

Two hit the ground, and she crouched again in her hidey-hole.

The rest turned and opened fire, killing the Enforcers guarding the corridor.

Once the gunfire stopped, Jàden bolted from her hiding spot.

They fired intentionally over her head, but she refused to stop. She dove into the corridor and dodged to the side, palming the door closed.

"Braygen!" she yelled.

The ship started to lift then bumped to the ground, the engines winding down.

"In here!" he called.

She raced down the corridor, but the door between them slid shut.

Jàden palmed the pad then slapped the door. "Braygen?"

Whatever he said came back muffled from the other side. The door at the far end slid open.

Frank stepped into the doorway, the blood-bound sword in one hand, a gun in the other. He palmed the door closed, his mouth curling into a sinister grin. "Take her out, Doc."

White hot needles seared into her skin from the top of her head down to her toes. Jàden screamed as the familiar, agonizing pain dug deep into her eyes and bones. She clenched her fists, fighting the invisible torture as she slid to the ground.

Frank crouched beside her and patted her cheek. "That's a good girl. You and I are gonna be together a long time." He tugged aside her collar, his finger sliding under the chain on her neck until the bloodflower spilled out of her bodice. "I don't fucking believe it."

Jàden clawed at her skin as he ripped the key off her neck. Silently begging the anguish to stop, she tried to grab the bloodflower, but her fingers curled inward like a seizure.

Frank swung the bloodflower back and forth in front of her like a pendulum. "A gate key? You were worth the wait, darlin'."

The steel door to the bay slid open.

Hard lines tightened Jon's features, his wild eyes filled with rage. A deep cut bled along his temple. He slammed his fist into Frank's jaw with a dagger clutched in his hand.

Frank's cheek ripped open as the dagger slid out of Jon's grasp and slammed into the wall as if magnetized.

The tension released, and Jàden fell over, breathing deep as the last aches faded. After two years of suffering, she hated that pain more than anything.

The door retracted.

She scurried toward the opening, smacking her hand on the lightpad. The hatch sealed again. With Bradshaw controlling the door, she and Jon were trapped.

Jon crashed against the cockpit door, blood trickling down his face.

Jàden charged Frank, bouncing off his broad back and hitting the ground.

He whipped around.

She scrambled to her feet and kicked him in the balls then slammed his nose against her knee. "Don't you fucking touch him."

Blood streaked Frank's cheek, dripping into his beard from a deep cut. His mouth curled into a vicious grin. He grabbed her arm and slammed her against the wall before clutching her neck.

Stars burst in front of her eyes. The gun and sword were stuck to the ceiling, Jon's dagger to the wall. Bradshaw must have magnetized everything, forcing her and Jon to fight Frank with no weapons.

"You and my son are never gonna be together." Frank clasped her tight and dug his fingers into her skin, hatred bleeding into his tone. "I'm going to stick him in a cage next to yours, and you'll watch him starve, wasting away to dust and bone."

Jon stumbled toward her, blood dripping for at least a dozen wounds.

But Frank snapped his fingers and silently ordered him back, his grip tighter on her neck.

"You're wrong," she said.

A gentle *domp, domp* whispered alongside her heart as a bit of wrapping fell loose from Mather's blade, dangling next to Jon's shoulder. He reached up to grab the hilt, barely wedging his fingers to hold the weapon in place.

His words, burning with Mather's grief, ripped through her mind. *Every man who stands between me and Éli Hareth will feel the sting of this blade.*

Jàden spat blood in Frank's face.

She slammed her fist into his chest, right where she'd shot him weeks ago.

"This is for Kale." She threw her back against the door and kicked his chest.

Frank flew backward, his head cracking into the tip of Jon's blade, his eyes wide and his arms dangling to his side. Blood leaked around the curve in his neck.

He didn't move again.

"Jon." Jàden rushed toward him, embracing him tight as tears streamed down her cheeks.

He clutched her, burying his head in her neck. "Oh, baby. I thought I'd lost you."

The walls demagnetized, and Frank's body hit the ground.

The door to the cockpit slid open.

"Holy fuck, was that a good fight." Braygen stood over two dead pilots, a headset over his ear. Wires dangled from an open console panel. "Hang on. Trying to get control back."

Jàden grabbed Jon's cheeks, his beard prickling her fingertips despite his blood. "Did you bond Éli yet?"

Jon pressed his mouth against hers and pushed her against the door to the bay. He deepened the kiss then pulled back enough that his mouth still brushed hers. "Baby, I'm Kale."

"Wha—"

Before she could say anything else, he pulled her into another deep kiss.

Jàden held him tight as his words slowly unfolded in her head. She pushed him back. "Wait, you're Kale? But that's impossible."

All the pieces clicked into place. From Frank threatening her on the *Darius* to the beacon towers to Braygen at her side.

"On the *Darius*, Frank was going to shoot *you*," she said.

"But you turned the gun on yourself." He slid his hand onto her cheek. "You saved me that day—"

She clutched him tight, a sob threatening to break loose from her throat. "I found you."

His jaw stubble prickled her cheek. She slid one hand into his hair and pulled him tight against her. Jon was the strength she'd craved, the other piece of her heart. But she'd wanted to save him from this nightmare, and it wasn't yet over.

"I have to get us out of here." Jàden palmed the pad to the bay.

The lights went out.

"No." She palmed the pad again as her feet drifted off the ground, the anti-gravity generators kicking on. "Bradshaw, turn the power back on."

She nudged Jon aside and pushed off against the door, floating down the corridor toward the cockpit. Shoving in beside Braygen, she brought up the HUD display, and the front blast panel shifted to transparent glass.

"Dammit!" Jàden slapped the console, pressing buttons and trying to turn the primary power on. Her mind turned as she tried to think of everything Kale had ever taught her.

The cockpit glass shifted from trees to a familiar face, spiked brown hair and a clean-shaved jaw.

Bradshaw met her gaze, something he'd never done the whole duration of her captivity. "You killed my tracker."

"And you stole my life, you pretentious fuck." Jàden slammed the console as Jon moved behind her, pressing the butt of the gun into her hand. "Turn off the Flame barrier."

"Not a chance." Bradshaw seemed distracted by something on his screen, and Jàden imagined him putting a fleet in the air.

Jon had already been beat to hell, and who knew if Éli was still alive.

She grabbed Jon and pulled him in front of her, pressing the gun to his temple. "I found the spark, and you can't open the gate without us."

Her heart lurched putting Jon's face on Bradshaw's camera, but he likely already knew everything Frank did.

"Call off your fleet and release the ship," she said, "or I'll kill him and then me."

Bradshaw's features hardened. "You wouldn't dare."

Jàden slid her finger over the trigger and moved the gun barrel from Jon's head to hers. "Watch me."

Bradshaw cursed and slammed his console.

The lights flickered on, and the door swished open.

"This isn't over, Ravenscraft," he said. "I know where you are."

"We have control," Braygen said, pressing several buttons. "Barrier off."

"You'd better run, Doc," she whispered. The Flame's power crackled through her veins. "I'm coming for you."

"I'll find you first."

She pressed a hand against the wall as the Flame's power surged through the shield holds. Lights flickered on, and the gravity pulled her down.

Sparks flew across the console and down the corridor walls.

"You bitch—" The rest of Bradshaw's words were lost as the glass shattered outward, the hull above their head cracking open.

Jon hit the ground, groaning in pain.

Letting go of the ship, Jàden dropped next to him and pulled his mouth to hers. Warmth bled into her senses, his beard prickling her jaw. "You all right?"

"You found me, and I ain't never letting you out of my sight." He tightened his grip, deepening their kiss until she could barely breathe.

Thomas shouted outside. "Captain?"

"In here." She helped Jon to his feet and wrapped his arm around her shoulder. "We need to get off this ship."

As the Flame ebbed from her veins, Éli's power surged, and Jon stumbled against her. "Flames. Must bond."

The ache burned in her chest as they stepped into the corridor. She leaned Jon against the wall and grabbed the bloodflower from Frank's hand, slipping the chain over her neck.

Frank's collar lay open, a chain around his hairy chest.

Braygen crouched over him, light pulsing over his palm. He slid a finger beneath the chain and pulled out an obsidian orb dangling on the end, pale blue light glowing from deep inside it.

"You gotta be shittin' me," Jàden muttered.

She'd once found a necklace with a small blue stone chipped from something much larger. The day she put it around her neck, everything changed.

"What is that?" Jon held his stomach like he was about to throw up. "Is that a gate key?"

Everything suddenly made a twisted kind of sense.

"It's the beginning," she whispered.

Dread tightened her stomach as Braygen pulled the pendant over his head. His stormy eyes found hers, that deep alien connection they shared forcing the words from her mouth.

"Don't ever let anyone know you have that," she said.

"Anything for you, Jàden." He grabbed the blood-bound blade and handed it to Jon. "Let's get the fuck out of here."

## CHAPTER 58

*Shadowrunner*

"You fought well," Jon whispered as they stepped into the cage room, blood and dead bodies everywhere. She hadn't stopped fighting and even killed the man who fueled her worst nightmares.

But dark power slid through him like oil as his vision blurred. "We need to find Éli."

And hope he was still alive.

Jon could barely keep himself upright as they searched the bay, the Enforcers dead. Dark cracks with burn marks covered several sections of glass as if something small and hard hammered into them.

"Gunshots," Jàden muttered. "Hang in there, Jon. We'll find him."

He let go of her and leaned against the wall, her soft whisper of breath leaving him. With the Flame barrier turned off, the sickness from the past week was back. "How long before Bradshaw finds us?"

"Not long." She spun in several directions then grabbed his hand and pointed toward a dark blot sitting against the far wall.

Death seemed to linger over his shoulder. Her light barely touched the darkness.

But he stumbled onward. He had to complete the binding.

Éli sat against a far wall, his hand to his side and sweat on his brow. He gripped the gun in his hand and aimed at Jon. "These things kill faster than you can reach me."

Jon nudged Jàden out of the way and crouched so the gun was pointed only at him. "I don't regret protecting my mother. But I do regret what you lost."

Éli snarled. "Don't lie to me, Jon. The only reason you haven't joined Sebastian is you are going to feel this anguish."

"I do. Every day." It wasn't a lie, and the pain of Mather's death struck him again. While part of him wanted to snap Éli's neck for kissing Jàden, Jon wouldn't risk another life without her. He held out his arm. "Bond me so we can both live, and I'll take whatever pain you want me to feel."

A smug sneer curled Éli's lip. But he coughed, and blood dripped out the side of his lip. That wasn't a good sign. "Promise me you will feel the full weight of my anguish."

Maybe he should kill him so it would just be him and Jàden again.

Then again, maybe Éli already had one foot in the grave. "Bring it, brother."

Éli scratched the side of his head with the barrel then tossed the weapon aside. "I'll give you what you want. In return, I walk out first—free and alive. And you don't dare follow me."

It sounded too good to be true, but Jon was too tired to care. "Done."

Grabbing Jon's forearm, Éli pulled himself up until they stood face to face, arms clasped. Black threads of the Flame's power wrapped his forearms and traveled to Jon's elbow, each man's energy tying to one another until something sealed.

Energy rushed into Jon, light and darkness, two pools of power begging for attention.

"Have a good life...*brother*." Éli pulled him close and slapped his cheek. Then he walked out of the bay and down the ramp like he barely had a scratch.

Jon turned to find Jàden and took her in his arms. He pulled her mouth against his, bright light rushing through his veins. The oily slick dissolved into a silky darkness twining with her light.

"Can we get out of here first?" she mumbled against him.

He traced a streak of blood across her cheek. "You found me. I'll go anywhere you want."

Jon lifted his palm, light and shadow and darkness swirling together in a trifecta of power. As he grabbed Jàden's hand to leave, sharp pain dug into his shoulders.

"What's happening?" he asked.

"I don't know." Jàden cried out and clutched her shoulder. "It burns."

He pulled down the fabric of her shirt. Her zankata tattoo glowed with deep indigo light. Jon traced his fingers over her birthmark. "The Flames are united."

The sickness burned away from his senses as his full strength returned, apart from the injuries Frank and Éli had beaten into him. Jon pulled down his shirt, the same indigo light glowing from lines around his brand. "Which am I, the horse or the wolf?"

He wanted to say more, but a young boy stepped off the ramp into the ship's bay.

Jon rubbed his eyes, certain he must be hallucinating.

When his vision cleared, obsidian black eyes stared back at him, filled with tears. "Uncle Jon?"

"Connor?" He bolted to his nephew's side, ignoring all the pain in his body. "Guardians be damned, you're alive."

Jon dropped to his knees, pulling Connor into a tight embrace. For one moment he held onto the hope that his family stood outside the ship. He scanned the field and between the trees, but the rain fell heavy over the dreary landscape.

"Where's your mother?" Jon asked.

"Dead." Connor sobbed against his neck. "He said she deserved it."

"Who?" Ice gripped Jon's heart as he stood once more.

But his nephew pointed off to the west. "My father."

## CHAPTER 59
*Westward*

Anger burned in Éli's gut as he leaned on Granger and limped through the trees toward their horses. He'd had to give up his prize for today, but he pulled her wadded shirt from under his leather breastplate and sniffed deeply of her scent.

"Commander." The hesitation in Granger's voice barely covered up the burning rage as he glanced toward the shattered sky beast. "I'll ride with you into death, brother, if that's what you wish."

"Not today, Captain." They'd pushed beyond their own limits and lost everything. Éli would have been dead if not for Evardo slipping into the minds of those soldiers and turning them on one another. But he wasn't about to walk away emptyhanded. Closing his eyes, Éli breathed in the softness of the Guardian and the strength of Jon Ayers.

Both Jon and his wife were a part of him now.

And he'd never let either one forget it.

Pulling on his own power, he traced dark threads of energy connecting him to Jon and his men, to Connor and to thousands of Rakir to the west and south.

After a moment, he let them all go, save one, drawing a trace amount of Granger's energy to help him heal faster.

Sebastian had always told Éli that he was born to greatness, and now he finally understood. His brand and loyalty no longer controlled him. Éli would still have to be careful about using his power but would never again be enslaved to another man's will.

"Today, we become shadows." He limped toward his horse and pulled himself into the saddle, trying to ignore the excruciating pain in his side. The gunshot burned, and he'd need a healer soon. "As we disappear from these lands, Jon will be left to deal with the all the gifts I left behind."

They'd never be apart now, and that knowledge would slowly drive Jon mad. A sneer curled his lip as he took one last look at his woman, her soft breath flowing in his veins as Evardo dropped to their knees, clutching her legs like a small child.

Stuffing her shirt under his again, Éli turned his horse and disappeared into the trees.

Granger was at his side. "You may have given up, but I still plan to take both Blakewood's eyes and leave him to rot."

"This is only the beginning," Éli muttered. "Every day Jon is with Connor, the death of his family will weigh on his soul. He will wonder if they're still alive and rotting away in a prison cell. That question's gonna eat his thoughts until he can't sit still. But that is only the start of his troubles. He has a wife he loves and a nephew he's loyal to, but Connor hates the Guardian. He's desperate to kill her for the terror she caused him."

Éli had fostered that fear over the past season, and now he couldn't help but wonder how much time would pass before Jon had to divide his loyalty between the woman he loved and the family he clings to.

"We need Evardo though." Granger glanced over his shoulder, almost as if he willed the dreamwalker to follow them.

A smile curled Éli's lip before the pain struck again and he doubled over, waiting for the sharpness to pass. "Evardo overextended their power, and they're like a beacon now that can't ever escape me." He nudged his horse to a faster trot as he clutched his side. "It might look like we've lost everything, but I did exactly what I set out to do: make Jon Ayers suffer."

"Where to now, Commander?" Granger kept pace with him as they passed beyond the last boundary of the village into the wildlands again. "You're gonna need to get that injury looked at."

For the first time in years, Éli smiled. "I'm in the mood for a strong réva and a good fuck."

"Now you're talkin'." Granger smacked the leather reins against his horse to put on more speed.

"After that, we're gonna steal us an army." Éli dug his heels into his stallion as they raced through a field with giant ferns.

They'd find a road soon and, with it, a village or another city. And once he was fit for travel again, it was time to find out exactly what Dràven held hostage that might bait Jon.

"But this time, I'll give the orders. Not those pretentious old fucks."

## CHAPTER 60
*Veradóra*

Jàden traced her fingers along the small, silver blade, tears in her eyes as she searched the sky for any of Bradshaw's ships. It had taken hours to find everyone when the gas finally dissipated, and as the Veradórans keened over the death of Ìana, Jàden and her brothers grieved for Andrew.

"This is my fault," she said.

Thomas laid a hand on her shoulder. "When are you gonna stop blaming yourself for everything?"

"When death stops touching those closest to me." She slid Andrew's small dagger back into the leather breastplate, a gift from Ashe to carry on his brother's spirit.

It didn't seem right, only seeing Ashe's grim face instead of two identical ones. She'd said as much when she'd etched her final farewell onto the arrow shaft and fired it into his pyre. Despite saving Ashe's life, she couldn't block out the guilt that she'd traded one brother's life for another.

"Andrew killed three of Frank's soldiers to protect us all. Don't dishonor his death by dwelling on your own guilt. He's my brother as much as he's yours, so we share this pain. Like family."

She clutched his hand. It would probably be the closest she ever came to Thomas calling her a sister, but she'd gladly take it.

"Training resumes tonight." He slapped her shoulder and rejoined Dusty and Theryn, the two bowmen still covered with bloody cuts and mud streaks.

Of fucking course Thomas would get her training before she had a chance to sleep.

Jàden grabbed Agnar's reins, her bags across his back. None of them had saddles anymore, but maybe

Kale had left her a replicator inside so she could forge them all new ones.

Alida touched her arm. "Sumaha wants to speak with you, when you're ready."

She nodded, heart twisting.

Ìana had been found dead, her body swollen so badly they almost didn't recognize her. The best guess Jàden could give the Veradórans was she must have had an allergic reaction to something in the knockout gas, though it did not satisfy their grief.

Sumaha snapped an orange blossom off her arm and slid it into Alida's braid. When she turned toward Jàden, her features were grim.

She clutched a pike staff tightly. "I am now leader of Veradóra, and you have brought war to our home. You will leave, with our peace upon you, but we will disappear with the wind and not return to this place."

Braygen stepped forward, peeling back the layer of his collar to reveal his ink. "Veradóra has been my home for nearly two hundred years, but I am Tahiró first. When Herana leaves, I will follow."

"Don't be a fool." Sumaha spat at his feet.

Tears filled Alida's eyes as she stepped away from her wife, tugging up the hem of her bodice. Guilt strained her voice. "You know my vows, my beautiful Orange Blossom."

Jàden laid a hand on Alida's arm. "Don't. Stay with your family. I have no wish for war."

"And yet, it is coming all the same." Sumaha tapped the pike against her shoulder. "Tahiró vows are stronger than family. Stronger than blood." She stepped closer until their noses were almost touching. "I know your plans to hide underground. Alida does not wish me to lead, and I do not wish her to follow any Guardian." Sumaha grabbed Alida's hand and held it tight, grief in Sumaha's dark eyes. "You will give her back to me when she is finished. Promise, Guardian."

Jàden laid a hand on the leader's shoulder. "She will be safe in the bunker. And who knows? Maybe one day Alida will show you the stars."

Alida grinned. "Gonna learn me how to wrangle one of them sky beasts. Then I'll rain down the fire over that Doc fella."

Jàden stepped back.

Jon tapped her shoulder and pointed to the sky. A small spot raced across the clouds. "Gotta go, baby."

Jàden nodded her farewell to the Veradórans and grabbed Agnar's reins. He tossed his head and shook out his fur, then they followed Jon into the bunker.

"Don't you worry," she said. "Kale always thinks of everything. If we're lucky, we'll have a holodeck in here for you fuzzy monsters."

The doors closed.

Her brothers stood beside their horses in the Temple of the Three Moons. Jon kept a hand on his nephew's shoulder, but uncertainty shadowed his eyes.

She stepped closer, but Connor glared at her and hid behind Evardo.

Sighing deeply, she turned over Jon's hand, light and shadow and darkness lifting from his palm. Untying his bracer, Jàden pushed up his sleeve, revealing the bloodflower tattoo.

"Enforcers tried to kill me once." She laid her hand on his forearm and looked deep into his eyes, her stomach fluttering at the gentleness of his thumb against her cheek. "But we're bound now, you and I, and I'll never regret my choice.

"I made a promise to you that I will not break," she said. "Two years of training to learn how to fight without magic."

Jon brushed a few stray hairs behind her ear. "I plan to be by your side a lot longer than two years."

For only a moment her gaze flicked to Braygen and the storm brewing behind his eyes. "I don't know what the future holds."

The Flame's power flowed between them as ink bled from his tattoo into her skin, the bloodflower pendant warming beneath her bodice. She smiled then lifted her arm, an identical bloodflower inked into her skin. "But this time we stay together until the end."

Jon pressed his mouth against hers, soft warmth from his lips whispering into her senses.

"Doc's coming," he said. "Let's figure out how to open this thing."

"Élon to the north, his divided lover Saheva to the south." She pointed at the female Guardian's statue, the only woman of the six to have a bonded sun. She walked toward Saheva's statue and laid her palm against the stone. Light zipped out from her hand, pulsing through the statue as gears started grinding.

The Guardian statues melted into the wall as the section in front of her shifted from telen to transparent glass.

Kale's face appeared on the screen. "I knew you'd find your way, baby. Welcome home."

Jon slid his arms around her waist as the floor dropped like an elevator. Kale's face disappeared, along with the wall. Dim lights flickered on over a giant docking bay several stories underground.

Jon tightened his grip, but she laid her hand over his arm to soothe his unease.

In the center of the docking bay sat her starship, the one she and Kale had prepped to leave *Hàlon*. Silver steel glimmered under the bright lights like a cage wrapped around an orange egg.

"What is that thing?" Jon muttered in her ear.

"That's my ship." Jàden lifted his hand and kissed his palm. "Once I learn how to fly it, I'll show you the stars."

THE END

# IRONSTAR

*Exclusive Preview*

Jàden leaned back in her chair and propped her feet on the console, fatigue pulling at her senses. She'd been up half the night watching the monitors, *Hàlon's* empty halls disturbing her more with each passing day.

"Figured I'd find you here." Braygen handed her a cup of coffee and sat beside her, a deep shadow in his stormy eyes. "Can't let it go, can you?"

She shook her head. "I've tried several different emergency beacons, and it's always the same. AI routes me to the tower and nothing. It's like everyone just walked off the ship."

*Or they were spaced out an airlock.*

Kale hadn't let her down either. Once she pressed her hand against the bunker's welcome message, some embedded program had given her access to areas of *Hàlon* she never knew existed. Though she didn't dare try to exploit that yet, not until she could figure out what had happened on the ship.

"Someone has to be alive," she muttered. "If the ship's a derelict..."

She sipped her coffee, unable to speak the rest of her thoughts. An empty starship meant it would only be a matter of time before basic functions failed. Then Sandaris would become a ticking bomb until the bionet generators stopped working.

Braygen laid a hand on her ankle. "Don't worry. We'll figure it out." Almost before he stopped speaking, he pulled his hand back. He set down his cup and rubbed his arm as if it ached.

"Give me your arm." She sighed and set her coffee aside, pulling her feet off the console. Like she'd done with Thomas on the *Darius*, she rubbed her hand along Braygen's forearm, massaging his aching muscles. "I didn't expect you'd be awake yet."

"I can't sleep." Braygen sighed in relief, unclenching his hand. "Some nights it's like fire and acid at war in my bones."

Jàden dug her fingers into his arm, working the muscles until that familiar tug in her chest became like a stinging hook. They were connected. She knew it as strongly as Braygen did. Perhaps they'd known one another in a past life, like she had with Jon.

Braygen wrapped his fingers around her arm as she worked. Caressing his thumb across her skin, he glanced at the daggers on her back before meeting her eyes. "Did I ever tell you about Marco?"

"Don't." She let go and swung her chair toward the console. The last thing she needed was Jon walking in here and throwing Braygen through a wall. Jàden pulled up the camera feeds from inside the bunker so they lined up on one side of the glass screen. She should make it very clear to Braygen that Jon is the man she loves, but her tongue couldn't seem to form the words.

"I lost Marco many years ago." Braygen slid one of her daggers free, the obsidian blade reflecting the low bridge light. He traced his thumb over the orb and dangling legs symbol. "He was dead before I could stop that... *thing*."

He sighed and leaned back in his chair again, holding the blade so the symbol on the hilt pointed at her. "This is what killed him."

"The symbol?" Jaden asked. "What does it mean?"

"It means, never go beyond the light." He laid the blade in her hand and wrapped her fingers around it. "I will follow you anywhere, Jàden Ravenscraft, but we cannot go where darkness rules."

She gripped the dagger, the sharp edge of the blade biting into her skin. "Braygen, spit it out. You're not making any sense. What's beyond the light?"

Jàden only knew one place apart from space where the darkness was constant: deep within the core of the moon. She shuddered at the memory of that place as an alarm chirped from her console. Thinking it was Jon from somewhere in the bunker, she turned toward her screen and pressed the receive call button. "This is Jàden."

Silence came through the speakers until a faint *click-plop-thop* whispered through.

"Hello? Jon?" she asked. Jàden set the dagger in her lap and turned up the volume. Or maybe he'd forgotten which button to push again. "Hit the blue one."

*Click-plop-thop.*

Unease tightened her gut. Was someone injured?

"Jàden." An eerie calm whispered through Braygen's voice. "That call isn't from inside the bunker."

"What?" She leaned over to his viewscreen where a map of the Dark Isle showed a flashing blue dot far to the south. She'd know that place anywhere.

Ironstar.

"See if you can pull up the video." No one outside the bunker should even know she was here, but she pushed that thought aside. Someone was alive.

Jàden kept the comm channel open. "This is Jàden Ravenscraft, Guild of Bioengineering. Can you hear me?"

*Click-plop-thop.*

A camera flicked on, and the screen illuminated a rippling obsidian goo that reflected light from a set of monitors. The substance solidified into a flat sheet, the orb and trailing legs carved into the black and glowing with bright green light.

"What is that?" Jàden asked cold settling in the pit of her gut.

"It's one of them," Braygen whispered. "Those from beyond the light."

The sound came again. Jàden reached across him, nudging a console button to pan the camera back. The blackness rippled. A pale tentacle touched the camera screen, soft suckers pressing the glass before it pulled away in a *click-plop-thop*.

Jàden clutched Braygen's arm. "Is that what I think it is? The creatures from inside the moon. They're on the surface?"

Text flashed on the screen: *I see you.*

Braygen laid his hand over hers, palm warm against her skin. "We are so fucked."

## NORTHMAN SPEECH

**Balé:** why?

**Borda:** eat.

**Dalan:** *pl. Dalanath.* Sleeping ghosts, specifically denoting the mysterious nature of hypersleep pod illusions of sleepers. In the north, folks use stories of dalanath waking up to scare small children into behaving.

**Ekki:** stop.

**Elbren:** Religious figures from the Golden City. They are spread throughout the southlands and are the caretakers of the Guardian temples, preaching that one day the Guardians will return to the sky. This is linked to a disaster earlier in Sandarin history where the stars disappeared from the night sky.

**Firemark:** see *shalir*.

**Gensana·darak:** the season of leaves. One of six Sandarin seasons.

**Hevkor:** a prestigious title given only to tradeship captains.

**Kóna:** wife. Used as both a relationship title for those who identify as female, and as an endearment between spouses.

**Kórante:** *plural kórantéth.* A prestigious title given only to the six powerful men of the High Council who rule the northlands.

**Màvon:** trees more common on the Northern Isle and in the Borderlands. Their pale trunks faintly glow when the sister moons are full at night. During gensana·darak their leaves turn a deep indigo. At the end of the cold season, the leaves turn to a bright wine color and the trees yield a dark green fruit.

**Melin oné:** no magic. An imperative statement warning any magic-wielders that they're in danger, usually out of self-preservation.

**Nakshirnén:** Bond of the Flame. This phrase is one of several types of spouse bonds, with the connotation that those who have forged this connection are bound for life and cannot be separated except by death.

**Níra:** relax. Often used to calm anxious people or horses.

**Norshad:** northern bred horse. Norshads are a horse/notharen hybrid. They travel in brother-herds, are able to change the color of their fur for camouflage, and always choose their riders.

**Notharen:** This unique line of equines has more in common with an octopus than a horse. Able to change the color of their fur to use as camouflage, these horses are stronger and faster than other equines and travel together in brother-herds.

**Oné:** a negative/inverse connotation usually meaning 'never' though can sometimes have a general no meaning.

**Rakir:** northern soldiers who serve the Tower and the will of the High Council. They are branded before training starts, and their brands are used to siphon energy away to feed the six kórantéth.

**Ranasen:** a sense of otherness. Outsider. Those who feel like they don't belong to their Guardians follow the lonely path to Herana, the Guardian of Lost Souls.

**Réva:** a tomato-based ale common on both *Hàlon* and Sandaris.

**Sahira:** a spider similar in look to a common tarantula. Native to the warmer jungles, these creatures have bright orange feathers on their abdomen. When hunting for prey, they spiral the feathers open to look like a flower, and spit venom when prey is near. One dose of their venom is enough to knock out a grown man.

**Sahirana:** *plural sahiranath.* Spider-shifter.

**Sanda le/sanda ven:** You're safe/we're safe.

**Sejhna:** poison. Its use is found most often in the north to put humans into a comatose state while the poison eats them from the inside. The victim feels everything but cannot wake up unless healed.

**Shàden:** a large, nomadic canid with a black leather hide. When it hunts, its body ignites with fire as it catches prey, burning it to nothing and feeding off the ash.

**Shalir:** Sandarin name for a firemark, a small glass orb that lights up or dims with a person's breath.

## VERADORAN LANGUAGE

**Denerada:** title of shame intended as punishment for bad behavior. The one who bears such a status must serve in the home of the offended until the debt is paid and the title removed.

**Kóra:** giant trees whose rough brown trunk can grow as wide as a house. Veradóra is located in a kóra grove, with many of the trunks hollowed out as homes. The leaves are green all year round, and the flowers do not bear fruit.

**Tahiró:** folks who have bound themselves to helping and protecting the Guardian Herana.

## NA'MASHKA SHE (Hàlon Common)

**Bareh ró:** she's awake.

**Kóro:** get out!

**Laoné lenä freon và naréa  Naréathana freon amshe faríoné  San 'endlan và drér fré  Vó e vastana ara zenathar o:** Light does not exist without darkness. Darkness cannot breathe without light. Bond them to create shadow, who both divides and unites.

**Nadrér:** a military starship built to create a blister and cut into the hull of an enemy ship. An intended attack vessel for quick boarding and escape.

**Naoné óra baría kar freon:** Courage cannot awaken without fear.

**Telen:** a highly dense manufactured stone created to withstand a millennia of intense storms and deep space vacuum.

**Vamahéa heriakór Jason Kale:** my name is Commander Jason Kale.

**Zankata:** crow-like bird with bright-colored feathers under each wing.

# FUN GOODIES FROM K. J. HARROWICK

**Free short stories!**
Want a peek behind the curtain at what Braygen was doing a hundred years ago? Check out his short tale and others on my website:
https://authorkjharrowick.com/short-stories/

**Subscribe to my newsletter**
Keep up to date on the latest book news, and get ready for *Ironstar*, the next installment of The Hidden Flames Artifact. Coming fall 2022.
https://authorkjharrowick.com/newsletter/

## FOLLOW K. J. ON:

Website
https://authorkjharrowick.com

Facebook | Instagram | Pinterest | Twitter | TikTok
@KJHarrowick

# ABOUT THE AUTHOR

K. J. Harrowick is a fantasy and science fiction author with a strong passion for blending grimdark worlds and futurist technology with threads of romance and revenge. She is the co-creator of Writer In Motion, a recurring WriteHive panelist, and has written articles for Science in Sci-Fi, Rewrite it Club, and Winterviews. With an unhealthy obsession for dragons, tacos, cheese, and beer, she works her gatory ways as a freelance web developer and graphic designer on a broad range of client projects before falling down the occasional rabbit hole. Her debut series, The Hidden Flames Artifact, brings dragons, sex, swords, and spaceships together in an epic mashup adventure.

# ACKNOWLEDGEMENTS

What started as a few role-play characters to pass the boredom in my earlier years has since blossomed into an entire fictional universe filled with hope, heartache, and the ideology that humans are connected to one another by much stronger bonds than a one and done cycle of life.

*Bloodflower* has been a passion project of mine for more than a decade, so it seems fair to start right at the beginning with the wonderful Heather Davis, Camille Wolfewood, Sherrie Mun, Sam Crossley, Derek Whitten and my HPH crew. Without you guys and the love and dedication you've shown in our years together, this book and its characters would not exist.

From that first draft more than a decade ago, I also want to thank my dearest friends Mirabella Kubinyi and the late Peter Kallay who have become the voices in my head pushing me to do better—to be better. Mira read a first draft of *Bloodflower* and I'm honestly shocked she didn't light it on fire right then.

This story got rewritten many times over the years, and for that I need to thank all the wonderful folks who had a hand it in. Abby Glenn, Ariel Ryan, Christopher T. Woolf, Christy Dirks, Ellen Mulholland, Ellie Doores, Glen Delaney, Jen Davenport, J. P. Midnight, K. S. Watts, Laura Hazan, M. A. Guglielmo, Maha Khalid, Megan Van Dyke, Melody Caraballo, Noreen Mughis, Rachel Brick, R. R. Fryar, Sanyukta Thakare, Sarah J. Sover, Sara T. Bond, S. Kaeth, S. M. Roffey, Stephanie Sauvinet, Talynn Lynn, and Tasha Livingstone. I'd also like to thank all the folks in The Writer's Craft Room, Rewrite it Club, Winterviews, Ocean's Eleven, World Flight, Mechanical Dragons, the original Space Bees, Writer In Motion, RevPit, and WriteHive.

And let's not forget my wonderful cover illustrator and RevPit sister, Rebecca Wilcox. She is the genius behind the art that binds this story.

I also want to send a shout out to Marc & Liz Williams at Williams Helde. You both have trusted me with your work for so many years, and that opportunity gave me the space to pull *Bloodflower* from the gutter to the bookshelves.

To the team at Portal World Publishing: Jen the Town Crier of House Davenport. Writer of explosions. Not the quiet one. Megan Storyweaver of House Van Dyke, first of her name, writer of twisted tales, lover of magic and kissing, promiser of happily ever afters. Melody Pie of the House of Caraballo, she drinks and writes things. Lady Talynn of the House of Lynn, Lover of Exquisite Vineyards, Chocolate Connoisseur, Teacher of Pleasantries, and Writer of all things fantasy and science fiction in the world of young adult. And to my two wonderful editors, Carly Hayward and Jeni Chappelle. I'd be lost without all of you! Thank you for all the time and dedication (and moral support) you put in for helping me bring this story to life.

Lightning Source UK Ltd.
Milton Keynes UK
UKHW021040070921
390174UK00010B/489